"YOU ARE AS A MAGGOT, FEEDING ON THE WOUND THAT IS THE ÆTHER, NEVER LETTING IT HEAL, ALWAYS CAUSING IT TO GROW."

"But our healers use maggots to consume dead flesh, so that the healthy flesh may return."

Kihantroh snorted. "Then let the maggots forgive the injury I rendered by comparing them to you. And now it ends. I know that your chair is an affectation. Stand up."

"You are a fool, Kihantroh," she said.

"Stand up!"

"Kihantroh, you cannot——"

"Enough! You have no say in what I can or cannot do. Stand now, so that I may strike you down!" The jewels flashed and the wheelchair shot away from beneath her; she fell heavily to the stone floor, and lay there for a moment, glaring up at the intruder.

Then, slowly, she stood.

I0589397

RAVELS

(The Conclusion of "Strings")

a novel

by James V. Viscosi

PRELUDE

THE ÆTHER

Chapter 1

BRENNENDAH STOOD ALONE at the edge of the world and stared into the Æther.

Things were always changing along this frontier, where the land was slowly being eroded by the grey mists that roiled and burbled out in the vast nowhere between the the far-off sea, the desertlike scrub of the Edgelands, and the grim wall of the distant Fists. The Rittandics had maintained an outpost here for centuries, observing and recording the behavior of the trackless void; Jordneh, witch-queen of the Ravels, was only the latest in a long line of monarchs who received reports on the state of the Æther, just as Brennendah was only the latest in a similarly long line of those who gave them. The monitoring methodology had not changed much over the decades. Like those who had come before him, Brennendah and his assistant Kaderleh—who had recently become his wife and, more recently still, an expectant mother—tracked the Æther's activity by setting up poles at fixed distance intervals from the crumbling border where land met vapor, recording the dates and times each was planted and when each was consumed by the nothingness. The growth of the Æther had, for many years, remained steady and inexorable; nothing halted the unraveling of the fabric of the world on whose face they walked, neither wishes nor walls nor witchcraft. Some wounds could not be healed; the spread of some infections could not be checked. All they could do was watch it happen, and write it down, and remember what had been lost.

When Brennendah had inherited the stewardship of the outpost, he had continued his predecessors' practice of spacing the poles a standard arm's-width apart, then over the course of tedious months recording the steady forward progress of the Æther, until finally one day the marker would be gone and the measurements would start over with the next one. On this day, when he had ventured with chalk and slate down to the very end of the earth to check on the pole closest to the Æther, to measure the distance of soil left between it and the abyss, he had expected to be recording the amount of earth that remained for pole number two thousand one hundred five—each was identified in a strictly increasing sequence by a stamped metal plate permanently affixed to its top—but when he arrived he had found that the pole with that number no longer existed. Nor did pole number two thousand one hundred six; nor did two thousand one hundred seven; and the encroaching mist had already chewed its way some distance toward the next-to-last pole that remained. Once he had somewhat recovered from the shock of seeing so many markers disappear so fast, he got down on his hands and knees and measured the margin that remained to the doomed number two thousand one hundred eight. After that, there was only one pole left. He would need to set up more, but they were running out of available poles, as well as land to put them on.

Measurements recorded, he put the grey stone tablet aside and crawled forward, to the very edge of the Æther. There he peered across the trackless fog, the abyss that had no sides, no depth, no bottom. Because of the way it blocked the winds from the distant sea, because no bird or cloud ever crossed it, some maintained that it had no *top*, either; they suggested that the void continued upward forever, invisible and unknowable, and that it only manifested as a frothy custard at this elevation because of the lands it had consumed. Brennendah had no idea if that was true or not. All he could say for sure is that it was eating his markers faster than it ever had since measurements had begun to be recorded all those centuries ago.

He reached forward with a tentative hand, paused, and, as always, pulled back before crossing the boundary between land and vapor. Perhaps some day he would be courageous, foolish, or desperate enough to breach the border between his world and whatever world the Æther inhabited, but that day was not this day. He withdrew instead, returned to the last pole, picked up the chalk and the slate, and retreated to the copse of gnarled, stunted pines where he had left a few soft clay tablets, wrapped in damp burlap and buried beneath a thin layer of soil, that were used to permanently record Æther observations. He transferred his latest findings from the slate to the topmost tablet, inscribing the chalk marks in the red, puttylike surface with a metal stylus. Once he verified that he had recorded the numbers correctly, he rewrapped the tablet—it was not quite full, and so not yet ready to be left out in the sun to bake—and buried it again, then erased the chalk marks from the slate with his sleeve.

"I am pleased to see you are not creeping around at the edge of the Æther this time," a voice like polished brass said.

Brennendah raised his head and glanced to his left as Kaderleh emerged from the trees, following the narrow path that led down from their semipermanent camp on the high ground a few hundred yards from the hole in the world. "Of course not," he said as she approached. "You told me not to do that anymore."

"And you always do as I tell you?"

"Of course."

She stopped a few yards away, chuckling. "Good. I do not want to have to explain to our child that, owing to excessive curiosity, its father was consumed by the Æther before it was born. That would set an unfortunate precedent."

"Indeed it would." Brennendah took his wife in, hair white as summer clouds, skin pale blue like the sky at the horizon, body slender and supple as a thin reed. Her silvery tunic still hung loose on her frame, though that would not be the case for much longer. He surreptitiously eyed her clothing, wondering if perhaps he could detect, just barely, a change in her outline.

"There has been no noticeable expansion of my girth since you left camp this morning," Kaderleh said, smiling; obviously he was not as discreet as he had hoped. Her gaze strayed to the remnant of the line of markers. She frowned. "I see that the same cannot be said of the Æther. Unless perhaps the storks have been gathering nesting material?"

She did not sound hopeful, because of course she knew better. Each marker consisted of a waist-high shoot of white-stained wood with the final hand's-width painted red, topped with the number-embossed metal disk that served both as its identifier and a strike plate when hammering the pole into the ground. The base went into a flanged metal spike that, when twisted after being driven into the earth, expanded into an anchor that prevented the pole from idle meddling or from being carried off by the large birds that dwelled in the nearby rock chimneys, known as the Fingers, that were the eroded remains of plugged fumaroles. Eons earlier, these had vented mineral-laden steam from the depths of the earth, forming spires that remained long after the surrounding earth had eroded away; now they were topped with massive, ramshackle nests, occupied by large families of squawking hatchlings. "No, I am afraid it was not the birds. There has been a jump. We need to assemble new markers, at least eight or ten."

"We have reeds, but we are out of spikes and plates," Kaderleh said. "I told you that when you set up this last group of poles, remember?"

He thought for a moment. "So you did." Picking up his slate, he said: "I have sunbaked tablets to deliver, and protocol requires that I report a jump to Jordneh immediately. I can get more of the metal parts from her smith while I am there."

"Mmm," Kaderleh said.

"What?"

"If you will be picking up supplies at the castle," she said, "I have a list to give you."

"Of course you do," he said.

~~~~

They walked back from the edge of the Æther in silence, long fingers intertwined. The sun was bright overhead, but distant—it always seemed distant here, a light-bending trick of the Æther, Kaderleh suspected—and the air felt cool and still, but not heavy; their passage stirred up the odors of dust and sand and the pitch that oozed from the small, scruffy, crack-barked pines. The oddly stunted trees grew only in a thin strip along the edge of the Æther and nowhere else, leading some to hypothesize that the species had in fact come *out* of the Æther, as if the trackless fog had belched forth a storm of pinecones that eventually became the scrub that bearded it. Kaderleh thought it more likely that they were simply mountain pines that had adapted to the low-water environment of this arid microclimate. Since becoming Brennendah's assistant not long after he assumed the mantle of lead researcher, Kaderleh had grown accustomed to the austere nature of the Edgelands. She missed the tall, verdant grasses of the prairies, but the fragile ecology here had a beauty of its own. She knew that the high desert plateau in the central Fists, underneath which the dwarves tunneled, was formed by the rain-shadow of the mountains. A similar phenomenon was at work here, but unlike the formidable mountain range to their east, the Æther did not actually wring precipitation out of the clouds; instead, the moisture-laden winds from the southern sea parted around the Æther much as a river might break over a large rock, then met again farther to the north, resulting in turbulent, unpredictable storms. The nature of the force that the Æther expressed remained poorly understood; it exerted some sort of positive pressure that kept the bordering seas from simply draining into the abyss, or the atmosphere from swirling down it in an asphyxiating cyclone. The Æther consumed, but only according to its own whim and schedule, and it radiated energies in ways that were beyond control.

This, of course, did not mean that no one had ever tried.

Five centuries earlier the witch-queen Untelleh had dwelled in a vast castle complex not far to the south of where they now stood, rumored to have enclosed an Æther vastly smaller than what now existed. A sorceress without peer, Untelleh had spent years examining and probing the misty realm; her studies had culminated in an attempt to cap it like a well, so that she could harness its power to augment her own abilities. The resulting explosion was said to have been audible over the whole of the plains, possibly the entire continent. Those few members of Untelleh's retinue who had been far enough away from the castle to escape the blast returned to discover an enormously larger Æther and no trace of her stronghold, its surrounding gardens and orchards and agricultural fields, its nearby shoreline, or even the ocean that had once lapped at the bluffs beneath her walls. This disaster marked the last time anyone had attempted to control the Æther, and was almost immediately followed by the appearance, over the mountains in far-off Abacar, of the monstrous Daras-Drûm. The resulting conflict preempted any serious attempt to discover if Untelleh and her people were still alive or if there was any way to reach them; and in the aftermath of the struggle to contain the death-wind, the Rittandics began their long, slow decline into infertility, sterility, and underpopulation. Few believed these subsequent misfortunes to be coincidental.

Since then, the Rittandics had studied the Æther from the outside, mostly, although a bold or foolish few still made attempts to penetrate the swirl of misty fog to learn more about its internals. This was strictly forbidden, but visionaries would not be deterred; thanks to them, an old theory had regained currency in the last few decades: That the Æther was not simple nothingness but was, in fact, a weak spot between worlds, an intersection worn through by a sort of friction, the way the fabric of a garment would eventually give way at the knee or elbow against the constant pressure of the joint beneath. She recalled that Brennendah's predecessor had, in fact, grown discontent with simply charting the disappearance of the poles, and had tried to enchant the markers to gather and transmit readings of temperature, pressure, atmosphere, and other statistics from the Æther back to a clay tablet, a sort of dumb remote writing. Whatever it had seen on those tablets was unknown; it had packed them up and brought them to Jordneh's castle, showing them to her and no one else, and for its efforts had been relieved of its duty. The tablets themselves were, according to rumor, covered with random scrawls that made no sense, though some whispered that the brittle surfaces contained encoded communications from Untelleh, lost out in the Æther. Most, however, subscribed to the theory that the monitor had scribbled the messages itself in a fit of madness, and had earned its dismissal.

Kaderleh did not approve of meddling with the Æther in such a fashion. Some doors were better left shut, lest they admit that which was not welcome. She considered the jump that had just occurred, and feared the battered gate Untelleh had once flung wide had creaked open yet again.

She and Brennendah continued through the Edgelands, the sandy ground shifting beneath their feet. Farther from the edge of the Æther, the bluish-green grass common in the rest of the Ravels began to appear in tufts between the stubby pines. They crested a hill that was half-sand and half-grass, ringed with conifers and barren on top. To the north and west she could see the rolling green and pewter downs that characterized this part of the Ravels; to the right, in the eastern distance, the Fists loomed, clenched hands of rock running from the far north to the south until they met the Æther and vanished. Crumbling half-peaks stood at the end of the range, as if someone had sliced through it vertically with a dull knife and carried part of it away. Where had it gone? If the Æther were a gateway, had unknown beings in some distant world looked on in shock as millions of tons of rock and earth had been vomited up in a catastrophic storm from their own grey puddle of mist?

The camp occupied the flat summit of the hill. As they entered the cleared area, Brennendah told her he wanted to relocate the outpost to a position farther from the Æther, which meant the tents would have to be struck and folded, the equipment packed and loaded and hauled and unpacked. A new deep well would need to be dug, a new observation tower and pole barn built, a new fire pit excavated and lined with stone. Perhaps they could dismantle the wooden structures, transport them, reassemble them at the new location; it was not as if there was so much wood in the Ravels that they could afford to abandon what was here. She must have made a moue while contemplating all the work that lay ahead, because Brennendah said: "I will return with workers to help us move everything."

She nodded, then said: "But I am not helpless. I will scout for a new location while you are gone."

"I do not expect to be away long," he said. "The smith should already have the parts made."

"You will be meeting with Jordneh. She always keeps you waiting in favor of her more *notable* callers."

"As you say," Brennendah said, "but this time, there was a jump. Once she learns of that, she will want to hear the details at once."

"Mmm. Once she learns of it."

"When I tell her advisors, word will get to her quickly. In a matter of this nature, there will be no delay."

"I hope so. This is not the time for us to be separated." She looked past the camp, toward Jordneh's castle far to the north, barely visible as a black and grey blot on the distant verdant highlands, swaddled by the spreading brown blocks of the surrounding village. Like a mirage, the far-off structures shimmered in a haze of pollen and water vapor from a recent autumn rain. The castle was distant enough that their camp needed its own water source and to be stocked with supplies, but also close enough that it did not take long to renew their cache when consumables ran low. She or Brennendah could take the wagon out in the morning and be back with food and equipment by nightfall. The roads in the Ravels were few, but good, and banditry virtually nonexistent.

Kaderleh followed Brennendah to the small barn near the main tent. The half-dead pines reached out to them with gnarled fingers. She would miss being surrounded by their stunted shadows, the scent of their dribbling pitch as it dried on their cracked surfaces, the way they popped and spit when they burned in the fire pit on chilly evenings. At least they would still be able to come back to the old site and cut them down for firewood. The wagon sat within the barn, and in the back, the horse contentedly munched its hay. Sun-baked tablets sat in a pile in the back of the wagon; Brennendah had allowed quite a stack to accumulate. He should have delivered them earlier but had been remiss, wanting, Kaderleh knew, neither to leave her alone nor to bring her along for the bumpy ride during these delicate early weeks. Now he had no choice; a jump mandated immediate notification of the witch-queen. "I could go with you——"

"That is not necessary," he said. "Although I must report it at once, another jump so soon after this one is, according to the historical record, highly unlikely. Stay here, safe and comfortable, and I will be back tomorrow afternoon with a team to help us move." He held a length of her hair in his fingers and ran it lightly between them. "We will build you a comfortable home a few hills away."

"With a proper bed, instead of a hammock?"

"Whatever you wish." Brennendah led the horse to the wagon and began attaching its harness, his long fingers moving quickly over the straps and buckles. "What else do we need, besides spikes, and number plates for the poles, and the makings of a proper bed? You said you had a list?"

"Yes, but I need to add a few more things to it before I give it to you."

"Of course you do," he said.

~~~~

By the time the horse was secured and the wagon loaded for the trip, it was late morning. That meant Brennendah likely would not arrive at Jordneh's castle until towards evening, but that was all right; he would make his presence known, explain the need and reason for a quick meeting, and then the functionaries who controlled Jordneh's schedule would rearrange things to put the two of them together sooner than might be the case under other circumstances.

"On the morrow, perhaps," Kaderleh said, when Brennendah spoke of the response he envisioned, "after Jordneh's morning constitutional, but before her daily flowerbed-planning session with her gardeners."

"That is unfair," Brennendah said. "She mostly allows the gardeners to plant the beds according to their own discretion." Then, looking to the south: "Rain. Feh."

"Perhaps you should stay until it passes," Kaderleh said, eyeing the distant sky. The day had started out clear and brittle, but now grey clouds had begun to accumulate out over the sea, far beyond the Æther, portending an autumn storm. Following its usual pattern, the system would split around the space above the Æther and form two separate tracks as it moved inland, eventually rejoining some distance to the north. That was where the risk of tornados was greatest but, threatening though the clouds might look, this was not the season for such severe storms. Brennendah might be caught in a heavy rain, but the roads were high enough to keep him safe from flash floods; and, of course, in the little desert of non-weather where their camp currently resided, Kaderleh should stay perfectly dry.

Brennendah glanced from the southern horizon to the wagon, then to the north. "Perhaps, but everything is prepared. The horse is ready to earn his hay. A glamour will keep me dry, and, if it comes to that, I have a tarpaulin to protect the tablets."

"And poor Horse?"

Her husband stroked the animal's mane. "Is that your name today, then? Poor Horse?" It whickered at him in evident agreement. "Poor Horse says that he enjoys the rain. It keeps the flies away."

She smiled. "So it does."

"It holds no such benefit for you, though. You should go inside and light the tent stove to keep warm."

"That is hardly necessary," she said, as her husband wandered off to check the horse's tethers and the wagon's wheels, and spread an oilcloth over the cargo. "It will not rain here. It *never* rains here." But as she spoke the words, something shifted; a central hump of vapor bloomed upward far to the south, spread and split like a pair of arms, then fell back beyond view. It happened so quickly that she almost questioned if it had happened at all. Almost. Had it really been the storm clouds, or had it been the Æther, belching like a drunkard? She felt a dull, icy dread rise in her stomach, with no source or reason, and looked at Brennendah, wondering if he had seen it, but he had ducked beneath the wagon, making a final check of the struts and panels before climbing on the buckboard and being on his way, and was in no position to have observed the sky or the Æther or anything but Poor Horse's hooves and the underside of the cart.

Returning her gaze to the storm, she could no longer tell what had roused her fear. They were just ordinary rain clouds, following an ordinary path. Perhaps it was had just been a trick of her condition. She had heard tell of such things.

Brennendah finished his inspection and straightened up. "Ready," he said. Then: "You will be all right? You seem pale."

"Fine. Just the light-headedness, I think. It happens, and it has passed."

"I see." He looked her over. "Do not feel that you must begin scouting new locations for the camp today. We have a good deal of time yet before the Æther will come this far."

"Do we? How can we know that? It seems prudent not to wait."

Brennendah nodded, acknowledging the point. "Do what you think best, but without overtaxing yourself. I have no wish to return and find, like one of Untelleh's field hands, that all I care about has been consumed by the void, but that is not the only fate to be avoided."

"You worry too much," Kaderleh said.

"Of course I do," he said.

~~~~

Kaderleh waited on the hillside near the barn as Brennendah drove the wagon away, trundling and rocking down the steep dirt track that years of arrivals and departures had worn into the terrain. That was another thing to look for when scouting their new location, she thought: It would need to be more easily accessible by cart than this one. In fact, she should start a list of requirements for the new site. Lists were good.

The cart bumped and swayed its way out of sight around the bottom of the next hill. If she fetched the spyglass and took it to the top of the watchtower, she would be able to spot Brennendah intermittently for much of his trip to the castle, but she had things to do and could hardly spend the entire day hoping to catch ever more

elusive glimpses of her husband's receding form. Leaving the vicinity
of the barn, she headed for the large central tent that served as their
primary living space. The shaded interior was cool; the camp stove,
reduced now to embers, provided a dim, ruddy glow, but she needed
better illumination in order to work on her list. She unbuttoned the
back flap and let it fall open, allowing the morning sun to fall on the
small desk near the cots. Light was one of the few things known to
pass over the Æther unmolested. A new experiment suddenly occurred
to her: They could try to compare the relative heat content of sunlight
that had passed over the Æther to similarly-angled sunlight that had
not done so, and thus learn if the Æther drained warmth from it. She
would recommend that to Brennendah when he returned; he would
know if it had been done before. She retrieved a blank slate and a
piece of chalk, sat down at the desk, and wrote *light* at the top of the
slate, underlining it to keep it separate from the remainder of her
forthcoming list. Before she continued, her gaze fell upon the spyglass
hanging from its peg on a nearby support pole.

Well, it would not hurt to take a *quick* look.

Laying the slate and chalk down, she fetched the telescope, put it to
her left eye, and looked out across the Ravels, sweeping the circle of
her magnified vision back and forth. There were the Fists, massively
solid, yet so riddled with dwarven tunnels that she imagined a good
blow might cause them to collapse. She knew that, unseen beyond the
rugged peaks, the elven forest of Torgonderrer sprouted on the
plateau, a mere remnant of the much more extensive ancient
woodlands that now lay submerged beneath the Boiling Sea.
Something dire had transpired in Torgonderrer recently; she and
Brennendah had observed a vast plume of smoke drifting southward
not long ago, as if a large woodland blaze burned. The smoke had
only persisted for a day or so, leading the two of them into endless
speculation as to what had happened. Perhaps Brennendah would find
something out during his visit with Jordneh.

Swinging the spyglass west, to her left, she scanned the downs,
searching for the small dust cloud that would be left by the wagon.
There it was. She caught sight of the dark shape of the cart itself just
as it vanished behind another drumlin, and moved the glass upwards to
where the road emerged from the other side of the low, rolling hill. As
she did, she noticed that the storm from the sea had begun moving
overland, two dark, chunky, oily arms of cloud reaching northward to
encircle the Ravels, overtaking the wisps that already drifted in that
part of the sky.

Kaderleh frowned. The other clouds were not moving with the same speed as the oncoming storm. Was this some sort of emanation from the Æther? She took the spyglass outside and, slipping it into one of the many concealed pockets of her robe, scaled the ladder to the top of the wooden observation stand—another structure that would need to be disassembled and moved—that allowed them to examine the void from camp on those days when close inspection was not required. Settling cross-legged onto the narrow plank at its top, she pulled out and extended the telescope and aimed it at the thick mists of the Æther. Nothing unusual seemed to be going on within; it belched forth neither riotous fumes nor hordes of monsters, and the weather rushing by overhead did not seem to have erupted out of it. Still, the system looked like no natural phenomenon that Kaderleh had ever seen. Her long fingers located and spun a dial on the side of the spyglass, rotating the mechanism inside; a specialized crystal snapped into the sightline between two of the interior lenses, adding a filter designed to bring enchantments forward into visibility. She drew a sharp breath, stunned by what it revealed: That the storm was riddled with strings of force, radiating and ramifying like the roots of a great tree or the neurons of a brain. Unlike a root system, though, she found it exceedingly difficult to trace the lines back to a central source; they connected and interconnected, split and merged, as if the entire system had been knitted together by a demented spider. She adjusted the lenses, trying to bring the storm into better focus, fading out the obscuring vapor and glial tangles, finally locating what looked like a central node in the back, beyond where the clouds parted around the Æther. The channels controlling the forward arms of the storm originated from there; but what was *that* attached to? A ship on the distant sea? She saw nothing connecting the point in the clouds with a point on the horizon. She adjusted the dial, rotating the enchanted crystal this way and that, worrying at the brain-like knot, causing her view of the strings to shimmer and warp. At that moment Kaderleh sensed a sudden shift in the air, and realized that she had made a grave error. If she had stuck to simple optics her scrutiny may have gone unnoticed, but when she brought the enchanted glass into the view, she had begun leaving traces, as if she were swabbing the clouds with a paintbrush.

Those traces led, inevitably, back to her.

She turned the dial to slide the viewing crystal out of position, and slowly lowered the spyglass, but it was too late and she knew it. She heard a growing rumble, as of a rockslide in the mountains, a stampede of Poor Horse and all his relatives thundering across the plains. She looked up as two thin tendrils of cloud emerged sideways, one from each distant arm of clouds, spinning around each other overhead, joining into a roaring helix that stabbed downward toward the camp.

In the last moment, as the winds picked up, Kaderleh lowered her head, closed her eyes, and imagined what her child might have become had it lived to be born.

~~~~

Brennendah had been making good time. Poor Horse was fed and well-rested; the wagon's load was light; the road was in good repair. Perhaps he would get to the castle in time to deliver his slates to Jordneh after dinner, inform her of the jump, acknowledge her concerns and admonitions, collect the spikes and number plates and the supplies on Kaderleh's list, and return to the observation post first thing in the morning. At least, that was what he thought before he noticed weather encroaching to the east and west, gloomy clouds the color of mud laced with mercury, moving forward with greater velocity than the cart. He pulled back on the reins, bringing Poor Horse to a halt; after a moment the beast started some reluctant grazing, not terribly enthused by the tough grass that grew in this area. While the horse masticated half-heartedly, Brennendah peered up at the sky, where onrushing clouds reached like arms from the sea to clutch the Ravels in a sinister embrace. The ostentatious display of abnormal atmospheric behavior elicited a growing suspicion, which Poor Horse seemed to share; despite the blinders he wore, the animal repeatedly lifted his head to the sky, ears flat, whites showing. The creature was clearly uncomfortable. Brennendah had anticipated being rained on, with a weak force-shell prepared and ready to fire when the precipitation began, but these clouds portended a different sort of threat.

The not-so-distant roar of a whirlwind from behind them snapped Brennendah's attention around; Poor Horse, too, raised his head, bits of dry, half-eaten grass flaking from the sides of his motionless jaws. They had stopped in a gully bounded by low, worn ridges, blocking his view of the surrounding terrain, but he spotted a funnel spiraling down from the pewter sky. He could not tell exactly where it was aiming to touch down, but it seemed to be in the vicinity of the outpost.

A tornado at this time of year, and in the *Edgelands*? Unheard of.

Unlike in the town around Jordneh's castle and the villages that lay to the north, they had no storm shelter at the camp. Why would they?

They had no weather. The closest safe spot would be the supply cave, a large cavity in an undercut bank in one of the nearby dry washes where they stored water and reeds and other dry goods. If the observation post were threatened, would Kaderleh be able to get to the supply cave in time? Would she even think to run to it?

Brennendah snatched up the reins and urged Poor Horse onward, leaving the good dirt road to ascend the drumlin to his right, hoping for a better view from the apex. If a tornado really was going to touch down nearby then a barren hilltop was hardly the best place to be, but he had to know if Kaderleh was in danger.

The wagon bumped and rocked its way up the slope. Although not intended for such a climb, the cart's wheels and Poor Horse's well-shod hooves proved adequate to the challenge, and they soon gained the summit, such as it was. Too late: The funnel had already touched down and begun to withdraw, spiraling back up into the malignant clouds that swelled overhead. He had missed seeing it make contact with the ground. But the clouds … The clouds now enclosed the Æther in a tight grip. The air remained open above the frothy boil, but everywhere else the azure sky was lost beyond a layer of ominous vapor. Brennendah sat on the buckboard, clutching the reins, incapable of telling Poor Horse what to do. He was supposed to be on his way to the castle, to meet Jordneh, but he had a grave feeling, a clawing fear in his stomach. The clouds should not look this way. Something dreadful had happened back at camp. Perhaps, as Kaderleh had feared, the jump had been a portent of something worse to come, and the Æther had belched forth some fresh doom to destroy them all.

He should not have left her.

He had to go back.

Poor Horse would move faster without the wagon, but the animal was unaccustomed to a rider; besides, the wagon carried no saddle or bridle for direct riding. Brennendah decided to lighten the load instead. He jumped down from his perch, hurried to the back, and unloaded most of his supplies—the water barrel, the stacks of prepared slates, a small bale of hay—to reduce the weight. He could pick them up again on his way out, after he had checked the camp and found all in order and Kaderleh had gently chided him for his foolish worry. That done, he leapt back to the buckboard, wheeled the cart around, and descended, taking the downward slope more carefully than he had the upward. At the bottom of the drumlin he turned left, back the way they had come. If Poor Horse found this odd, he gave no indication, though the beast continued to cast glances at the sky, ears flattened, eyes wary. Brennendah slapped the reins to urge greater speed but the animal mulishly refused to accelerate, as if they were heading toward some destination known to be unpleasant; yet Poor Horse was well aware that in this direction lay his stable, his hay, his water. The creature's lack of enthusiasm for the return journey disturbed Brennendah immensely.

The rumbling sound arose again, closer this time. Another funnel? Where was it? This gully was narrower; the glacial moraines blocked his view of the surrounding sky and he dared not try to climb one of them again and expose himself to whatever was coming. He slapped the reins again; Poor Horse plodded onward without adding a whit of speed. They emerged from the cluster of pimpled hills at a slightly lower elevation than where they had entered, but at least he could see a bit farther. Brennendah scanned for signs of the second tornado he had heard, and quickly spotted a funnel withdrawing into the sky just to the north, leaving behind a nearby hilltop scoured of grass as if it had been shaved with a razor. Debris littered the barren hump and lay scattered across its flanks: Fragments of flat stone, pieces of curved planking, squares of tile. Feathery amber scraps—hay blasted back into straw—drifted lazily in the wind.

Brennendah's dark eyes widened. That wreckage was all that remained of the supplies that had lately occupied the back of his wagon, and that he had laid out on the hilltop in order to gain some speed. The churning storm continued rolling northward on its way to Jordneh's castle, but had paused in its seemingly purposeful march to extend a swirling finger and touch the spot where, not long before, he had stopped to look at it, almost exactly the way one might lower a languid thumb to squash an ant that had paused to taste the air near one's picnic lunch.

He squeezed his eyes shut, feeling terribly short on time, but needing to think for a moment. So: It was widely known that weather systems possessed a great deal of inertia in their behavior. If a storm such as this one were under the control of some entity whose primary attention was focused elsewhere or who was not particularly experienced in commanding atmospheric forces, then there could well be a delay of several minutes—as wind patterns shifted, temperatures changed, water vapor condensed—before a command to, for instance, have a tornado to touch down at a specific spot could be carried through to completion. Such a delay might allow enough time, perhaps, for an unwitting individual who had been at the targeted location to move away, and then to look back upon where he had been, to see the spot devastated by the wind, and pause to consider the implications of that destruction, exactly as Brennendah was doing right now.

Brennendah recognized the leap he was making. So far as he knew, not even Jordneh could direct weather on this scale. She could make it rain on selected crops when conditions were favorable; she could summon cool breezes down from the Fists to break local heat waves. But conjuring up a system large enough to blanket the Ravels? That was far beyond her ken. If she possessed such power, the village around her castle would not need to be riddled with shelters to preserve lives from the tornadoes that plagued them. Yet this unnatural storm behaved as if directed by a malign intelligence. Its primary objective clearly lay to the north, judging by its motion, but it had taken note of Brennendah and been bothered enough by his scrutiny to make a lazy attempt on his life. Would it make another? And who had been its first target, if not Kaderleh and the camp?

He cast another glance in the direction of Jordneh's castle. It was not visible from here, but would present as a black smear in the misty distance if he were on higher ground. It hardly mattered if he could see it or not. He knew there was no chance that he could outrun the storm and get there in time to warn the Queen of what was coming, just as he knew there was no chance that he would return to camp and find it intact and Kaderleh waiting for him with a quizzical smile, wondering why he had come back so soon.

He could attempt only one impossible feat today. Which would it be?

Brennendah gave Poor Horse another slap with the reins, and urged him onward, back towards the observation post.

~~~~

Jordneh, Witch-Queen of the Ravels, sat at her desk in the small office near her apartments, regarding the human who had recently arrived from Abacar bearing a sealed message from Lord Korrin. "I have reviewed Korrin's proposal," she told him, looking down at the rolled-up scrolls she held in her long blue fingers. The man had given her to understand that, unlike some lesser couriers who were mere deliverymen, he knew the contents of the papers he carried and was authorized to discuss them. "Korrin must, of course, understand that we Rittandics sustained terrible losses when we helped his forefathers contain Daras-Drûm and neutralize its worshipers. Terrible losses. The curse inflicted on us then remains unbroken to this day, and continues to spread through our bloodlines. We are not eager to suffer similarly in repelling the Banderlundi."

"Of course." If the fellow found her insufficiently respectful for not using his master's honorific title, he had the good sense not to say so. "But the Banderlundi are neither the death-wind nor its cultists."

"Indeed they are not," Jordneh said. "The Banderlundi have an army. They have a navy."

"But at least they are *alive*," he said, with the narrow focus of one charged with arguing a single issue from a predetermined perspective.

"As were the ones who styled themselves the priests of Daras-Drûm. Though the same cannot be said of their footmen."

He made a derisive noise. "The death-wind was no god, and its priests were no priests. Sorcerers who sought to draw on its vampirism to power their own necromancy and enslave the mindless undead who trailed in its wake, yes. Clerics, no."

She regarded the messenger for a moment—he had an unusually nuanced understanding of the ancient threat, to be sure—then asked: "What of the others? The elves, the dwarves, the Pelts? What have they to say about the matter?"

"We messengers parted ways at the pass some time ago, so I cannot speak to the reactions of the other kingdoms, but I am confident that the children of both forest and mountain will perceive the wisdom of Lord Korrin's request."

"Mmm. No doubt you are right, although the wisdom they infer might not be that which was intended."

He gave her a puzzled look. "I am sorry. Does her majesty find Lord Korrin's meaning unclear?"

"No, not at all." She smiled and shook her head. "You humans. Always thinking everyone sees the world the way that you do. If you tell the dwarves that the sea will be rising past their doors, they will make the doors waterproof. If you tell the elves that the sea will overtake their trees, they will collect seeds from every plant they can find and move to higher ground. If you tell the Pelts that the sea will drown them, they will just grow gills. Do you understand? None of those whose aid you seek will immediately take up the sword you offer and begin slashing at the waves."

"Surely neither the dwarves nor the elves nor the Pelts are so eager to let the 'Lundi yoke them, your majesty."

"We are all yoked to something."

"Some yokes are donned willingly, and some are imposed. Which is easier to bear?"

Like a good diplomat, this man had an answer to everything. "Tell me, then: What would Korrin have me do? Does he think I can sink the fleet that lurks offshore, or afflict its sailors with more scurvy than they already—" She broke off as one of her advisors, the neuter Lemdenoh, burst into her office. Its chest heaved, as if it had arrived here running through the castle at top speed. Hoping that her request to be undisturbed would not have been dishonored without good reason, she turned to regard the intruder rather than immediately berating it.

After a moment Lemdenoh spoke, its voice hoarse and winded. "A storm approaches, your majesty."

"A storm?" It was time to issue the deferred reprimand. "Such news hardly seems worthy of interrupting my meeting with our esteemed visitor, Lemdenoh."

"Not normally, my queen," Lemdenoh said, "but this storm has already spawned tornadoes in the southern downs."

"Tornadoes? This is not the time of year for tornadoes."

"Indeed not, your majesty."

She considered the information for a moment. "The system will not dissipate in the South?"

"The observers do not think so. When it was noticed, the spotters went to their towers. They report that the storm behaves oddly. It has generated two funnel clouds thus far, and both appear to have been ..." Lemdenoh trailed off, looking uncomfortable, then said: "Targeted."

Lord Korrin's messenger, speaking out of turn, as humans so often did, said: "What do you mean, *targeted?*"

Lemdenoh cast a questioning glance at the man, then at the queen; Jordneh gave the barest of nods, granting the neuter permission to speak freely. Turning to the messenger, Lemdenoh said: "The spotters believe the funnel clouds were used to attack specific points on the earth. Each descended, stayed on the ground for a brief period, and then withdrew without significant motion away from the spot where it touched down. That is *highly* unusual for a tornado. For one storm to do it twice in quick succession is without precedent."

"From such a distance, how can you tell what it did? Magic?"

"We have four towers equipped with fully rotational telescopes mounted on precise compasses, containing a complement of adjustable lenses. They are spaced sufficiently far apart that we can compare the angles of the compasses of any two of them when focused on the same point and, because the distance from each tower to each other tower is known, we may use a parallax calculation to determine the position, direction, and speed of the subject under observation."

Noting the emissary's blank look, Jordneh said: "You may consider it magic." Then, to Lemdenoh: "Take me to where I can see this storm for myself."

"We believe there is a danger, your——"

"I know what you believe. Show me this storm, Lemdenoh."

"As you wish."

The neuter moved to grasp the handles of her chair, but Lord Korrin's messenger, displaying the impulsive helpfulness not uncommon in his species, took hold of them himself. "Lead the way," he told Lemdenoh.

They departed the office, traveling with unaccustomed speed through the castle. Jordneh twisted her head around to look up at the man propelling her wheeled conveyance. From his startled expression, she realized that to him it must look like she had just snapped her spine; among their many other limitations, most humans could rotate their necks a mere ninety degrees at best. How tedious *that* must be. "Thank you for your assistance," she said. "I did not ask your name, before, but I would know it now."

"I am called Kendrick. Tell me, your majesty, have you no healers who could let you walk again?"

"Some injuries are beyond the skill of even the most gifted of healers to repair, I am afraid." They bumped onto one of the wooden ramps that partially overlay all the stairs in the castle that the witch-queen might desire to traverse, going up it to a higher level of the castle. "You realize, young Kendrick, that if Lemdenoh is correct about this storm, you may be putting yourself in jeopardy by accompanying us."

The man grinned with half his mouth. "I am not *that* young, your majesty."

"Young or old, there are shelters available for all, as protection from the tornadoes that plague the Ravels."

"I do not fear the wind, your majesty. We get some fearsome cyclones off the sea in Abacar in late summer."

"Yes, I am familiar with your hurricanes. They are indeed impressive, but there is a reason some refer to our funnel clouds as the Fingers of Death."

"Fingers do not frighten me unless there are five of them and they close into a fist."

Still with the ready answers. She nodded. "As you say."

They soon arrived at a third-floor landing, where Lemdenoh pulled open a heavy wooden door to reveal a circular verandah, arcaded near the castle but open to the elements farther out. Kendrick pushed her through the door, following Lemdenoh along the curve of the balcony until they reached a spot that allowed them to see across the southern Ravels toward the Æther and the distant sea. Clouds streamed in from that direction, thick and grey and chunky as congealed fat floating in cold soup, rushing along the underside of the sky as if pressed between angled panes of heavy glass. Despite this, a perfect circle of sky directly above the castle remained clear and utterly empty, even as the clouds blotted out every other scrap of blue from the surrounding mountains all the way to the Edgelands. She saw no signs of funnel clouds for the nonce, but Lemdenoh was right; this storm was unnaturally threatening.

"I thought you said the weather was still over the southern downs," she said as she stared at the writhing clouds.

"So it was, your majesty, when I came to get you."

"Then it should not be *here* now," she said. "Not so quickly."

Kendrick moved away from her wheeled conveyance, going to stand near the balustrade, away from the sheltered overhang, looking up at the malignant bloom overhead. "This sort of … *weather* … is commonly seen here?"

"No," Lemdenoh said, "it is not."

"Come away from there, Kendrick," Jordneh said.

"We should all be taking shelter," Lemdenoh said, "not exposing ourselves to possible—" As if in response to the tension in Lemdenoh's voice, the bells in the storm-warning towers that ringed the town began to ring a clangor that signified dangerous weather, drowning out the rest of its statement. The advance notice was far from adequate. In the spring bell-ringers would be on duty day and night, but tornado season was months away; given the evident speed of this storm, it had likely arrived before the bell towers—which were separate structures from the observation towers, so that the vibration of the massive chimes would not disrupt the delicate mechanisms of the telescopes—could even be unlocked and the clappers freed of their dampers. She hoped her subjects had already realized the danger, and had begun to seek shelter even before the alarums prompted them to do so.

Lemdenoh was right. This phenomenon was being directed.

Weather was difficult to manipulate in any region, and even more so here in the Ravels, where the Æther's influence disrupted atmospheric patterns in ways that no one fully understood; whoever was behind this must, she thought, have only the barest level of control over the maelstrom. If she could nudge the winds in the proper way, perhaps she could neutralize it, crash it like a cart that had lost its steering pin. Clutching the arms of her wheeled conveyance, Jordneh focused on the spinning inner ring of clouds, suspecting that it was the anchor that kept the system coherent. She reached out with her mind, unconsciously raising her left hand as she did so, directing a probe through the wards to touch the circling band of clouds, see if she could peel some of the energy off, turn it back on itself, and destroy it with its own power.

Jordneh felt an immediate, crushing pain in her fingers, as if they had been closed in a vise, and realized at once that she had made a mistake. The power behind the storm had been waiting for her to reveal herself, and now she had; but before she could do more than gasp, an immense, unseen pressure settled over her, immobilizing her, welding her to the chair. Something shifted within the clouds, a ripple, like the muscles beneath the skin of a snake as it prepared to strike. She could feel a static charge gathering, prickles on her skin; Kendrick's body fur stood on end, and the fine hairs of his head began to quiver. Did lightning gather? If so, the metal tubing of her chair would make it a dangerous place to be. There was, however, no rumble of thunder; instead, the inner ring of clouds above the castle lurched into motion, spinning widdershins around the castle. Simultaneously, a number of tendrils of vapor dropped and thickened. She counted three, then six, then, finally, ten. Ten fingers. Enough to make *two* of the fists Kendrick feared. How could this unnatural horror deploy that many tornadoes at once and not tear itself apart?

Unable to move or speak, the witch-queen could only watch as Lemdenoh went to Kendrick, took his arm, and tried to shepherd him back to the ostensible safety of the castle. They both took flight before Jordneh's eyes, swept up and carried off by a debris-laden wind that roared through scant yards from where she sat, untouched, unmarred, pinned like a prized butterfly in a glass case. The fingers of death touched down and pirouetted through the village like a troupe of wicked dancers. They never closed into the fist Kendrick had feared, but they hardly needed to as they raked the town over and over and over again, destroying it as thoroughly as the pounding of a giant's club. Then, as if dissatisfied with the destruction they were wreaking, they coiled on themselves, turned sideways, sought out the shelters, pounded and pulled and worried at the doors until they gave way. Despite the dust and wreckage that obscured the town, she could see the funnels doing their evil work, reaching beneath nearby buildings, sucking out the occupants like marrow slurped from bones. The air must surely be full of screams, inaudible over the roaring of the wind; her ears rang with it. She felt, indistinctly, a battering from all sides, as spiraling currents tore through the halls of the castle behind her, scouring it of inhabitants, of furniture, of wall hangings, of everything it contained that could be picked up and carried away. Windows and shutters and doors exploded outward, blasted from their supports and their frames, blown into the maelstrom of debris that chewed the town with grinding force. The storm devoured her village, and passed it as rubble; and throughout it all she sat, safe and helpless, enclosed in the incapacitating protection that had been imposed upon her, unable to act. The enchantment did not force her to watch, but she was unwilling to close her eyes.

After some time, the wind abated. The pressure that had held her in place, that had protected her from the storm's wrath, eased. Jordneh had no idea how long the onslaught had lasted; she doubted any of the chronometers in the castle had survived. She took hold of the rims to propel herself forward, hoping to get a look from the balustrade at the devastation, but a battered, bloodied corpse thudded to the balcony in front of her, blocking the wheels. It was Korrin's courier, bashed and beaten by windblown projectiles, and now dropped directly in her way. The odds of this happening at random were minuscule, so it must be a message. Where, then, was the messenger? She looked up as the wind deposited the answer on the balcony nearby: A Rittandic, upright and unharmed. For a moment she thought the storm had by some bizarre design returned Lemdenoh to her; but, no, this was someone else. Of course it was someone else: The architect of the destruction, come to claim credit for his work. "Greetings, my queen." The Rittandic looked down at Kendrick's body, nudged it with a foot. "You still consort with lesser beings, I see."

To her surprise, she realized that she knew this creature. She said, "Kihantroh?"

"Ah, you remember me. Good."

"Of course I remember you. It was not so long ago that—"

"That you dismissed me from your service, stripped me of my purpose, and sent me away? No. It was not so long ago at all. This human wears the uniform of Abacar. What business did you have with him?"

"He ... he brought me a message from Korrin," Jordneh said. "Kihantroh, why—"

"A message?" The huge eyes closed for a moment, and when they opened again, she saw the fading remnant of a rheumy human iris in their black depths. What dark glamour lay behind that artifact? "Yes, yes, I remember. My Lord Korrin dispatched four riders, one to the Pelts, one to the dwarves, one to the elves, and one to you."

"What know you of Korrin's messengers, Kihantroh?"

"I know the dwarves still have theirs, shut up like an honored prisoner beneath the mountain while they pursue the machinations, long-planned and oft-deferred, that his warning finally set in motion. I know that yours, of course, lies dead at my feet. Of the one sent to the Pelts and the one sent to the elves, I know not their fate, save that they failed to return before events overtook Lord Korrin and he passed from this world to find whatever reward awaits him in the next."

"Passed from—Kihantroh, what have you done?"

A faint shrug. "I have done as the Tellehi said I must."

"The … Tellehi?" Now a term of disparagement, this had once collectively referred to the followers of the sorceress Untelleh, who had with their mistress been cast into the Æther during her disastrous attempt to harness its energy. In modern use it was derogatorily applied to those who displayed a blind willingness to go along with any ill-starred venture. "What do you mean, the Tellehi?"

"I mean the Tellehi," Kihantroh said. "Do not think to deceive me with a mask of false ignorance, my queen. The Tellehi told me the truth about the Æther, and about *you*." Its thin lips pulled into a smile, or a grimace; perhaps it was both. "All those years I spent studying the Æther, bringing you those slates, waiting on your convenience as you attended to matters of more importance than a mere researcher—all those years, my queen, you lied and dissembled and feigned interest in the information I brought you; and *all those years*, the shadows knew your secret. They only needed one who would hear their whispers."

"And that one was you? You think something communicated with you through those slates that you cast into the—"

"Something *did* communicate with me thus. I know that is why you had the slates destroyed, and why you sent me away."

"I relieved you of your position because your experiments with the Æther were becoming dangerous."

"Dangerous to *you*, perhaps, as the runes revealed the truth which you sought to hide for so long."

"And what truth is that, Kihantroh?"

"They followed me, you know," it said. "The Tellehi. After my experiments with the slates, I had gained their attention. They found a way to communicate with me across the void, despite your efforts, despite the distance between me and the prison which contained them. Because what is *distance* to one who is smeared across all reality like dye seeping through fabric? What is *time*? You sent me away from the Æther, but in truth I never left it. Or perhaps it never left me."

"You still have not told me what secret knowledge you think you have gained. What could possibly impel you to come striding back here like some barbarian chieftain, destroying your own——"

"Barbarian? I am hardly that. You see, your majesty, I know the true history of the Ravels now. I know who you are. I know *what* you are. The Tellehi told me all. Your *long-term study* of the Æther? A sham, a pantomime. You already know why the Æther seethes and how the Æther spreads. You sit in your chair and you unravel reality itself to power your glamours. You batten on the land like a leech. Yes, I know you! You are the very same sorceress who dwelt in the North in the times when Untelleh lived. You lolled on your throne while she cast herself and her people into the void, then claimed the power thus released as your own. You style yourself a great witch-queen? Feh! I name you the worst kind of parasite. You sacrifice the land, the people, the very *world*, so that you can siphon off the energy released when the bonds of matter are broken and stuff churns to nothing. Yes, the Tellehi told me. You are as a maggot, my queen, feeding on the wound that is the Æther, never letting it heal, always causing it to grow."

"Yet do our healers not use maggots to consume dead flesh, that the healthy flesh may regrow?"

"Sophistry." Kihantroh snorted. "Then let the maggots forgive the injury I rendered by comparing you to them."

"And those who lived in the village?" She gestured with a gnarled and useless hand at the ruined town. "What did *they* do to earn their deaths?"

Kihantroh shrugged its narrow shoulders. "They were there. When one parasite dies another takes its place, unless all have been eradicated. And so, my queen, your long, useless life ends. I know that chair is but an affectation. Stand up."

"You are a fool, Kihantroh," she said.

"Stand up!"

"I know not whence came these Tellehi that *enlightened* you, but they have ladled up a soup of lies beneath the thinnest skin of fact."

"Lies? Then let me show you some truths." Kihantroh plunged its hands into its voluminous pockets, and pulled out two objects. She drew a sharp breath, immediately recognizing the Maul of Abacar, the Jewel at its tip casting a kaleidoscope of light through the gem-encrusted head.   The other item was a crude iron claw, evidently of Kihantroh's own creation, the ends folded into tines to enclose and protect a second glowing stone.   This must be the Illata, she realized—or, depending on one's point of view, the Brisindeld. "You see what I possess, my queen?   What the Tellehi led me to obtain? Where are the lies in them?"

"Kihantroh, you cannot—"

"Enough! You have no say in what I can or cannot do. Stand now, that I may strike you down."   The jewels flashed and Jordneh's wheelchair shot away from beneath her; she fell heavily to the stone floor and lay there for a moment, glaring up at the intruder.

Then, slowly, she stood.

~~~~

As the wagon approached the outpost, Brennendah began to note debris scattered along the sandy track and in the tall grass. Most of the wreckage consisted of pieces of wood and the occasional bit of twisted metal, although at one point he spotted something gleaming and, stopping Poor Horse—who had become much calmer now that the storm had moved on—he retrieved the remains of their spyglass from the roadside berm. The large lens was gone and the tube had become packed with soil when it had been driven into the earth. Even though it was useless now, he shook it out, watching the clumps of dirt fall and crumble on impact, and brought it back to the wagon. He was unsure why he took it, and decided it was because he thought he might have it repaired one day by the lens-crafter in the village at Jordneh's castle. If he planned to get the spyglass remade, that meant the lens-crafter would still be there, which meant the castle would still be there, which meant his fears about the storm were overblown.

The thought was entirely irrational but it was, at least, a little bit comforting.

Unfortunately, there was no comfort to be had as he neared the crest of the hill. First he came across the shredded canvas of their tent, ripped from its moorings and draped across several of the scraggly trees in the dead grove that surrounded the cleared ground. One end of it fluttered limply in the light breeze that wafted across the downs. He halted Poor Horse again, and climbed down from the wagon to inspect the fabric. Kaderleh did not lie beneath it. He extricated the tarpaulin from the stunted pines, being careful not to tear it further, then folded it several times and stuffed it into the back of the wagon. It filled nearly the entire space. He could hardly deny now that he was merely being maudlin, that he was collecting these worthless, broken things because Kaderleh had used them, had touched them, had been around them. He was mourning her already, even before finding her body, and he wondered when he had realized she was dead. It had been, he supposed, when he came to understand that the storm had deliberately tried to kill him.

Setting Poor Horse back in motion, he continued onward. Closer to the observation post, the scrub trees themselves were splintered and broken, the grove littered with wreckage: Scraps of clothing, spars from the pole barn, unused slates half-buried in the ground like the unmarked tombstones of tiny graves. The camp itself had been obliterated, scoured off the hillside, with only a few battered pilings and worn paths through the low, dead trees to show where it had once been. Still, Brennendah spotted a bale of hay that had somehow survived the wind more or less intact, a loose wad of buttery yellow feed spread in a compact lump across the hilltop. He halted the wagon there and released Poor Horse from the harness, letting the animal browse while he prowled the campsite searching for clues. The demolishment was so complete that it was difficult to reconstruct what had happened, but he thought he discerned a pattern in the grass, indicating that the funnel had touched down at the watchtower and then run in an outward spiral to devastate the remainder of the camp. It had confined itself to the hilltop rather than wandering in a roughly linear fashion as tornadoes normally did, but Brennendah hardly needed that additional bit of information to convince him that the destruction had been intentional. The wind had methodically devoured the outpost, leaving no large piles of debris for him to search, no rubble to be excavated, no timber to be shifted, no shelter upon whose door he could knock to announce that the danger had passed.

Where, then, was Kaderleh?

He wandered to the highest point of the hill, where the observation tower had stood. All that remained was one thick support, twisted and splintered just below knee height, leaning at a drunken tilt. He noticed something glinting in the crescent of soil around the base of the post, a trinket which had fallen and remained there somehow, perhaps protected by the lee of the sturdy beam: Kaderleh's birth-pendant, which she would have passed along to their child when it was born. He knelt and picked it up, traced his finger along the inscribed double helix, a representation of the encoding that made each of them what they were. Two stones were inlaid at the top, one for the father and one for the mother, each the origination point of one part of the helix. He lingered over the empty spot at the bottom where little one's polished stone would have been inserted to finish the design. No stone would ever be placed there now. The pattern would remain incomplete forever.

Choosing a sharp stone from the loose rocks mixed in with the soil around the support, he scratched a few runes into the unadorned backside of the amulet, a brief epitaph to the one around whose neck it had once hung. Then, clutching the pendant, he stood and cast his gaze to the north. From here he could just barely see the ugliness transpiring in the distance, malignant clouds massing above the spot where Jordneh's castle stood. The storm seemed to have sprouted multiple funnel clouds, writhing and squirming like a monstrous polyp. If the spyglass were not broken and filled with dirt, he could have looked through it to better see the destruction; he could have used the enchanted crystal filter to observe the lines of magic that directed the tornadoes. Yet doing so would be unwise. Whatever intelligence controlled this system had already demonstrated an extreme distaste for being watched; but he, she, or it seemed rather occupied at the moment and was, perhaps, unlikely to notice a simple spell of location, especially one created far away by someone with no interest in the weather or who was manipulating it.

All Brennendah wanted to do was find his wife. Surely he would not be destroyed for *that*.

With some murmuring and waving of hands, Brennendah invoked a small, highly targeted glamour, insulating it as best he could from the influence of the nearby Æther, whose sole concern was to tell him where Kaderleh's body could be found. For an agonizing number of seconds, the glamour hung in the air, as puzzled as its caster; Kaderleh was nowhere nearby, but that had already become apparent. He carefully extended it, slowly expanding its range, until suddenly the emanations of the Æther flooded into the glamour, breaching the parameters he had put around it and causing it to surge outward in a sudden flood. The signal spread beyond Brennendah's control like a seizure impulse traveling through the nervous system, strings touching other strings, telling them where Brennendah was and what he wanted to know, until finally, from far away, the response came back. Kaderleh's strings were found. She was at Jordneh's castle, still inside the storm, carried like a bit of foam, a scrap of flotsam. Not content with killing her, the winds had carried her away from him, that he might not even lay her to rest among the small pines, murmur a few words, bury her with the pendant folded in her hand.

He gave the distant clouds a furious look, and realized that the column of destruction had withdrawn. Whatever havoc it had been wreaking there was finished, or at least in temporary abeyance. Brennendah knew his inquiry had been detected. That burst from the Æther had betrayed him.

Poor Horse, who had been contentedly munching on hay nearby, raised his head and whickered nervously. A moment later Brennendah was beside the animal, holding the reins with a trembling hand.

The storm was coming back.

~~~~

Jordneh and Kihantroh faced each other on the balcony, while around them, the twisting, twining funnel clouds withdrew into the atmosphere. They had done their work; Kihantroh had moved on to other concerns.

"So?" Jordneh said. "I am standing, as you demanded. What now? Do you expect me to offer you access to this power you think I have? Do you wish to hear me beg for my life?"

"I know you will not beg, and power is something I have in abundance."

"Yes, I see that," she said, "but what has it cost?"

"Do not lecture me about *costs*, you, who burns the very land itself as if it were fuel for your hearth."

"You name me a leech and a parasite? Then what are you? You have gained your power from possession of the gems, yet you have no idea what feeds the crystals, do you? As the fire consumes the wood that sustains it, so they must consume something. At least I know whence *my* power comes."

"So you admit it."

Confound it. "I did not *make* that wound in the world, Kihantroh," she said, "and it was not up to me to save Untelleh from her own arrogance and greed. She chose her path and would not be deterred. The monitoring of the Æther is in truth a safety measure to ensure that—"

"Enough. I have heard enough. The Tellehi did not tell me wrong."

"These *Tellehi* who you think spoke to you, whatever they may be, can have no connection with Untelleh. You must understand this. There is no return from the void."

"You are wrong, my queen. With the gems in hand, I have the power to restore what was lost."

Understanding dawned at last. "You … think you can bring her back?"

"Yes."

"You think you can restore the lands that were consumed?"

"Yes. The lands, the castle, the lives."

"And you think justifies the destruction of scores of *other* lives, who never did you any measure of harm?"

Kihantroh merely shrugged, as if the matter were of no consequence. "The way must be cleared."

"By what right do you——"

"Feh! Do not speak to me of *rights*. You have forfeited any claim to such high concepts, you who have grown fat on the blood of the world."

"Be that as it may," she said, struggling to keep her voice from becoming a screech, "the fact remains that Untelleh is gone. She is *gone*, Kihantroh! Everything she took with her into the nowhere is *gone*. Not even you can deny that."

"I can and do deny it. You know as well as I do that matter cannot be created or destroyed, but merely changed. What the Æther consumed still exists in some form. Dispersed, enfeebled, attenuated, yes, but it exists. Now that I have stopped you from gnawing away at the Ravels, I can use the gems to undo all the harm that you have done. I will roll your glamours back, feed the energy into the Æther, and reverse the process of consumption. Untelleh and her lands will return, and the world will be healed."

She stared at Kihantroh, aghast. "You intend to unmake *all* my enchantments?"

"That is as it must be."

"You cannot! Kihantroh, the implications … Think of the binding on Daras-Drûm! The death-wind yet lingers in the caves beneath the black cliffs of Abacar. Is it really your wish that the monster should walk again? You know it was the source of the curse that has devastated our race with sterility, with infant mortality, with those born like …" She trailed off, shook her head.

"Those born like me? You may say it. I will not take offense." Then, when she did not respond: "The timing of the death-wind's appearance, so soon after Untelleh's misfortune, is hardly coincidental, is it? I know it slipped into this world through the gap created when the Æther was torn open. You say Daras-Drûm is the source of the curse on our species, but I say *you* are. Yet another crime to be written on your ledger, my queen."

"So it is *my* fault that Untelleh was so reckless, and it is *my* fault that the death-wind stormed the Slash, and it will be *my* fault when it returns after I am undone? Such a neat package of blame, Kihantroh, and none of it yours. Perhaps you *have* been learning from Untelleh after all."

"Once the hole in the world is healed, Daras-Drûm may simply disappear, banished whence it came with no further effort; and if it does not, then we will bind it once more, Untelleh and I. What was put down must be raised up again, to return to the state before. And then there will be ..." Kihantroh trailed off, cocked its head as if it heard something unexpected. Did it think the Tellehi spoke to it? Were they whispering lies into its tympanum even now? Jordneh had no idea. She said nothing; there was aught else to say. Kihantroh was beyond reason. Anything she told it would simply be twisted into fuel for its obsession. The moment passed and Kihantroh's attention returned to her. "And then there will be peace," it said. "Thank you, my queen, for confirming what the Tellehi told me. I bid you now farewell."

Jordneh heard a rumble, as of a stampede approaching from out of the sky. She looked up and saw a whip-thin funnel cloud descending toward the balcony, carving a ragged path toward the spot where she stood. She tried to step away, but found her feet were rooted in place; while they had stood there debating, Kihantroh had caused the stone floor to quietly grow up around her ankles, locking her in place. The attempt to move caused her to lose her balance. Sharp pains shot up her legs as her knees twisted and she fell onto her back, looking up at her approaching doom. From the corner of her eye, she saw Kihantroh spread its arms wide, holding its garment out like a sail; a gentler wind than the one she was fated to meet caught the fabric and billowed it out, lifting the sorcerer into the sky like an untethered kite. It soared up and away and out of sight.

Then the deadly tendril touched down, and the witch-queen saw no more.

~~~~

Kaderleh had once surveyed all the small pocket caves and overhangs in the dry wadis that surrounded their camp; as far as he knew she was the first to have ever taken an interest in them. Ever organized, she had compiled a list of all the larger ones, complete with a map, with assignments of what supplies could or should be stored in each. She had shown it to Brennendah once, and he remembered it, as he remembered most things, with a clarity that allowed him to lead

Poor Horse on a hurried rush through the ragged trees down into a long-dead wash and toward a nearby chamber where he could hide among the boxes and barrels and, perhaps, go undiscovered until the enchanter's attention turned elsewhere.

At the sharp bend where the overhang could be found, Brennendah stopped. Poor Horse snorted uneasily. Why had he brought the animal along? It could not be coaxed through the low opening. Casting nervous glances at the sky, he removed Poor Horse's bridle and let the animal flee—little encouragement was required; the frightened creature was already strongly inclined bolt—and then, getting into a crouch, he crawled through the low opening into the eroded underside of the bank. The space beyond was surprisingly large, cool and dim, full of the dark shapes of casks, barrels, cases, and bundles. Kaderleh had been astonishingly industrious in transferring supplies over, freeing up space in the barn and tent. He had hardly noticed, so intent had he been on what was going on in the Æther. Now she was gone, and his days of scratching information onto slates were clearly behind him, and this small storehouse stood before him like a reminder of his neglect.

Crouching, he peered out from beneath the overhang. With a gesture he erased the tracks poor horse had left in the sandy ground. The chalky white dust that had hung in the air settled to earth, restoring it to an appearance of spindrift, though a careful observer might note a certain orderliness in the whorls and patterns. It would have to do; he had no more time to work on careful concealment. Outside his improvised shelter, the telltale roar of a funnel became audible. He had already seen that the force directing this phenomenon was able to move the storm at astonishing speeds; perhaps it also had the power to observe everything that crawled along the land beneath it. Every cloud could be a hunter's blind, every sunbeam a searching eye. He would have to move as if he were constantly being observed, eschew any further use of probes that the invisible enemy might detect, avoid doing anything that might attract attention. This burrow might become his home for some time.

Retreating to the deepest part of the cave, he caused the slope outside to collapse, mimicking a natural landslide, burying the entrance to the cavern and leaving him in utter darkness. He closed his eyes and turned his attention inward, settling himself into a trance, instructing the synapses in his brain to shut themselves down. He would be a stone, a rag, a piece of clay. The tornado would not find him. A perfunctory search, perhaps a quick, malicious stab at Poor

Horse——the animal truly earning the casual nickname he had bestowed upon it——followed by the attacker's withdrawal: That was the best outcome Brennandah could hope to achieve. And afterwards, when the storm had retreated and the skies were clear, he might make his way to the castle, and find out what had happened there; he might locate Kaderleh's body, and give her a proper farewell. He could almost hear her gentle voice telling him she had a list of the things she wanted him to tell her about, if he ever found her again.

"Of course you do," he murmured, and then he slept.

PART ONE

THE DEATH WIND

Chapter 2

CONSCIOUSNESS SLOWLY RETURNED to Bernard, grudgingly, from somewhere far away. He coughed, spitting up water from deep in his chest; lukewarm liquid dribbled from the side of his mouth like thin blood. He gradually became aware that someone nearby was mumbling gibberish. He lay there a little while longer, coughed two, three, four times, each hack expelling a bit less fluid than the one before. The mumbling stopped, started, stopped, started again; he couldn't tell what was being said. Finally one last paroxysm flipped him onto his side, where he vomited up several gouts of rank seawater. It flowed away along rough grooves in the angled floor.

Trembling, he rolled onto his back. He felt something chafing around his wrist, realized it was the leather strap that they'd used to hang him from the cable. It had come loose from his left hand. He fumbled with the remaining knot until he got it off, then cast the waterlogged hunk of metal-studded hide away. He never wanted to look at that thing again.

The atmosphere felt close and clammy, thick with the rancid, stale smell of a shore where the water had retreated and left behind clumps of grey, drying seaweed riddled with dead fish. For a moment he thought he might have washed up on some nighttime beach, but the darkness was too complete, the air too still, the waves too silent. Remembering the last thing that had happened before he had blacked out, he decided that he must be in a cavern; somehow the current that had seized him and sucked him under had deposited him here, in a pocket of breathable air. He had no idea how that could have happened; he should have drowned. Maybe he *had* drowned, and he just didn't know it yet.

Who had been mumbling? Brannoc? It was dead silent now; if it had been Brannoc, he had stopped when Bernard woke up, which made sense in a way. Nebandalex had told him that while he, Bernard, had been unconscious after nearly being strangled by that minstrel, Brannoc had animated his body, talking to Nebandalex, plotting an escape that had never occurred. If they had switched places then, maybe they had switched places again when Bernard passed out in the water from lack of oxygen. Had Brannoc suddenly awakened in the watery dark? How horrifying would *that* be, to suddenly find yourself in possession of a body that was deep underwater and out of air? He could hardly imagine.

But no, he didn't think the mumbler had been Brannoc. The

rogue's presence was missing from Bernard's mind in a way that seemed different from his usual absences when Brannoc would go away to sulk. That left unpleasantly open the question of who *had* been making the sounds—some creature gibbering in the dark?—but Bernard wasn't ready to deal with that thought just yet. He sat up, suffering through a few moments of vertigo as his head spun around the drain a few times. He coughed again, but no more liquid came up from his lungs. Taking a careful look around, he realized that the darkness was not as complete as he'd originally thought; there was some faint illumination here, like on a night when thick clouds couldn't quite hide the full moon. The light emanated from the walls themselves, generated not by the glowing lichen of myth and legend, but from an endlessly repeating series of runic squiggles that seemed to be scrawled along the entire length of the tunnel, which from here consisted of a single long tube slanting upward into the unknown. Peering around, he identified a disk of black water in the floor nearby. Maybe he had entered through that opening, in which case he might be able to exit that way again. He crawled over to it and ran his fingers along the edge of the pool, feeling the unmistakeable texture of crumbling brick. A thin, gritty paste of rotting mortar adhered to his skin when he touched it. He stuck his hands in the water and shook it off, disliking the feel of the stuff on his skin, as if thousands of tiny sharp mouths were gnawing at him.

Scuttling away from the water—he didn't quite trust his legs yet—he carefully stood, then tottered over to the nearest wall for a closer look at the luminous sigils. The writing didn't appear to be etched or scratched into the stone; it just sort of floated slightly above the surface, as if the tube had been lined with shellac laced with radiant script. The intensity of the glow lacked consistency; it would flicker and fade, then strengthen again, like a fluorescent light on its way out. He wondered if that meant the magic was failing, or if it was supposed to do this according to some kind of cycle. At its darkest, the cave was nearly black; that had been its condition when he had awakened. From its nadir the illumination fitfully strengthened to moonlight level, where it stayed briefly before decaying back into dim obscurity.

Obviously this was some sort of enchantment; he didn't need Ambrosia the Sorceress to tell him that. But what was it for? Bernard retreated from the magic walls, put a bit of distance between himself and the dark water, and sat down on the floor to think.

So. Okay. He was in a sea cave, probably below the cliffs opposite

Abacar. It seemed highly unlikely that any natural action of the current that sucked him under would have deposited him here, so how had he arrived in the tunnel? He didn't really think Brannoc had swum into it under his own power. Had something reached out from the darkness, latched onto his ankle, and reeled him in? Why? Bernard couldn't think of any reason that would be beneficial to him. He eyed the nearby inky pool in the dimness. It just sat there, smooth and placid as the smile of a contented psychopath. The fact that he could breathe—the air was thick and moist and stale, but hardly noxious—argued for some sort of oxygen exchange with the world above, but the sea water wasn't rushing up out of that pool to fill the space, which implied that the cave was airtight. Yet intelligent beings had obviously been here once, as evidenced by the brickwork around the pool and the ominous scribbles all over the walls. They might have come and gone through the water, or some sort of medieval airlock, or even a portal like Mercy created using the Illata. In any case he doubted that their means of egress would be available for his use.

Where were the others? Bernard had no idea if Nebandalex or Cynidece had survived the fall, but he was pretty sure that the other two prisoners had perished. He was certainly the only one to have ended up in this tunnel. He stared off into the distance, where the glowing runes seemed to converge into a starry pattern, a wall of squiggles. If he wanted to find out where it went, he would have to go exploring. He slowly got to his feet, feeling sore and unsteady and short of breath; his soaked leathers creaked and tugged uncomfortably, resisting his effort to stretch his limbs. He spent a bit of time limbering up, getting some suppleness back, before moving on along the tunnel. At least it seemed to slope upwards. The squiggles in the walls were omnipresent, casting their dim luminance, the entire endless screed glowing and fading in unison. The flickering seemed to be changing, getting more erratic. He had a feeling that portended nothing good, and hoped it wasn't a reaction to his presence.

The diameter of the passageway gradually increased as he moved away from the pool, so it wasn't until the floor leveled off that he realized the tunnel had ended and he had entered a very large chamber. It, too, was lined with glowing runes, which was why, from below, it had seemed as if the tube ran off into a galaxy of sigils. Gawking at the luminous script that surrounded him, he tripped over something and nearly fell across an old, moist, dismembered skeleton, its components lined up across the floor as if someone had been playing jacks with them. It wasn't the only one; the floor was strewn with almost-connected remains, carefully laid out in circular ranks, a spiral pattern of bones. Bernard had stumbled over a femur. He picked it up, thinking it might be useful as a club. It was cold and slippery; holding it seemed to numb his hand, as if he had picked up a chunk of ice. It dawned on him then just how frigid it was in here; he started to shiver, his body trembling from head to toe, until, with an effort he released his grip on the bone and cast it aside. The shivering subsided. Thrusting his hand into his opposite armpit—which, being sodden and leather-clad, did nothing to warm it—he gave the skeleton a baleful glare, then backed off with a start as the femur slid across the floor and returned to its original position.

Okay. Messing with the bones in here was a bad idea.

He picked his way back to the tunnel entrance. In the sanctuary of the relatively vacant edge of the circular chamber, he waited until the glow of the runes was on an ascendant cycle, which revealed a mass of remains littering the floor, bones gleaming pallid white in the gloom. It seemed like an entire graveyard had lurched over and vomited into this stone pit. The roof arched high overhead, supported by a series of masonry ribs that met at a stone ring at the highest point in the center of the dome. The ring circumscribed a uniformly illuminated disk that faded and strengthened in time with the runes. He couldn't tell if there was rock behind the disk or not; perhaps it was a seal on the way out. Not that he had any way to reach it. This was the oubliette in Abacar all over again, on a much vaster scale. He imagined the owners of these skeletons milling around beneath that ring, hoping for it to open, only to fall one by one, die and decay and become the field of bones that stretched out before him. Though if that was what had happened, he didn't think they would be arranged in quite so orderly a fashion.

Tearing his gaze down from the roof, he saw that in addition to the tunnel in which he stood, there were seven other openings in the round chamber, equally spaced, like the spokes of a wheel or the arms of an octopus. Did each lead down to a pool like the one he had emerged from? If they were the equivalent of tentacles dangling in the water, thinking of the octopus analogy, they would grab whatever came into range, right? So maybe the others had ended up in one of the other tubes. It was worth checking. Staying close to the wall, he headed toward the nearest opening. As he approached it, he began to hear faint scuffing sounds coming from somewhere. He stopped moving at once. He didn't think the sounds emanated from his target archway, but it was impossible to tell in this vast echo chamber. He darted to the nearest supporting rib and squeezed into the joint where it met the wall, trying to flatten himself as much as he could without actually coming into contact with the runes, the rock, or the brickwork. Bad enough he had to touch the floor with his leather-shod feet.

Before long, he noticed movement partway around the chamber: A pale figure emerged from one of the openings, dragging something behind it. The dragging was the source of the sound he had heard. He squinted through the gloom, trying to discern what this apparition might be. Ghost? Ghoul? Goblin? None of the above: It was Cynidece. He could tell from the jet-black hair, the ropy muscles, delineated by shadows even in this dimness. He could see dark rings of scrapes and bruises around her wrists where the leather straps had held her suspended for days above the chasm. She dragged another former denizen of the cable along behind her, using his leather strap as a handle for pulling. Bernard called her name; Cynidece immediately let go of her burden, dropped into a fighting stance, and looked around. "Over here!" He stepped away from the wall and waved his arms. "It's me, Bernard!"

She spotted him, straightened up, grinned in a broad and slightly deranged manner, and beckoned him over. He hurried along the perimeter, in his haste accidentally kicking a few bones that lay in his path. Even through his boot, touching the bones made his foot go numb; he slowed down after that. He didn't want to fall down and sprawl across these accursed remains, worried that if he did he might just freeze to the floor and never get up again. Nor did he look behind him to where, he was sure, the dislodged body parts would be sliding back to their original positions. By the time he reached Cynidece, she had scuffed a little ways back into the tunnel from which she had emerged, hugging herself as if to keep warm. Nebandalex lay on the floor at her feet, pale and still, but the elf's chest was rising and falling in a shallow rhythm so obviously he was alive. "So cold," she whispered. "I have not been so cold since I was last in the mountains."

"Don't touch the bones or you'll feel ten times worse. Listen, did you wake up near a pool of water?"

"Yes. A current stronger than I could swim against pulled me under. I thought I would drown. Instead ..." She trailed off, looked down the tunnel, which ran downward into a sigil-lit gloom. "Your friend was beside me. He would not wake up, so I dragged him away. What *is* this place?"

"I don't know," Bernard said. "Nowhere good."

A sudden clatter echoed out of the round chamber; Cynidece

flattened herself on the floor beside Bernard as a shape stumbled out from one of the other tunnel openings, awkward and shambling, knocking bones this way and that. What looked like a few loops of viscera, glistening in the dim, fluctuating light, swayed from its abdomen as it shuffled out into the ossuary, heedless of the remains it kicked aside like so many dead leaves. The fingers and feet and skulls skittered back into position after the intruder passed by.

Bernard heard Cynidece's sharp intake of breath. "Poddock," she said.

"Poddock? But he's …" Bernard trailed off, unwilling to finish the thought.

"Dead," Cynidece whispered, as the figure fell out there among the bones and did not get up again.

~~~~

Ambrosia the Sorceress was trapped in the ice cave, surrounded by enemies.

But that wasn't right, was it? Chilly though it might have been, the crypt below Korrin's castle was neither made of ice nor a cave; and Ambrosia the Sorceress was no longer a character being directed on-screen in a game. No. Mercy herself had been trapped; Ambrosia was just a persona she had assumed, and into which she had temporarily disappeared; and although she *was* surrounded, it was not by enemies. Not really. They were just statues, dumb stone figures animated by an enchantment, whose only purpose was to prevent the Jewel in the Maul from leaving the crypt, a purpose at which they had already failed, though they were unaware of that fact. The gem had been carried away by her *real* enemy, the Rittandic disguised as the ancient astrologer Rumad Kram, who had left behind a glamour to fool the guardians into thinking that the crystal around Ambrosia's neck was the one they were charged to protect. Only the figures guarding the entrance remained at their stations, though they had turned sideways to block the way out; Kram had simply opened a portal and vanished, rendering such security measures laughable.

The statue which had caught Mercy lifted her off the ground and then, as if it couldn't tell the difference between Mercy and the jewel that she wore, half-dragged, half-carried her across the moisture-slicked floor toward the sarcophagus that Rumad Kram had smashed to get at the Maul. The dog statue that once adorned it had animated along with the others, but the old man had shattered it to get at the prize beneath, depriving the carven creature of the lower half of its body and one of its front legs. Its jaws opened and closed as if trying to bite or bark, and its one remaining leg scrabbled futilely against the slippery stone, causing it to turn in a jerky circle. Mercy found herself oddly disturbed by this, as if it were a real animal that had been harmed; she wanted to repair it, but of course she couldn't. Even if she knew a glamour to mend a broken statue, she couldn't have summoned enough focus to cast it, or, indeed, anything else. With her free hand she fumbled with the chain around her neck from which the gaudy, enchanted pendant depended; if she could remove it and leave it in the sarcophagus, maybe the statues would lose interest in her. Maybe. But the thing refused to come off; the harder she tried to pull it away from her chest, the more it resisted, until finally it tore itself out of her grasp and settled back into place. She couldn't find a clasp to undo, and the chain was so tight around her neck that she couldn't slip it over her head, even though that was how she had put it on originally. It seemed as if half the links had vanished. Was that Kram's doing, too? She thought back to when Korrin had insisted she wear the jewel, how he had seemed relieved once it was in place. Since then, she'd had the gravest difficulty concentrating when she tried to cast anything; she'd only managed a few glamours that, like her last veil, had been weak and ineffective. Was that a coincidence?

Her captor stopped when they reached the dog's open-faced tomb. It was about the same size as a large wicker chest of the sort that might stand at the foot of a bed, full of warm clothes and blankets and slippers meant for colder months. It really did contain the skeletal remains of a dog-like creature. The bones lay curled up around a depression in the stone, into which the Maul must have fitted until Kram had stolen it. Mercy had a moment to wonder what esteemed canine this must have been to rate a place of honor among Korrin's ancestors; then her captor hauled her up and deposited her on the edge of the ossuary. She fell partly into the opening as its stony hands tried to stuff her into the sarcophagus, apparently thinking that laying her to rest within would satisfy its duty. The polished sides felt icy cold against her body, and the bones of the royal pet poked her in the hip; she went limp and folded herself into the space, hoping the stony hands might let go of her once she was within, giving her a chance to scrabble out. The other guardians clustered around, sightless faces turned toward the sarcophagus, as if it were a bathtub and they had all come to stare as she scrubbed herself clean. She wouldn't be able to break through that circle of defenders. The golem reached for her legs, which were still outside the crypt; she quickly pulled them in, not wanting it to snap her in half while trying to stuff her into the opening.

Suddenly she realized that the others were reassembling the shattered lid, passing the fragments around like a bucket brigade, piecing them together with the unerring precision of a team of jigsaw puzzle experts; only a few chunks remained to be incorporated into the slab. As each shard was added to the others, the seams rippled and vanished. They had already managed to reassemble the broken dog statue; it paced around the box as if it were a real canine impatient for its bed to be ready.

They were going to seal her up in here, just like the Maul had been.

She tried to take hold of the sides of the tomb and pull herself out, but couldn't seem to raise her arms enough to do it; the higher she lifted them, the stronger the desire became to return them to her sides. Afflicted with some sort of magical inertia, she couldn't even rally the strength to sit up. It must all be part of the protective enchantment on the receptacle; items placed in it wanted nothing more than to stay in it. Whatever was in the tomb belonged in the tomb and should not be removed, be it the Maul, or the dog's bones, or Mercy herself. If the false Rumad Kram had not possessed the Illata, he would never have been able to extract his prize from its resting place. But he *had* possessed it. She had brought it to him.

The statues were finished assembling the cover. How long had it taken for them to find all the fragments? She had no idea. Time seemed to have become thick like syrup, slow and viscous. The statue of the canine sat expectantly, stone tail slashing scratches across the floor, as the guardians moved the lid back into place. She shrank away from it, fully occupying the space beneath, withdrawing her limbs to avoid having her hands or feet crushed crushed as the capstone settled into place, locking her in the blackness, a buried treasure, cuddled by the bones of a well-loved, long-dead pet.

Mercy heard stone clacking against stone as the carved representative of the dog jumped back into position atop the lid, turned a few circles, and lay down, as if to join her in sleep.

~~~~

After Poddock's shambling body collapsed among the other remains, a soft clatter went up from the chamber, as if he had knocked down the first in a vast array of dominoes. The bones seemed to be responding to the addition of a fresh corpse, readjusting themselves to maintain the pattern that Bernard had noticed. Bernard and Cynidece, without saying a word to each other, picked up Nebandalex and retreated a little way down the tunnel, away from the room of the dead. As they settled the elf back down on the floor he coughed weakly a few times, spitting up a bit of dark, phlegmy water. His eyes flickered open, dull and unfocused. For a moment Bernard feared that Nebandalex would shuffle up to join Poddock among the bones, but then his head tipped to the side and his gaze settled on Bernard's face. "Ribbit," he said, his voice hoarse and weak.

Cynidece looked a question at Bernard, who shrugged. "It's sort of a password," he said. Then, to Nebandalex: "It's all right. I know you're you."

"Who else would he be?" Cynidece asked.

"You'd be surprised." He knelt down and helped Nebandalex sit up, then removed the leather strap that bound his hands together. Gently rubbing his wrists, the elf examined their surroundings with something resembling curiosity, although mostly he just looked spent. "We're in a cave," Bernard told him.

"I see that. Are we under the ocean?"

"So it would seem."

"How?"

Bernard glanced at Cynidece. She shook her head; she didn't have any idea either. "I think ... something reached out and took us."

She raised an eyebrow.

"Well think about it," Bernard said. "I'm here. You two are here. *Poddock* is here, and he was dead before he hit the water. None of us swam in."

Her eyes narrowed. "You are saying we were *collected.*"

"Right. Yes. Exactly. Whatever this is place is, it's gathering the bodies that fall into the sea."

Nebandalex said, "For what purpose?"

"I don't know. Maybe something here eats them and leaves the bones."

"Stop thinking like a hungry human," Cynidece said after a moment. "This is not about meat."

"It's not?"

"No. Believe a predator when she tells you such a thing."

"Um, all right," he said, unsure of exactly how to take that remark. "Then what *is* it about?"

Instead of answering, Cynidece crept to the nearest wall and ran her fingers down the air in front of it, as if the glowing runes were text that she could read by touch. Bernard and Nebandalex both watched her. Bernard said: "Are you some kind of sorceress?"

She laughed. "No. Far from it. But I know an enchantment when

I see one. This is a binding, very strong."

"It doesn't look strong. The way it flickers——"

"Do not be deceived by that. This is powerful magic."

"Okay. So, a binding? That means something is being kept imprisoned here?"

"Oh, yes," she said. "Something bad. *Very* bad."

"How did we get in, then?"

"You are equating it to a set of physical bars. That is another mistake. This binding is not designed to keep things out. If it were, it would have been constructed differently, and would require more power to maintain. Someone decided that was an extra precaution not worth taking." She was silent for a moment, then said: "Or, perhaps, it is so that the captive could claim the bodies that were hung out over the chasm."

"Why would they want to let it do that?"

"As a tribute. If you have chained a beast whose hunger could consume you, you would be well advised to keep it fed."

"Why keep a beast like that chained at all?" Bernard said after a moment. "Why not destroy it?"

She looked at him over her shoulder, then turned away. "Some beasts cannot be destroyed."

While Bernard thought over the possibility of an indestructible monster, Nebandalex said, in a quiet, hoarse voice: "You know what is here."

"I *think* I know," she said.

When she failed to offer any further details, Bernard said, "Care to share?"

"No. Not while we remain trapped here."

The whispering of the bones from the massive chamber finally died down, leaving them in silence until Nebandalex spoke again. "If this is the thing that you think it is," he said, "then why are we three still alive?"

"This binding is very, very powerful. I suspect that it prevents the … entity from exercising the abilities it possesses. It would likely be accustomed to collecting those who have died on the cable and rotted out of their bonds; it just drags in whatever lands out there in the sea, and amuses itself by arranging their bones in a pleasing fashion."

"But Poddock *walked* in, and he was dead."

"Was he walking, or was he *being* walked? There is a difference."

"But the … it must sense that it has taken living beings this time," Nebandalex said. "It must know we are here."

"Would you expect tree roots growing through the earth to know that worms are crawling by?"

"Depending on the tree, yes, I would."

She chuckled at that, and shook her head. "I should know better than to ask an elf such a question." She turned away from the wall and came back to join them. "Whether it knows we are here or not, it cannot act against us directly. Not now. The binding prevents it. When we perish of thirst or starvation, then it will claim us, and add us to its garden."

Evidently Nebandalex had realized what Cynidece thought they faced; Bernard was the only one missing that critical piece of information. He thought about the feeling that had surged through him when he'd picked up the bone, the chill, how it had seemed poised to suck all the warmth out of him, all the life. Like a conduit, a needle connected to a suction tube and plunged into an artery. "So there's something here," he whispered, "and it feeds off life?"

"No," Cynidece said. "It feeds off death."

"But death isn't a thing. It's the absence of a thing."

"How do you know that?" she asked. "Have you died?"

"Well, no," he said. "Not exactly." Then: "We obviously can't stay here."

"Obviously." She cocked her head at him. "And you have a plan for escaping, do you?"

"Yes. Let's try to get out the way we came in."

Cynidece gave a soft, clipped laugh, almost a bark. "Through those pools of water, back into the current? Even if we could swim against it, this place would just draw us in as it did before."

"You have a different idea?"

"Not yet." Cynidece aimed a finger toward the large room. Her nail looked thick and tough; he wouldn't want to go up against her in a face-scratching contest. "But let us go back to the room of bones. I want to have a closer look at something."

~~~~

Kihantroh had not been able to properly observe or direct the storm that it had sent back to the Edgelands around the Æther, whence the faint probe that arrived during the last moments of its confrontation with Jordneh had originated. That spell, a tracking glamour, had not been directed to find Kihantroh, nor had it been particularly powerful; its caster seemed to be a sorcerer of only middling ability for a Rittandic, and not looking for a fight. Still, Kihantroh felt obliged to respond, if only to discourage further meddling from that direction. Even though Kihantroh was armed with the powerful gems, the static and fog of the Æther exerted a vexatious effect on the working of glamours, a difficulty that increased along with distance from the target. Kihantroh had, essentially, programmed the storm and sent the system southward with instructions to drop a few tornadoes around the observation post—which should be a more than sufficient deterrent against further meddling from whatever scientist had worked the conjuration to find his missing assistant—then dissipate. For the next part of its task, Kihantroh could not be occupied with swatting flies and managing the weather. The *real* work was about to begin.

Now that the castle had been scoured of the witch-queen's court and her influence, and the surrounding town had been cleared of its residents, the area was psychically blank, free of interference. It was time to begin undoing Jordneh's enchantments.

There were limits to what this could accomplish. If someone had died as a result of Jordneh's magic, that person would not miraculously return to life; if a spell had had an irreversible effect, the change it had wrought would not be undone. Every piece of wood Jordneh had caused to catch fire and burn to ash would not be reconstituted from smoke and carbon and be returned, pristine and untouched, to its place in the hearth. Still, as Jordneh's active enchantments were canceled one by one, the power she had been expending to maintain them would find its way back to the Æther, to be reconstituted as the matter it had been before she had stolen it to fuel her witchcraft. The energy would know where it must go; it would remember what it had once been. And after Jordneh's impact had been erased, Untelleh would become recoverable; she would return to her seat of power in the South, with an understanding of the consequences of what she had done. With no one drawing on it to energize unnaturally potent sorcery, the Æther would be contained, no longer a threat to the stability of the reality in which they lived. The ignorant masses might never know that the world had been in such peril, but those who mattered would remember Kihantroh's name, and speak it with respect.

This part of the plan, rolling back Jordneh's glamours up until the point that Untelleh's region had imploded, would be the most difficult of Kihantroh's undertakings. It knew this. Her enchantments were strong and ancient and widespread. To find and undo them, Kihantroh needed to enter the witch-queen's own frame of reference as much as possible. The absorbance glamour, so successful against lesser beings, could not have been used for this purpose; attempting to subsume a consciousness as old and as powerful as Jordneh's into Kihantroh's own mind would be inviting disaster, the utter loss of its own identity. Obliterating her corporeal form and setting her spirit adrift had been the safer thing to do, but it still needed some link to her, some way to assume her perspective. This was why Kihantroh had forced her to stand: Not just to make her demonstrate that she could, but to preserve her wheeled conveyance after she had been destroyed.

The witch-queen had not sat upon a proper throne in hundreds of years. Though her reliance on the mobile chair had been feigned, she had carried out the charade with rigorous discipline, leaving it during her waking hours only on the rarest of occasions, as when stately duties required that she occupy the seat in her great audience hall. If anything in this place held an imprint of her consciousness, it would be that wheeled device. Kihantroh called it over now, inviting it to right itself and trundle across the debris-strewn balcony. As it approached like a favored pet, Kihantroh turned and, feeling the seat bump the backs of its legs, settled into the place where Jordneh had spent so much of her life. Yes. As Kihantroh had suspected, the wood and cushioned leather had soaked up and retained a powerful echo of the longstanding connection Jordneh had created between herself and the Æther. Its aura enveloped Kihantroh with a sense of being back in the Edgelands, at the frayed edge of the world, communing with the void. This was the conduit by which it would gather up the energy Jordneh had expended, feed it back to that decaying realm of grey vapor, and force it to yield up that which it had consumed.

Sitting in the dead queen's chair, in her dead castle, in her dead village, Kihantroh raised its arms, spread them wide, and began reeling in all the strings that Jordneh had touched in her long, long life.

~~~~

The interior of the ossuary was dark and quiet and secure; the cold lessened as her body heated up the space. Mercy didn't quite remember why she had been fighting so hard against being put in here. It was like being in bed with the covers pulled up over her head and a favorite pet curled up next to her. The bed was made of marble, the cover was a slab, the pet was only bones, but all of that had ceased to bother her; she could almost feel the soft cushions against her back, the luxurious sheets, the warm, silky fur that the dog would have worn when alive, however many centuries ago that had been. And so she lay in the dark with the gentle breathing and steady heartbeat of her imagined canine companion, while the air grew moist and close and unbreathable.

She had just started to drift off to sleep when something brought her back to wakefulness. She couldn't say for sure what it was. Not words; it was silent in here, as a tomb should be. Not a touch; nothing could reach her in her stone sanctuary. It was more of a sensation, as if someone were dragging a loose silk shawl across her skin, starting at her head and her toes, moving inward toward her core. No, even that was wrong; the feeling wasn't on her skin, it was *in* it, as if thousands of tiny roots were being withdrawn. Phantasms faded. The dog next to her was not alive, not a pet, not warm; it was dead, it was bones, it was icy cold. The sarcophagus was not a cozy place to rest; it was a grave. She was shivering. A pounding sound penetrated her consciousness: Her fists, beating a tattoo against the underside of the lid. Her hands ached as if badly bruised. Had she been battering the stone the whole time, even while her mind had fantasized cuddling with the dog, had tried to pretend she was safe in bed?

As the last wisps of fog departed from her brain and she slammed her knuckles into the stone one last time, a spiderweb of glowing hairline cracks spread outward from the point of impact, like black ice splintering over luminous water. Scrawled runes flashed across the dark interior, then faded, leaving an afterimage of squiggles in her vision. Without a sound, the stone cover shattered. Mercy squeezed her eyes shut tight, expecting to be covered in rubble or crushed by the statue of the dog falling on top of her; instead, she felt herself sink a few inches, as if the layer of stone beneath her had suddenly become insubstantial. She opened her eyes. The cover was gone, leaving her coated with a thick layer of pale grey powder, as if it and the dog statue on top of it had dissolved into their constituent matter, then fallen down to cover the next available surface, which was her. The smooth marble lining of the box had disintegrated too, settling into the cracks and crevices of the rough, raw stone beneath, coating the dog's sad little bones. She sat up in an ash-colored cloud. After coughing a few times, she shook off the grit, then traced a line down her left forearm with her right index finger and held it up to her eyes. It reminded her of the fine dust that accumulated on a shelf or on top of the refrigerator.

So the dog statue was gone; what about the others? She looked around, half afraid that the golems would be advancing on the tomb, but they no longer seemed to be interested in her or in anything else. They stood immobile, as statues ought, each frozen in the act of returning to its appointed location. Whatever enchantment once animated them had lost its force. As she watched, they began to crumble all around her, losing form and definition, fuzzing into dust and spilling across the floor. Only those few icons that had never left their posts were unaffected by the spreading dissolution. What was going on? She was still gawking at them when she suddenly became aware of an absence against her throat. Her hand went to the spot where the jewel had been. It wasn't there anymore. The chain still loosely encircled her neck, but all that depended from it now was the gilt claw that had once held the faceted stone, empty as an eagle's claw after its prey had escaped. The gem seemed to have sublimated into the atmosphere. She easily removed off the chain and threw it across the room. Good riddance.

Mercy was almost afraid to get out of the sarcophagus, lest it trigger some renewed attention or attack; nor did she really want to face the long climb back to the castle or the guards that must be roaming the halls in search of her. But she couldn't stay here. Taking care with her injured left knee and sore ribs, she clambered out of the box, settling herself on the cold stone floor. Her gaze lingered for a moment on the skeletal dog that lay within the ossuary; she knew it had just been the effects of the spell, but still, she couldn't shake a strange feeling of loss, as if this really had been a beloved pet that had died and now lived only in her memories. She reached in and lightly touched the small, elongated skull, imagining it warm and furred, with soft ears and wet nose and large, liquid eyes. She took a last look around at the decaying figures. Pieces of Lord Korrin's body were scattered among them, shriveled mail-clad bones coated with dust and rubble. Nothing she could do for him now. She turned and limped toward the entrance. The atlantes that had blocked the way out had crumbled, leaving behind a pair of plain columns, previously concealed by the bulky statues, that actually did the work of supporting the archway. She paused just inside the door, gathered her thoughts. Could she focus enough to cast a veil, so that she could, perhaps, move through the castle undetected? She thought so, and now would be the time to do it, when she was alone and undisturbed. She concentrated, moved her fingers the way she used to when she had been Ambrosia. After a few sluggish moments of indecision, the room flickered a little, shimmered in a familiar way. It had worked. The glamour was cast.

"Mercy the Sorceress escapes the ice cave," she whispered.

~~~~

The three bedraggled ex-prisoners huddled at the threshold of the big, domed room, eyeing the densely-runed circle at its apex. "This is the capstone of the binding," Cynidece whispered.

Bernard squinted at it. "The capstone," he said.

She nodded, her stringy, wet black hair bouncing against her cheeks; everything took forever to dry in this damp, fetid abyss.

"So what does that mean?"

"It means this is the center of the enchantment. The knot that ties the strings."

"And the strings would be ... ?"

"What the knot holds together."

"Um. Where I come from, we call that circular logic."

"That is quite a phrase. Here, we just call it magic."

Nebandalex gave Cynidece a narrow look. "For one who claims not to be a sorceress, you seem unusually capable of understanding spells."

"Some Pelts have certain sensitivities," she said, glancing at the elf. "I am such a one. I can see and read most enchantments well enough, but I cannot cast spells, nor break them." She turned back to look at the ceiling again. "Unfortunately for us. Or perhaps fortunately, in this case."

"Fortunately why?"

"Because I would not wish to see this enchantment broken. What is bound here should not be released."

"Right. The mysterious *thing* that no one will tell me what it is."

"Knowing would not make you happier."

"Really. You think I could be less happy than I am right now?"

"Yes." Nebandalex and Cynidece both spoke at the same time; Cynidece started to chuckle, but then it froze in her throat and turned into a croak. Nebandalex, too, drew a sharp intake of breath. It took Bernard a moment to realize what had provoked their reactions: The runes, which until now had merely been flickering, seemed to be unraveling, the jagged symbolic lines straightening, flashing, then fading, progressing upward from the farther reaches of the tunnel in which they crouched.

"Cynidece, what's going on?" Then, when she did not answer: "It's going away, isn't it? The spell? It's shutting down?" Still no answer. He started to reach for Cynidece's shoulder, thinking he would give her a shake, get her attention, then decided not to. For some reason he thought he might end up with the stump of an arm if he proceeded. "Is this because of us? Because we're here?"

"I think not."

"Then why——"

She cut him off with a look at said he was being obtuse.

"Okay. So what happens when … *if* … what's in here gets let go?"

Cynidece and Nebandalex exchanged a glance. Whatever they thought was imprisoned here, it was so bad that neither of them wanted to talk about it. Finally Nebandalex said: "They called it the death-wind. It appeared in Abacar long ago and spread misery across the entire Slash."

"Everyone suffered," Cynidece said. "Corpses lay in the fields like crops left to rot. Fires spread unchecked across the plains. We Pelts died by the thousands when the Acarians abandoned us along the river. The dwarves shut themselves up under the mountains and never really came back out. The Rittandics were blighted with sterility."

"Hundreds of elves perished as well—elves we could hardly afford to lose—and their bodies had to be burned, along with whole swaths of infested woodland. In their cups, the elders still speak of battles waged at the edges of the forest, how hard they fought with steel and spells to keep them out of Torgonderrer."

"Keep *who* out?"

"The dead, of course."

"Those who fall beneath the death-wind will stir and walk again while in its presence like marionettes," Cynidece said, "just as Poddock did. They cannot think or fight as they did when alive, but they hardly need to. They swarm and hold, and keep the puppet master's prey from escaping." Then: "You should *know* this. How can you not know this?"

"I'm not from here."

"Are all Banderlundi so ignorant of the history of the realm they would conquer?"

"I'm not from there either," Bernard said, as the runes around them flickered out. The dim glow from the other tunnel openings faded as well. Now only the domed room remained illuminated. The disk of light in the center of the ceiling began to sag downward, becoming something pendulous, reminding Bernard of a cartoon tonsil—an *infected* cartoon tonsil, he thought, as the swollen center grew dark and malignant beneath the glow, like a lump of coal wrapped in Christmas lights.

"I was wrong," Cynidece murmured, staring at it. "That is not just a capstone. That is the death-wind. It was the key to its own binding."

"*That* thing?" Bernard said. "It's just a … a blob."

"It is not fully free yet, and it must be weak after centuries of being held captive. But ..." She trailed off as a putrescent wind erupted from the sagging thing, as if it had been gathering up and storing all the dead fish from the fathoms, savoring the stench of decay before letting it all out in a flatulent blast. It nearly knocked them over; Nebandalex might have tumbled away if Cynidece hadn't caught hold of him. Behind them, from the depths of the tunnel, Bernard heard a wet gurgling sound. The wind must be forcing the water down out of the pools, he realized, purging it like blowing air through a straw. Along the bottom of the cliff where the tunnels emerged, Bernard thought, the sea must be boiling, though he doubted anyone would detect it in the spume and churn from the waterfall. Maybe they would notice the stink.

A clattering sound came from the dome room. The bones had begun to move, not pushed by the wind, but drawing together, reassembling themselves like stick puppets bound by strings. It seemed that Cynidece had been right. The dead were going to walk.

"We have to go," Bernard said, turning away from the macabre scene. His leathers creaked softly as the wet material stretched and scraped against itself.

Nebandalex said: "Go where?"

"Back to the pools."

They stared at him. Neither moved.

"There's nowhere else to go. I'm hoping the wind will push us out."

Nebandalex said: "You cannot be serious."

As if it had heard him and taken his words as a challenge, the gale suddenly intensified; Bernard could have sworn he heard screams carried on it, as if from a distant battle. "Bernard is right," Cynidece said. "We have nowhere else to go."

Nebandalex still didn't move, but he offered no resistance as Bernard and Cynidece dragged him off down the tunnel like a pair of press-gangers, away from the dying light, into the darkness. Without the luminous runes Bernard couldn't see a thing, but it seemed that Cynidece could, because she suddenly said, in a commanding tone, "Stop."

Bernard halted immediately, and felt forward with his toe. The stone floor ended just ahead of them. The wind was even stronger now, intensified by the narrowing tube; they had to lean back against it to avoid being blown over. Was there any water left in the pool, or would jumping into it be like falling into a pit? "What does it look like? Can you see? Is it a well?"

"No, more like a slide," Cynidece said. "At least at first. Let us hope it stays that way. Hold tight when we jump."

"All right," Bernard said, even though if he held onto Nebandalex's arm any tighter he'd cut off the elf's circulation. "On three? One—"

But the death-wind, which cared nothing about numbers, gusted on one and blew them into the hole.

~~~~

Mercy ascended the steps slowly, favoring her injured knee. It seemed to be slowly improving as she used it, but it still ached, and she simply had no energy to go any faster. Part of her still didn't want to return to the residential levels, where she would have to deal with the fact that her friends had been hung out over the chasm to die, while the man who could have had them brought back lay in desiccated pieces on the floor of the cold stone crypt she had left behind. Still, she kept going. What else could she do?

She finally reached the narrow opening at the top of the stairs. Beyond it lay the hall of icons, where she had hidden after Kram blasted her out of the throne room. Here, the statues were all intact; they were just normal sculptures, not part of whatever aborted enchantment had guarded the Maul. She poked her head out for a look around. The hallway was empty. Guards were surely searching for her, but they weren't looking here right now. The audience hall stood off to the right, but there was nothing for her there anymore, no potential allies or sympathetic ears, just an angry dwarf and watchmen waiting to clap her in chains. Straight ahead, the corridor shrank into a dim, cobwebby passage. Ribbed supports entered it at a perpendicular angle near the ceiling in the left-hand wall and angled upward before exiting through the right. Buttresses. That suggested the narrow hallway ran close to an exterior wall; perhaps there would be an exit in that direction. She tottered into the chill shadows of the abandoned passageway, hoping to find a postern gate, a window, a door, anything that would let her slip out of the castle undetected. No torches burned here; she suspected a human eye would have trouble making out any details in the dimness, but with her elven vision she saw as well as on an overcast day, and avoided obstacles—stacks of bricks, rusted stone-working tools, piles of moldering fabric—with little difficulty.

Soon the corridor curved and arrow-slits appeared, cut into the wall between the buttresses to her left. Each was set into an elevated nook where a man could stand with room to draw and fire a bow. They admitted a feeble, filtered light; dust motes swirled in the slanting rays, disturbed by her passage. She climbed into the nearest niche and cleared the clingy, shivering cobwebs away from the arrow-slit. It ran from the floor of the nook to its ceiling, irregularly notched to the left and right to provide a wider field of fire than a simple vertical opening would allow. She put her eye to it peered through to the outside. The buttresses extended outward and down into the cracked flagstones of a wide, empty courtyard surrounded by a defensive curtain wall. The open space appeared forlorn and windswept, with dirty sand spread across the pavers and drifts of dead leaves and small branches heaped up against the walls. Mercy guessed that, for whatever reason, the area had been abandoned. That was good; if she could get into it, there wasn't likely to be anyone there to spot her. She couldn't see enough to get her bearings relative to any part of the city she had visited before they'd been captured; the tops of a few buildings were visible over the curtain wall, but she didn't recognize any of them. She was about to withdraw when a guard slowly paced into view along the top of the wall, always looking outward, never toward the castle. He didn't seem to be in any particular hurry. Whatever alarms had gone off when Kram had launched his sneak attack didn't seem to have resulted in any agitation yet around the perimeter of the complex.

She climbed down from the platform, absently wiping her cobwebbed hands on her hip, thinking about what she'd seen. The view through the arrow slit reminded her of when she had looked through similar openings in the stockade wall in Torgonderrer, just after she and the others had left Yexandor's hill following their first confrontation with the Rittandic. There, she had witnessed the incongruous sight of a dwarven fleet floating past, and had called down a lightning strike to destroy the lead ship and block the river. Of course, she'd had the Illata in her possession then, making her far more formidable than she was now; but beyond that, she had been a different person: More Ambrosia, less Mercy. Things had changed. Even if she had the capability, she didn't see herself blasting the guard and blowing a hole through the wall. All she wanted to do was sneak out and find her way back to somewhere safe, like maybe the inn. Aldric probably wouldn't be very happy to see her, but she couldn't think of anywhere else to go.

First, though, she had to get out of the castle.

She turned left and continued on through the dimness, hoping to find a door.

~~~~

The stinking blast of wind propelled them down the formerly

water-filled chute. It banked steeply forward like one of those extreme slides at the water park—not that Bernard had ever gone on one, but he had seen the thrill-seekers lining up for a five-second plunge while he floated lazily along a fake river on a fake inner tube. That was more his speed, not this wild plummet through the darkness along slick rock smooth as glass, heading for a questionable splash pool. A sense of increasing pressure prompted him to capture a deep breath scarcely a second before they hit the water; the ocean was being forced out of the subterranean complex, too, but not as fast as they were. They swirled and spun along with the sea, but he somehow managed to keep hold of Nebandalex's wrist and could only hope Cynidece was doing the same, and that they didn't get their brains bashed out on the floor or ceiling, and, most of all, that the pressure driving the water's movement didn't suddenly change its mind and suck them all back in.

When the tube spat them out into the bay the quality of the water changed, like passing through a membrane that kept waste on one side, as if the water in the cave had been saturated with some gross essence that had been filtered out while they had been let through. Bernard, eyes squeezed shut, couldn't distinguish up from down, but he felt a tug on the hand that clutched Nebandalex and, hoping that meant the elf knew which way to go, kicked his legs to follow. His head soon broke the surface. Gasping, he gulped down breath after breath of air. It was mostly free of the rotten stench from the cavern, although the water churned and bubbled all around them, bringing with it the whiff of decay. The cataract roared not far away, its drifting spume obscuring the view across the chasm, helping to neutralize the odor. He felt waterlogged and exhausted, and looked longingly at some rubble heaped at the base of the nearby palisade, but Cynidece indicated the opposite direction with a tilt of her head. She wanted them to make for Abacar, the city responsible for hanging them out over the chasm, evidently considering it preferable to whatever was stirring in the caves. Bernard could hardly disagree.

Swimming through the chop and surge of the falls would have been difficult even if he hadn't already been worn to a nub by everything that had happened in the last few days. His creaky, waterlogged leathers were far from bathing gear and weighed him down. The others, clad in lighter garments, had less difficulty; Cynidece in particular took to the water like a seal, coming back to help Bernard or Nebandalex when either of them slowed down. More than once, she hooked an arm around Bernard's waist and swam for a while one handed, her feet kicking up a prodigious wake behind them.

He thought he caught a glimpse of webbed hands and feet, but it must have been a trick of the water and the mist and the slanting light of the afternoon sun, because he knew she didn't actually have either. At last they reached the rocky shore beneath the city and hauled themselves out, panting and exhausted, onto jagged rocks stained white and yellow-brown from generations of sea bird. The current flock had, it seemed, recently departed in a hurry, leaving behind claw-scratched stone and grotesquely disemboweled fish still moist in the saturated air. Bernard imagined the entire group squawking and taking flight when the sea had begun to boil. Those birds had the right idea. He would have done that himself if he could, but right now he didn't even have the energy to sit up. When he finally did, he located Nebandalex and Cynidece nearby, crouched down behind a particularly large boulder, staring across the water at the opposite cliff. "What are you looking at?" Bernard said.

"Nothing," Nebandalex said.

"No bubbles, no blobs, no monsters rising out of the water," Cynidece said.

"But the air pushed us out."

"Yes, it did," Cynidece said. "And that was your second clever thought of the day. You are a good man to have around in a bad situation."

"It was?" Then: "I am?"

She nudged Nebandalex. "Has he already forgotten that he saved us on the cable?"

"I have found that Bernard rarely recognizes his own contributions."

"Um. Yeah." Suddenly embarrassed at being credited with rescuing anyone, Bernard crouched beside them. "So if the bubbles stopped, the air in the cave must have reached equilibrium. Nothing coming out or going in. Maybe the binding held after all?"

"That is *not* your third clever thought of the day," Cynidece said.

"Yeah, I know." Turning his gaze upward toward the looming precipice, he said: "How do we get back to the city? I'm too tired for rock-climbing."

"The only way up is the Harbor Road," Cynidece said. "We could swim to the docks—" Here she gestured vaguely to their right, in the direction where the chasm widened into open sea. "—but they might not let us through the gate where the road begins. Perhaps if we wait until—"

"I see a boat coming from that direction," Nebandalex said.

After a moment Bernard spotted it too, a small dark smudge moving slowly across the water. Bernard could barely make out four occupants, two working the oars, two scanning the water from the bow and stern. "What are they doing? Looking for bodies?"

"No, bodies fall into the water all the time," Cynidece said. "They care nothing about that. But the cable breaking ... That is without precedent. They may be searching for it so they can bring it back to shore and haul it up the Harbor Road."

"In that thing? It's hardly big enough to carry the cable. All that metal must weigh a ton."

"If they locate it, a larger boat will come and pick it up."

The three of them slowly moved to keep the boulder between them and the boat, peering over the top or around the sides as the rowers brought their vessel close to the opposite cliff where the cable should be dangling. The openings to the sea cave must be in that vicinity, too. He squinted, having difficulty seeing through the drifting mist, and he soon lost track of the little dory. "Where are they? I can't see them."

"You cannot see them because the boat sank," Nebandalex said.

"What?"

"Something pulled it under," the elf said, "the way a large fish might seize a small bird paddling on the surface."

"Was it the death-wind?"

Neither of the others answered.

Bernard turned to Cynidece. "That plan you had where we were going to get back in the water?" he said. "I think I'm against it."

Chapter 3

MERCY REACHED THE end of the arrow-slit corridor without ever finding a door or window to the outside. Which, she supposed, made sense; you wouldn't want your enemy bashing its way into the very hallway from which your archers were trying to shoot them. Still, the result was disappointing; she really didn't want to have to make her way through the castle trying to find another way out.

The hallway ended in what had once been an archway, now stopped up with bricks of a different color and texture from the walls. The stonework surrounding the former opening were cracked and soot-stained; there had been a fire here, and in its aftermath the corridor had been permanently closed up. She ran her fingers along the stone, wondering if freedom waited just a few inches beyond her reach. Frustrated, she banged on the wall with her fist as if she might be able to bash her way through, then spun and leaned up against it, watching dust and bits of cobweb drift through the weakening shafts of light that angled in through the slots. Her gaze followed the pallid sunbeams to the floor, where a few leaves that had found their way in from the outside had collected in the joint where a buttress column met the wall. If only she were a leaf, Mercy thought, then she could flutter through the arrow-slit and escape.

Hmm. A leaf.

She climbed back up onto the nearest archer platform for another look through the arrow slit. It was about the width of her hand, taller than she was, with three horizontal openings at various spots along its length. If she made herself thin enough—if she made herself into a leaf—she could slip through it, drop to the courtyard on the other side, and find her way out. But how could she do that? She didn't have the Illata anymore, and maybe it was true that without it she was nothing special, but she had managed to escape from her bonds in Torgonderrer without the assistance of any super-powered gems. She closed her eyes and concentrated for a while on becoming narrower, until she became impatient and, even though she didn't feel any different, she nudged the slot to see if anything had changed.

Nope. She still didn't fit.

Mercy bumped into it a few times like a stubborn fish trying to squeeze into a cave that was too small for it, then stepped back to think some more. Maybe she was going about this the wrong way. She didn't need to change herself so much as she needed to convince the wall that she was skinnier than its arrow slit. She jumped down, carefully picked up a dry, dusty leaf, and climbed back up. She held the leaf in front of her face, studying it, the desiccated veins, the long-dead stem. Roughly the size and shape of a human hand when viewed from the front, it looked too wide to fit through the opening, just as she was too wide to fit. Holding it by the stem, she turned it sideways, so she was looking at it edge-on. Now it looked barely as wide as a sheet of paper, although its actual size hadn't changed at all. She didn't really have to change her size either. It was all a matter of perspective. She turned the leaf so she was looking at it from the front again, then slowly spun the stem between her fingers. A strange tightness settled over her, as if she were being constricted by invisible rubber bands. The world shifted, becoming curiously angled, as if it were a pop-up book. The leaf fluttered to the floor.

Feeling hopeful that something had happened this time, Mercy shuffled around, lined herself up edgewise with the slot in the wall, and carefully inched sideways. Rough stone plucked and grabbed at her front and back, scraped at her nose and forehead, but she was able to move through the opening. The wall was relatively thin here because it had been scooped out on both sides, to create the archer's nook on the interior and give a wider field of fire, and she soon emerged onto the crumbly, sloping brick surface of the scalloped exterior. The flagstones of the courtyard lay six or seven feet below. She turned her back to the castle and steadied herself for a moment; because the wall thought she was so thin, she was able to brace against it like a cardboard cutout perched on a narrow rail. In that awkward pose she inched her way to the right until she reached the reinforcing rib where, wedging her elbows into the corners, she allowed herself to slide to the ground. She stayed flat against the buttress and sidled along it to the end, then peered out to take a quick look around. The courtyard looked as disused as she had hoped: The skeins of sand and grit seemed undisturbed by the passage of human feet, marred only by a few bird prints and the tracks of some small, claw-footed animal. To her left, the curtain wall banked sharply inward and ended at the side of the keep, perhaps where it met the edge of the chasm; she saw no exits of any kind in that direction. To her right, a thick, squat tower jutted out of the main body of the castle, forming a wall across the courtyard. It was made of the same sort of stone that she'd encountered at the end of the corridor.

She exited from the niche between the buttresses and moved out into the courtyard. Spiky weeds, grey and withered, sprouted from gaps in the flagstones; lumpy tarpaulin-covered stacks lined the outer wall of the low tower. The protective fabric looked cracked and faded. It reminded her of the unfinished section of her neighborhood back home, where the developer had started building more houses and then ran out of money, abandoning construction material to the elements until someone turned the cash spigot back on. She headed for the tarps, figuring that if that was where the builders had piled their crap, then there must be a big opening nearby through which such stuff could be hauled. She quickly found it, a massive overhead door half-hidden behind the heaps. A few gentle tugs told ger that it was bolted to the floor on the inside, too heavy for her to lift, or both. Leaving it behind for now, she continued exploring, and soon discovered that the new tower didn't quite reach the curtain wall; there was a gap between the two structures of perhaps half a foot, with a runoff channel cut into the floor. She could see light on the other side of the dim and exceedingly narrow passage. Because she was still a leaf, this could be a way out, although the distance she would need to cover was much, much greater than the arrow-slit had been. She suffered a sudden vision of her glamour failing partway through, causing her to expand and get stuck forever in there. The thought paralyzed her and she recoiled, just as footsteps approached on the curtain wall overhead. Mercy flattened herself against the wall, forgetting to breathe for a moment; but then, looking up at the outward-tipping crenellations overhead, she realized the sentry couldn't possibly spot her from up there unless he held out a mirror on the end of a pole. Still, she stayed put, not moving or making a sound, until the sentry reversed direction and moved back off the way he had come.

Okay. She couldn't stay here forever. The big door was a non-starter unless she magicked it open, and who knew what she would find on the other side? A gate that big was going to make all kinds of noise, especially if she used a glamour to rip it out of the floor. At least with the narrow space between the tower and the wall she would be able to see what she was getting into at the end of it. Deciding to chance it, she sidled into the gap. It was somewhat wider than the arrow slit had been, so she could move along it without scraping all the skin off her face. The unbroken brick of the tower scrolled by in front of her eyes like tedious wallpaper. Partway through she stumbled into a spot where the floor had been cut away at an angle, creating a small channel that emerged from a dark gap beneath the tower in front of her and exited under the wall behind her. Some sort of drain, she thought. It could be a way out, but where did it go? She paused, then carefully lowered herself, bending her knees out to the sides; she didn't have the space to turn around, or even really to crouch, so she had to explore the opening blindly by pawing around inside. She felt a layer of grit and soft debris—food waste, not sewage—but little else. The sluiceway didn't appear to be blocked by bars or grillwork at this point. She was pretty sure she could fit through it, as long as her narrowing glamour held up, but it would be an awkward shimmy, and if it funneled into a narrow pipe or it took a sharp turn or its ceiling closed in she might end up wedged forever beneath tons of masonry. Future archeologists excavating the place might find her bones there and theorize that she had been interred beneath the wall as a sacrifice to whatever gods they had worshiped when the place was built. Now there was a lovely thought. She hesitated, looking off to the left, toward the far end of the tower, where it opened up again to daylight. She could hear indistinct voices from that direction, and shadows moved as people passed by. It seemed to be a high-traffic area, but what was the traffic? Guards? Peasants? Tour groups? She still had the veil glamour, so she should be able to emerge from the gap undetected; surely that option was safer than entrusting her fate to the unknown architecture of a drain. Too bad she couldn't turn herself into water.

Having thus decided, she began shuffling again. The opening drew tantalizingly closer, closer, closer. Soon she would be out of the press. But as she neared the end of the narrow passage, she realized that one of the passers-by had stopped and was staring at her. It was a small and rather grubby girl, perhaps the daughter of a servant, standing there splayed-foot with two fingers jammed into her mouth, gawking.

This girl could see her. Had the veil glamour failed? Mercy raised her arm and looked at her hand, trying to figure out what had happened. The child, evidently taking the gesture for a wave, responded in kind, then grinned and toddled forward as if planning to join Mercy in the tiny alley. An arm came in from the right and snatched her away. Mercy heard a woman's scolding voice and the child's breathlessly protesting one—no doubt the girl was trying to explain that a person was moving through the ribbonlike space—but fortunately the adult did not take this claim seriously and come back to investigate. Mercy took a deep breath, trying to relax and get a grip so she could reinstate the veil glamour. The attempt was an abject failure; her fingers felt flat and stupid, and the confines of the space weighed on her mind and interfered with her concentration. It was clear that she wouldn't be able to cast anything under these circumstances. She would have to get out of here and let herself expand again first, which would mean returning to the blocked-off courtyard. But then she would need to make herself flat again, and maybe the effort of maintaining her status as a leaf was what had broken the veil glamour in the first place. Not a very impressive performance. What kind of two-bit sorceress would fail to keep two spells going at once?

Okay, she couldn't just squeeze out among all those people while she was visible; she would get caught immediately. She glanced in the direction of the courtyard, thinking maybe there was some other way out; her gaze fell on the dark hole in the floor that she had explored earlier and rejected. Was she really going to have to try that?

Yes, she was.

Mercy crab-walked her way back to the cutout and positioned herself to slip through it; then, realizing that she would not be able to bend properly to slide backwards under the curtain wall, she slowly lowered herself into a sort of sitting position, pushing her legs forward into the black space in front of her. She didn't encounter any obstacles, and ended up on her back in the sluice with most of her body beneath the tower. She imagined her grimy legs and feet sticking out into a kitchen washbasin, sending some scullery maid fleeing in panic. It was a silly thought, but it made her smile a little. She reached into the drain and ran her fingers along its roof. It was rough and ragged, with plenty of finger holds; she could kick and drag her way along it. High overhead, the outward bump at the underside of the parapet nearly touched the tower wall, with only a thin line of illumination separating them.

She took a deep breath, then exhaled. All right. Time to say goodbye to the light for a little while.

Mercy pulled herself under the curtain wall, squirming and wriggling along on her back. Blackness fell as her body blotted out the gruel of light that seeped in, but she kept going, hauling herself through the cramped, chilly space, trying and mostly succeeding to suppress the lurking trepidation that she would end up trapped here forever. But then she got stuck.

Like a ship encountering a sand bar, she ran aground on a particularly dense, gritty deposit. It stopped her for a few seconds, which eventually became a few minutes, as she tried to move forward or backward and was prevented by hard, roundish nodules—Unshelled nuts? Fruit pits?—that caught against her shoulders and spine and prevented her from sliding like the ball in a rope-trick bottle. Nervousness gave way to fear, and then to panic, until finally the sand shifted beneath her, allowing the pebble-like refuse to roll. She was moving again, sliding onward, debris grinding into her back, and then——

And then she was looking up at filtered daylight, squinting in the relative brightness. Her head had emerged from the narrow sluice into a sewer. Overhead, a metal grate showed her the sky beyond the outer edge of the curtain wall, which loomed whitewashed and massive over the near side of the grill. She had made it through. Pulling her arms free of the drain, she planted her hands on the wall to either side and pushed with all her strength, pushing herself farther out. Gravity did the rest, taking her on a short tumble into a damp channel that ran beneath the street or road or whatever it was above her. She lay there, panting, unable to catch her breath, her lungs seemingly still constricted by the squeeze she had put herself through. Of course. She was still a leaf. Mercy held her hand up edge-on in front of her face and, turning it wide, felt herself expand back to normal width. She lay there for a little while, watching shadows of passers-by on the wall, listening to their footfalls, just *breathing*. It felt wonderful.

At length, she sat up, grateful that there was room to do that here. Her fingers were scraped and bloody, her clothes stained with dirt, her hair matted and filthy. She had lost a shoe somewhere along the line. Aldric's ministrations and Korrin's fine clothes notwithstanding, she looked like a sewer rat again, in which case she was right where she belonged. She eyed the brickwork tunnels that entered and exited the catch basin in which she lay. She could probably squirm through them, but that didn't mean they would take her anywhere she wanted to go. Rusty iron rungs in the wall ascended to what looked like a hinged portion of the grille; that seemed like a much better way to exit rather than scraping around in questionable tunnels beneath the city. Well, except for the part about emerging from the underground directly in front of a castle where everyone thought she had launched a most ostentatious attack in the throne room, and where she would probably be on the Most Wanted list for murdering Lord Korrin once they found his body.

She felt safe enough here for the time being; no one would think to look for her in the sewer. Even if anyone remembered that the drain existed, they wouldn't consider it as an escape route. She could rest for a little while, and think, and try to figure out her next move.

Mercy leaned back against the moist stone wall, closed her eyes, and pretended she was back in detention, trying to stop time.

~~~~

Arran Blackhawk, not quite believing what he had been told, said:

"*Where* was this, again?"

"The large basin in the cookery, sir."

"So this scullery maid claims to have been cleaning vegetables, or whatever it is they do in this basin, and——"

"And a pair of feet and legs emerged from the drain slot in the back, then withdrew, leaving this behind."

Arran Blackhawk regarded the gold-filigreed purple slipper that the guard had brought with him as evidence to support the kitchen girl's claim. His immediate thought was, of course, that Ambrosia had been wearing it. He could poll those in the throne room, but he doubted that any of those fops and dandies and chattering ladies would be able to give him a useful account of what the elf had worn on her feet; yet obviously his brother must have shod her in *something* when he had taken her to his room, and it was highly doubtful that anyone else in the castle possessed such an ostentatious set of footwear.

"The maid thought it must be the ghost of a girl killed in the fire," the watchman offered.

"A kitchen-wench ghost who leaves behind a royally-colored shoe? Unlikely. No, this could only be the witch." Korrin, Kram, and the elf had all vanished in the chaos after an explosion of light had temporarily blinded almost everyone in the throne room. No one could tell him where they had gone; all he had were a bunch of courtiers, sycophants, guards, and one extremely irate dwarf, all with red eyes and tear-streaked cheeks, none of whom had seen anything remotely helpful after the flare. "This drain is *how* tall, exactly?"

"A handspan, perhaps a bit more."

Not tall enough, in other words, for even the slightest of elves to crawl through, let alone one as amply proportioned as Ambrosia. Arran Blackhawk closed his eyes and visualized the layout of the castle; part of his job was to be intimately familiar with the layout, architecture, and vulnerable points of the complex and its surroundings. The cookery in question was in a relatively new tower, isolated from the rest of the structure by stone barriers to prevent a repeat of the disastrous kitchen inferno that had destroyed a third of the castle. Its thick firewall interrupted a corridor that girded the old keep. No one went that way anymore; why would they? Its defensive arrow slits were obsolete, its statues musty. Now it was just used for the storage of things no one needed, or for the occasional interment of some august personage down in the crypts that held the bodies of the honored dead, and, of course, the …

Oh. Yes. That.

Arran Blackhawk leaned back to think. He had practically ordered his brother to put a suppressor gem on the elf to interfere with her use of sorcery, and knew that he had done so, on the pretext that it was jewelry. Once donned, this ornament—which had been enchanted by Jordneh, witch-queen of the Ravels—could not be taken off by the one who wore it. Unless the elf was more powerful than Jordneh, which seemed *highly* unlikely, she would have been unable to invoke the potent glamour that had robbed everyone in the throne room of their sight; and while there was no consensus among those polled as to exactly what Ambrosia had been doing just prior to the flash, everyone *did* agree that Rumad Kram, who had arrived late to the audience, had been carrying the witch's pack, and that the old man had goaded her into opening it. Furthermore, while all that had been going on, the cable over the chasm had snapped, sending its burden of prisoners—including Ambrosia's cohorts, snared along with the elf-witch in Kram's unauthorized dragnet—down into the hungry sea.

It was all so very neat, how events had played out. *Too* neat. Arran Blackhawk didn't like it.

Of course, he also didn't like the fact that the three of them—Korrin, Kram, and Ambrosia—had vanished at the same time, or that the elf had apparently left her shoe in a sink via a drain that was much too small to admit her. That suggested her abilities had returned, but how? Had someone removed the gem from her neck? Kram would certainly not have done it, given his antagonistic behavior towards her. What about Korrin? Why would he have wanted Ambrosia to be able to cast spells, except to help defend against *another* sorcerer? And who might *that* have been, if not Rumad Kram? But the astrologer was no magician. At least, he never had been before.

Arran Blackhawk thought some more, and finally came to a conclusion. "Form a squad and go down into the crypt," he told the guard, who had been quietly standing by awaiting instructions. "Take care. Be on guard against the astrologer."

"The astrologer? But, sir, if the witch is in the drain—"

"At present, it is not the witch who worries me."

The guard clearly found this strange, but, like a good guard, said: "Yes, sir." The man swept out of the room.

That done, Arran Blackhawk returned his thoughts to the matter of the basin, the drain, and where it led. It would run, as most simple sluiceways did, through a narrow aperture beneath the wall and out into the surrounding system of sewers that ran throughout the underside of the city and ultimately emptied into Chasm Bay, near the waterfall. He closed his eyes and pictured himself walking along the curtain wall opposite the cookery tower. Recalling the layout, he imagined himself passing a grate in the flagstones, kneeling to examine it, noting the large space beneath for accumulating runoff.

He opened his eyes. Yes. That was the spot. If the witch had somehow used her magic to escape through the drains, she might well have found her way into that catch basin, and might have lingered there to rest. Certainly her goal would be to escape, but it could not be easy to remake oneself into a shape and size that could slip through such a passage, which was, after all, designed to be traversable by water and small amounts of refuse and nothing else. Even such a deadly and masterful sorceress as Kram alleged the elf to be must pause now and then and catch a breath.

Kram. He shook his head. To hear the astrologer spin the tale, one would need to assemble an entire platoon to capture the witch by force, and even then—unless she were taken unawares and possibly drugged, as in that embarrassing spectacle Kram had orchestrated at Goldshine's inn—one would expect to forfeit a goodly portion of one's men. Arran Blackhawk could, of course, scrape together a small team out of those watchmen not otherwise occupied with searching for the missing Lord Korrin, maintaining order around the city, and dealing with the aftermath of the broken cable, but why should he, when Ambrosia could supposedly dispatch them so handily? Why put so many men at risk?

Why not just go himself?

~~~~

From the concealment of the tumbled rocks, Bernard and the others watched the goings-on in the bay. After the first rowboat vanished beneath the foamy waters a brief period of inactivity ensued, after which the harbor began disgorging a number of small boats to ply the waters. Dories of varying sizes and levels of occupancy skimmed across the water, most forming up into a line, although some noodled around near the spot where their scouting pioneer had been lost. Perhaps they were looking for it, this endeavor met with disappointment. Then a larger vessel emerged from the breakwater; its furled sails showed it to be capable of longer voyaging, though at the moment it operated strictly under the impetus of several sets of oars, which provided better control in the perilously close region of rocky walls and shallows and erratic winds. It took up a position along the opposite side in the vicinity of the sunken dinghy, displacing the small searchers, which moved off to join the others, completing a chain that stretched all the way back to the quay.

While the scows finished assembling themselves into a floating bucket brigade, some men on the schooner operated a long hooklike apparatus, fishing around in the depths. Looking for bodies? Bernard had no idea, and half-expected the probe to be seized and yanked beneath the waves, but eventually they came up with the cable, dangling and dripping like a massive grey eel. They swung it around to the first rowboat in the chain, which passed it to the next, which passed it to the next, and so on; but the thick, braided metal was so heavy that it acted like an anchor, threatening to capsize any individual boat. It seemed to be difficult for the sailors to keep hold of, slicked as it was by water-resistant grease; they would get it partway along to dry land only to have some butterfingers lose his grip, causing the cable to splash back into the water and begin to sink, at which point all the other boats in the line had to drop it as well lest it pull them down into the depths.

The third time that happened, Bernard murmured: "You'd think they would've had a better plan for dealing with this."

"Why would they?" Cynidece said. "The cable was enchanted by one of the old Rittandic witch-queens. It is supposed to be immune to rust and decay, and unbreakable."

"Looks broken to me."

"*Supposed* to be," Cynidece said.

Bernard grunted. Part of him wanted to stand up, shout, and wave his arms to draw a boat over that could take them off this miserable glob of rock and bird droppings, but these were the very same people who had hung them out over the chasm in the first place, and if they were discovered they would most likely end up back in chains or summarily executed. Perhaps now, while so many were engaged in the recovery operation, would be a good time to swim for the docks; whatever force had sucked the first boat under the waves—that malignant pendulous blob that swayed beneath fading runes—seemed to be quiescent, maybe digesting its last meal, maybe unable to decide which boat to attack next. So many ships, so little time.

"I see the boat that sank," Nebandalex said.

Bernard and Cynidece crept over to where the elf lay sprawled on one of the low rocks. "Where?" Cynidece said.

Nebandalex indicated the direction with a tip of his head. Bernard spotted the boat not far away, upside-down, a dark brown shape bobbing low in the rough water, just the hull, no sign of oars or occupants; if the death-wind had really taken them, then it had tossed the dory aside like an empty pea-pod, and the current induced by the roaring cataract had drawn it towards them rather than pushing it out to sea. Or had it? "Do you think it *really* drifted over here, or is this some sort of trap?"

"The death-wind does not set traps," Cynidece said. "Subtlety is not its tactic."

"In that case, do you think we could——" Bernard broke off as Cynidece pushed forward off the rocks and slipped into the water, easy and silent as a seal that had spotted a scrumptious penguin. "I guess she does," he said, watching Cynidece's lithe, inky form shoot away just below the surface toward the overturned boat. In a second she was lost to sight beneath the foam and chop.

"Our new friend is not one to hesitate when she sees a path she wants to take," Nebandalex said.

"No, she's sure not."   The Pelt reached the boat much more quickly than Bernard had thought she would; the capsized vessel turned in the water, and after a moment it started to move their way in a direct and purposeful manner. He supposed she must be underneath it, propelling it along with powerful kicks. Didn't she ever get tired? And how was she navigating? As far as he could tell she was completely submerged, and her head never once broke the surface to have a look around, yet somehow the boat found its way unerringly to where they lay hidden. Only when it was bobbing broadside just off the rocks did any part of her emerge, and that was just her hand, beckoning them to join her. Bernard didn't really want to get back in the water, but neither did he want to remain trapped on the rocks indefinitely; the sun was moving steadily along, casting them into chilly shadow, and he had a feeling that by the morning they would be dead of exposure if not of more nefarious causes. He exchanged a glance with Nebandalex, who shrugged, then slid into the sea.   Bernard followed, the two of them making their way the short distance to the partially submerged hull, then ducking under and up again into the deeply shadowed interior.   Some light leaked in from the water, illuminating it about to the level of a movie theater between the darkening of the lights and the start of the film. The air was close and wet but, compared to the atmosphere in the sea cave, positively salubrious.   Cynidece hung inside, arms outstretched, long fingers curled around the oarlocks, her pale face almost glowing in the indirect light, a sharp contrast to the utterly black hair that framed her visage.

Nebandalex braced his hands on the curved side of the boat, while Bernard took hold of one of the seats. "Now what?" he said, his voice muffled and echoey at the same time in the water-bound space.

"Now we make for the docks," Cynidece said. "We should be able to get close enough to swim for the ladders before they spot us."

"But then what? You said they wouldn't let us through the gates to the road up to the city." Bernard thought for a moment. "You know what? We're going about this wrong. If we try to sneak through, we look suspicious. If we swim back with the boat, we look like we were out on the water helping with the cable and had an accident. Then they might just let us through."

"True. To most observers, even to city watchmen, those given over to the chasm are just shapes swaying in the wind. Given all the activity, we may not be recognized as escapees."

"Unless someone at the gate was involved in arresting us or hanging us on the cable" Nebandalex said.

"I doubt they would have dragged a harbor-gate guard all the way up to the inn just to arrest you lot."

"You were not there. The inn had more guards than guests."

"Even so," she said, "Bernard's plan is a good one; I have no better suggestion than to swim the boat back and act like we belong there, and see what happens."

She let go of the oarlocks and disappeared. Bernard and Nebandalex regarded each other in the semidarkness. "This is mad," the elf said.

"Well, we can't stay on the rocks forever."

Nebandalex sighed. "No, I suppose not."

Cynidece's head reappeared.

"For this scheme to work," she said, "you have to come out from under the boat."

~~~~

Mercy wasn't sure how long she had been asleep, but she knew what had awakened her: The insistent sound of metal tapping against metal. Feeling sore and stiff, she blinked and looked around. It was still fairly bright out, though the patch of sunlight shining through the grate had moved some distance along the masonry wall of the sewer, becoming increasing elongated as it shifted position. A shadow obscured the spot of illumination; someone was standing on or near the grill. This person seemed to be the cause of the tapping sound, as if some citizen with a metal-tipped cane were waiting impatiently for the arrival of public transportation. *Tap tap tap.* Pause. *Tap tap tap.* Pause. *Tap tap tap.* Why didn't this person move on like a normal passerby? Feeling the first stirrings of suspicion, she slowly crawled over to get a better view of the grate, but couldn't make out any details of whoever was up there. All she saw were the bottoms of his shoes and the sweep of his cape.

Then, to her surprise, he spoke.

"I know you are down there," he said. His voice was pitched low, for her ears only, and while his tone was gruff, he did not sound overtly hostile. "You still reek of Korrin's scented oils."

She did? When had Korrin put scented oils on her? She gave her arm a sniff, and detected a faint, flowery aroma underneath the stink of sweat and grime, but hardly anything she would call a reek. She shook her head; how she smelled was of little importance at the moment, and certainly whoever was up there hadn't found her by wandering around the castle grounds scenting the air. Not unless he had a bloodhound with him.

"Very well," the voice said. "Pretend you are not there, if such is your desire. But unless you wish to take up *permanent* residence in the sewers, you would be well-advised to come out and talk to me."

After a moment, she said: "Who *are* you?"

"Ah, you do have a voice! Good. I am Arran Blackhawk, Korrin's half-brother. We have met, but you would not remember me; you were unconscious at the time."

"I was … When did—"

"In the dungeon, after Kram had you drugged and arrested."

"Oh." Then: "Are you here to arrest me again?"

"That depends on you. Korrin and Kram have both vanished. My men are scouring the castle looking for them, and for you. The dwarf wants your head. The cable bearing your friends has fallen. You are alone. If I unlock the cover, will you come out peacefully?"

"How do I know you don't have ten archers standing there waiting to shoot me full of arrows?"

"If I wanted you full of arrows, I would have had it done through the grate as you slept. Trust me, I am as alone as you are."

This situation was absurd, her sitting in the catch basin whispering through a grate to an unseen interlocutor as if engaged in some sort of sewer-based confessional. Still, she was in no condition to fight, and she didn't relish the idea of crawling through sewer pipes with no idea where she was going. "All right," she said. "I won't trust you, but I'll come out."

"Fair enough." The shadow moved away from the grate; she heard some clicking and scraping from the cover, and then it lifted away, allowing more light to pour into her miserable hiding place. She clambered up the ladder; her sore knee made climbing difficult, and when Arran Blackhawk took hold of her and half-hauled her the rest of the way out, she was grateful for the assistance. This Blackhawk was a much smaller man than Korrin, and darker, with a hardness to his face and eyes that his half-brother had not possessed. She noticed a dagger in his free hand; he could easily have planted it in her stomach when he was helping her out of the sewer, and no doubt would have if she had done anything remotely threatening.

This, she thought, was not a man who was likely to dress a strange elf up in fancy clothes and daub her with scented oils and take her to see his garden.

Never moving his gaze off her face, Arran Blackhawk closed the grate and kicked a sliding latch across it, barring it shut. Then he retrieved a dark cloak from the ground at his feet and tossed it to her. "Put this on," he said. She complied, slipping her arms into the sleeves, eyeing her surroundings as she did. It turned out that she hadn't really escaped from the castle; between the curtain wall and the rooftops she had seen beyond it, there was another, lower barrier, separated from the inner parapet by a cobbled track. Yet another line of defense. Who did they expect to attack them here?

"And the hood," he said.

She started to pull the hood up, then stopped and said: "I don't ... your brother gave me a necklace to wear, and it did something to keep me from—"

"I am aware of what he did. But you are too recognizable, and this is merely a cloak, nothing more."

"But you said *your* men were looking for me. If you're in charge, and I'm with you, why do I have to hide under a hood?"

"The *guards* are mine, but the *castle* is Korrin's. Everything is in disarray, and Kram has been telling everyone with ears that you are some manner of master enchantress. If we were are seen together, the immediate assumption is likely to be that you have somehow put me in thrall. So it would be better for you to remain unidentified for the nonce." The man hesitated, then said: "If you would prefer to conceal us with an enchantment, you may do so. I will refrain from cutting your throat while you cast a glamour. *One* glamour."

"Um, all right." She did feel slightly better after her too-brief rest, and had used the veil glamour so often that it had become routine; if she could manage any spell under these circumstances it would be that one. With some effort she succeeded in enfolding herself and Blackhawk within a cloak of obscurity, seeing the familiar blurring of her surroundings that meant it had taken effect. "It's done."

"Very well," he said. "Now walk with me, and tell me what Kram has done."

So they walked, and Mercy talked, and somewhat to her surprise, Arran Blackhawk listened.

She started at the end and worked backwards, telling him what had happened in the catacombs, how a Rittandic sorcerer wearing an old man's body had killed Lord Korrin and escaped with both the Illata and the Jewel in the Maul, then how she and the others had arrived at the city, and had been assaulted in their camp outside the walls by a renegade watchman. She left off the finer point that the man had surrendered before Nebandalex killed him. Finally, she related the events in Torgonderrer, when she had acquired the Illata from the elves, thus wrapping her tale back around to the events in the catacombs. She did not mention where she really came from or who she really was or how she had gotten here, figuring that she had already given Blackhawk more than enough to think about. Besides, adding those details would probably just make him think she was insane.

By the time she finished, she realized that he had guided her to a set of gates that, like an airlock, stood open on either side of the perimeter track along which they walked. Both gates stood open, but were guarded by men with pole-arms on who subtly scrutinized those who came and went. Traffic was light at the moment. She glanced at Arran Blackhawk. "Are we leaving?"

"*You* are leaving. I have matters to deal with yet."

"You're letting me go?"

"I believe that you have told me the truth. Your story conforms to my own reasoning and conclusions. I have suspected for some little time now that Kram has been manipulating events for his own reasons. Whether he was a disguised Rittandic or a Pelt or some demon from the void, or merely himself, I do not know, but his role is apparent in hindsight. What you did in the forest with the elves is not my concern. Your companion killed Marjack, one of my watchmen, but Marjack was marauding and your friend has been punished. I see little reason to hold you here, and less to bury a blade in you."

"But Korrin—"

"I will shortly confirm what you told me about Korrin. I had already dispatched men to the crypts before I found you. My half-brother will be just as dead whether I keep you or set you free." He handed her an amber-colored piece of thin metal with a hawk engraved on one side. "Find your way back to the inn where you were to tell your stories. Give this to Goldshine or his lackey behind the bar." Blackhawk's mouth quirked into an ironic grin. "They may recognize it. Tell them I will be calling on you soon, and will expect to find you waiting for me there."

"I—" She broke off as Arran Blackhawk simply turned and walked away from her, back into the shadows the way they had come, moving out of the range of her veil. If anyone had been looking their way, he would have seemed to have stepped from an invisible doorway, but no one was.

She watched him until he was out of sight around the curve of the wall, then put the badge into one of her new cloak's many pockets and slipped away herself, passing into the questionable freedom of unfamiliar city streets.

~~~~

The three of them swam the rowboat toward the distant docks, making steady—thanks mostly to Cynidece, who had taken up a position at the stern of the rowboat—progress despite the resistance of the strange currents that tried to draw them back toward the falls. Bernard was much more concerned about being seized and pulled beneath the water by the mysterious force from the sea cave than he was about being spotted by the boats plying the mist-shrouded bay, but neither occurred; the ships were occupied with their cable operation, and the monstrous gob from the sea cave seemed to be quiescent for the moment. Maybe it was digesting its earlier victims; or maybe they were just too far away to grab.

As they passed beneath the promontory from which they had been dispatched onto the cable, Bernard couldn't help giving it a long, unfriendly look. He imagined the scene from down here, a thin black line across the sky with dark shapes sliding along it until friction overcame gravity and momentum and they stopped, swaying like flies trapped on a filament of web. He was glad the barbaric thing had broken, and would provide no more meals for the spider. Then he remembered that the spider was the thing beneath the waves, and that, deprived of—or freed from—its web, it would soon be coming out to hunt, and decided maybe he wasn't so glad after all.

Once past the outcropping, they soon neared the docks, which were housed in a large concave space where the cliff bowed inward toward the city. It looked like a massive rockfall had occurred here in the distant past, converting a huge quantity of stone into tumbled rubble. The local residents, industrious things that they were, had exploited this material by hauling it out to form a pair of breakwaters encircling what must be a fairly deep harbor, judging by the size of the few ships that floated within. There were only two, and they both looked like refugees from a naval battle that had gone badly; one seemed to have been burned rather extensively, while the other had a broken mast, leaving its sail draped like a shroud.

Alongside the cliff, a narrow channel had been left open to allow small boats to come and go without getting in the way of bigger merchant vessels. To Bernard's relief, Cynidece aimed them at this opening; there weren't any large ships coming or going that might run them down, but the side-door approach kept them well away from the trawling cable-crew and the opposite side of the chasm, where that malignant polyp lurked beneath the slate-grey waves. The low ridge of tumbled stone that separated the passage from the rest of the marina stood two or three feet above the surface, studded with brazier-topped pylons that probably served as warning beacons for nighttime navigation. Both beacons and breakwater were thickly coated with bird droppings, but, like the rock pile they had left, no birds were present. Bernard concluded that the avians around here knew something that the humans didn't.

"You there!"

At the shout, Bernard turned away from the breakwater. Another rowboat—this one right-side up, unlike theirs—had entered the channel. It carried yet another set of cable-recoverers, two at the oars, one in the bow wearing thick leather gloves up to his elbows, presumably to protect him from poky bits of braided cord. Bernard feared that they had been recognized, but all the gloved man did was gesture impatiently for them to move to the right and, when they failed to adjust course quickly enough, bellow at them to get out of the way. "Sorry, sir," Cynidece said as they kicked and shoved the capsized boat sideways through the water. "She's harder to steer when she's upside-down."

"In the future, you lot might do better to stay on land," the gloved man said as his boat passed theirs. He wasn't even looking at them anymore, gazing instead in the direction of the distant flotilla. Bernard turned to watch them exit the channel and turn right, passing behind the high outer jetty.

"You're certainly right about that, sir!" Cynidece called as the other boat disappeared from sight. Then, in a murmur: "This scheme was your third good idea of the day, Bernard. Well done." Bernard, inordinately pleased by the praise, felt himself flush a little with embarrassed gratification.

Soon they emerged from the channel. Cynidece, who had obviously been here before, steered them to the right, toward a stubby outcropping of flattened stone. A wooden shack, in shape and odor not unlike a large outhouse, occupied most of the space. It appeared to be a stand where fishermen could buy bait and gear. Surrounding this noisome structure was a series of mushroom-shaped posts, moorings for small boats, though at the moment the shack stood alone; all the tubs that usually occupied these spaces must be out helping to recover the cable. They paddled up alongside, reaching shore with a few final exhausted kicks. Now that they had a solid surface to brace against, it was easier to manipulate the hull; as Bernard and Nebandalex set about righting the capsized boat, Cynidece abandoned them, scrambling up the rocks and out of sight. Once the dory was floating properly again, Bernard dragged himself out of the water and caught the dripping line that Nebandalex tossed him, securing it to a post by looping it a few times and then pretending to tie a complicated knot according to the elf's bewildering instructions. As he went after the Pelt, Nebandalex was already unraveling his handiwork, obviously intending to redo it properly.

He found Cynidece at the counter of the shack, greedily drinking water from a large wooden cup. She had another, full, cup in her other hand, which she immediately started quaffing as soon as the first one was drained. Then she plunged both cups into a nearby barrel and started over again. Said barrel was full of bait in the form of small, wriggling, shiny fish; Cynidece, less than careful with the filling or the drinking, must have been chugging down a good number of minnows with each mouthful. The proprietor of the shack, a hoary fellow with one eye and fewer teeth, stood staring at her from behind the split, stained, knife-scarred counter with a slack expression of amusement, which became open guffaws when Nebandalex, soaked and bedraggled, appeared beside them, looking more like a half-drowned muskrat than a woodland sprite. The one-eyed man said something that Bernard found unintelligible, but apparently Cynidece understood it; she put the cups down on the counter and pushed them back toward him. "Almost," she told him, wiping her mouth with the back of her arm, "but not quite."

Bernard sniffed the barrel. It smelled strongly of fish, but not of salt, and at this point he didn't care how rank the water tasted as long as it was fresh. He reached for one of the cups, but the old man's hand shot out and pinned his wrist to the counter. Cynidece said something in a sharp tone and the man let go, then snatched away the cups and stowed them out of sight. "Sorry," she said. "He wants you to pay for the bait, and you have no money."

"I don't want bait, I just want water."

"If you think you can get water out of that barrel and not get bait with it, you are more clever than I am." Her tone suggested this could not possibly be the case.

"How did *you* pay for it, then? You don't have any money either."

"No, but I have credit. We will find you something to drink, just not here. The proprietor lacks a certain *generosity of spirit*." The one-eyed man laughed heartily at what was evidently some sort of inside joke the two of them shared, but his good humor was unaccompanied by any increase in his generosity of spirit; the cups didn't come back out. Cynidece shook her head, then indicated a narrow wooden catwalk that connected the bait shack's platform with the main part of the wharf. "That way leads to the gate."

Leaving the shack and its unavailable water behind, they went to the catwalk. Bernard eyed the ramshackle structure. Age-blackened posts, driven into holes in the cliff, supported it at a crooked angle; a rotten-looking braided rope ran through rusted iron rings in the rock face at roughly waist level, providing something to hold onto, but there was nothing along the opposite side to prevent a drunken fisherman from tumbling into the sea. Bernard suspected it wouldn't take much weight or vibration to detach the whole thing and send it splashing into the water; thinking of all the little boats that had been pressed into service recovering the cable, all those feet tramping along this funhouse contraption, he was mildly surprised it hadn't collapsed already. At least it'd be a short fall. The wall curved outward and he couldn't see much of where the catwalk ended, except that it was a more-or-less flat surface of crushed stone. "Are you sure that can hold all three of us?" Bernard asked.

Cynidece laughed and smacked him on the shoulder. "How much do you think I weigh?" She started off across the creaking boards. Bernard waited until she got a little distance away, then followed. Nebandalex brought up the rear. The catwalk groaned and shifted underfoot, but it delivered them safely to the other side. This was revealed to be the main body of the wharf, from which the quays radiated like spokes. To their right, where the cliff wall bowed inward, a high, thick wall of masonry and stone topped with outward-facing spikes stood. Passage through the barrier was controlled by a massive gate of wood and rusted iron, standing open at the moment, flanked on either side by small, unattended guard posts. Bernard could see a cobbled track rising sharply beyond the opening. That must be the Harbor Road. Little traffic was moving through it at the moment: No merchandise coming or going, no sailors or stevedores moving cargo around, no carts or wagons or hopeful anglers. The few people who were present had gone out onto the jetties to gawk at the cable-recovery operation and weren't interested in the activities of a trio of soggy ragamuffins. Bernard's gaze moved on. He eyed the ships that floated out in the deep water. From here they looked even more woebegone, as if they had been piloted by ghosts and left behind when the spirits fled to haunt the city.

"We should go before the guards return," Nebandalex said, reminding Bernard that they were escaping, not sightseeing. He followed the others through the gate and up the road as it turned hard to the right, narrowed to about the width of a wagon, and ascended for some distance along the curving wall before making a sharp left into a ludicrously steep switchback. This pattern would surely be repeated many times before they reached the top.

What a day. Zip-lining down a cable, plunging hundreds of feet into the water, sluicing through a sea cave, swimming across the splash pool of a waterfall, negotiating a broken-down plank bridge, and now, slogging up a mountain. He wasn't looking forward to this climb. Feeling like an adventure tourist who'd been abandoned by the company that had promised safe fun and excitement, he said: "I don't suppose we can call a taxi down to get us."

"I do not know what a *taxi* is," Cynidece said, "so I am going to say *no*."

~~~~

Beyond the gate Mercy encountered yet another barrier, this one merging in toward the outer fortification of the keep, forming a dead-end off to her left. She recognized it as the wall that ran along the top of the chasm. It was punctuated with stubby towers and pierced here and there with small, barred windows through which she could see blue sky and the black rock of the cliffs on the opposite side of the bay. She might have gone to one and taken a look into the depths, but gawkers were clustered around each one and she didn't want to risk detection; Arran Blackhawk would probably not be amused if she got herself captured immediately after he had let her go.

Keeping close to the castle wall, she moved off to the right, away from the dead-end and into a nearby residential area where small shops mixed with large communal rowhouse-type dwellings. The structures had the uniform look of barracks and she wondered if this was where castle guards and town watchmen who were not billeted in the castle lived with their families. The neighborhood stretched off to her right, away from the cliff. She stayed on the road that ran along the wall, keeping to the middle, well back from the spectators who jostled for positions at the viewports. Ahead, she saw one of the cable viewing platforms that she'd noticed from Korrin's cliffside garden; it was crammed with people trying to get a better look into the crevasse. The spillover of people milling around waiting to climb the steep ladder to the overlook bulged out into the middle of the street. She could hardly get up to the platform while concealed by the veil glamour; attention slid off of her like water off glass, but that wouldn't protect her if she tried to shove her through a crowd. She took up a position nearby and hung around for a little while, watching and listening to the throng, trying to get an idea of what the attraction was. From the murmurs of conversation she soon gathered that they were watching ships down in the bay trying to recover the cable, but she heard no mention of what had happened to those who had been hanging from the wire when it fell.

Much as she would have liked to get a look into the abyss that had claimed her friends, she had to find her way back to the Goldsmith Inn before Blackhawk came looking for her. If she wasn't there, he might think she had fled the city, which wouldn't cast a favorable light on anything she had told him about Rumad Kram. She wasn't sure what sort of reception she would get from Aldric, but the only way to find that out was to show up, right? She slipped past the line and continued on her way, keeping an eye out for any familiar landmarks, but soon encountered another distraction: A gap in the wall, crowned by an arched catwalk of wrought iron, beneath which large gates had been drawn open. Platforms similar to the observation deck perched atop the walls on either side of the gate, but guards were stationed at the ladders to keep them clear, so the curious had accumulated in a good-sized group at street level, peering and pointing through the gates. Mercy glanced to her right, into the city, where the cobbled thoroughfare that emerged from the chasm ran straight through in a gradual downward slope to a large open space from which other streets radiated like spokes. In the distance, she thought she could make out the bazaar surrounding where she and the others had entered the city. If she went that way, she would probably end up on more familiar ground, from which she could locate Aldric's inn; but the chasm was *right there*. How could she not go look?

She sidled toward the gap, giving the other spectators as wide a berth as possible. Most of the observers had gathered at the left side of the gate, which, presumably, offered a better view into the chasm, so she had room to get close on the right side, between the people and the guards keeping them off the deck. Beyond the wall, the road plunged into a series of very steep switchbacks interspersed with flat sections that ran along the edge of a vast crescent-shaped rockfall, deep and rugged, ending in a sheltered harbor far below. A fin of reddish-grey igneous stone, obviously more durable than the black surfaces that surrounded it, protruded from the middle like the spine of some giant creature. A number of vessels plied the roiling water within the chasm; from here they looked like toys, a train of boats all connected to a thick, glistening rope. That must be the cable. Her gaze followed the line inward, then traced the path of the road as it switchbacked up the cliff. Because each lower switchback was offset outward from the one above, she could see almost the entire length of the road, from water to top. It pierced the reddish fin via dark, narrow tunnels, one over the other. Some small figures caught her attention as they emerged from one such passage, perhaps halfway down, trudging wearily upward. Slanting afternoon light glinted on carrot-colored hair.

Mercy squinted through the shimmer, not entirely trusting what she thought she had seen. That couldn't possibly be *Bernard*, could it? He had fallen into the chasm. But it looked like him: Gawky, wiry Bernard, clad head-to-toe in dark leather. He'd lost his hat; maybe it was still at the inn. If that was Bernard, then the slim brown-haired figure behind him had to be Nebandalex. She had no idea who the third climber might be, with that mass of spiky black hair and a pale hatchet face atop a body almost as gangly as Bernard's, but the other two … it was them. Her friends. It had to be. She watched them for a little while. She didn't think she had ever seen either of them move so slowly, tottering forward at the pace of the exhausted and the injured; but after plunging so far into the water and managing to come out alive again, she was amazed they could move at all.

She couldn't stay here until they reached the gate. She had to know sooner.

Mercy slipped through the gate and started down the Harbor Road to meet the travelers on their way up.

~~~~

The climb from the harbor was even more of a slog than Yexandor's hill had been. Sore, thirsty, and bone-tired, there was no way he would be bypassing the path and going straight to the top this time. This time, Bernard was taking the slow route, just like everybody else.

It was only in the hairpins that the road got steep, but those were *very* steep. There, the surface had been cut into washboard-like ridges for better traction, with wide sections above and below chipped into the rock where a slower cart or wagon could be pulled aside to allow faster traffic to pass. The stone bore the marks of innumerable wagon wheels, but at the moment, the only traffic on the road consisted of the three of them. It made him feel highly conspicuous, like a cockroach crawling across a gleaming white kitchen floor.

Partway up the road, a spine of something like granite began to protrude from the wall like a fin. On its first few passes, the track bowed out and detoured around the bulging vein of harder rock, but as they climbed higher and the ridge protruded farther, the road-builders had started tunneling through instead. The bore-holes began as little more than archways, each with a thick iron gate set into it; these stood open, swung back into the black rock wall and secured with latches, but it was apparent that they could be closed and locked. Shutting them would turn a major inconvenience into something close to impassable; the way the cliff sloped back toward the city, defenders above could rain down all sorts of projectiles on any invaders as they marched up the road and stalled at every barrier. Bernard thought again of what they had seen in the tunnels, the malignant glob, the clattering bones, dead Poddock shuffling around with eyes like the belly of a fish. "If they close the gates, will it keep that thing from the cave out?" he asked, as they passed through one of the increasingly-long passageways. This one had a door at each end, like an airlock. Cynidece and Nebandalex both looked at him, then at each other, then away. Obviously the question was so stupid that it did not rate an answer.

They kept going, nobody saying much, wanting nothing more than to get out of this vast water-filled cleft in the earth. They plodded around switchbacks and shuffled through dark burrows, until finally while passing through the shadowed confines of yet another tunnel, a soft voice came at them from out of the darkness, saying: "I thought you were dead."

Bernard and Nebandalex stopped walking immediately, but the Pelt pounced like a cat, leaping forward and grabbing at nothing, her arms and head and torso fading from view. Bizarrely, while this was going on Bernard found his attention wandering to the half-seen walls and floors, as if they were far more interesting than whatever invisible thing Cynidece grappled with; but then her unseen opponent emitted a shriek of dismay, bringing his focus back to that space he couldn't seem to look at.   He belatedly recognized the effect and, even more belatedly, the voice that had emanated from it. "Cynidece! Wait!"

She froze. He couldn't see her face, but he had the sense that she was giving him an expectant look.

"That's our friend. I think."

"You *think*?"

"Yes. Mercy? Is that you?"

"She cannot answer while my hand is around her throat, whoever she is. How sure are you that this is a friend?"

"Very sure. Positive." Then: "Almost."

There was a brief pause while Cynidece considered this, the momentary silence broken by faint choking sounds that seemed to come from nowhere. "Well then," the Pelt said as she finally pulled back, "a friend should know better than to sneak up on another friend in a dark place."

"I wasn't *sneaking*. I was *waiting*." The veil effect faded and Mercy stood there in the shadows, battered and filthy, with a fresh, shallow cut bleeding along her cheek and another on her neck where Cynidece's nails must have raked her skin. She raised an arm to dab at the injuries with a dirty sleeve and said, "So who's *this*, Bernard?"

"This is Cynidece. She was on the cable with us. Cynidece, this is Mercy … I mean, Ambrosia—"

"You mean *Mercy*," she said.

Bernard opened his mouth, closed it again, then said: "I do?"

"Yes.   We can discuss it later."   Mercy cast a baleful look in Cynidece's direction. "She was on the cable? So she's some kind of criminal?"

"No. Um, well, I'm not sure. But she helped us get back here safely, so—"

"I heard the tale of your arrest," Cynidece said.   "We are all criminals here, are we not?"

"Some of us were set up."

The Pelt laughed. "Of course! As were all of the prisoners in the dungeon and every innocent lad sent to the executioner's block. But we three—" Here she indicated Bernard and Nebandalex with a toss of her head. "—have had the good luck to cooperate and survive, and it seems to me we should continue to conspire a while longer. But perhaps we can let you join our group of thieves and miscreants."

Mercy looked like someone had just stuck her with a pin. "Perhaps *you* can let *me* join *your*——"

"There's trouble coming from under the water," Bernard said, hoping to forestall a nasty fight. "Let's just get out of here, okay? Then we can redo the introductions without arguing."

He could tell from the set of her mouth that Mercy wasn't happy about the interruption. She started to say something, stopped, then said: "Fine. That's fine." Her tone suggested it was anything but. "I'm supposed to go back to the inn, anyway, so I don't have time to stand here and argue."

Nebandalex said, "The inn? Where we were arrested?"

"Like the criminals you are," Cynidece said in a merry murmur.

Mercy glared at her. "Yes, that inn. I have to meet a … a person there and I shouldn't be late. Listen, half the city is up there gawking into the chasm like they're watching a gladiator meet or something. So I'll veil us and we can go, as long as *someone* doesn't try to throttle me when I start casting. Can we agree to that please?"

"You're worried about being late to meet someone?" Bernard said. "Are you sure you're really Mercy?"

"Ribbit," she said, and stuck out her tongue at him.

~~~~

Mercy didn't much care for Bernard's new friend—her bleeding cuts and bruised windpipe were evidence of the ruffian's obviously overreactive nature—and would have been happy leaving her behind on the Harbor Road to fend for herself, but she could tell Bernard wouldn't go for that. He thought he owed the scrappy ruffian something, and Mercy knew better than to suggest abandoning her. She made a veil wide enough to conceal all four of them and, in tight formation, they resumed their trudge back to the top. Along the way, the others filled her in on what had happened to them between the roundup at the inn and their reunion in the tunnel; Nebandalex did most of the talking about Korrin's dungeon, while Bernard took over the story for the events in the sea cave. They shared narrative duty for the parts where they had both been conscious. Cynidece shared nothing. Mercy asked very few questions, as she spent most of the climb gasping for breath; several times they had to line up against the wall or at the edge of the precipice to avoid running into small groups of men coming down with wheeled cases or mysterious parcels and, once, a wagon loaded with crates. Mercy was grateful for the brief rest breaks that each of these pauses afforded.

When they finally reached the top and put a bit of distance between themselves and the gate, Mercy called for another break in a shadowed spot away from the crowd. She was sure Blackhawk must be waiting for her at the inn by now, but if she didn't rest for a few minutes they were going to have to carry her the rest of the way. Her inferior endurance was proving to be way more troublesome than she had anticipated; the experience of actually having to stop and lean against a wall because your head was spinning was a lot more unpleasant than merely having to switch your on-screen avatar from a sprint to a walk while an energy meter replenished itself from red to green.

Once she was ready to move again, they headed into the city, the others following Mercy along the avenue that ran from the harbor to the front gate. Now it was Mercy's turn to talk; she gave the others a quick rundown of what had transpired after she woke up in Lord Korrin's bedchamber, a detail that elicited a knowing smirk from Cynidece, who obviously thought she was leaving something out. Whispers of Lord Korrin's behavior with the young ladies of Abacar apparently extended well beyond the castle walls. Well, the woman could think whatever she wanted; Mercy didn't care. She just kept telling the story. As she described crawling through the drain and holing up in the sewer, they entered a large flagstoned circle with a dry fountain at the center. Wide streets radiated from it like the thick spokes of a wagon wheel. Mercy made to go around the fountain and continue straight toward the distant gate, but Cynidece put a hand on her shoulder to stop her. "I thought you said we were going to an inn. There is no inn that I know of along this road, which means there is no inn along this road at all."

"We just have to go to the bazaar at the front gate, then go along the wall to——"

"What? Why go around the highwayman's barn? Tell me which inn it is and I will find us a more direct route." Then, Mercy didn't say anything: "Is it a *secret* inn?"

"Um, no. I'm just not sure you'll really want to be there, is all."

"That is quite considerate of you, but I have already decided I *do* want to be there. What can you tell me that might change my mind?"

"I can tell you who's there waiting for us. Waiting for *me*." She fished in her pocket, pulled out the little metal shield, and showed it around to everyone. "We're meeting Arran Blackhawk. Lord Korrin's brother."

"*Half*-brother," Cynidece said.

"He's the——"

"Head of the city watch," Cynidece said.

Mercy folded her arms. Obviously there was nothing she could tell Cynidece that the woman didn't already know. Bernard, scandalized, said: "What? Mercy, they *arrested* us! One of them tried to *strangle* me!"

"They hung us on the cable," Nebandalex said, rubbing his wrists.

"I know, I know," Mercy said. "The situation has changed. Lord Korrin is dead, Kram is gone, Arran Blackhawk is in charge, and——"

"That makes it all the stranger that we would be meeting with him," Cynidece said.

"If you'd let me *finish a sentence*, I'll explain." She glared around at them, daring anyone else to interrupt her. Nobody did. "Okay, so, Arran Blackhawk found me in the storm sewer, I don't know how. He let me out and I told him everything I just told you. He wanted to meet me at the inn so we could talk some more without anybody doing anything, um, stupid."

"So Blackhawk is now our friend and we are meeting him for a chat? In that case, I solemnly promise not do anything *stupid* when I see him." Cynidece grinned, showing an unusual number of very white teeth. "Now forget your elaborate wandering and tell me the name of the inn."

Mercy eyed the woman, trying to decide what her angle was. Why was she hanging around? What was she after? It couldn't possibly just be that her time on the cable and under the water with Bernard and Nebandalex was such a traumatic bonding experience that the three of them were now inseparable boon companions. Unfortunately she couldn't think of a way to get rid of her that wouldn't alienate the others. Mercy sighed, then said: "Fine. It was called *The Goldsmith*. Lead on, then."

"Oh, my. Goldshine's little palace?" Cynidece raised a spiky black eyebrow. "You lot do like to get get arrested in style." She pointed a long finger at a road that exited the circle at an angle to the left. "This way."

True to her word, Cynidece got them to the inn much more directly than the way Mercy had intended to go; instead of trudging all the way to the bazaar and then sneaking along the wall, they went a little distance down the angled road, then turned right onto a smaller street that jogged between the overhanging backsides of cheek-to-jowl buildings. They emerged onto another wide avenue, where they turned right again and soon passed the narrow opening between the outer wall and the first row of buildings, from which they had emerged the other day. Mercy saw Nebandalex cast a glance at the alley, and figured he was wishing for his bow, which was, she hoped, still hidden in the pile of rugs; but as they were going to meet the city's head of law and order, carrying weapons was probably not advisable, and she didn't request a detour in that direction.

The inn looked just the way Mercy remembered it, with its nominal fence and deep yard and wide, shaded porch; the guards hadn't cordoned it off or burned it down or confiscated it. The smithy next door stood idle, though smoke still drifted out of it, scented with an iron tang. The farriery and other nearby businesses had very little trade going on either. Mercy wondered if this was normally a day off from work, or if the lack of activity was just because the entire population had drifted over to the chasm to watch and gawk.

They passed through the opening in the fence and crunched up the gravel walk. It had been raked recently, erasing the tracks of the numerous city guards who had passed along it while hauling them all away. It sort of reminded her of the little rock area outside Yexandor's fallen tree, with its combed crushed white stone and curving benches. This wasn't a place for sitting and reflecting and taking in the view, though; this was a place for passing through on your way to somewhere else. Shaking off the memory of Torgonderrer and what had happened there, she proceeded to the porch and up the short steps. In the shadows, Mercy dismissed the veil that had concealed them. They wouldn't be needing it now. She looked a question at the others: Were they ready to meet Arran Blackhawk? Bernard shrugged; Nebandalex nodded; Cynidece grinned and cracked her knuckles against the side of her head. Close enough. She pushed open the door and led them inside. The invisible bell tinkled overhead, announcing their entrance. The interior was neatly arranged, ready for patrons who hadn't shown up. A low fire burned in the central hearth, giving the room a pleasantly smoky odor; short, irascible Bertram stood behind the bar, polishing things that didn't need polishing. One would never guess the city watch had recently staged a large police action here. A table near the back was occupied by Arran Blackhawk, three watchmen, and a small, elderly, wizened fellow with a stack of scrolls and parchments in front of him. They all looked up at the sound of the bell. Bertram did, too; an expression of distaste briefly crossed his features, followed by startled recognition. He made a clicking sound behind his teeth, then went back to moving his rag around the fittings, a little more quickly now, perhaps, as if by wiping faster he could erase all of these intruders from his dining room.

"You are late," Arran Blackhawk said. Then: "You brought

friends."

"So did you," she said, eyeing his little band.

"A precaution," he said. "Trusted men, selected by me for their skill and their discretion." He tipped his head at the old man. "Or, in the case of young Yardle here, for his collection of scrolls. Barkeep!"

Bertram determinedly kept wiping the fixtures, but could be heard to mutter: "What now?"

"Three more place settings, if you please." Arran Blackhawk examined the group. "And a larger table."

"You've already got the largest."

Blackhawk looked around. "So we have." He pointed at Bernard. "You. Help us rearrange the furniture."

While Bertram called for more plates, Cynidece and Nebandalex moved chairs out of the way and young Yardle, forced to vacate his seat, hastily gathered up his scrolls to protect them from being pinched between surfaces or, even worse, falling on the floor and getting stepped on. Bernard and the three watchmen dragged a nearby table over and butted it up against the first one. Arran Blackhawk stood off to the side observing the operation with all the sternness of a field commander ensuring the proper execution of his crafty battle plan. More chairs were arranged and everyone settled in, as if for a birthday gathering or retirement party, or maybe a peace conference hastily called to end an ill-conceived war. Yardle spread his scrolls out in the middle and started pawing through them. Mercy wondered what he was looking for.

As Yardle shuffled papers, Aldric emerged from the kitchen carrying a tray loaded with steaming mugs. A serving girl followed, eyes downcast, bearing another tray with more mugs and a plate of bread and cheese. Seeing their approach, Yardle spread his arms and body over the scrolls, afraid that his careless companions would spill something on the precious documents; then, apparently realizing that he made an inadequate shield, he bundled them all up, retreated to a different table, and resumed his search there. The food and drink service, which had paused during Yardle's relocation, resumed and proceeded silently. Bernard grabbed his mug as soon as it was offered, sniffed it once, then drained it. As he set his mug down, Aldric—who had moved on to set a beverage in front of Mercy—leaned over and whispered in her ear. She grinned in response; after the innkeeper moved on, Bernard, with a curious look on his face, leaned over. "What was that all about?"

"He said I was even dirtier than the first time he saw me."

"Oh." Then: "Well, maybe he'll give you another makeover."

"I think I've used up my allotment of free spa visits." She sipped her beverage; it tasted something like cider, but with a strong hint of strange berries. Just juice, she thought, no ale, no potion to knock her out. She took another small drink and surreptitiously watched Arran Blackhawk nibble a piece of cheese that looked almost as hard the stare he aimed at Aldric and the serving girl. The two of them circled the table refilling cups, then split up, the serving girl collecting Bertram and taking him into the kitchen while Aldric locked the front door, crossed the room, and disappeared through the curtains into his apartment.

"My men found what was left of Korrin in the crypt," Blackhawk said, turning that gaze toward Mercy. "The scene is as you described. It seems clear enough that Kram—or whoever it was masquerading as the old man—killed my half-brother and made off with the gems, and orchestrated it so that you would suffer the consequences. The question is why? And what will he do next?"

"He is ending our enchantments," Yardle said from the other table, not looking up from his scrolls. "We have ample evidence of that."

Mercy said, "Well, I'm glad you don't think I'm the one who's doing it."

"Hardly," Yardle said, his tone suggesting that Mercy had been boasting about how she'd turned all the statues into dust and, while she was at it, had hung the moon and set the sun on fire. "A pretty face and the skill of a hedge-witch may suffice for some purposes, but not for this."

"I'm not a hedge—"

"Yardle lacks tact, but he is not wrong," Blackhawk said. "You simply lack the power to overcome these glamours, else I would not have found you hiding in a sewer, would I? The very point of the protective enchantments is that they were supposed to be unbreakable, just as the cable over the chasm was supposed to be unbreakable. Have you found the other information we require in your heap of worthless scrawls, archivist?"

"Not yet. If we had done this in the castle library, with the proper indexes, rather than hastily gathering up everything from the—"

"Yes, I heard your complaints the first two times. The castle is not where I wish to be right now, so we will do this here." To Mercy: "There are matters of succession. Korrin has no official heir, so the posterior that will be warming the hawk throne is, for the near term at least, likely to be mine. Once that happens, I will have so many claims on my time that I will be unable to accomplish anything of substance."

Nebandalex said: "Surely whoever is responsible for making sure someone is sitting in this throne of yours would understand if you told them you had important tasks to perform, and that their schedule must wait."

"That may be how things would proceed among the elves," Arran Blackhawk said, "but you are woefully unfamiliar with the workings of a *human* court. Once it seizes hold of me, any *real* work will stop, at least for the short term."

"Real work?" Cynidece raised a bushy eyebrow. "What sort of work might that be?"

"Keeping the death-wind out of the city long enough for most of the population to escape," Blackhawk said.

Chapter 4

KIHANTROH SLUMPED OUT of Jordneh's wheeled conveyance and collapsed to the stone floor of the balcony. If it had been able to sweat, its clothing would have been drenched from the exertion required to unravel the endlessly knotted ribbon of enchantments that the ancient witch had left behind; but Rittandic bodies did not cool themselves in that fashion, and so Kihantroh's skin was hot but dry, its head pounding, its lungs working furiously as they expelled overheated air. And still the task remained unfinished! Without the gems, it would have been impossible to even contemplate continuing.

The exhausted sorcerer dragged itself to the edge of the balcony and hauled itself up to lean on the balustrade, almost wishing it still wore one of its stolen human forms so that it could stand with arms outstretched and let the perspiration evaporate from its skin, taking excess warmth with it. Slowly its breathing steadied and it could take a moment to look at the town beyond the castle walls, now reduced to rubble and timber and piles of brick. Thorough as the destruction had been, surely some few villagers had escaped the funnel clouds that had demolished the buildings or had been out in the plains and had returned to find their homes destroyed, their families obliterated. Was what Kihantroh had done here, to them, so very different from what had befallen those who had survived the catastrophe in the South, when Untelleh's lands had disappeared?

Kihantroh shook its head. That was Jordneh's way of thinking, her influence sowing doubts in its mind. The witch-queen and her followers had all been lobes of a tumor that needed to be excised from the flesh of the world. The way had to be cleared for Untelleh's return. Kihantroh cast an unfriendly glance at the chair where it had sat for hours, marinating in its former occupant's essence even as it unrolled her glamours. Though nothing like the overwhelming assumption of a persona effected by the absorbance glamour, the process did affect Kihantroh's perceptions; it was as if Jordneh lingered nearby whispering unsolicited advice into its tympanum. Even in death, the witch-queen was a font of self-serving lies.

Of course, she had told the truth about *some* things; the prison that contained the death-wind beneath the sea in far-off Abacar was of her making, and Kihantroh sensed that it had already failed. That was an active enchantment, maintained by the steady drip of power she lent it, and it—along with any other glamour that she kept empowered in a similar fashion—had ended with the witch-queen's life. Daras-Drûm was a blight upon the world, but it would be weak from its long imprisonment, and less than the elemental force of death and mayhem it had once been. If the entity rampaged through Abacar for a time, if it sloughed southward across the Slash, was that such a high price? What in the Slash—a miserable warren of benighted humanity governed by the Jordneh's bootlickers, their loyalty bought with trinkets and enchantments—merited rescue? Banderlund would starve or slaughter them soon anyway. Perhaps the death-wind was merely another tool to clear the way for a new regime, one in which Untelleh could negotiate a new diplomatic arrangement, rather than letting Korrin drag the Slash into a futile war against the superior forces of the encroaching northern empire.

Well, these were matters and concerns for a later hour. The dizzy overexertion had faded, still required rest in order to avoid utter collapse. In a sudden fit of nostalgia, Kihantroh decided to repair to the cubby reserved for the scientist studying the Æther, who normally dwelt out in the field but returned on occasion to report on the process of erosion occurring in the Edgelands, waiting on Jordneh's convenience to be allowed into her august presence and tell her things she already knew. Kihantroh had spent no small number of nights sleeping in that room; perhaps there would be some comfort to be found among its familiar walls, though the sparse bedding and furniture that had once occupied the space would, of course, have been splintered and spat out into the courtyard or the bailey by the scouring winds.

Leaving the chair out on the balcony, Kihantroh shuffled off into the castle in search of one night's peace.

~~~~

Before Arran Blackhawk could elaborate on how he thought they might thwart the death-wind, even temporarily, the archivist made a satisfied clucking sound and brought a small parchment over to the table. He unrolled it in front of them, weighing the corners down with small, highly-polished rocks that he evidently carried just for this purpose. The document contained a sketch rendered in charcoal, depicting a cavern very much like the one from which Bernard and the others had recently escaped. It seemed to have been drawn from the perspective of a person standing at the entrance to one of the tunnels and looking toward the center of the ribbed dome, at a scabrous pendulum depending from the apex. The swollen, noxious thing seemed to pulse with malignant energy, although that might have been Bernard's brain filling in the details based on what he remembered from that deathly pit. The only thing missing was the field of bodies.

"That's what we saw in the sea cave," Bernard said.

One of Arran Blackhawk's heretofore-silent companions said: "You saw the death-wind?"

"Yes," Bernard said.

"And you *lived?*"

"Um. Yes."

"Obviously," Cynidece added.

"This is a sketch of part of a tapestry, since lost to fire, depicting the original binding of Daras-Drûm," the scribe said. "If you saw the monster in this state, it means the binding has started to fail."

"No," Cynidece said, "it has *completely* failed. Tell them, Bernard."

"Me? Why me?"

"Because you had no idea what it was, so you will just say what you saw and not what you already knew."

"Um. What? Well okay. So, yeah, at first there were all these runes on the walls, but then they sort of faded, or they got pulled back into the top of the dome, where that … thing was squashed into a sort of disk. Once the runes went out, the disk turned into a blob like in the drawing. When it came down from the roof this wind started up, I guess, and that pushed the water out through the tunnels. We jumped in and rode it back to the surface. Like getting blown through a straw."

Nebandalex said: "A what?"

"A hollow tube for air."

"I see. Like a breathing reed."

"Yes, just like—"

Yardle loudly tapped the table with one of his small rocks, signaling an end to the digression. Once Bernard fell silent the archivist said, "The enchantment that has held Daras-Drûm in check for all these years was maintained and supported by Jordneh, as it had been by her predecessors. That support has now been withdrawn, as is evident by the breaking of the cable and the account given by these … individuals."

"I agree," Blackhawk said.

"The death-wind draws in the bodies that fall from the cable and feeds on what remnants of vital force clings to them. This is the entire reason the cable exists; it supplies a small part of the fuel that has sustained the binding over the centuries. But the energy supplied by executed criminals has never been sufficient to maintain the spell in its entirety, and so Jordneh and those before her have always augmented it with their own power. Her power also animated the golems in the crypt, and various other enchantments that we have long relied upon for security. That all of them have failed over the course of a day cannot be coincidental."

"I agree with that as well. None of that is at issue. What *is* at issue is why it happened, and what to do about it."

The other watchman spoke up. "Perhaps Banderlund has pressured or bribed her?"

Blackhawk shook his head. "Jordneh is hardly susceptible to threats of violence or the lure of gold, and even were she, Banderlund has no more interest in seeing the death-wind freed of its prison than we do. They would rather starve us out than wave their swords at what cannot be cut. No, this mischief is the work of a third party. Of that, I am sure."

"You mean this supposed Rittandic impersonator," the archivist said. "Yet why would this creature go to the trouble of assuming Rumad Kram's form and arranging to eliminate them—" Here Yardle indicated Mercy, Bernard, and Nebandalex, with Cynidece included just because she was sitting in their vicinity. "—only to erase the enchantments that would have ensured their deaths?"

"Because their deaths were incidental," Blackhawk said. "These three were obstacles to its goal of obtaining the Maul and the Illata, nothing more. Once that goal was achieved, their fates were no longer of interest. The same is likely true of Daras-Drûm; its release is incidental to some other purpose. What *that* purpose is, we do not know; what we *do* know is that Jordneh no longer sits the throne in the Ravels. If she did, she would not have allowed her enchantments to be ended so abruptly."

Yardle frowned, causing his features to recede into an even deeper morass of wrinkles before. "So you believe this Rittandic, or its puppet, now rules beyond the Peltish Downs, and that soon the death-wind will emerge from the chasm and into our streets."

"Yes. And we have no one with the power to stand against it." He gave Mercy a significant look. "Or do we?"

A brief silence ensued, broken by Mercy. "If I had the Illata, then maybe," she said. "But I don't, and without it ... Well, maybe I *am* a hedge-witch after all." She looked at the governmental side of the table. "You don't have any spellcasters in the castle who can deal with this thing?"

"No."

"What about, like, priests? Clerics?"

"Prayers to gods of water and the hearth and fertility will not hold the death-wind in abeyance any more this time than they did before," Arran Blackhawk said. "We need sorcery now, not entreaties upon deaf spirits."

"Abacar has long relied on the good will of the Rittandic queens in matters of strong enchantment," Yardle said. "We have healers, of course, and a few invokers who can start fires or cure plants of blight, but none with the ability to put down Daras-Drûm. Humans who can wield magic are rare enough. Those who can wield *powerful* magic are all but nonexistent. I could name a finger after each one mentioned in the texts and still have——"

Arran silenced him with a waved hand. "Your point is made, unless you can use your scrolls to actually conjure up one of these powerful human wizards from the annals of history."

"If sorcerers could be conjured from paper, the last necromantic war would have ended much more quickly than it did."

"Just so. I have long found both paper and those who wield it to be rather useless." Blackhawk fell silent for a moment. "Very well. We must withdraw from the chasm, close the gates, and hope we can hold the death-wind off until we find a way to bind it again." To the men he had with him, he said: "It is as we feared. You already have your instructions for this situation. Execute them."

The watchmen nodded, stood, and clanked their way out of the inn. Cynidece twisted in her chair to observe their departure, then turned back to face Arran Blackhawk again, a thin smile on her face. She said: "Regarding executions——"

"I have not forgotten who and what you are," Blackhawk said, "but your crimes were against my half-brother's regime, and I have larger concerns than you at the moment."

"Fair enough," she said. "You will of course understand if I choose not to linger while you sort those *concerns* out."

"Flee or stay, if we fail to stop the death-wind here, eventually it will reach you where you hide and carry out your sentence." Then: "To those who do *not* intend to abandon the city, let me illuminate the plan that is now in motion. Our immediate purpose is twofold: Try to delay Daras-Drûm in the chasm, and deprive the monster of prey by evacuating as much of the population as possible. To the first end, we will close the Harbor Road, lock all the gates that face the chasm, and post as many men as I can find along the edge of the cliff."

"Which accomplishes what, exactly?" Mercy said.

Blackhawk shook his head. "Nothing much, to put it plainly. We can only hope to slow it down long enough for most of our citizens to disperse, and possibly get word to others who can assist us. The Pelts, the elves, the dwarves, perhaps even the Rittandics."

"The Rittandics? You think any refugees will make it over the mountains in either direction at this time of year?" Cynidece snorted. "Unlikely. And even if they do, you yourself said that Jordneh must be dead. The most powerful Rittandic sorcerer you have available at the moment is the one who brought this calamity down on you in the first place."

"Likewise with we elves, I fear," Nebandalex said. "With Yexandor killed, we have no enchanter able to work glamours on the level you need."

"The dwarves cannot help you. They are about as magical as this table." Cynidece rapped a bony knuckle on the wooden surface. "Their inventions could not stop the death-wind before, and will not stop it now. And as for we Pelts, you know full well that we are not spell-casters. And if we were, we would not again make the mistake of trusting any Lord of Abacar."

Silence. Bernard looked at Mercy. She sat there for a long time without speaking; she had a look on her face that Bernard recognized from after-school homework sessions, when she was chewing over some particularly tricky assignment. Finally she said: "Okay. So what we need to do is bind Daras-Drûm again, squash it back into a prison. All the big guns, the major sorcerers who could maybe have done that, are gone. A few dozen little sorcerers put together will be useless. The dwarves can't kill it with artillery. The elves can't kill it with magic. The Pelts won't get involved and would be useless if they did. Is that what I'm hearing?"

"These others are all here to tell me the ways in which we cannot succeed," Blackhawk said. "I had thought you might have a different sort of suggestion to make."

"I do," she said. "Let's get the Illata back."

~~~~

The bathhouse at the back of the inn looked just as welcoming as the first time Mercy had seen it, with its bubbling sunken basin and its chaise lounges on the other side of the room divider and its fresh linens stacked like books waiting to be shelved. She knelt down and swirled her hand in the hot water, while the others stood by looking at what they'd missed out on the first time they were here. Bruised and battered as they all were, a soak would do them good, but they were not being offered the use of the bath, just of the building. This small distinction proved no impediment to Cynidece, who made a delighted sound, stripped off her filthy garments, and slid into the tub like a penguin into the icy ocean.

"Of course," Aldric murmured. "Feel free."

"I always do," Cynidece said, eyes closed as she luxuriated.

Arran moved past Aldric to stand near Mercy. "You wanted to come here. Why?"

"It's relaxing." She stood, wiped her hand on her hip. "It's quiet. I'll need a place like this when I try to find the Illata."

With a sidelong glance at Cynidece, Arran Blackhawk took Mercy's arm and guided her toward the back of the room, where the divider still stood. She remembered falling asleep behind it, exhausted from her journey, soothed by the warm water, the luxurious towels, the soft blankets. Mercy heard Cynidece say: "Don't go. Stay. They're going off to have a private chat." Mercy peered around the divider; it looked like Bernard had begun moving to join her and Arran, only for Cynidece to extend an extraordinarily long and flexible leg to intercept him. Nebandalex hung back near the wall, out of the woman's reach. Prudent of him.

Bernard said: "Mercy, do you need—"

"It's fine," Mercy told him. "Stay with Cynidece."

"But—"

Laughing, Cynidece flicked her leg in a move Mercy couldn't follow; Bernard went down, splashing into the tub, clothes and all. Water sloshed over the sides and across the floor. Aldric turned an unusual shade of pink. "Really, I can't allow—"

"Leave us," Arran said. "Attend to your guests."

"I have no guests, thanks to you."

"As if you cannot afford to be closed for an afternoon. Go."

Aldric pressed his lips together, then shook his head, turned, and headed for the door. "Please do try to leave *some* water in there," he said over his shoulder as he departed. "It is awfully tiring watching my girls haul buckets from the well to refill it." Cynidece only snorted in response.

Arran drew Mercy back behind the screen, cutting off her view of the others, though she could still hear the others splashing around. "What's with the secrecy all of a sudden?" she said.

"The elf does not concern me, but the woman is a known spy for the Pelts, and the man is clearly of Banderlundi descent. They have already heard much more of our business than I would like."

"Well, I don't know anything about Cynidece, but believe me, Bernard's Banderlundi heritage barely even goes skin deep."

"Even so." Blackhawk pulled her deeper into the corner, then said softly: "Realize that I know nothing of sorcery, and explain to me, if you can, using small words, how you hope to retrieve the Illata from your enemy across such a distance?"

"Um. Okay. Well, so, when I touched the Illata, it did something to me. It, like, *imprinted* itself on me, or something."

"Imprinted?"

"Uh-huh. Kind of like … like, a wax seal? You push a signet ring into the wax and it leaves a mark that stays behind. The Illata is the ring, I'm the wax. I think I can use the impression it left to call it back to me."

"And you think its new owner will permit that?"

"Um. Well, I'm not sure it can stop me. But I'm hoping it hasn't realized I'm still around."

"*Hope* is such a wan and feeble warrior, long past its battlefield prime." Blackhawk moved away and beckoned to Nebandalex around the divider. "You. Archer. Come here." The elf sidled around the tub, carefully staying out of Cynidece's grabbing range, and joined them behind the partition. "You elves held the Illata in your village for decades. This little one proposes to summon the gem back from the Ravels, across the mountains. Do you think she might succeed?"

"I possess little expertise on the workings of the Illata," Nebandalex said, "but I have seen her do things with it that no other could, including Yexandor. If she believes she can bring it back, then I will not be the one to say she cannot."

"She made the claim that she has touched the stone, but it is well-known that to do so means death. Ask my half-brother."

"It is no mere *claim*. I saw her carry the Illata as if it were an ordinary rock found lying on the ground. Yes, it destroys most who touch it, or even spend too much time near it, but not her. She endures."

Arran Blackhawk gave Mercy a long, evaluating look. Finally he said: "Very well. Make your attempt. If you succeed, you will use the stone's power to re-bind Daras-Drûm beneath the waves."

"Yes," she said. "Or however else I can bind it." Then: "I wouldn't stop your other preparations, in case I can't get it back."

"Oh, I have no intention of building an entire castle on the foundation of your efforts," Blackhawk said. "How much time will you need?"

"I don't know. As long as it takes, I guess."

Blackhawk grunted. "Understand: You have until dusk, or shortly thereafter. No longer."

"What happens if I can't finish before then?"

"Then you will likely never finish at all," he said.

~~~~

They left her to it; Arran Blackhawk cleared everyone out of the bathhouse except for Bernard, who insisted on remaining, keeping watch over her. Of course. What else would he do? But he stayed on the other side of the partition, so quiet that Mercy couldn't even hear him breathing as, lying on the blankets behind the screen with her eyes closed and her thoughts turned inward, she hunted for the Illata.

It might be very far away, it might be in the next room, it might be on another continent or in another dimension; its physical location was largely irrelevant. When she had touched the Illata it had seeped into her like dye, and even though it was gone from her vicinity, the link remained intact. In a way, the Illata was everywhere and nowhere at once; it was the threads in the fabric, and the color in the threads, and the space between the warp and the weft. She could follow the weave anywhere, find anything, as long as she had enough time and paid close enough attention. But at the moment, time was in short supply. Instead the search was on fast-forward, as if she were hunting for a scene in some movie where her favorite actress made a cameo appearance. Mercy still felt some disjointed traces of Ambrosia the Sorceress as she ran quickly through her own mind, again like a video being played back too fast, where a character might flicker across the screen and disappear almost before they registered. She thought Ambrosia had disappeared when she'd been locked in the ossuary, marinating in Jordneh's magic, but—

Wait. There it was, a spark, the afterimage the Illata had burned within her. It was suddenly everywhere, as if all the Illata contained had been replicated and stored inside her. Feeling the radiance coming from her internal copy of the Illata, she wondered if she could use *this* as a power source to restore the bindings that had failed. She studied it, eyed the thick lines that connected it to the rest of her existence, and concluded that she could not. It was too closely tied into her own existence, and if she tried to draw on it she would, in effect, be using *herself* as the battery to power Daras-Drûm's prison. That might work for a little while, but the way everyone talked about that thing, she knew she wouldn't be able to contain it for very long. You didn't get to be nicknamed *the death-wind* unless you had some kick.

This trace of the Illata really did look like some vital internal organ, she realized, isolated but connected to the rest of her being thick variegated trunks, multitudes of strings bound together into ropes, thrumming with a cardiac pulse. Somewhere along the line she had started thinking of it the way everyone else did, as merely a powerful gem, but this was a reminder of what it was supposed to be: The shattered Heart of a fallen god. Was there really a cosmic entity named Tyndallëau waiting to be restored to life, an Ushgaluk lurking outside the walls of reality, seeking an opportunity to reenter the world and destroy everything in it? Maybe Ushgaluk and Daras-Drûm were one and the same; after all, things could have different names in different places. Another reason not to try to use this to cage the threat. It would be hooking herself up to some source of vast corruption. Kidney dialysis in reverse.

Threads led from the impression of the gem off into the wider world, threads that anchored it and her in the reality of the city, the Slash, the lands beyond. Some of these threads had to lead back to the original Illata. She couldn't follow them one by one, there was no time for that; could she follow them all at once? Sort of dividing her consciousness into myriad little pieces? It seemed risky, but perhaps worth a try. She moved closer to the Illata, extended imaginary arms towards it; it obligingly shrank to fit between her hands, becoming immeasurably brighter, and incredibly dense. Her fingers found the seams between its facets and before she realized what she was doing, she had started to open it up, peeling off its skin and separating it into sections, like an orange. A riot of images flashed across her vision; a cacophony of sounds shattered against her ears; a miasma of odors flooded her nose. She tasted a melange of flavors on her tongue, felt a variety of fabrics sliding across her skin.

Overwhelmed, she released the gem and staggered back. The surface sealed itself, the glow dimmed. She shook her head as the sensory assault faded and cleared. Was that what everyone else experienced in the instant before contact with the gem killed them? It had flung her out of herself, back into the real world, but she realized immediately that where she had landed was not where she had started. She no longer lay behind the screen; she wasn't in the bathhouse. Instead, she seemed to have found her way into a seat on a balcony in some faraway place. The air smelled different here, laced with strange pollens and the tang of dust, with no trace of the sea. The sky stretched off in all directions, and in the distance she saw a range of thick mountains punching at the sky like a series of clenched hands.

And the Illata—the actual thing itself—was nearby. She could feel its energy crawling over her skin.

Instead of bringing the gem to her, it seemed she had taken herself to it. Which meant the Rittandic was nearby.

Oh, crap.

~~~~

Bernard sat alone on the bench on the other side of the partition from Mercy, and waited for her to save the world.

Every once in a while he got up and peeked around the divider to check on her, trying to move as quietly as possible so as not to disturb her. She never opened her eyes when he was looking at her, so either he was doing a good job being silent or she was ignoring him. Whatever she was doing seemed to involve exertion without movement; in the lantern light, he could see sweat glistening on her pale skin and across her brow. He wondered if he should dampen a towel in the tub and lay it across her brow or something. Probably not. The whole reason they were in this shed of a bathhouse was so she could avoid distractions, such as people piling cloths on her head.

Returning from one such check, he was surprised to find that Aldric had slid open a narrow pocket door in the back wall and was laying an armload of clothes on the bench Bernard had lately occupied, along with the leather hat Brannoc liked to wear and which had been lost during the chaos of their arrest. The innkeeper's ever-present cat-thing rode on his shoulder, eyeing the hat with greedy intent; Bernard was pretty sure he saw small tooth-marks in the brim. Noticing Bernard looking at the pile, Aldric whispered: "I know I am not supposed to be here, but I thought Ambrosia might like to change into clean clothes after she is finished with ... well, whatever it is she is doing. And I found your hat in one of Trouble's treasure-caches. She nibbled on it a bit, I fear."

"Oh," Bernard said, surprised; he'd expected Aldric to be angry with them for getting his inn commandeered by the city watch not once, but twice. "Thank you. And thanks for giving clothes to Mer ... um, Ambrosia, before, too. When she was supposed to tell stories for you."

"As she is trying to rescue the city from the death-wind, another change of outfit seems a small enough gift." The man glanced at the screen behind which Mercy lay. "And before, well, you were all rather less than presentable when you first came here. I could hardly have her standing in my dining room looking as if she had just emerged from the sewer, could I?" Then, after a moment: "You understand, I hope, that what ... *transpired* ... was none of my doing."

"Yes, of course."

"Good. Good. I would not have it be thought or said that Aldric Goldshine colludes with the city watch against those who stay at his inn."

"We didn't think that. How are the preparations going?"

"I have no idea, really.   Arran Blackhawk has taken over my apartment as his temporary headquarters and I am banned from entering it. My own apartment! I can only imagine the uproar at the castle, with Lord Korrin dead and his half-brother's whereabouts unknown to them, but he cares not. The archivist has carried word back that Blackhawk is safe and operating from an, er, undisclosed location. The evacuation is underway, but no one seems to expect it to be finished before nightfall. Your friends are waiting in the room I gave you before. I delivered some clothes to them as well, though whether that—" Here he wrinkled his nose a little.   "—*woman* chooses to wear them rather than continue to go around in her shift remains to be seen."

"So Cynidece is still here?"

"Yes, she is."

"Good," Bernard said, oddly pleased that the Pelt hadn't fled yet; he'd thought she would be gone as soon as the gates were opened.

"If you say so," Aldric said. "Personally, I—" He broke off as a blue light suddenly flared from behind the divider, suffusing the room with a cyanotic glow.   Aldric's pet creature hissed and leapt off his shoulders, fastening her sharp claws onto a wooden crossbeam that ran lengthwise through the bathhouse, hanging upside-down and wide-eyed. Her sleek tail had gone all bushy with surprise.

"Trouble!" Aldric said in a hoarse whisper.   "Come down from there!"

The cat-thing, uncooperative as cats tended to be, instead scuttled along the underside of the beam, her nails scraping notches into the wood, until she was over the spot where Mercy lay. Once there, she clung tightly to the beam, staring down, the illumination staining the white portions of her fur blue. Bernard knew that color.

"She did it!" he said, looking at Aldric.

"Wonderful! What did she do?"

But Bernard was already hurrying around to the other side of the divider, even as the glow began to fade. "Good job, Merc—"

He stopped.

Aldric said: "Is something wrong?"

Bernard didn't answer, just stared.   Mercy's nest of blankets lay empty. Aldric came to join him, took in the scene. "She is supposed to be there, is she not? With the gem?"

"Um. Yes."

"Where is she, then?"

"I ... don't know. Somewhere else."

Aldric's cat-creature dropped off the beam and landed on the innkeeper's shoulder, making a soft, nervous chirping sound.

"I was never here," Aldric said, heading for the narrow door, taking all the clothes—and even Bernard's hat—with him as he left.

~~~~

Okay. So. She was on a balcony in a castle in some place that was not Abacar. The Illata was close, but it wasn't here. An open archway that had once been a doorway stood nearby, offering admittance to a dark and wreckage-strewn corridor; but before she started wandering around inside, Mercy decided to go to the railing and see how things looked from there.

They didn't look good.

The balcony wasn't high up on a tower like Lord Korrin's had been; it was actually rather low on the wall, maybe the equivalent of the second or third story of a building. But the castle itself was built on top of a flat-topped rise in the middle of what looked like a small, irregular depression, perhaps the bed of an ancient lake. A stone bridge that might have once been a causeway ran off across the basin, connecting this keep to another on an adjoining former island. The plains surrounding the two structures was littered with debris and rubble, the smeared remains of houses and buildings, as if someone had come through with a gigantic rolling pin to crush and flatten everything and spread it along the floor like so much pie dough. The wreckage looked quite fresh, splintered wood bright and unweathered, no overgrowth of weeds or grasses. She crept along the balustrade, staying low so she could avoid being seen from the ground, but it really didn't look like there was anyone out there to spot her. The view was the same from every angle of the curving verandah. She didn't see any structures left standing, everything mowed down to a uniform few feet of height. She saw no bodies, but no sign of survivors, either. No movement, no excavating, no bonfires to provide light and warmth. Except for the sound of wind rustling through the tall grass between the ruins, the basin was silent as a graveyard long after dark. Where were the rescuers digging through the rubble? Where were the people crying over their buried loved ones? What had happened here?

Mercy reached the end of the railing and turned back toward the place she had started, and stifled a gasp as she saw a Rittandic sitting in the wheelchair, staring at her.

For a second she thought this was the sorcerer whose gems she had come to steal, but no, if it were she would've been blasted off the balcony already.   Besides, this figure seemed flickery, vague, transparent, more like the apparition Yexandor had presented to her the first time she saw him back in Torgonderrer.   It didn't beckon to her as Yexandor had; it just sat there, the black pits of its eyes deep and sad, looking in her direction.   Not sure if the ghost could actually perceive her, Mercy cautiously approached, moving low along the balcony like a supplicant; the wispy face tracked her movement, which settled the question of whether or not it knew she was there.   She stopped a little distance away, not wanting to get too close.   The specter watched her with vacant eyes.   Mercy opened her mouth but the phantom shook its head, the movement leaving behind faint lines of fog that caught up and merged with the translucent flesh.   Suddenly the chair rolled towards her across the balcony floor.   Startled, Mercy scuttled backwards, then caught herself as the chair stopped in front of her.   The apparition had faded almost to invisibility, but gradually became more substantial again as its vapor trail caught up and rejoined the main body of the phantom.   Mercy stayed crouched nearby, watching, wondering what this was all about.

The phantom opened its mouth and said, *I am Jordneh, once witch-queen of the Ravels, now only a memory. This is where I died.*

Her voice echoed in Mercy's head, reminding her of those dreamlike occasions when she had talked to Ambrosia directly.   Was she dreaming now, too?   Was she asleep behind the divider in Aldric's bathhouse?

You are not sleeping, Jordneh said.

Mercy started to speak, but Jordneh shook her head again and put a diaphanous hand to her mouth, then to her temple.   Evidently she wanted Mercy to think her responses rather than utter them aloud. She wasn't exactly comfortable with the idea that the ghost of the Rittandic witch-queen was reading her mind, but—

If you use your voice, I will not hear you. I no longer exist at that level.

"They think—" Mercy broke off, shook her head. *They think you're dead. In Abacar.*

And so I am, Jordneh thought, *but yet I linger. Kihantroh has started to realize that it is not so easy to erase such a long scrawl across the world as the one I left.*

Mercy thought: *Kihantroh?*

Kihantroh. The one who killed me and destroyed the village. The one who took that which you seek.

Kihantroh. Now she had a name to go with the changing faces of her enemy. Good. Then: *Wait, how do you know what I'm looking for?*

Did you think you were so subtle? I detected your inquiry and what it sought, and I blended it with what little power I retain, so as to obscure its origin and purpose. Had I not done that, Kihantroh would have already found and destroyed you.

Oh, Mercy thought. *Okay. Um. Thank you?*

I do not seek your gratitude. Kihantroh, too, realizes that something has happened, and has begun searching for an intruder. You should not have brought yourself to this place.

I didn't mean to. I saw the Illata, and I touched it, and then … I was here.

In her mind, Mercy heard the equivalent of a spectral grunt. *Kihantroh is drawing back all my glamours. Even though it paused to rest, the process continues on its own; these phenomena have an inertia to them. You must have been caught up by the inward flow and carried along with it.*

You mean Kihantroh brought me here by accident? Like a … a piece of driftwood?

Even so. It would hardly be the first to unwittingly invoke its own downfall. I can conceal your presence for a little while longer, but my power and endurance are limited. We must not waste either. Kihantroh will not be confounded for long; it will soon understand that I am the source of the disturbance it senses, and will come here looking for me. It will bring the gems with it. You may then be able to reclaim what was once yours, if you are quick enough. The spirit stared at her. *Are you quick enough? I wonder.*

I can be quick, Mercy thought, annoyed that everyone seemed to have such a low opinion of her abilities lately.

Then prepare yourself. The spectral being's gaze turned to the vacant archway leading into the castle. *The Illata is coming.*

The chair pivoted and rolled back towards the door, leaving Mercy to stand alone in the waning afternoon light.

~~~~

Bernard found the others in the small room, where Aldric had said they would be. Cynidece, contrary to Aldric's doubts, had put on the clothes he'd brought for her; she now sported a loose-fitting brown tunic sashed at the waist with a rope belt, along with clean breeches. She looked healthier in them, less pale, scrubbed and fed and almost wholesome, a development explained by the empty serving tray in the hall outside and the scummy water in a washbasin on the fireplace hearth as well as by the change of garb. Nebandalex, though, still wore the same filthy garment he'd been wearing when they were arrested; after a moment Bernard noticed clothing in what seemed a more traditionally feminine cut and color in a neatly-folded pile near the door, evidently having been rejected by its intended recipient.

Cynidece had put on the outfit meant for Nebandalex. Bernard somehow failed to find this surprising.

The Pelt and the elf appeared to have been arguing, which stopped when Bernard entered. "I thought you were staying in the bathhouse with Mercy," Nebandalex said after a moment.

"Well I was," Bernard said, "except she's … not there anymore."

"You lost her after having only just found her?" Cynidece shook her head. "Careless."

"Did she go through a portal, like the one she made at the river?"

Bernard shook his head. "No, she just … disappeared. I don't think it was on purpose."

"Did the Rittandic take her?"

"I don't know." He glanced at the wall, in the direction of the common room. "I suppose I have to go tell that Blackhawk guy it didn't work."

"He never expected it to work," Cynidece said, "which is why he has been taking steps to protect the city in a more conventional way, which will not work either." Then: "We should leave before things get worse."

Bernard looked at her. "Leave?"

"Yes. Leave. Get out of the city. As I was *trying* to explain to your friend Nebandalex, it is only late afternoon. If we go now, we can put enough distance between us and the city to—stop shaking your head, this is a good idea."

Bernard didn't stop shaking his head. "Is that what you two were arguing about? Whether or not to ditch Mercy and me?"

Cynidece looked confused. "Ditch?"

"Leave without."

"Oh. Well, no, of course not. I meant *all* of us. We would have stopped to get you."

"Sorry, I'm not abandoning Mercy."

Cynidece frowned. "But you just said she disappeared. If anything, *she* abandoned *us*."

"No. She didn't. And when she comes back, this is where she'll—"

"*If* she comes back, you mean."

"*When* she comes back—"

"Daras-Drûm will have turned Abacar into a city full of puppet-corpses. I would prefer that mine not be one of them."

Bernard crossed his arms. "Fine. Leave. I'm staying, and I'm going out to talk to Arran Blackhawk now. Lex, are you with me?"

The elf glanced at Cynidece, then stood moved to Bernard's side.

"Males and their idiotic heroics on behalf of beautiful females," Cynidece said, rolling her eyes. Still, she followed them out the door and into the dim, short hallway. Bernard could hear her back there, muttering to herself, though he couldn't make out any words. She was probably trying to persuade herself that staying in Abacar was not the stupidest thing she had ever done.

They pushed through the curtain of wooden beads and into the empty dining room. From his accustomed spot behind the bar, Bertram said, softly, without looking up: "If you're seeking our new lord, you may find him in Aldric's room." The little man flipped open a section of the bar nearest them, allowing them to pass through. As they filed by, he said, apparently to Cynidece: "And I see you looking at the till."

Cynidece snorted. "If I intended to rob you, you would not see me looking."

They entered Aldric's apartment, Bernard in the lead. Arran Blackhawk leaned over a writing desk there, examining scrolls that had been spread across the surface. He gave them a glance, then fixed his gaze on Bernard. "I had not thought to find you out of the bathhouse except in the company of the sorceress and the gem," he said. "I take it that scheme has gone awry."

"Mercy disappeared. I think she accidentally went to the Illata instead of the other way around."

Blackhawk straightened up. "You are sure it was not of her own volition?"

"Yes." Then: "Pretty sure."

"Pretty sure?" The man grunted. "Well. If the witch could easily transport herself in such a fashion, I would not have found her hiding in the sewer outside the castle, would I? The most likely explanation is that her attempt to retake the Illata was detected and thwarted." He looked down at the documents again. "Certainly she is beyond receiving our assistance, or rendering assistance to us."

"What are you saying?"

"That she is most likely dead. Have you two got weapons?"

Bernard said: "Huh?"

"You and the elf. I mean to post you to the upper Harbor Road gate, and if you have weapons cached nearby, I would like you to fetch them. Our armory is not bottomless."

"You're recruiting us?"

"Press-ganging, more like," Cynidece said. "I told you we should have——"

"We do have weapons," Nebandalex said, cutting her off. "My bow and Bernard's quarterstaff are hidden in a pile of carpets near the market."

"Good. You will go and get them. Two of the men stationed on the front porch have already been instructed to accompany you." To Bernard: "You and the Pelt will stay here."

Nebandalex, looking a bit nonplussed, departed. Cynidece watched him go, a little smirk on his face. "He told me he wanted his bow back," she said. "This is probably not how he expected to get it."

"Do not let your smile grow too wide," Blackhawk said. "I am posting *you* to the harbor gate as well. Consider it a way to earn your pardon from the cable. I expect you require no weapon from the armory?"

"We Pelts carry our weapons with us."

"Oh, I am aware of that." He returned his attention to the documents on the table. "You two are dismissed."

Once Bernard and Cynidece had returned to the common room, he said: "If this thing is coming up the harbor road, and the only way to stop it is with magic that we haven't got, then I don't understand what posting us to the gate is supposed to accomplish besides getting us killed."

"*That* question, at least, has an easy answer," Cynidece said. "It gets us killed first."

~~~~

Kihantroh had been dreaming that Jordneh had arisen again and begun roaming the castle, whispering what might have been the key to a long and complicated spell, finishing just as she entered its room and came to stand beside its cot; jolting awake to an empty room, Kihantroh quickly sent out probes throughout the castle, seeking any unwanted presences, any lingering influences, that might need to be dispelled. It soon discovered something lurking on the balcony where the witch-queen had perished, as if some echo of her had clawed its way back through that curtain separating the living from the dead. A memory of her essence still enwrapped the wheeled conveyance—that was why Kihantroh had spared it, after all—and it could have formed a nucleus around which such energy might gather. Although not an immediate threat, it still required dispersal. Though still unrested,

Kihantroh dragged itself out of bed and picked up the jewels from the space beneath, then stumbled out into the hallway to head back toward the verandah where it had left the chair.

The walk was a relatively short one, taking Kihantroh through echoing, wreckage-strewn corridors. Kihantroh knew them well, having walked this way many times during its tenure as Jordneh's servant, bringing reports to her about the state of the Æther, thinking in its ignorance it was helping to control that canker on the earth. Now it knew that it had merely been helping the witch-queen assess how much damage her activities were causing. The effort it expended now on Untelleh's behalf would atone for its earlier abetting of Jordneh's regime. Kihantroh felt vaguely ashamed about having stopped to rest, but undoing centuries of powerful enchantments was exhausting work. It paused for a very brief rest at the bottom of a curving stair partially covered by a ramp. A few splashes of grey-blue blood stained the steps, nearly indistinguishable from the stone, but there was no body. Kihantroh did not want to be stepping over corpses, and had instructed the wind to carry all of them away and spread them across the fields beyond the village. Kihantroh was sure Untelleh would want to visit the castle once she returned from her exile, and one did not leave the husks of swatted flies lying about one's home, especially when expecting a distinguished visitor.

The walk had helped clear its head, and it felt Jordneh's presence more strongly now than before, though it remained but a faded facsimile of the powerful entity she had once been. Still, it was conceivable that the echo possessed enough coherence to present a threat. Tightening its grip on the Maul and the iron claw that held the Illata, Kihantro proceeded up the stairs to the hallway at the top. From here it could see the opening to the balcony. The door was gone, smashed by the wind, and a gauzy shadow occupied the space just beyond, feathery and insubstantial, sitting in the wheeled conveyance, peering into the castle with uncomprehending eyes. The shade was Jordneh's. Was it even aware of its surroundings? Did it remember what had happened? Its gauzy face bore the expression of someone presented with an unexpected and baffling puzzle. Kihantroh moved closer, holding the jewels in front of it, creating a barrier in case the entity proved to be capable of an attack. When none came, Kihantroh was emboldened, and moved closer. "Why have you manifested?" it asked.

The phantasm did not respond, or even react.

"Can you speak? Can you communicate at all?"

Nothing.

"Look at you. A phantom, a shadow. There is no substance to you. There never was."

Again, no response. Kihantroh shifted its vision to the level of the strings. The witch-queen's ghost was inextricably tied to the chair in which it sat, and which had given rise to it. Probably it was Kihantroh's own doing; by occupying the seat itself while reeling in Jordneh's glamours, some bit of energy must have bled off and formed into the shape that the chair knew best, just as hot metal poured into a mold took on the likeness of that which the mold had once enclosed. This echo seemed to have about as much awareness of its surroundings as did that hot metal, but still, any shard of Jordneh was dangerous, and not to be tolerated. The difficulty was that Kihantroh needed the wheeled conveyance, but not that which occupied it. Some delicate surgery would be required to excise this cancer.

Wielding the gems like a pair of the finest scalpels, Kihantroh began cutting away at the ties that bound the specter to the chair.

~~~~

From their assigned position at the top of the Harbor Road, Bernard could see a team of watchmen moving up from below, shutting each gate behind them as they climbed. At the same time, throngs of people and carts and wagons moved through the city streets in the opposite direction, away from the chasm, towards whatever exit was closest. Some ancient emergency plan, put in place for the eventuality of the death-wind's return, had been activated and was now in motion; Bernard was impressed with the level of compliance, and troubled by the amount of fear it bespoke. You didn't get this many people willing to evacuate in the face of an invisible threat unless they were genuinely frightened about what was coming. Having seen the death-wind's stirring firsthand in the cave beneath the sea, he rather envied those who were free to run away from it; if Mercy had been with them, he might well have sided with Cynidece when she had argued for leaving.

Several regular members of the watch were stationed here, some at street level with Bernard and Cynidece, and others, armed with bows, up in the observation deck with Nebandalex, where they were well-positioned for firing arrows down onto any unwelcome visitor that might lurch up the road. Taking a few steps to the partially-closed gate, Bernard peered at the chasm. It seemed the cable had been retrieved and secured to a stone piling at the base of the opposite cliff, but any further work had been abandoned for now. No surprise there.

He eyed the metal gate. It seemed quite solid, but no one else thought it would protect them and neither did Bernard. He idly ran the butt of his quarterstaff along the bars. The noise startled the watchmen, earning him surprised looks and a glare from their leader, a dour fellow named Haldabyr. Behind him, Cynidece chuckled and said: "Go ahead and break your staff on the gate. That silly piece of wood will be of no use against the death-wind anyway. None of your weapons will."

"The wench speaks from envy, as she has no blade," one of the guards said, drawing and waggling his sword, to the chuckling amusement of his fellows.

She turned to face him and said, in a mild voice, "This wench does not *need* a blade. Would you like me to show you why?"

Pinch-faced Haldabyr blanched a little and ordered the impudent watchman to sheath his weapon. The man complied, mumbling something that sounded vaguely placating. Remembering the wary regard Arran Blackhawk had displayed toward Cynidece, Bernard found himself wondering what, exactly, she was capable of, and why she was the only one here who was not armed; but when she turned back to Bernard, saw him watching her, and flashed him an exceedingly sweet smile, he decided not to ask.

From the observation platform, Nebandalex called down: "I see Aldric approaching."

Bernard looked around and spotted the innkeeper hobbling towards them from out of a nearby alley. For once, his cat-thing was not with him. He wore an ill-fitting belt buckled too low on his waist, with a sword in a bouncing scabbard that seemed to interfere with his movements. "I have been *recruited* into the *watch*," he said as he arrived at the gate. He drew his weapon, swung it around a few times, then held it up in the air; the rust-streaked metal looked dull and pitted. "Where is the enemy?"

"Put that away before you run one of us through," Haldabyr said.

"Or yourself." Cynidece caught hold of the sword by the blade and inspected it. "Not that the edge is sharp enough to do much damage," she added, running her thumb along it. Aldric, looking cross, tugged it away from her and sheathed it, missing the scabbard on the first two tries.

Bernard said, "Are you drunk?"

"Of course not. Well, perhaps a little. I was sampling ale in the cellar when Blackhawk found me and sent me to the armory. After they gave me this, I requested to be posted to my front porch, but they apparently think it is unimportant to guard my inn."

"What fools," Cynidece said.

"Where's Bertram?"

"He was deemed too old for duty."

"And too short," Cynidece said.

"He and Trouble are heading out of the city, to my estate in the downs. Perhaps they will be safe there for a little while."

Bernard was not surprised to find out that Aldric had a country estate. "How rich are you, exactly?"

"Rich enough that he never had to carry a sword before," Cynidece said.

"I know a thing or two about swords! You hit and stab things with them." The innkeeper tugged his blade free again, and dropped it this time; it failed to penetrate the ground, ending up lying on its side like some sort of unintentional metaphor. Looking down at it, Aldric said: "This weapon is defective. I should ask for another."

"I suspect they gave you that one so that you would not hurt yourself or those around you," Cynidece said.

Aldric stared at her for a moment, then turned to Bernard and said: "I prefer your elf-friend to this one." He managed to pick the sword up and fumble it back into its sheath. "She is more polite."

Bernard couldn't remember anyone ever referring to Mercy as *the polite one* before.   It seemed safest to avoid getting involved in comparing her and Cynidece, so he ignored the statement and turned back to the chasm instead. The crew that was locking the gates on the Harbor Road was perhaps three-quarters of the way up now; he figured they would reach the top either just before or just after dusk. They seemed to be in quite a hurry, not wanting to be caught outside the city once the light had failed, although from everything he'd heard about what was coming he doubted it would make much difference which side of the wall they were on when the death-wind boiled out of the chasm.   Feeling idle and discontent, he leaned his quarterstaff against the wall and climbed up to the observation deck.   The two human archers, lounging on benches against the near wall, looked at him with uninterested suspicion; his appearance marked him out as a Banderlundi, and although that fact had been rendered temporarily moot by the thing that lurked out there beneath the rocks and waves, the archers' gaze still served notice that he hailed from an enemy nation, and was not one of them. Clearly Nebandalex was not one of them either; he stood at the far corner of the platform, peering down into the chasm as the bottom slipped into darkness. Bernard joined him there. "Look at the shadowed water," the elf said, "and tell me what you see."

Bernard had been eyeing the promontory where they had been put onto the cable—those who had been on this platform that day would have had an excellent view of the process—but now he turned his attention downward. The yawning split in the earth opened roughly parallel to the sun's track, so that even the very bottom remained illuminated for most of the day, but portions of it had begun to slip into the shade where irregularities in the rock blocked the light. The water that swirled and eddied within those alcoves was darker, of course, than the water out in the open, but aside from that he didn't see anything special. "What am I looking for?"

"The water is changing. Can you see it? A green light on the surface?"

"No, it just looks like regular water."

"Nebandalex is right," Cynidece said at Bernard's elbow, making him jump a little. He'd had no idea she'd followed him up here; she moved as quietly as a cat. "I see it too."

The two archers joined them at the wall, apparently feeling left out now that they were outnumbered by Bernard's group, but they could not make out the suspect tinge in the water either. "Well, keep an eye on it," Bernard said, trusting in Peltish and elven eyes more than his own in this matter. "I'm sure it's going to spread."

"As am I."

Bernard climbed back down to his post on the street, Cynidece trailing along behind. Arriving there, he discovered that Aldric had wandered through the harbor gate to the top of the road; he had unbuckled the scabbard and left it on the ground near Bernard's quarterstaff. The team coming up from below was only a few switchbacks away from the top now. "You know, I own a small boat, but I have never seen it," Aldric said.

"Why not?"

"I never go down to the harbor. It is in such an inconvenient location."

Cynidece snorted. "Putting a harbor at sea level. Insanity."

"Why do you have a boat if you don't use it?"

"I hire men to take it out and catch fish for the inn." He gave Bernard a look of immense seriousness over his shoulder. "If we should survive this, I am going to go out on the boat once."

"Um, okay," Bernard said.

"Why would you want to do that?" Cynidece said. "Do you like being seasick? Do you enjoy the smell of unwashed sailors?"

"Just so I can say I have been out on the ocean."

She laughed. "You certainly are a melancholy drunkard." To Bernard: "He will start singing maudlin ballads before long."

Aldric shrugged and turned back to the water. He did not start to sing.

Instead, he said: "Is it my imagination, or is the water turning green?"

~~~~

There wasn't anywhere to hide on the balcony, so Mercy had flattened herself against the curving wall, out of sight of the door that Jordneh had blocked with the wheelchair. She waited there, scarcely breathing, as Kihantroh confronted the specter of the witch-queen. She hoped the sorcerer wouldn't detect her through the interference that Jordneh exuded. She could hear Kihantroh speaking to the phantom, unaware, it seemed, that the ghost was not able hear anything it said; then it began working some enchantment, a spell to excise the witch-queen's essence from the chair and banish it forever. If Mercy was going to steal the Illata back, she had to do it now. Once the witch-queen was gone there would be no more magic chaff obscuring her whereabouts, and Kihantroh would find her.

She could tell the Illata was right there, could feel its radiance, along with that of the Jewel in the Maul. She couldn't get a solid fix on the Jewel, though. It felt less real somehow, less *present*, maybe because she had never touched it. She could tell there was no chance she might pry that one away from Kihantroh, not under these circumstances. She needed to concentrate on the gem she might be able to take, rather than try to grab them both and lose everything. She inched sideways along the wall until she could just see the witch-queen's chair in her peripheral vision, then stopped, afraid to get any closer. Kihantroh might not be able to sense her, but it would hardly fail to notice her if she blundered into its field of vision.

Now she could see the blue light of the gems spilling out from the interior of the castle, enfolding Jordneh's chair in a cyanotic glow. The witch-queen's ghost had begun to fray, streamers blowing off her like fog fading in the sunlight. Kihantroh was unraveling her to nothing. Some of her dying energy must run back to Abacar, Mercy thought; Jordneh had been maintaining old enchantments there. That could lead her back. She felt her arms moving almost on their own, her left one reaching out toward the unseen Illata, her right one toward the distant mountains and the city by the sea that lay beyond them.

Jordneh's ghost raised its arms in mimicry. The chair lurched forward. Mercy heard Kihantroh's short, sharp exclamation as the phantom—which, it seemed, was not confined to the chair after all—sprang to its feet and closed its fingers around the Illata. Or were they Mercy's fingers? Suddenly it felt as if the shade of the witch-queen were Mercy's puppet, a disguise she was wearing, a secret skin. That was *her* hand clutching the gem. She had it in her grip. Now she let the bands that stretched from here all the way to the Slash snap her back, hoping the Illata would come with her. Vertigo suddenly overwhelmed her, a sense of twisting, of falling, of sliding through a twisting tube in utter darkness. A moment later she thudded down into something soft.

Mercy opened her eyes, and saw the ceiling of Aldric's bathhouse above her. She lay on the divan behind the partition in Aldric's bath, in the warm, dim quiet; and, clutched in her hands, pressed to her chest, she held the Illata.

It had worked. Holy crap.

She lay there for a few minutes while the spinning in her head subsided, wondering if Kihantroh was going to come screaming through a gate to reclaim what she had just stolen. It didn't happen. As far as Kihantroh knew she was dead, torn to pieces or beaten to a pulp by the statues, right? She didn't think it was aware that she had been at the castle; Jordneh's screen of static had obscured her presence even until the very end. Maybe Kihantroh would think the witch-queen had done it herself, stolen the Illata and cast it away or hidden it somehow. Still, it would soon start searching for its lost treasure, just as Mercy had done. Eventually it would find her. She had to make good use of the stone before that happened.

When she thought she could stand without falling over, she got up and stumbled into the main room of the bath. Bernard wasn't there anymore. The water in the tub still steamed gently, but the fire in the converted forge was almost out, reduced to a low pile of dull orange embers; it had obviously been closed up and left unattended for some time. How long had she been gone? The daylight had been fading when she'd been on the balcony in the Ravels, but with no windows here to show her the sky, she couldn't tell how near it was to full dark now. She wrapped the Illata in a small cloth from the linen rack, then put that inside a larger towel and swung it around a few times to make sure the Illata didn't fall out. Then, slinging the makeshift sack over her shoulder as if she were comically running away from home, she tried the pocket door next to the bench. It didn't budge. She went out the other way, stepping onto the garden path.   The sun had gone, mostly, leaving behind its slanting rays to paint the purple sky in streaks of fading orange-gold.   She made her way along the path to the inn proper, passing unlit lanterns that swayed on thin metal poles in a light breeze.   The building had the deserted feel of an outdoor restaurant after all the diners and staff had gone home, so she wasn't surprised to find that the back door was locked.   She moved on, staying in the shadows near the building, not liking the exposed feeling that settled over her when she was out beneath the open sky.   She pushed through ornamental shrubs with scents vaguely reminiscent of lavender and rosemary and sage.   They plucked and scratched at her as she slipped between them and the wall.   She reached the side of the front porch, where she slid under the railing and sidled to the front door.   Also locked.   Turning, she eyed the street.   Deserted.   Keeping her gaze on the sidewalk, she gave the front door of the inn a few light raps with the back of her knuckles.   She didn't expect an answer, and didn't get one.   Everyone was gone, but to where?

Well, the death-wind was expected to arise from the chasm, so that seemed like the logical place to go if she planned to intercept it.

She moved away from the inn, down the gravel path.   As soon as she came out from under the shelter of the porch roof, she had that feeling again: Wide open and observed, as if some malign influence had covered the city, making note of every living thing within. Reaching the street, Mercy hesitated, looked left, looked right. The sea air had grown chill and clammy while she'd been gone, with a putrid diffusive shimmer as if from a light mist. She didn't think it was spray from the waterfall.   Maybe the death-wind was already here, a pestilential cloud adrift among the buildings, entering her lungs, clinging to her skin. She could hear sounds in the distance, clattering movement, wooden wheels rolling over uneven stone. People were still leaving town, she thought. Unless Daras-Drûm could be stuffed back into its prison, corked like an evil genie, sealed like toxic waste, their escape would only be temporary. They might be caught on the road or in the forest instead of in the city; they might be caught tomorrow or next week instead of today; but they would still be caught. It was up to her to stop that from happening.

With the Illata bouncing against her back, Mercy turned to her right, and headed for the sea.

~~~~

As dusk settled over the chasm, the sickly cast of the water finally became apparent to all observers, even the human ones.   Bernard watched as it spread out from the shadowed area beneath the cliff face not far from where they had fallen, seeping across the undulating waves like time-lapse footage of mold consuming meat. At first the slick of green seemed to be spreading in a rough semicircle, but as it bulged outward it became distended, turning into a threatening finger jabbing toward the harbor. The breakwater turned the putrid current aside; it curled back on itself, forming a luminous spiral on the surface, a nasty lime ripple treat. As the swirl became more defined the water in the center seethed into a fizzy brew, raising a cloudy lather that roiled above the water. This swelled up and began to rotate just beyond the quay, coalescing into something that, from Bernard's perspective, looked like a tiny hurricane, complete with an eye in the center. The water surrounding this microcosmic storm whipped into a choppy froth; the flags on the docked ships snapped and fluttered sideways in a rising breeze, though the air high above at the gate remained mostly still.

"I see why they call it the death-wind," Bernard said, regarding the dwarfish cyclone.

"Not yet," Cynidece said, "but you will."

The central eye of the maelstrom congealed into a greenish-brown disk, then bulged upward like a polyp before coalescing into the corrupt gob from the sea cave, standing up like some thick gelatin mold rather than hanging down. Within the subtly luminous, semitransparent mass, Bernard thought he saw dark shapes drifting, blurred shadows moving like blots across the translucent glow. Were those arms? Legs? Heads? Sidling over to Cynidece, he whispered: "What are those things inside it?"

"Bodies of the dead. They are carried in its winds and sometimes pass through the center. When it arrives, it will spew them at us, and they will try to hold us here while Daras-Drûm overruns us."

"Oh," Bernard said. He thought of the field of skeletons and bodies that had reposed in the central chamber of the sea cave. Was Daras-Drûm bringing every one of them along to hurl against the gate? This just kept getting better and better.

The entire cloudy mass began to move forward through the gloom, gliding toward the harbor like some sort of ghastly haunted hovercraft. The viscous leading edge piled up against the breakwater, then bubbled up over the top and spilled down the other side, spreading across the water between the ships at their moorings. The glowing central mass barely quivered as it crossed the barrier and tipped into the harbor, illuminating it like a ghastly lantern. The death-wind didn't bother going around the ships, it just flowed over them, obscuring them beneath fog and foam. Distressed wooden creaks and groans echoed from the smothered vessels as their hulls splintered. With the boats to provide scale, Bernard realized just how large the entity was; it loomed nearly as tall as the main mast of the largest ship in the harbor, with a circumference over half again as big as the ship was wide. It exited the harbor, leaving crumpled, listing wrecks in its wake, just as the crew working its way up from below rounded the last switchback. They were only a few dozen yards from the top now and, abandoning any pretense of orderly motion, broke into a flat-out sprint toward the putative safety of the walls. Haldabyr stepped through to the edge where the road pitched sharply downward and hollered at the men to run faster, even though Bernard was sure they were already going at top speed. They reached the gate and stumbled through, followed by Haldabyr, who shouted for the gate to be closed. Those assembled took hold of the heavy metal bars and rolled the barrier along the track, slamming it into place. Haldabyr spun a thick bar and secured it with a giant lock, which under other circumstances might have seemed comically huge but, in the face of the stormy mass brewing below, was laughably inadequate.

Moving steadily forward, Daras-Drûm reached the cliff edge, where the Harbor Road rose toward the city. The sticky clouds accumulated in a growing pile at the bottom until finally they began to slowly flow up the rock wall, completely ignoring the road, the switchbacks, and the gates that had been so assiduously closed against it. Bernard heard the twang of a bowstring, then another. He couldn't see the arrows fly, or if they struck home, but they could hardly miss such a large target when it was coming straight at them. The death-wind gave no indication that it even realized they were shooting at it, let alone that it had been hit. It was going to reach the top within minutes, spill over the wall, and swamp the city with its fetid exhalations.

One of the bowmen climbed down from the observation platform, his bow on his back. Reaching the street, keeping his gaze on the ground, he turned away and dashed up the central avenue, just as a group of watchmen entered the intersection from the direction of the castle. Arran Blackhawk was with them. "Bring that man back," he said, pointing at the fleeing archer. Three of the newcomers broke from the group and sprinted after the deserter, who dodged into a side street. The pursuers plunged in after him, while Blackhawk led the remainder of his group forward, directing them into a semicircle around the gate. He had archers with him as well as footmen, Bernard saw, and a bucket brigade bearing torches and containers of black pitch. Evidently he was planning to set something on fire. As the men began to lever flagstones out from the pavement, a trough was revealed beneath, cut into the stones around the gate. Evidently this, too, was something that had been planned for in advance.

Stepping up to the gate, Blackhawk stared down at the luminous monstrosity slurping its way toward the city, his face sickly in the green glow. "The forecasters thought it likely to attack from the waterfall," he said, a commentary on the inaccuracy of weathermen. "I see they were wrong, as usual." He cast a sidelong glance at Bernard and Cynidece. "Perhaps it is drawn to you who escaped it earlier."

Cynidece said: "Would you like us to run, and see if it chases us?"

"It is chasing every one of us, and all we can hope to do is slow it down. *Light and fire!*"

Seconds after the command, a hail of flaming arrows zinged down from the observation deck, tracing orange lines through the air. This time there was no question but that they had hit their target, thudding into the gelatinous mass at nearly the same time, each to be snuffed like a match smothered by cold jelly, leaving little except a series of fading smudges across the glowing, gelatinous surface.

Slow it down? Ha. They weren't going to *slow it down*. This thing was going to roll over them like they weren't even here.

Wherever Mercy had ended up, Bernard hoped it was somewhere safe, and that she stayed there.

~~~~

As Mercy tried to find her way back to the harbor gate, the city became increasingly shrouded in a mist that seemed to be rising from the sewers; perhaps it had flowed in through the pipes and tunnels beneath Abacar's main streets forcing its way up through the grates and drains that normally carried runoff into the chasm. The basin in which she had earlier found refuge was probably full of cold fog now. She didn't like smell of it, or the taste of it on her tongue, or the feel of it on her skin and hair, a faint greasy sheen, as if it were an atomized blend of water and rancid fish oil. Was it backing up into the castle, into people's homes and shops and apartments? She imagined rooms filled with vapor, a clammy chill reaching into every corner, every hiding place, settling into the lungs of those within like a pale, unhealthful perfume. She couldn't imagine breathing it in any sort of concentrated form without passing out.

Between the disorienting sheets of drifting grey mist and the mild dizziness that inhaling it induced, she missed the turn onto the side street Cynidece had taken them along earlier, and soon realized she was wandering through a part of town she had never seen before. She moved closer to the buildings on the left, hoping to spot one she recognized, or maybe find a sign or a person to tell her which way to go. Not that she had much hope of either; no one was out on this sinister night, not around here. She was in an abandoned no-man's land between the defenders standing along the chasm and the defended fleeing through the gates, and had no guide to show her the way.

Eventually she became aware of running footsteps somewhere ahead of her. A refugee? Someone who might pause in flight long enough to point her toward the harbor? It was difficult to tell exactly what direction they were coming from. She hurried forward almost got knocked off her feet by a man who suddenly came sprinting out of a narrow alleyway between two shuttered, darkened shops. Mercy was by far the smaller but the man was overbalanced, looking over his shoulder as if pursued; he went sprawling in the road while Mercy spun, grabbed the icy iron post of a nearby unlit oil lamp, and managed to stay on her feet. She reoriented on the runner as he picked himself up. He wore the uniform of the city watch, and sported a bow and a quiver on his back; a few arrows had spilled when he fell and lay on the cobbles, pointing at the archer as if in accusation. She started to ask him where she was, but then three more watchmen came pounding out of the alley. Two of them seized the runner's arms; the third got hold of his kicking ankles. Ignoring Mercy just as thoroughly as they ignored the man's cries of protest, they picked him up and carried him back into the darkness of the alley. Assuming the man was a deserter running away from Daras-Drûm, following those who had grabbed him seemed like a good way to find whatever forces of law and order remained operational. And so, without really thinking about it, Mercy snatched up the arrows from the street and went after them.

The fishy stink in the alley was worse than out in the open street; the noxious vapor that had risen up to fill the city was more concentrated where the air was still and close and the buildings pressed in on each other. Although her night vision was usually excellent, the mist interfered with it so much that she could barely see the dark shapes of the watchmen up ahead of her. The captured archer's squeals continued to carry through the fog, though, so she was able to keep up, at least until she entered a four-way intersection where a second pair of buildings abutted the first, offset from each other by a short jog to the right. The sounds made by the guards were faint and confusing here, echoing around one of the corners. She couldn't tell which way they had gone; the damp, muddy, puddled cobblestones had recently been smeared by so many feet that they yielded up no information about which way her quarries had gone, even if she'd known the first thing about tracking, which she didn't.

Now she realized why she'd taken the arrows.

Switching one of the projectiles to the hand that held the Illata, she let the other one balance on the heel of her palm, and instructed it to point toward the man who had been carrying it. It swayed and bobbed and then—she felt a little thrill—it gradually swung around to indicate one of the corners. She hadn't used the Illata to make this happen; she'd done it herself. It was a small thing, but it was hers, a tiny glamour she had invented on the spot, and it had actually *worked*. Who needed Ambrosia the Sorceress anyway? Not her!

Following the point of the arrow, she hurried up the alley toward her date with the death-wind.

~~~~

The outer bands of Daras-Drûm's cloud reached the gate well before the luminous bulk of the creature did, and paused there as if waiting for reinforcements. Bernard could see what Cynidece had meant about the dead being carried in the wind; the skeletal corpses spun by a few yards away from the bars, reaching out with bony, clutching fingers as they were swept along. It was like watching a slow tornado that had siphoned out the contents of a cemetery. "Why isn't it throwing them at us yet?" he said, shrinking back from the grotesque show.

"Are you so eager to find out? It will strike all at once, when it is close enough to quickly overwhelm us. Just wait."

Below, the death-wind bubbled and frothed up one switchback after another, building up behind each ridge, cresting, then spilling over to begin slurping up the next, the gelatinous core wobbling slightly as it passed over each one. As it crossed the last few switchbacks the swirling dead began gathering near the front, darkening the translucent green mass. The first trailers of thick fog curled around the bars as Daras-Drûm slouched over the final switchback. Bernard imagined its arrival at the gate; it would loom over them and then burst like a pimple full of pus and zombies, vomiting its dead minions over the wall. Wouldn't *that* be lovely? But before that happened, the three men who had gone in pursuit of the deserter returned, carrying the archer who had tried to flee. The other watchmen parted around them as they deposited their cargo at Blackhawk's feet. He looked down at the man with obvious distaste. "I see you are missing a few arrows," he said. To those who had brought him: "Did the coward fire on you?"

"No, he ran into an elf-woman and fell," one said. "He must have lost them then."

That got all of Bernard's attention. "Elf-woman? What did—"

Blackhawk held up a hand, motioning Bernard to silence, then said: "Describe her. Be quick."

"Apologies, sir, but it was very foggy and I did not get a good look. I noticed the ears, but—"

One of the others said, "She had pale skin and hair the color of spun silver and wore ragged clothes that were once white. Had Derrow not collided with her, I might have thought her a ghost."

"She's back," Bernard said.

"So it seems."

"She's probably lost. We have to go find her. We're almost out of time."

"No," he said, as the pallid mist beyond the gate took on the greenish shade of the death-wind, "we are *already* out of time." Raising his head, he shouted: "What are you all waiting for? *Fire!*"

Another round of burning arrows flew from the observation deck, smacking into the gelatinous surface, setting it aquiver and marring it with small smudges even as the flames snuffed out on impact. The threatening vapor rushed forward and spilled through the gate, frothing into the city like steam through a grill. Denser mist crested the wall and poured over it in an overwhelming wave, extinguishing the fiery pots that the archers had been using to light their missiles. They abandoned their perch, scrambling down the ladders, pursued by cascading treacle. Nebandalex didn't have time for climbing; he jumped, passing over the head of one of the other bowmen who not quite nimble enough, stumbled at the bottom of the ladder and was engulfed, his cry for help ending abruptly as the fog flowed over him. Nebandalex hit the ground just ahead of the surging clouds, rolled to his feet, and joined the main body of the group. They all fell back as Daras-Drûm crashed like a wave against the gates. The metal groaned and fell inward, clattering to the ground beneath the luminous glob. At a nod from Arran Blackhawk, two men cast torches into the pitch-filled trough in the street. It flashed into a crescent of fire, suffusing the fog with ruddy light even as the death-wind finally disgorged its cargo of dead bodies out into the road. Mist popped and sizzled where it touched the flames, emitting the noxious odor of rotten, burning fish. The wind picked up, causing the fire to whip and crackle. More mist poured into the trench. Bernard didn't know if the death-wind was deliberately trying to extinguish the flames or if it was just moving inexorably forward and didn't even know the fire was there. The drying-seaweed stench in the air grew stronger. Corpses stumbled through the inferno. Only a few—the most recent victims, Bernard thought, like Poddock and the archer—had any flesh to burn; the rest emerged as blackened, skeletal things, animated by invisible strings, marionettes of the dead.

The smothering froth surged forward. The orange glow that had lit the fog died away as the fires went out.

Then a blue one appeared to take its place.

~~~~

Despite the drifting mist, Mercy spotted the death-wind as soon as she emerged from the alleyway; she could see it swirling off the edge of the cliff like a malignant little hurricane, could feel its icy breath sweeping across the cobbles. She hurried forward, unwrapping the Illata from the concealing fabric, and raising it up before her as if it were a lantern. Viewed through the glow of the stone, the death-wind was revealed as a tangled knot of absence, a moving hole in the world, a doorway leading who-knew-where. The clouds that swirled around it were not clouds at all, but the fraying ends of matter that peeled apart as Daras-Drûm consumed it. She suspected it was the sort of entity that would roam the unraveled void that Ambrosia had warned her against, devouring and devouring until there was nothing left. In a way, it was strange, dark cousin to the gate she had created back in Torgonderrer when she had banished the dwarven raiding party. *That* opening had led to another place within this reality; she had no idea where *this* opening led, and didn't really want to find out.

As she approached, the thing's leading edge caught an archer and smothered him. She could see him unraveling within the cloud, the strings that gave him life peeling away from the ones that gave him substance, slurping into the singularity at the center of the storm, to be replaced by new green-tainted ones, the color of the thing's putrid radiance. The new strings spun roots into the body's head and arms and legs, reanimating it. The corpse shook and quivered and staggering back to its feet as another of the death-wind's puppets. By now Mercy had reached the small group of watchmen; at Arran Blackhawk's wordless signal they parted to let her through. She arrived at the edge of the defunct fire-trench, ignoring the drifting smoke, the gem held high, a beacon against the dark. Fog roiled all around but did not touch her as she moved forward, as if she pushed a plow that turned the mist aside. She knew the defenders were falling back behind her as the death-wind continued to encroach, except for one who moved closer. Bernard, of course. Mercy sensed him coming up beside her, a knotty tangle of tightly-wound strings. The others around the gate seemed utterly insubstantial in comparison to how she perceived Bernard; they were made of clouds and cobwebs and tattered scraps. Little wonder Daras-Drûm pulled them apart with such ease. She and Bernard were different from them in some crucial, fundamental way that she still didn't understand, and perhaps never would.

The malign entity raged around them, and Mercy realized she couldn't banish it or destroy it; some piece had been removed from reality to create it, and until that piece was replaced, the fabric of the world could never be fully repaired. Closing this hole would open another one somewhere else, and the death-wind would slip through. No, she had to contain it, capture and neutralize it and keep it from consuming anything else. Focusing on the luminous strings that it sent back out to animate the bodies on which it fed, she turned the death-wind's hunger back on itself, feeding its own strings into the maw. The green glow intensified as the feedback loop grew tighter and tighter, as Daras-Drûm ate itself and became increasingly constrained. Through the swaddling towel, she felt the Illata growing icy cold, as if the death-wind had begun leaching energy out of it. That wasn't what she had intended. How had it gotten its hooks into the gem? She tried to sever that connection and suddenly realized that she and Bernard were alone, sealed in a cloud of roiling fog. The rest of the world had disappeared, as if in trying to entrap the death-wind she had instead invited it to cover them, to chew its way along the strings leading to the Illata, to get inside the gem and consume all the energy it contained. She couldn't let that happen, but her brain had grown sluggish and stupid and she couldn't figure out how to stop it. Her muscles began to quiver. The Illata felt heavy in her hand, so heavy, accreting mass like a giant hailstone gathering ice before it plummeted out of the sky. Her arm drooped; her grip on the stone loosened. The mist pressed closer.

Then Bernard's fingers closed around her wrist and lifted it up again. He said nothing, but he put his own hand on the Illata, holding it with her, adding his energy to hers. Bernard didn't know if he was immune to the Illata's degenerative aura, had every reason to think that being this close to it, actually *touching* it, was tantamount to suicide, but there he was, doing it anyway, trying to save her. She sensed the Illata's power flowing into him, through him, back out again, stronger after the round-trip, like a rocket gaining momentum from the gravity assist of some star or massive planet. It supplemented her flagging strength; she felt vigor returning and, marshaling the potential he had lent her, pushed back against the death-wind, rerouting its hunger and bending it inward once again.

Around them, the mist began to boil.

~~~~

Nebandalex fell back when the others did, retreating as the death-wind overran the walls and flowed into the city. In the tumult he managed to lose his bow, and then when Mercy suddenly appeared carrying the Illata, he was so shocked he failed to retrieve it before it was lost beneath the odious treacle. He watched her pass through the ranks, heading straight for Daras-Drûm. Blackhawk formed the defenders into a line behind her, well back from their original position, spread into a wide semicircle one man deep. It was quite obvious that if Mercy failed they would not be able to hold the gate, but still the man refused to order a retreat. Nebandalex supposed that might be praised as admirable and heroic, but it could also be cursed as stubborn and futile. Which would win out depended on whether or not Mercy could carry the day.

The archer who had fled before had fled again as soon as everyone's attention was diverted, of course, so Nebandalex helped himself to the man's abandoned bow and badly-fletched shafts. Such crude weaponry, but it could hardly be less effective than his own arrows had been. Thus prepared to join hopeless battle, he moved back to stand with the others in a perimeter that slowly widened as they moved further back from the encroaching fog. Mercy, now joined by Bernard, stayed right at the cloudy edge, holding out the Illata as if offering it to the death-wind, a bribe or inducement to leave the rest of them alone.

"What are they doing?" Cynidece whispered into Nebandalex's ear, startling him; he was unaccustomed to humans being able to sneak up on him, even at times like this, when most of his attention was elsewhere. But of course Cynidece was not human.

"She is trying to invoke the power of the Illata to stop the death-wind," he said, thinking it rather obvious.

"But ... she is *holding* it. In her hand."

"Of course she is. We told you she could. Did you think we were lying?"

"Yes." Then, a moment later: "How interesting that you were not."

He watched the wall of fog as it curled in around the two figures before the gate, enfolding them like the wings of some pallid bird of prey. Was that what they intended to happen? He did not think so. Aldric drifted past just then, edging toward the back of the line. No one else seemed to notice him break ranks. Nebandalex kept still, and let him flee unremarked; the man's utter ineptitude with a blade made him more of a liability than an asset, although, really, none of their weapons would avail tonight; Mercy would stop the death-wind here, or no one would. When Nebandalex glanced behind him a few moments later the innkeeper was gone, his sword-belt and scabbard lying on the cobbles, the belt still buckled, as if he had evaporated from inside it.

Suddenly a powerful gust of fetid wind erupted from the cloud, stinking like the rankest swamp in the lowlands. The wall of fog surged forward, covering Ambrosia and Bernard, overrunning the line they had made in the cobbles. Obscure figures shambled out of the mist, Daras-Drûm's dead puppets, moving forward ahead of the cloud. Nearly all were skeletal, though a few recent victims still looked like the living beings they had once been. They moved jerkily but with precise coordination, a set of marionettes controlled by a single puppeteer. Bees in the hive had more autonomy than these sad parodies. Slow and stupid, their purpose was to hinder escape, to grab and hold while the death-wind smothered and feasted. The defenders fell back in a chaotic fashion as everyone tried to avoid being caught by the draining fog or seized by the corpses. Several of the men broke and ran, only to be brought up short by Arran Blackhawk's roared command to hold. Incredible; what did they think Blackhawk would do to them if they fled that inspired them to stay and face certain death?

Cynidece moved forward, alone, wading into the mass of the dead. They swarmed her like giant grasshoppers. Pieces went flying as she moved among them, striking with seemingly bare hands that moved faster than Nebandalex could follow. Blackhawk's men, inspired by his words or shamed by the Pelt's example, reassembled and stood their ground, staying just out of reach of the expanding fog-bank; they hacked with swords and bashed with cudgels as Daras-Drûm's creatures shuffled forward. What was already dead could not be killed again, but their bodies fell when their legs were removed or crushed, and their clutching fingers and enfolding arms became less effective when their arms were severed from their bodies. Nebandalex opened fire, though his arrows were largely useless; he may as well have been throwing pebbles. The corpses he shot continued lurching around, no more inconvenienced than they would have been by the bite of some annoying insect. He threw the bow down, and the quiver, and looked for steel. Aldric's shoddy, abandoned sword would have to do. He reached the scabbard in a few bounds, snatched it up, drew the weapon, swung it a few times. It felt unbalanced and was undoubtedly dull—the innkeeper had not been wrong about that—but smacking the dead with the flat of the blade would be more effective than shooting them. Nebandalex turned. The death-wind's puppets continued to shuffle forward, silent but for the scuffing of their feet. Their ranks had grown, augmented by defenders who had been overcome. Some still carried their weapons, though they seemed unaware of doing so; others were now unarmed. Somewhere nearby Blackhawk was shouting commands that Nebandalex could not interpret; they seemed to be in some sort of code that the watchmen understood. Off to his right, the dead clustered around someone. He could not see through the swarm, but from the flying body parts he guessed it was Cynidece in the middle of that pile. The Pelt was giving an excellent account of herself, but the enemies had immobilized her and the mist was closing in. Nebandalex moved in that direction, thinking he might use Aldric's worthless weapon to pry her out of the heap.

Before he got anywhere near her, Daras-Drûm began to glow.

The oozing mist sizzled and popped, emitting a stench like burning swampland; then it exploded outward. Crumbled scuds of clotted foam and froth spewed in every direction, covering the walls, the gate, the living and the dead; then that, too, evaporated, leaving behind a faint cobwebby residue that quickly faded. The misty shroud that had draped the cliff behind the death-wind sighed into the harbor. The walking corpses tottered and fell and did not rise again. Cynidece was revealed at the center of a pile of shredded bodies, filthy and grinning like a madwoman. She seemed to have been enjoying herself immensely.

Bernard and Ambrosia—Mercy—still stood where they had been when the mist had overtaken them. Bernard had hold of Mercy's wrist. As the fog evaporated he let go of her, stumbled back a pace, and fell down hard, shaking his head as if trying to clear frigid water from his ears. Mercy simply collapsed straight down, like a wild beast felled by an arrow through the spine. Nebandalex changed direction at once, heading toward those two instead of Cynidece, who obviously did not require his assistance. Before he reached them, Bernard seemed to have gathered his wits a bit, and crawled over to where Mercy lay. She was still clutching the Illata, but something about it had changed; Nebandalex saw hints of green in its depths, like leaves rotting at the bottom of a pool. Something had happened to it; was the death-wind imprisoned within? Remembering how Bernard and the other humans had not seen the taint in the waters of the chasm at first, Nebandalex wondered if this contamination would be visible to them.

Cynidece arrived and the two of them hauled Bernard to his feet. "I feel like I got run over," he said, leaning heavily on his quarterstaff. "Did anyone get the license number of that truck?"

Another one of their strange idiomatic phrases; Nebandalex gathered that Bernard felt as if he had been trampled into the ground. "We thought the death-wind had taken you both," Cynidece said.

"Almost," Bernard said. "Not quite."

Leaving him propped up against the Pelt, Nebandalex went to check on Mercy. She was still sprawled on the cobblestones, but seemed to be conscious, at least. He knelt beside her. "And you? Did you also get … run over by a … truck?"

She laughed weakly, then groaned. "You're cute when you try to use slang." She fumbled with the Illata, wrapping it up in a towel that lay by her side. Nebandalex was not sorry to see its suspect luminosity smothered in fabric. He stood and helped her up; she leaned into him for support as he guided her around to face the others. A smile flickered across her lips. "Nice job, Bernard," she said.

"You too, Mercy."

Abruptly the four of them were surrounded by watchmen; Daras-Drûm had vanished, so their erstwhile co-defenders seemed to have adopted them as a new threat to be isolated. Nebandalex felt the others shifting around him, the four of them coalescing into a compact group, back to back to back, eyes in every direction. If it came to a fight, Nebandalex feared the result; Bernard and Mercy were in no condition to defend themselves. But the men did not attack, and after a moment Arran Blackhawk appeared, passing through the ranks and to stop nearby. He circled their little band once, regarding them as if their eight legs formed a large spider that might be venomous. Finally he said: "The threat is ended? The death-wind is contained or banished?"

"Yes," Mercy said.

"Then walk with me," Arran Blackhawk said. "We still have things to settle, and not much time."

~~~~

By the time Bernard's head had cleared enough to pay attention to where Arran Blackhawk was taking them, they were back at the gate from which he and Nebandalex had emerged when they'd been removed from the oubliette and carted off to the cable. The realization of where they were drew him up short, attracting Blackhawk's attention. The man looked a question at him. Bernard said: "Isn't this the way to the *dungeon?*"

Blackhawk grunted. "Yes, but I am not returning you lot to the oubliette. I need you off the street while my men clean up the mess the death-wind left at the gate. This is likely the last chance I will have to operate freely for quite some time, and the cells are beneath the notice of the fancy folk of the court." He spoke as if he were going to end up a wretched prisoner rather than lord of the city and most of the Slash; Bernard felt like telling him to try spending some time in the stinking straw of a pit or hanging from his wrists over a chasm, but it was probably best not to annoy the man in charge, so he shut up and followed the group through the gate. No one jumped them or drugged them or clapped them all in chains, so that was an improvement. Once inside the castle, they followed a different route from the one Bernard remembered, soon arriving in what seemed to be a mess hall attached to troop quarters; through a wide archway, Bernard saw a long room tightly packed with bunk beds, all presently unoccupied. The men who normally slept there would be spread across the city as part of Blackhawk's evacuation and defense plan. Most of them probably didn't yet know that the creature had been neutralized; Bernard imagined them standing around in nervous groups, wondering when and from where Daras-Drûm would strike, coming ashore like a sinister hurricane.

Their host gestured for them to take seats around a wide, barren plank surrounded by benches, while he himself paced around, then abruptly dismissed most of the watchmen who had accompanied them, saying: "Find whatever runners you can and tell them to distribute the message that Daras-Drûm has been ... Well, just say the threat is contained for now, but the evacuation command is *not* rescinded. No civilians are to return yet, and those who ignored the order to leave must remain in their homes. If anyone is found on the street without authorization, they are to be arrested."

Those thus instructed exited to carry out their mission, leaving only

Blackhawk and a couple of his men. Bernard remembered them from the original group at the inn. Blackhawk continued to stand, looking as if he was waiting for someone; this turned out to be the ancient and querulous scribe, Yardle, who plodded into the room ahead of a pair of guards who didn't *quite* have to prod him along him at spearpoint. He sat down far from the rest of them, muttering something about his scrolls. Blackhawk did not acknowledge these complaints, instead leaning over the edge of the table near Mercy. "You did well enough, regaining the prize that was stolen from you, but you were unable to retrieve the Maul."

"Yes. The Rittandic—Kihantroh—still has that."

"Better to have recovered one gem than neither. May we see it?"

Mercy hesitated, then unwrapped the towel that concealed the Illata. Bernard thought he could feel its radiance prickling on his skin, making the fine hairs along the backs of his hands shiver; it cast weird, threatening shadows that seemed to move on their own when Bernard viewed them from the corner of his eye, but not when he looked at them directly.

"Can you explain what you did to the death-wind back there?"

"Not really. Well, sort of. I turned its own power against it. I made it try to eat itself, and that tied it in a knot."

Blackhawk looked a question at the archivist, who said: "The records indicate that a similar trick was used to bind the creature originally."

"It's not a *trick*," Mercy said. "We're not talking about a rabbit hidden in a hat."

"Yet the death-wind *is* trapped within the crystal, is it not?" Blackhawk said.

"Um. Yes. It tried to draw on the Illata, I guess, and pulled itself inside. Now it's stuck there."

"When we saw it in the cave, it was flattened into a disk," Bernard offered.

"A disk in a cave, a knot in a gem, it makes no nevermind to me, as long as the binding holds." To Mercy: "*Will* it hold?"

"I think so."

"You *think*?"

"We know Daras-Drûm's not going to stop chewing on its own tail, so it should be self-sustaining, as long as no one reverses the spell."

"The old spell was also self-sustaining," Yardle said, "until it was undone by this Rittandic sorcerer after you lost the gem."

"Well maybe if no one drugs me and puts a stone around my neck that keeps me from using magic, I'll be able to hang onto it this time."

"And by that you mean you will take it with you?" The new Lord of Abacar studied her. "Out of the city. Away from here."

"Well, I certainly don't mean to leave it behind."

Yardle said: "My lord, you cannot allow the safety of the Slash to rest on her thin shoulders. What is to stop this Rittandic—"

"Kihantroh," Mercy said.

"—This *Kihantroh* from besting her again, and taking the gem, and loosing the monster within? For that matter, what is to stop her from threatening us with its release herself? The artifact is too dangerous to leave in their hands."

"Yon archivist is impolitic, but his blade has a point. Can you protect the Illata? Would it not be better hidden away in the crypt or elsewhere, safe and unseen?"

"How'd that work out for you last time?" Mercy said.

Silence.

"Uh-huh. Exactly. The Illata won't be safe anywhere until Kihantroh is dealt with, and the only one who can do that is me. I need the Illata to match the Jewel, so it's coming with me when I go. Any objections?"

"My lord, you must make the responsible choice—"

Blackhawk raised his hand and the sage fell silent. "You are right," he said, looking over his shoulder at Yardle. "I must make the responsible choice, which is this: That poisoned thing cannot stay within these walls. The elf is correct; we are not able to keep it safe or hidden. Who will craft the spells to conceal it? Who will develop the wards to protect it? Kihantroh will come for it again, and we will not be able to protect it." Yardle pressed his lips together and shook his head, but made no further comment. Blackhawk turned back to Mercy. "You will leave now, while things are still disorganized and the citizens are outside the walls or shut up inside their homes, that your departure may go unnoticed and unremarked. You will not stop to tell stories. You will not tarry for a bath at the inn. These two—" Here he indicated Bernard and Cynidece. "—will not pause to steal anything. Am I understood?"

Mercy nodded, but Cynidece said: "We are not ready for an overland journey to the Ravels. Do you expect us to walk across the mountains with no food or gear and only these rags to wear?"

"I expect you to leave the city. After that, your choices are your own."

"Yet removing this Rittandic creature will be doing you a service.

Do you want us to succeed or not? Is banishing us with nothing but what we now carry the *responsible* choice, Lord of Abacar?"

Blackhawk grunted. "Fair enough. You need to be equipped. Yet I can hardly have you raiding closed shops or pillaging the bazaar, can I?"

"Is the keep so understocked that you have no food or warm clothing to spare?"

"I can give you some things from the dungeon stores, but I have not the sort of kit that would see you across the mountains." He fell silent, looking thoughtful, then said: "Very well. This is what I shall do. Your friend Goldshine fled the gate; I will have the cheerful scribe Yardle prepare a writ instructing him to equip your merry band for this expedition, such supplies to be given or paid for by him, as full recompense for his dereliction of duty. If he complies, no further action will be taken against him. He is a prudent fellow; he will do what is requested, especially when his alternative is to be hanged for cowardice." To Cynidece: "The innkeeper is known to have an estate along the Peltish Way. I assume you know where that is?"

"Of course I do," Cynidece said. "You realize that hanging Goldshine for cowardice would be like hanging a dog for going on all fours?"

"*You* stayed at the gate, condemned criminals that you are. Should I expect less from a wealthy citizen?"

"Probably," Cynidece said.

Arran Blackhawk snorted. "Well, I do not," he said.

"I had no idea you were so naive."

"Not so naive as to believe that you, Pelt, will not be back within the city walls making mischief before the season is out. Nevertheless, I will still grant you pardon and safe passage out of the city, said pardon subject to revocation when you return, as I know you shall."

Cynidece grinned and nodded and didn't bother to deny it.

"Good, it is settled thus. You will guide these others to Goldshine's estate; you should be able to reach it with a day or two of hard walking. I will give you traveling cloaks, and water and food enough to get you there without thirst or pangs of hunger. No doubt you will receive a fine welcome, and he will be quite generous in offering you supplies for the balance of your journey."

"Thank you," Mercy said.

Blackhawk shook his head. "Save your thanks for after you have confronted your foe," he said, "lest you spend them all now, and have none to spare then."

Chapter 5

THE FOUR OF them soon left the keep, writs in hand, features concealed by musty hooded cloaks that had been brought up from some dungeon storeroom. Bernard carried a scrawled map of the way to Aldric Goldshine's country estate, scratched onto cloth with charcoal and stuffed into his pocket. Cynidece said she didn't need it, but Mercy wanted something that showed them the way in case the Pelt decided to disappear after all. What goal was the Pelt pursuing? Did it really align with theirs? She obviously had all kinds of history with Abacar and the Blackhawks, and maybe even with Aldric, and something about her just triggered a reflexive suspicion in Mercy.

Well, if the Pelt double-crossed them, she would deal with it when it happened. But still, she wanted her own map.

Outside the castle, Cynidece guided them into a narrow alley between two buildings, which soon turned into a maze of narrow brick-walled passages running by closed doors, the backsides of shuttered businesses. Perhaps these were the shops Blackhawk had warned them against robbing. Cynidece moved fast, turning right, then left, then right again, zigzagging through the dimness. Were they even heading for a gate, or was she leading them into some sort of ambush? Why had Arran Blackhawk appointed as their navigator someone he manifestly didn't trust? Finally Mercy planted her feet and stopped, bringing the others up short, and said: "Wait."

Cynidece glanced back at her. "For what? Were you listening to Blackhawk? We must get out of the city at once. I realize you must be tired already, but we may rest once the gates are at our backs."

"Yes, I was listening." Mercy *was* tired, actually, and could have used a rest, but she hardly intended to admit that to Cynidece. "*Are* we going out of the city? Because it seems like we're just getting deeper into a maze."

"I know my way through these alleys. This will take us to a side gate that is rarely used."

"Why not just go out the front way?"

"Are you *sure* you were listening? We were told to avoid people. Have you seen any people along this route?"

"No, but——"

"Blackhawk instructed me to be your guide, but I can only do that if you let me. Follow me, or find your own way." Without waiting for a reply, Cynidece turned and continued along the dark and claustrophobic space. The others looked at Mercy; muttering, she started moving again, hurrying after the Pelt on her winding path between the buildings.   It wasn't long before the alleys started widening; soon they emerged from a cluster of row houses and shops near a spot where a jagged ridge of black stone sprouted from the earth. The city wall incorporated it as part of the barrier against the outside world, so that a watchman on patrol along the top could continue walking over the toothy upthrust as if on level ground. Cynidece took them toward the jumbled pile of rock.   As they approached, a cavelike opening came into view where a broken monolith leaned drunkenly against its neighbor. The space between had been mortared up and set with a thick iron gate. This exit had, it seemed, gone unused during the evacuation, perhaps because it was small and hidden and out of the way, or perhaps because no one could open it; the barred panels were secured by a large, rusted, ancient-looking chain, held together by an equally-corroded lock. Cynidece stopped at the opening and made a grand gesture of presentation. "Behold," she said. "A gate."

Mercy rattled the chain, and favored Cynidece with a raised eyebrow.

"A locked gate is still a gate," the Pelt said.

"Here, maybe I can pick it," Bernard said, stepping up and pulling out a length of stiff wire that evidently had been secreted somewhere in his leathers this entire time. Mercy stepped out of the way as he inserted this into the keyhole and began working it around, his tongue sticking out of the side of his mouth as he concentrated.

At length, Nebandalex said, "Perhaps Mercy can open it with a glam—"

"No no," Bernard said. "She needs to rest. I've got this." Then, muttering: "This is my Brannoc impersonation. I've got this."

Cynidece said: "Who is Brannoc?"

"Somebody we used to know," Mercy said, not looking at Cynidece.

"Ah," Cynidece said. "A missing party member? Like Ambrosia?"

Mercy said nothing, but Nebandalex was right: It would be faster if she magicked it open. Still, she wanted Bernard to succeed, or at least to *think* he had. She turned away and pretended to cough into the crook of her elbow a few times, then quickly reached out to the lock's strings, found the tumblers, and gave them a little pull.   The lock clicked open, eliciting a please sound from Bernard. He put the pick away as the gate swung inward on protesting hinges, opening just enough to let them out, single file, onto a narrow strip of rocky riverbank. The falls roared somewhere to their left; Cynidece took them in the opposite direction, picking their way along the uneven boulders, until finally the river veered away and they stepped out into the clearing along the city wall that faced the plains. From here they could see the throng of evacuees, most of whom evidently had nowhere to go and continued to mill about near the front gate, in the nearby meadows, and along the road. A number of city watchman stood guard, both on the ground and on the parapet, monitoring the citizens. Mercy saw that the four of them would have been *very* conspicuous forcing their way through that crowd in their dungeon cloaks, hoods up, concealed weapons forming odd lumps and bulges beneath the fabric. It seemed that Cynidece had been correct to take them along a different route, even if she'd led them to a gate that was nominally impassable.

Staying close to the river, they moved across the grassy yard and into the woods. Nobody in the crowd or its minders spared them a glance, as far as Mercy could tell. Given that the gate was ringed with torches while the four of them slunk through the darkness in garb the color of charcoal, she doubted they were even visible, and she didn't bother with a veil glamour. Once among the trees, they cut to the right, emerging onto the road some distance away from the city. They soon passed the area where they had camped on the night Marjack attacked them. Mercy glanced in that direction from underneath her hood, then looked quickly away, not really wanting to reminisce about the episode.

"Did something happen there?" Cynidece whispered, suddenly appearing beside her.

Startled, Mercy said: "What?"

"The look you gave that spot tells me this is a location of some significance to you." She ostentatiously examined the trees. "To me, it looks like any other stretch of roadside. What does it look like to you?"

"Nothing I want to tell *you* about," Mercy said.

"We spent the night there and were attacked by a highwayman when … our sentry fell asleep," Nebandalex said, evidently having overheard the exchange. "He tied Mercy up and had a blade to Bernard's throat before I shot him."

This characterization, technically accurate though it might have been, made it sound as if the man had been holding the knife to Bernard at the moment Nebandalex killed him. In fact, he been retreating. It certainly wasn't Mercy's job to clarify the situation, though.

Cynidece said: "And so you two were put on the cable, and this one was put in Lord Korrin's bedchamber?"

"Yes," Nebandalex said.   "We were … careless."

"Well, it would have happened anyway, or something like it," Mercy said.   "With Kihantroh already in there impersonating Rumad Kram, if we hadn't given him that excuse to arrest us, he would have found another one."

"I see.   Well.   The important thing to remember is this."   Looking past Mercy to Bernard, she said: "When you are on watch, you do not fall asleep, lest a thug tie up your friends and put you to the blade."

"I'm aware," Bernard said, turning a shade redder than usual.   "It won't happen again."

"It had best not, at least while we are traveling together," Cynidece said.   She gave him a very sweet smile, and added: "If it does, I may have to put you to the blade myself."

Despite the Pelt's cheerful expression, Mercy was pretty sure she wasn't joking.

$$\sim\sim\sim\sim$$

The travelers continued onward for some time through the night, leaving the city walls and its surrounding cultured fields and manicured woodlands behind.   They passed various intersections and turnoffs but kept going straight until finally, as dawn approached, they came upon a smaller road that diverged to the southwest, bending inland and sloping upward to a plateau of rolling hills and grassy swells.   Cynidece guided them onto it, so this, apparently, was the Peltish Way.   Mercy had thought it would be bigger.

Their mostly level walk alongside the river now became a steady uphill slog.   Footpaths like hiking trails in a nature preserve exited at erratic intervals, vanishing up and over other hills or dipping into low, flat, lightly-wooded hollows where small clusters of buildings and cottages nestled among fields of produce left fallow for the season. The snapped and crumpled stalks of whatever common crops grew here stuck up out of the ground like broken, half-buried spears, as if they were failed and trampled defensive perimeters around the hamlets.   They continued plodding along across the threshold of sunrise, into the morning, then the early afternoon.   Despite frequent rest and snack breaks, Mercy found herself getting more and more exhausted, until finally she had to ask Cynidece to look for a place where they could halt until tomorrow.   The grinning Pelt obliged, and soon took them off the road and down a short decline, stopping next to a stream at the bottom of a shallow, sandy ravine.   The creek swung in from the south to parallel the road briefly, then turned away again and opened into a broad, flat glen that contained a few ramshackle houses with gardens and a small mill pond. Thin smoke drifted from several chimneys. Preferring to keep their presence unadvertised, they stayed inside the trees, well away from the cleared areas, huddled together in a little pod beneath the trees. Mercy imagined they must look rather like a mushroom faerie ring as they sat hunched over in a circle in their fungi-colored cloaks, nibbling hard bread and dried meat and drinking water that had acquired a leathery aftertaste from the water skins, complementing the musty flavor it already had from sitting in a barrel in Arran Blackhawk's dungeon. Not exactly traveling in style.

They drew sticks to determine the order of the watch. Mercy got the first one. Bernard settled in next to her as the others curled up under threadbare dungeon-issue blankets. They sat a while in silence. Eventually one of the others began to snore. Bernard said, "Is that Nebandalex?"

"I think so."

"Elves never snore in stories."

"No, not usually." She nudged him with her elbow. "You should do some snoring, too, you uncouth human."

"Ha ha. If anything, *you* should be the one sleeping, after what you did back there."

She shrugged. "The short straw has spoken."

"Mmm." Then: "I wanted to ask you something. About the Illata."

"Yeah?"

"Yeah. About, um … what's inside it now?"

"Uh-huh. What about it?"

"Well, with that *thing* in there, can you still use it? Or will that let it out? I mean, like, are we going to get where we're going, and you try to use the Illata against the Rittandic, and all of a sudden the Daras-Drûm is there? I really don't want to *ever* see the death-wind again."

"You won't. I've got it locked up. Don't worry."

"Well, I'm worried." He sighed. "I touched the Illata."

"Yes, you did, and that was very helpful of you. So thanks."

"You're welcome. And I didn't die."

She snorted.

"Ha, yeah, right, of course I didn't. So listen, when I touched that thing, it was like … like I was home again. I mean, like, I saw home, for a little while. Except Brannoc was there, too, sort of hanging around. Like we were separated and he came to visit? I was me again, and he was him.   But then afterwards, it seemed like we were back together, even though he's not in here anymore——" Bernard tapped the side of his head.   "——Even though he *is* there, just not the same way as before. Sorry, this is coming out all nonsense."

"No, it's okay. Something like that happened to me, too, with me and Ambrosia, the first time I touched it. I'm not really sure what it means. How do you feel now?"

"Oh I'm all right. I'm fine. It's just … I hadn't heard anything from Brannoc in a long time. Since the sea caves, I guess. Nebandalex said while we were in the dungeon Brannoc was in control of my body, walking and talking and trying to figure out how to escape. But now he's gone. I thought he might have died or something, you know? Like maybe he drowned and the death-wind ate him. But then he was there again with the Illata. I don't understand it. It's like he … like he's inside the Illata, and when I touched it he was there and climbed back in my head, except he still doesn't talk to me. But now I kind of know Brannoc stuff, and that's why I thought I might be able to open the lock on that gate, see? And it worked."

She didn't have the heart to tell him that it hadn't worked, that *she* had opened the lock. It wasn't his fault; the mechanism was probably seized up and unworkable. Besides, what he was telling her was exactly what Ambrosia had said would happen when she had been in Mercy's head, urging her to touch him with the Heart—the Illata—while they were camped outside of Abacar. Maybe if she had listened, things would have turned out better. "Well, I mean, it's good that you picked up Brannoc's skills and stuff, and you really didn't need him talking in your head. You two argued all the time."

"Well, yeah, but still, I don't like to think Brannoc's dead and I, you know, *absorbed* him or something. It's creepy."

"He's not dead," Mercy said. "He never existed. You and I are the real ones, remember, not Ambrosia and Brannoc. They're fakes. We're not."

"That's not what Brannoc used to say. He used to call me a demon and said I stole his body."

"Well, Brannoc was wrong."

"I guess."

"What do you mean, you *guess*? Are you a demon?"

"Well, no, but I——"

"Stop right there. There's no *but*. You created Brannoc in the game, and——"

"*You* created him in the game, you mean."

"Fine, *I* created him, but I created him for you because you couldn't make up your mind. A *scout?* named *Bernard?* Really? I couldn't let you do that."

"Yeah, sure, and I'm ever so grateful."

She couldn't help but smirk at that, but sensing a serious question lurking in the background, said: "Think about it this way. We needed skills to survive here, and we didn't have them. Putting us in with Ambrosia and Brannoc was maybe a way to ease us into learning our way around."

"Maybe so, I was, like, having conversations with an imaginary friend who wasn't even my friend. He took control of our body when we needed to do rogue stuff, while I just watched. And when you became Ambrosia, you didn't even remember you used to be Mercy. Why not just give us skills directly instead of saddling us with split personalities?"

"I don't know. Maybe if we had all that information shoved into our brains, our heads would have exploded. You want your head to explode?"

"Those are our only options? Split personalities or exploding heads?"

After a moment she said: "Yes. Yes they are."

"Well, I think you forgot you were Mercy because you *wanted* to forget you were Mercy. As long as I've known you, you always wished you were someone else. Remember those dolls, when we were younger? You made a whole elf family out of them. You cut pointy ears out of construction paper and glued them to their heads, and you glued a bigger set onto *your* head and insisted we all had to call you *Ambrosia?* And you wanted to glue a set on my head, too, but your mom said—"

"God, Bernard, stop. Don't remind me about *that.*" Mercy spread her arms. "Anyway, fine, I get the point. It's all my fault. I made you play the game, I created Brannoc for you, and then, I don't know, you got downloaded into his brain, and I got downloaded into Ambrosia's brain, and there we were. But we're okay now. You're fine, I'm fine. Everything's fine."

Bernard snorted. "Oh, yeah. Everything's super duper."

"Great. Now go get some sleep so I can wake you up later."

Bernard sighed, moved away, and lay down on the ground near the others.

A moment later, she heard Cynidece say to him: "You two have the strangest conversations I have ever listened to."

~~~~

Morning presented itself with a sky the color of old smoke and air heavy with the threat of rain. The clouds bulged down toward the earth like a grey skin laden with water; as they prepared to depart from their cold and cheerless camp, a chill shower began to patter on the leaves overhead, flowing from one to the next to the next before finally dripping onto their heads and necks like melting ice water. They bundled their cloaks around them, raised their hoods, and made their way back to the Peltish Way. Cynidece took the lead again as they traipsed along the dirt road. Its surface was quickly turning into mud; the precipitation, while not hard, was steady and soaking, the sort of autumn rain that turned fallen leaves to rot every year. A light, shifting wind blew in from their back, sending the tiny raindrops into a patterned dance that found its way through any gap in their cloaks, of which there were many. Conversation dampened along with everything else, they walked in a companionably miserable silence, meeting no other travelers along the way. The hamlet near which they had camped was the last they encountered for some time, and when Mercy finally did notice another one in a shallow valley to the right, the houses there looked tumbledown and abandoned. She began to wonder if Cynidece was leading them out into the uninhabited plains for some nefarious purpose, but when she consulted the map during a relatively dry rest break, it seemed to comport with the route they were taking. Cynidece, of course, noticed her looking at the document, and gave her a knowing smirk, but said nothing.

Toward midday they came to a crossroads where a wagon-thin track intersected the Peltish Way. This path ran down into the lowlands to the right and up into higher downs to the left. Each corner of the intersection was guarded by the statue of an animal. The Pelt paused in the center of the crossroads, looking at each of the statues in turn: A creature that resembled a large hare, one not unlike a fox, some sort of predatory cat, and a clawed, fanged, web-footed amphibian beast that looked like a variety of the creature that had hauled itself out of the pond in Torgonderrer on the very first afternoon Mercy had arrived in this world. She eyed that last statue with a certain amount of unease, wondering if those things lived in the watering holes of these hills. She hoped not.

Cynidece went over to the cat statue and start stroking it behind the ears. The drizzle continued unabated. At length, Mercy said: "What are you doing, exactly?"

"I never thought to see these totems again. This one was always my favorite."

"Mmm. Well. This doesn't seem like the time to stand around reminiscing and petting the statues."

"No, I suppose not," Cynidece said, although she kept on doing it.

"Are we almost there?" Bernard asked.

"Yes. Goldshine's estate is in the next dale to the south." She tilted her head to the left, where the narrow, rain-darkened wagon track climbed crested the fell and vanished from sight, like a brown ribbon stretched across a mound of grey-green fabric.

"You ... have visited it before, I take it?" Nebandalex asked.

"Oh, I have trespassed on his grounds more than once," she said, favoring the elf with an oblique smile. "Not that your innkeeper friend ever knew I was there. This will be my first visit as a guest, if *guests* is what we shall be."

"Well, we won't find that out until we get there," Mercy said.

"So impatient when you are not exhausted." Leaving the cat statue, Cynidece strode up the mud-slicked track, moving with her customary confidence; the others followed. The hill proved to be deceptively tall, the incline unexpectedly steep, the trail treacherously slick; the others all took it easily enough, but Mercy found it difficult to keep her footing as the slope increased. She began to fall behind. Nebandalex, noticing her trouble, drifted back and offered a supporting arm to help her. As the lower ground fell away, the road back to Abacar was revealed, shrouded in grey mist and drizzle, the distant trees in which they had camped nothing but cottony shadows scribbled beneath the fog. Nebandalex kept glancing back that way, until finally Mercy asked: "What are you looking for? Is someone following us?"

"No," Nebandalex said. "I am just saying farewell to the trees. There are no woodlands ahead of us."

"You may yet encounter a few more forests, melancholy elves," Cynidece called back. "The Fists are not *entirely* rock and stone, you know."

That woman was all ears, and she seemed to file away whatever she saw or heard—which was everything—for future reference. There would be no more sensitive discussions when Cynidece was around, Mercy decided, although Bernard probably told her everything anyway. Those two, and to a lesser extent Nebandalex, had become fast comrades after their shared experience on the cable and in the sea cave with Daras-Drûm. It suddenly occurred to her that perhaps the reason she was finding it so difficult to accept the newcomer into their group was that she was jealous of her friendship with Bernard, and didn't like how he and Cynidece had become so close so quickly. God, was she really that petty? Maybe so. When you didn't possess many friends, you needed to hang on to the ones you *did* have, right?

Bernard and Cynidece paused at the top of the hill for her and Nebandalex to catch up, standing up there like a couple of explorers peering down into uncharted territory while they waited for the struggling porters to arrive with their gear. "Can you see Aldric's house?" Mercy asked.

"No," Bernard called back, "but we can see his mansion."

When she and Nebandalex joined them at the summit of the drumlin, Mercy understood what he meant; Aldric's so-called country home stood at least twice as large as his inn, consisting of a huge central structure with two angled wings that ran back like a pair of opposing barracks. The building seemed to have been built entirely of logs, now stained black by the rain, with a slate roof colonized by clumps of moss distinguishable from the grey stone only by their softly-rounded contours. Split rail fencing surrounded the structure, running off into the fog, which grew steadily denser toward the back of the valley. The place seemed to be emerging from the mists of some other land, projected out of a forgotten past or an unrealized future. A small covered wagon stood off to the side, its fabric top soaked and dripping, water running down the sides, making the swirls of gilt inlay glimmer in the ashen light. Was it paint, or actual gold? "That cart reminds me of something you'd see on a merry-go-round back home," she said.

Cynidece snorted. "*Now* who is standing around reminiscing?"

They descended at an angle along a track that followed a gentler, longer slope along the backside of the hill. Another road ran off to the west, dropping sharply before winding off into broad scablands and disappearing from sight. Mercy wondered where it went; she could barely make out the shadow of high, bulky peaks in the distance through the shrouding fog and rain. Cynidece had mentioned crossing mountains to get to the Ravels; maybe those were the ones she had been talking about. It looked like a very long slog followed by one heck of a climb, and she began to doubt she could make it on foot at all. Maybe Aldric would give them horses.

After reaching the bottom of the hill, they walked a little way along the fence to the open gate, where a crushed-stone drive diverged from the muddy path. They crunched along the trail of pea gravel until it widened into a parking area that could accommodate quite a few carts and carriages, although at the moment its only occupant was the colorful cabriolet. The small wagon stood off to the side; Cynidece detoured to investigate, giving the wagon a cursory inspection, while the rest of them stood around in the cold, incessant drizzle. A small, rustic portico over the front door would have afforded shelter, but as if by unspoken agreement they waited for the Pelt to get back before proceeding. When she did, Mercy said: "Blackhawk told us not to pause to steal anything."

"Blackhawk knows I am not a thief," Cynidece said. Then she grinned and added: "But the wagon carries nothing of value anyway. The yellow is merely paint, and if Goldshine sent his cash box out of the city, it has gone into the house along with those who brought it."

"Speaking of the house," Bernard said, "let's go there."

They closed the rest of the distance to the mansion and gathered under the porch roof. Lanterns burned within; they glowed fuzzily through fogged, narrow windows. The door sported a massive black iron knocker which Cynidece ignored, preferring to rap with the back of her hand. The sound of her bony knuckles striking the wood was shockingly loud, as if she were hitting it with a hammer. No need to worry that anyone in the house might fail to hear *that*. Yet no one answered; Mercy might have thought the place unoccupied, but they wouldn't have left the lanterns lit in the front hall when they went out, would they? She hoped they hadn't done anything foolish before the specter of certain death; she could imagine Aldric sitting comfortably, his cat-monkey-thing purring in his lap, his feet up by the fire, knocking back a mug of poisoned ale, killing himself before the death-wind arrived and did it for him. She moved forward and reached for the knocker, stopped at the sound of a bar being withdrawn on the other side of the entrance. Someone was alive inside after all. A moment later the door swung inward, revealing Bertram standing there. He still had a rag slung over his shoulder—possibly the very one he was constantly using to polish the brass at the inn—and his expression of distaste upon seeing them was the same as always.

"*You* lot again," he said, as if they showed up here all the time despite having been told to stay away.

~~~~

They didn't need to display the letter from Arran Blackhawk to get invited in; shaking his head, Bertram stepped back and motioned them forward, watching from the side as they filed into the dim, smallish foyer, where it was marginally warmer and considerably drier than out in the drizzle-soaked plains. "Is Aldric here?" Mercy said, as they stood dripping water onto a stained, rather threadbare rugs that was clearly here for the purpose of collecting the damp and dirt of the outdoors before it could be spread to the more reputable floors and carpets elsewhere in the house.

"No," Bertram said.

"Oh." Then, when no additional information was forthcoming: "Um, where is he?"

"The last time I saw him was when he sent me away in the wagon. Perhaps *you* should tell *me* where he is."

"Er, we thought he would be here."

"Well, you were wrong. Did you come all this way just to see him? I thought you had been posted to guard the Harbor Road from the death-wind." He ostentatiously looked past them at the front door. "Was that it behind you? It just looked like regular fog."

"That's because it *is* just regular——"

"The death-wind has been dealt with," Mercy said, interrupting Bernard's attempt to answer Bertram's snark as if it had been an actual inquiry. "Now we're on our way to … somewhere else. Arran Blackhawk said we should stop here for supplies. You're sure Aldric hasn't shown up?"

"I think I would know if Aldric were here," Bertram said. "He is difficult to miss. No, the only ones in residence are me, the estate staff, and Aldric's *cat*, though the cat ran off somewhere a little while ago, and good ridd——wait, Blackhawk sent you *here* for supplies? Why would he do that? Does he think we run an outfitter's shop?"

"The manor is largely self-sufficient, is it not?" Cynidece said. "You have horsemen who spend days and days out in the fields driving your beasts between field and meadow. Surely you have material we could use on our journey. Dried food, blankets, warm clothes?"

Bertram had started shaking his head partway through her statement, and didn't stop after she was finished talking. "Yes, we are self-sufficient, and one good reason for that is that we do not just give our supplies away to anyone who asks for them. If Blackhawk wanted you equipped, why did he not do it himself? What is all that?"

At a nod from Mercy, Bernard had produced the bone tube in which their various scrawled documents resided, and was shuffling through them with a chagrined expression on his face; evidently he couldn't read whatever language the scrolls were written in. Cynidece took them away from him, found the appropriate one, and began reciting from it. "Aldric Goldshine, citizen and acting watchman of Abacar, was stationed at the Harbor Road in defense of the city and fled his position without authorization. He is therefore guilty of and his life in jeopardy for dereliction of his duty——"

"*Dereliction of duty?* Aldric's no soldier, no watchman. Blackhawk had no business trying to make him one."

"They were issuing weapons to every man who could hold a blade," Cynidece said. "Even you probably would have gotten one, had Goldshine not tucked you into his fancy cab and given his horse a smack on the rump to make it run along home."

"The point," Mercy said, shooting Cynidece a look that she hoped would shut the Pelt up, "is that Blackhawk understands why Aldric left and isn't really interested in pursuing the matter, as long as you help us on our way."

"So you are agents of the Blackhawks now, is that it?"

"Free agents, whose interests happen to be temporarily aligned with his, more like," Cynidece said. "We have all kinds of writs that talk about it. You may keep the one that says Goldshine will not be hanged if he accommodates Blackhawk's request."

"So he thinks to extort supplies by threat?" Bertram seemed about to spit on the floor, but restrained himself, and after a moment said: "Very well. What sort of supplies do you need?"

Mercy said: "Well, we're going over the mountains——"

"Will you be needing goats to ride, then? Or are we expected to give you horses?"

"A wagon would be nice," Bernard said.

"No," Cynidece said. "At elevation, the rain we came through will be snow or sleet. A wagon would get stuck."

Bertram gave her a long look. "Are you serious?" he said. "You intend to go through the Fists at *this* time of year?"

"We do."

The little man shook his head. "Madness, but no more than I should expect from you three, I suppose, let alone from *you*." This last was directed at Cynidece, a hooligan so dire she required separate denunciation. "Very well. You lunatics are going over the mountains." He folded his arms across his chest. "Warmer clothes, tents, bedrolls to sleep in, yes, we can spare those. We are not well stocked with food that will keep on a long journey, but I believe the cook has been salting meat for the winter, and there is some hard cheese and bread. You can have enough of that to see you through a few weeks. Will that do? Or are we expected to send along a minstrel to memorialize your heroic deeds for all posterity?"

"No minstrels," Bernard said.

"But I believe you mentioned horses," Cyindece added.

~~~~

Grumbling, Bertram led them down the central hall and then along a chilly back corridor into the northern side of the mansion. There, he dragged open a heavy wooden door in an archway to reveal a short connecting passageway that ended in a beaded curtain similar to the one separating the dining area from the guest rooms back at Aldric's inn. The curtain clicked and rustled in a cold, damp breeze scented with the aromas of straw and manure and animal sweat. The cranky bartender led them through this curtain and into a large stable. Bertram had not been joking about the goats; Bernard spotted them huddled in a stall near an open gate that faced the southern wing, which loomed across the open courtyard like the side of a becalmed ship. A couple of boys paused in the work of forking hay into their pen to give the group a curious glance, but perhaps put off by Bertram's scowl or Cynidece's feral grin, they asked no questions and quickly got back to work. Other small barnyard-type animals—dwarfish sheep, chickens, ducks and geese, a few miniature pigs—milled around loose or in enclosures in the space between the buildings. Only the waterfowl seemed to be enjoying the weather. Considering what Cynidece had said about horsemen, Bernard supposed there must be cattle and other large herd beasts somewhere, too, maybe out in the valleys behind the manor, tended by drenched and miserable wranglers. Aldric didn't strike Bernard as the ranching type, but perhaps he was a hands-off gentleman farmer as well as a hands-off fisherman. Bernard could picture him sitting on his patio enjoying a freshly-baked buttered scone while his employees tended to the crops and livestock. There *was* a patio at the back of the house, Bernard saw, sheltered beneath a second-story projecting verandah, with a little table and a few chairs, though in the current pall of weather no one was using it.

They came to where a small office stood, separated from the rest of the stable by a wall that, while half again as tall as Bernard, did not come close to reaching the ceiling. It had a door that could be closed and a window that could be shuttered, although at the moment both were flung wide. Within, a vastly broad fellow sat behind a desk, talking with a much narrower man, clad in the soaked black hood and garments of a highwayman, who stood near an inefficient-looking stove, holding out his hands over the metal surface in search of warmth. They both turned to look at the newcomers as Bertram brought them over, and Bernard realized that the reedy fellow was Aldric; his garment was in fact dark blue, and had only appeared black because it was soaked with water, but it had begun to dry out at the cuffs, showing its true color there. The innkeeper saw them and raised an eyebrow and opened his mouth to speak, but before he got any words out Bertram said, sounding even more annoyed than usual: "I told this lot you were not home, and yet here you sit chatting with Strond, and me ignorant as to your whereabouts. Nicely done."

"Ah, yes, well, I would have gotten here sooner, but there was an … incident in which I stumbled into a ditch and fell asleep for the better part of a day," Aldric said. "And it was quite warm in here, so I—"

Bertram made a clucking sound. "Drunk, were you?"

"Well, I could hardly face the death-wind sober, could I?"

"You hardly faced the death-wind at all," Cynidece said, earning herself an elbow from Mercy.

"When that *cat* of yours disappeared, I should have realized you had arrived," Bertram said. "She always knows when you are here, even if *some* of us are not informed."

"You know she hates it when you call her a cat," Aldric said. Then: "Where is she?"

"Who can keep up with that animal? I assumed she was in the kitchen stealing knives again."

"Cook threatened to stab the creature if it came into the kitchen one more time," the big man at the desk—Strond, apparently—said in a musing sort of voice, as if this were a puzzling attitude that he had been pondering for a while.

"Cook should know better than to try that, unless he wants to give her another piece of cutlery. Trouble is much too quick to be skewered by the likes of—oh, there she is." Just then a weight landed on Bernard's shoulder, tickling his cheek with a furry touch. Before he could react it had relieved him of his hat, and leapt off, its claws leaving tick marks in his leather shoulder pads. Bernard stared into the rafters as the monkey-cat creature fled with her swag, swinging off into the shadows. "You will never see *that* again, I'm afraid," Aldric said, watching his pet vanish into some distant corner of the big room. "But I am sure you did not come all this way just to bring Trouble a new toy. Since all of you are here, and *she* is back—" Here he indicated Mercy. "—I assume that after I, ah, left the city—"

"Fled the gate," Cynidece said.

"—some method of … of dealing with the death-wind presented itself?"

"Yes, it did," Mercy said. "Now we're on our way to take care of another problem, and we could use your help one more time."

"Blackhawk sent them," Bertram said. "We are admonished to give them supplies for their journey, in exchange for ... well, they brought a writ from him, anyway. I will not summarize it, you can read it yourself if you are of a mind. They asked about horses, which is why I brought them here, to see if we had any nags they might borrow, though I doubt that anything we lend them will ever be returned."

"Nags?" Strond was scandalized. "We keep no *nags* here!" To Aldric: "Your *bartender* knows nothing of horses, or what they—"

"Please, please." Aldric made a calming gesture with his hands. "I am sure Bertram meant no aspersion against the stable or those who manage it."

"I think he did," Strond said.

"His concern regarding the fate of any valuable livestock that we might loan to our associates is quite understandable." Aldric gave them a narrow look. "They do tend to get involved in risky situations."

"It's not always our fault," Mercy said after a moment.

Aldric chuckled, then glanced at the stableman. "Would you be so kind as to go to the kitchen and ask Cook for hot mulled wine? Our guests look nearly as cold as I feel."

"Getting rid of me now, is it? Secrets to discuss?" The fellow stood; he was even larger than he had appeared when sitting down, easily capable of picking Bertram up and breaking him in half, but he seemed back in a good humor. "And how long should I annoy Cook with my presence?"

"Mmm, long enough for him to prepare a new batch of wine, at least. Fresh bread would be welcome, too."

"Bread takes a long time to bake," Strond said. "I am not sure I can spend that long in Cook's presence without stuffing him into his own stove."

"He must have some baking already in the brick oven. That *is* what I pay him for, after all. Go and find out if he is doing his job, if you would."

With a grin and a wink at Mercy, the stableman departed, brushing past Bertram, who stood with arms folded by the door. "You had best not expect to dispose of *me* on some foolish errand as well," the little man said after Strond had gone.

"Of course not. Do shut the door and window, though. Perhaps we can get this draft-ridden room to retain some warmth." As Bertram moved to close up the office, Aldric dragged the stableman's chair from behind the desk and planted himself in it near the stove. Looking at Mercy, he said: "Is this journey taking you where I think it is?"

"I don't know. Where do you think we're going?"

"Well. To the Ravels, of course. You must have retrieved one of the gems in order to put down the death-wind, but if you had them both you would hardly be here in my stable carrying ominous paperwork from Arran Blackhawk." He looked at each of them in turn. "Am I wrong? You are planning to cross the Fists, yes? The mountains will not be kind to you at this time of year. I can give you supplies, but Bertram is not incorrect to suggest that any animals we lend you are likely never to see their stalls again."

"You have another idea?"

"Mmm. Consider. You sent yourself to the Ravels from my bathhouse, yes?"

"That was an accident."

"Can you not do that again, but on purpose, and for your entire group?"

"What, send *everybody* to the castle?"

Aldric looked at her as if she were being obtuse.

"I don't know how I did that," Mercy said. "It just sort of happened. And Kihantroh knew someone was there. The only reason I got away with the Illata was that there was some … interference covering me. That won't happen again."

"I see. Well, it is hardly my place to advise adventuresome sorts such as yourselves—" Here, Bertram coughed loudly. "—on what mode of travel they should employ, but even on horseback you will be lucky to get through the mountains in under a fortnight, if you get through at all."

"Giving Kihantroh plenty of time to find us, or to prepare for our arrival," Cynidece said.

"Exactly. And when you do reach the Ravels, hungry and exhausted from your journey—"

"Kihantroh will destroy us," Cynidece said.

"Mercy summoned a storm to put out the fire in Torgonderrer, with no time to prepare," Nebandalex said. "I would wager she can transport us across the leagues if she tries."

"Um. This is different from playing with the weather. I don't know if I can make a window and control it well enough for us to go through it safely," Mercy said. "I mean, I sent Kihantroh through one once, and then a bunch of dwarves, but …"

"But you just sent them away," Bernard said. "You weren't trying to get them to somewhere specific, and it didn't matter if they got there safely."

"No. But maybe I could target a location. I mean, I sort of did it already, with the Illata."

Bernard snorted. "Hey, get on this plane, and maybe you'll get to your destination in sort of one piece."

"Ha ha. That isn't helping." She trailed off, looking thoughtful, and Bernard realized she was starting to seriously consider the idea. "I would have to practice a little first."

"Practice a *lot*," Bernard said.

"If I aim for the village around the castle—"

"Then Kihantroh's big red intruder alert light starts flashing and the sirens go off and the flying monkeys come out."

Aldric said: "This enemy of yours has flying monkeys?"

"No, no, there's no flying monkeys," Mercy said. "That's just a figure of speech."

The innkeeper looked disappointed. Bertram, sounding alarmed, said, "If you find and adopt a winged version of that *cat*, Aldric, I swear I will quit."

"Forget I mentioned flying monkeys. The point is, there's no telling how far out from the castle would be safe to teleport into, is there?" Bernard said. "We know how powerful this guy is, not to mention sneaky. You told me Yexandor had a network of magic-detecting wards all around Torgonderrer and Kihantroh basically hacked them. Anyone who can do that, you can bet they can set up a serious monitoring system of their own. Maybe the entire *country* would be wired up."

"Not the entire country," Cynidece said. "Even with the gems, that is beyond anyone's ability."

"Why?"

"Because of the Æther."

They all looked at her.

Mercy said: "The what?"

~~~~

They moved from the office—which had finally begun to warm up—out into the entry area of the stable, because Cynidece wanted to draw pictures in the dirt.

The rest of them stood around and observed as, using a wooden peg, the Pelt sketched out the terrain of their present location in the highlands of the Slash, then the rolling plains of the Ravels, and finally the tall, blocky mountains that separated them. "We are in this area, more or less," she said, indicating the hilly region she had laid out to the east of the mountains. "It would take us at least two days to reach the Fists, and several more to cross them. This is if we were on decent riding horses, mind you, not farm horses such as they have here. Not calling them *nags*, your worship," she added, with a sidelong glance at Aldric, "just making clear they are not the sort of steeds accustomed to long hours of riding, especially through the mountains."

"Call them what you like," Aldric said, "at least until Strond gets back from the kitchen."

Cynidece snorted as if the stablemaster's pride in his animals were of no concern to her, which of course it wasn't. Resuming her travelogue, she said: "Coming down the other side, we would enter the eastern Ravels. Jordneh's castle is halfway across the plains, surrounded by watchtowers. They're for spotting funnel clouds, but any eyes Kihantroh might have put on them will certainly see us coming."

"You've been there?" Bernard asked.

"No, but I've been told about it. It's my business to know such things."

"Is that *business* what landed you out over the chasm in Abacar?"

She gave Mercy half a smile, but didn't answer. Turning back to her scribbled map, she said: "Now, at the southern end of the Ravels, we have the Æther. This is a region that was once ruled by a Rittandic sorceress named Untelleh, but something happened there centuries ago and now it is a cloudy void."

"A void?" Mercy said.

"Yes. Again, I have not seen it, but that is how it was described to me. The Rittandics, being analytical sorts, keep a station nearby to monitor the Æther, which apparently has been growing slowly since the ... incident, whatever it was. Now, none of this is a secret, exactly—how could it be, an ocean of clouds where there should be land and sea?—but neither is it something they shout from the castle walls. But this is whence the Ravels now gets its name. Because it is where the world unravels."

Mercy gave Bernard a sharp look. Here was evidence that what she had saying all along was, in fact, happening: The world was coming apart. She caught his gaze, and thought she saw understanding in his eyes, a comprehension that she was right. She hoped so anyway. It had been a while since he had talked about bailing out or asked to be sent home, but she was sure he continued to entertain the thought that this was an optional journey that she was indulging in for kicks.

"So you would have Mercy open a way for us into this Æther?" Nebandalex seemed dubious. "It sounds … unstable."

"Into it? No, we will not be jumping off *that* cliff. And yes, it is somewhat unstable, but that makes it unlikely to have detection wards around it. Waste of time and energy. Nobody can approach on foot from that direction, and you would have to be mad to try to open a window to a region that might not exist when you get there. Fortunately, we clearly are all a little bit mad. We need a place where we might arrive unnoticed, and the Æther is the obvious choice."

"It might be the obvious choice, but is it a good one? How can we be sure we won't end up in the void?"

"By making the trip in hops," Cynidece said. She jabbed her peg into a spot between a couple of small excrement piles, which she had previously identified as the pass through the Fists that they would use should they travel on foot. "There is a small mountain lodge here in the pass. It caters to travelers between the Ravels and the Slash. As it happens, I know the proprietor. His name is Grunsandrovar." She pointed the peg at Mercy. "If you can get us to the pass, we can reconnoiter from there. An overlook nearby commands a view of the Ravels from the mountains to the Æther. We can find a spot close to where the land ends but not so near that we are likely to fall in, and then our esteemed sorceress can transport us there."

"You're sure we can see the Æther from there? It's not too far away?"

"Grunsandrovar has an enchanted tube that lets him see long distances."

Bernard said: "What, like a telescope?"

"He does not call it that, but you can, if it pleases you."

"Why does an innkeeper need to see long distances? Is he looking for guests?"

Cynidece shrugged and gave Mercy that grin again. "He is in a good position to observe things on the far side of the Fists, and so he does. And if on occasion people visit him and would like to know what he has seen, he tells them. For a price."

"People."

"Yes."

"Like you?"

"There are very few people like me," she said. "But yes."

"What are you, some kind of spy?"

Cynidece laughed. "Of course I am," she said.

"Pelts are notorious spies and villains," Bertram said. "They have no country of their own and pledge fealty to no lord on either side of the mountains, so they survive by subterfuge and trickery."

"Some might put it that way." Cynidece had stopped laughing, and her voice had become rather brittle. "Others might put it that we have no country because it was taken from us long ago, and in the taking, we learned that loyalty paid to a lord is currency poorly spent."

"All right," Mercy said, jumping in to divert the conversation before Cynidece did something unpleasant to the little man. "So you're a spy, and this Grunsandrovar is one of your sources, is that it?"

"We provide each other with information. It is a mutually beneficial relationship, unlike *fealty* to some *lord*."

"Is Grunsandrovar a dwarf?" Bernard said. "That sounds like a dwarf name."

"He is, but he has no ties with those who rule in Dolvendelve, if such is your concern."

"Yeah, but other dwarves must stop by now and then to have little chats and compare hammers and stuff, right?"

"As do elves, humans, Pelts, and Rittandics."

"Still. We don't want the dwarves to find out where the Brisindeld is, so it's best he doesn't know what we've got with us."

"Very well." Cynidece gave Bertram a sidelong glance. "Not because he is a dwarf, but because too many needlessly know our business already."

"To that end, you cannot simply *appear* at the door of this Grunsandrovar's inn," Aldric said. "You must look the part of the exhausted traveler, or he will be suspicious. Perhaps you should use this ... ability ... we are discussing to arrive a few miles away, and walk from there. Get a bit of the road on you."

"Perhaps they should go now, while they are properly filthy and bedraggled," Bertram suggested.

"Ha ha," Mercy said. "No. I need a few days to work on opening and controlling windows. Aldric ... I hate to ask you for more help, but——"

"Yes, you can stay here while you practice," he said. "There are spare rooms in the servants' wing where you can sleep. I will leave word with the staff that you are not to be approached, but if any should wander by, try not to send them across the mountains or to the other side of the world. And please do remember that this is not my inn. The accommodations will be spare. The food will be simple.

There will be no minstrel to entertain you in the common room after dinner."

"That should suit them," Bertram said. "They have a prejudice against minstrels."

~~~~

Aldric seemed to have a rather lofty standard as to what constituted *spare accommodations*; the unoccupied quarters he put them in were larger and airier than the stuffy, closet-sized space to which they'd been consigned when Mercy was telling stories at his inn. Perhaps the beds were a bit thin, the sheets a bit rough, the furnishings worn here and threadbare there; but a roaring fire in the corner hearth quickly beat back the chill that seeped through the walls, and the crackling flames coupled with the steady thrum of rain outside made for a very cozy refuge from the winter storm. Add a fish tank and some books and she could stay on indefinitely as Aldric's house conjurer, Mercy thought, making sure no sheep got lost and no blight took the potatoes and the cream didn't spoil. But domestic wizardry wasn't what she was here to do. The information Cynidece had shared about the Æther and its consumption of the surrounding lands proved that she needed to finish the job, put the shards of the Heart back together, stop the Æther from spreading further and eating this entire world, and the one next to it, and so on, until there was nothing left.

No pressure.

She had managed to banish the Rittandic from Yexandor's fallen tree and to send the dwarves away when they had come to attack the elves, but in neither case had she attempted to reach a specific location; she had opened the windows in her imaginary attic to bring rain and extinguish the forest fire in Torgonderrer, but that had been a different sort of trick, creating a junction with herself in the middle. As for sending herself to the Ravels, well, that had been an accident. This jaunt they were contemplating had to land them in the right spot, at the right time, without sucking in everything around them the way the gate she'd used against the dwarves had started to do, and without dropping them into the Æther itself. And she needed to figure out how to practice doing it without sucking Aldric's entire mansion through an opening the size of a door.

Again, no pressure.

Aldric had assigned the rooms by gender, so she was bunking with Cynidece. It hadn't been a bonding experience so far. At the moment the Pelt was idling near the fire watching Mercy as she sat on the floor with a pillow—really, a sack filled with seed husks of some sort, not unlike the kind of rustic cushion found in the barracks of Colonial reenactment sites back home—and tried to induce it to travel from the floor in front of her back to the bed from which it had come. She had been trying to do this without relying on the power of the Illata, but it soon became obvious that she couldn't; she lacked both the power and the skill to open a portal on her own, and while she would have preferred to operate without having to use the gem as a crutch, saving the world was a big job, and if it required an external battery then so be it. She fetched the stone from its pouch and set it in her lap. Green threads swirled through the blue depths in eye-bending whorls and eddies, as if the essence of Daras-Drûm were the oil to the Illata's vinegar.

"It seems more active now than it was before."

Mercy glanced at the Pelt. "I'm not sure I should comment on that," Mercy said, "what with you being a notorious spy and all."

The woman laughed, then got up and moved to the cot from which Mercy had requisitioned her test subject. She sprawled across it, lying perpendicular to direction in which one was supposed to sleep, heedless of the fact that her own bed was on the other side of the room. "You do realize that you are focusing on the wrong thing?"

"What?"

"It seems to me, as a careful observer and notorious spy, that you are trying to induce the pillow itself to go from one place to another. But you told me you were going to open a trapdoor such that the pillow would fall through it. So stop targeting the object, and start targeting the door you wish to make."

Mercy stared at her. "Just what sort of spy are you?"

"The sort who can tell whence attention is directed. You have spent most of the afternoon staring at that pillow as if you hope it might speak to you. Believe me, it will not."

Mercy had, in fact, been concentrating on the pillow itself, trying to force it to jump from one spot to another and, to her immense irritation, Cynidece was completely correct; that wasn't really what she wanted. She wasn't trying to teleport something, she was trying to open a portal, which was an entirely different concept. Perhaps because of her earlier disastrous experiences with way-opening, she had been going about this experiment all wrong. "Yeah, well, maybe I'm staring *through* it, at the floor where I'm trying to open the portal," she said.

"Oh, of course. Clearly I was mistaken. Carry on, then."

Annoyed, Mercy fluffed the pillow, inasmuch as one could fluff a five-pound sack full of seeds. She glanced at the bed again. The Pelt still lay on her back, her head in the spot where the pillow had come from. Mercy ran her hands over the rough fabric of the cushion. She didn't look at it, just sort of measured it out with her fingers, how thick it was, how wide. She closed her eyes and, rather than imagining the pillow moving, imagined a trapdoor opening beneath it. That wasn't so hard to picture, was it? After all, she'd come and gone through a trapdoor in her attic room for years. This one would just move the opposite way, swinging down instead of up, and at the same time it opened here it would also open behind her, in the ceiling above the bed. The pillow would not end up in the room below them, but in a different spot in the same room it started from. It would—

The pillow fell away from her hands.

Mercy opened her eyes just as an iridescent ripple spread across the floor and faded, as if something had vanished beneath the surface of a puddle of oil. From the bed, Cynidece made a pleased sound; she sat up and retrieved the pillow from where it lay across her feet, brought it to the head of the bed, and set it back where it belonged.

"Well done," she said, "and I appreciate your not dropping it on my face."

~~~~

Dinner at Aldric's mansion took place in the late afternoon, in a room on the second floor of the main house, with a verandah that overlooked the broad, flat, alluvial valley stretching out behind the estate. The rain had tapered off as the daylight waned; the fog had begun to thin, revealing more of their host's holdings beyond the immediate courtyard and gardens. Standing at the railing of the elevated porch, Bernard could see a couple of separate paddocks for large animals that appeared to be of a bovine or ursine nature. A faint lowing was occasionally audible, drifting in when the winds favored it. Beyond those lay several discrete fields, separated from each other by low stone fences; then the cultivated areas gave way to scrubby woodlands surrounding a large outcropping of brownish-red rock. Dark, thin tendrils of smoke wafted from the vicinity of the outcropping, leading him to wonder if there were people camped out there, Aldric's cowboys, perhaps, guiding cattle to and from distant pastures beyond Bernard's sight.

It was chilly on the verandah, and Bernard was about to rejoin the others—just Aldric, Bertram, Mercy, and Nebandalex, for now, with Cynidece having mysteriously absented herself—inside, when he felt something settle onto his head. Surprised, he reached up, then found and removed his hat. He glanced to his right. Cynidece stood nearby, smirking at him. "I hope you didn't have to fight Trouble for this," he said, looking it over. There were a few small tooth marks in the leather brim, a few claw scratches, but the cloth and leather construction appeared otherwise unblemished after its theft.

"I know when I am overmatched. I tracked the little beast to her lair beneath the attic boards, and stole it back while she was elsewhere."

"Thanks," he said, wondering how Cynidece had managed to wriggle through whatever openings Trouble used to get into her hidey-hole, let alone how she had crawled through the rafters to reach it. He slipped it back onto his head. "How do I look?"

"Complete." She took his arm by the elbow and held it. "Why are you out here by yourself?"

"Just looking around. Getting some alone time." He pointed at the smoke rising from the distant rocks. "I something on fire?"

"No, that comes from the furnaces outside our host's gold mines."

"Aldric has gold mines?"

"His family is called *Goldshine* for a reason."

"And you know that because … you're a spy?"

Her eyes tracked the smoke. "No."

"Then how—"

"The first mines in this area were dug, long ago, by us Pelts. When we were decimated in the first necromantic war against Daras-Drûm, we lost our territory to the men of Abacar. There were too few of us left to hold it. Now, the only ownership we retain lies in the names of the Way and of the Downs."

Realization dawned. "*This* is the country that was taken from you?"

"Yes."

"And that's why you knew where Aldric lived? When you said you had tresp—"

"Probably best not to speak of that quite so loudly, with aught but an open door between us and him," Cynidece said. Then, in a softer voice than he'd ever heard her use before: "I have been involved in certain … *operations* … throughout this region. Including here."

"Stealing gold?"

"Is it stealing if you take back what is yours?"

"Um. Right. So that's how you wound up over the chasm?"

"Among other reasons."

"Are you … do you think we can get it back for you? Your land?

With the gem?"

Cynidece shrugged slightly. "I have no such expectation." She gave him a measured look. "But it seems to me that if I help you do something for your people, you might later be willing to help me do something for mine."

"Huh." He thought about that. "I'm surprised Blackhawk let you go, if he knows that's what you're thinking."

"He must know it; he is far from stupid. But executing me will hardly deter we Pelts from our goals." She grinned. "Perhaps the threat of the death-wind and the loss of the Maul unhinged him and made him foolishly merciful."

"Mmm. He didn't seem unhinged. Or merciful, actually."

"He is neither. Ah, dinner is served."

She said this just as Mercy poked her head out onto the verandah and said, "Bernard, the food's—" Her gaze moved to Cynidece, then to their linked arms, then back to Cynidece. "Where did *you* come from?"

"She, um, she brought me my hat."

"So I see. Well, come and eat, and then there'll be a demonstration." Mercy withdrew without waiting for a response.

Bernard glanced at Cynidece. "You didn't go through the dining room to get here?"

"What fun would that have been? I climbed down from the roof." Then: "Let us go eat, and see the show, and find out how much trouble you are in with your fair friend."

~~~~

After most of the food had been eaten and the plates cleared, it was time for Mercy to demonstrate what she had spent the day practicing. After all, she could hardly ask them to trust her to transport them across the miles before they had at least seen her move, say, a candlestick from one side of the table to the other without turning it into a sterling silver knot. Well, maybe not a candlestick; Aldric seemed reluctant to subject any of his candelabra or other finery to her skills, so a rather undercooked piece of meat—which no one but Cynidece had been interested in eating—was chosen as the unlucky victim. Sitting all fat and pink on a wooden carving board beside a bloody knife, it had no idea what was in store for it.

The others lined up against the wall behind her, as far away as they could get without actually leaving the room, and with a handy exit nearby in case there were any accidents. Mercy felt like a performer again, sort of like when Aldric had engaged her to tell stories in his inn, although this time she wouldn't be conjuring up any people and places from her imagination; this time she was playing the magician, not the bard, and she wasn't just doing tricks, not sawing a lady in half or pulling a rabbit from an empty hat or popping flowers out of her sleeve, abracadabra! No, she had to prove, to herself and to the friends who would be coming with her, that she could position a window with enough accuracy that no one going into the mountains would end up inside a boulder or off a cliff over a thousand feet of empty space.

Her plan was to transfer the meat from the plank on which it sat to an empty plate at the other end of the table, leaving behind both the cutting board and the knife. Achieving this goal would require a tiny trapdoor of exactly the right size to open, just for a second, underneath the meat but above the blade-scarred wood. It was not unlike sliding a sheet of paper between them, Mercy thought, although that was the wrong sort of analogy for what she was doing. No, she was inserting something zero atoms thick between them. Even that was wrong. The windows she hoped to open weren't *things* the way papers and doors were things; she needed to stop trying to equate them to physical objects if she was ever going to really get her head around this process.

The others were waiting for her to do something. She heard them breathing and shifting their weight, and one of them seemed to be humming a tune she had never heard before. "Okay," Mercy said. "Are you all ready for some hocus-pocus?"

Nobody answered, not that she really expected them to. She closed her eyes, keeping the image of the table in her mind: The place settings, the scattered silverware, the lace doilies beneath the candles; all of those things were going to stay right where they were, unaffected by the window. There would be no vacuum, no black hole effect; the rest of the contents of the room would not be sucked into the opening she was trying to make. This was just for the piece of meat. She could feel it when the trapdoor opened; the strings that underlay the room changed, sending a little shiver through the skin of reality. At almost the same moment, she heard Aldric hiss a warning and, wondering if he felt it the change as well, she opened her eyes, just in time to see the innkeeper's pet cat-thing bounding in through the door to the verandah, which had been left ajar. The creature leaped at the table, front legs extended, claws out, reaching for the piece of meat. It was too late to stop the doorway from opening; the crack was made, the split in the world was there, the meat was falling through it. Trouble sank her claws into the prize and went with it, both of them disappearing through a blank nothing. The last thing that Mercy saw before the gateway closed was Trouble's clever tail curling around the butt of the knife and pulling it after her.

Nothing landed on the target plate.

For a moment, no one spoke.

Then Bertram said, "Where is the cat?"

"Yes." Aldric looked at Mercy. "Where *is* the cat?"

Before she could answer, scuffling noises emanated from underneath the table; then Trouble scampered out from the shadows there, carrying the undercooked meat between her teeth, tail still wrapped around the handle of the blade. She bounded back out to the verandah and vanished with her prizes, scurrying up the wall outside, a white blur in the darkness.

"Well, the cat seems to have survived unharmed," Cynidece said, "but you missed the plate."

~~~~

After another day's practice, during which Mercy had gotten progressively more accurate with her short-hop portals, she decided she was ready for the real thing. The travelers, plus Aldric and Bertram, gathered on the ground-floor patio between the wings of Aldric's manor, in an area not visible from outside the property. The house employees had been given things to do that had taken all of them to other parts of the estate: The stable boys had been charged with rounding up escaped goats, while their master had been enlisted to help the groundskeeper repair the mysteriously-damaged fence through which the goats had fled; the gardeners were harvesting late-fall vegetables to be roasted for dinner; the oft-whispered-of but never-seen Cook remained in the kitchen with his helpers, preparing meat and bread for an end-of-season dinner party Aldric had decided to host for his distant neighbors. With most of the staff thus occupied and out of the way, only those who already knew what was going on would observe the unusual departure that was about to take place, or wonder why their four guests were all wearing heavy coats and mittens taken from the house's store of winter clothing, as if they would soon be someplace much colder than where they were now.

Aldric and Bertram stood well off to the side, just in case anything went wrong; Mercy and the others clustered together as she concentrated on opening a vertical doorway big enough for a person to pass through, connecting—she hoped—the courtyard with the far-off mountain trail that Cynidece was describing. Mercy had her eyes closed, the better to listen and concentrate as Cynidece spoke about the pass, how it looked, how one would get there from here, what landmarks were nearby. Never having seen their destination herself, Mercy relied on Cynidece's words to help her locate the place, sliding her mind along the strings that connected everything, searching for a topography that corresponded to what the woman was saying. The Fists in the area they were targeting, worn and rocky, offered any number of valleys and passes that *might* have been the one they sought; but Mercy couldn't be sure, and she didn't want to send them all to a spot where they would fall off a cliff or be trapped in an inaccessible canyon or set off a rockslide that would sweep them away. And so she kept looking, sending her mind wandering along mountain pathways and valleys, looking for the one that matched, that felt right. It didn't seem to be going very well. Every time she thought she had found it, Cynidece would say something negatory that made her realize it was the not the right place: The pass they were looking for was narrower than the one Mercy was inspecting, the road was steeper, the slopes were rockier, the trees were scrubbier. How Cynidece always managed to come up with a reason why Mercy was wrong just when she thought she had it, she had no idea. Finally, she opened her eyes in frustration and said, "Look, this isn't work—" She broke off because a shimmering curtain hung in space directly in front of her, as if someone had stretched a soap bubble across an invisible frame. A smear of colors came through it, whites and grays and browns, as if there were some scene beyond it, a blurred and unrecognizable whirl. "How long has *that* been there?"

"A while," Bernard said. "When it's blurry like that whatever is behind it changes, like it's moving around. Then it comes into focus, and—"

"And I tell you you have the wrong place," Cynidece said.

"—And then you move it again, and the next place is a closer match. But still wrong. Didn't you know you were doing it?"

"Um. No. I didn't. You said it's focused when it stops moving? Why is it still blurry now?"

"I think the appearance of movement is an illusion," Cynidece said. "It is your own attention that makes it focused or not. You stopped between targets this time, so it shows nothing coherent."

"Oh. That makes sense. Okay, hang on." Mercy concentrated and, slowly, the scene on the other side came into focus. It was a mountain valley, to be sure, but not one that seemed to be used by travelers passing through the range. A shallow, rocky creek bed ran through the left side, black water skinned with ice. The stream was edged with overhanging banks that the water had cut through the thin topsoil and rock; withered grasses hung down over the rubbled bed like hanks of unkempt hair. Beyond, dark pines shot into the vast blue sky. A mountain loomed over the scene, only partially visible behind the obscuring trees, its reddish-brown heights obscured with bands of dirty snow. It did look like a clenched hand; there was even a ridge along the side that could have been a thumb.

Cynidece leaned in and examined the scene. "I do not know this place either, but it is in the correct general area of the Fists," she said. "See how the summit curls on itself? That is typical of the mountains to the northeast of the pass where the inn is." She crouched down and looked upward, as if trying to see the sky through the window of a train. "Can you raise it up into the air? Grunsandrovar will have his hearth lit and we should be able to spot the smoke column. There will not be many fires burning in the Fists this time of year."

"I can try." Mercy concentrated on lifting the window away from the earth and into the sky, in order to reveal more of the surrounding area while retaining the clarity of the image. It responded sluggishly at first, as if overcoming some gravitational resistance, but then it began to rise at a steady rate. The stream and forest fell away, becoming a carpet of mottled green and brown and rust and white, the shallow creek a shimmering black ribbon snaking through it. Farther still, and the peaks themselves receded, the Firsts becoming a broad field of massive rugged boulders, the hands of a buried army. The others all watched the image in fascination, but none more intently than Cynidece; her gaze flickered all over the changing scene, searching for something she could identify. Finally she made an exclamation that prompted Mercy to freeze the window where it was. "Do you see it?" she said.

"I believe so." The Pelt moved closer and pointed at a tendril of grey smoke that rose to some little height before being caught by a wind off the high peaks and smeared into a thin, flat cloud. If she hadn't been able to trace it back to its origin in what looked like a rather distant valley, Mercy would have thought it was just another wisp of vapor scraped from the sky, like a thin curl of frost peeled off a window by a fingernail. "That is chimney smoke. Move closer to where it rises, then to your left, and we should find a spot where we can arrive on the road and walk the rest of the way to the inn."

Mercy nodded; the effort of speaking her previous short sentence had left her out of breath. Keeping the image sharp while moving it was much more taxing than sending pillows and small animals across a few yards; it almost felt as if she herself were at the altitude of the window, where oxygen was scant and warmth was absent. Her upper lip was wet again. She touched it with her tongue and tasted blood. Bernard stood nearby with a cloth, but seemed reluctant to approach her, or the portal. She could hardly blame him. The mountains scrolled by beneath the window as she moved it closer to the source of the smoke and the valley came into view. Barren and rocky, it hardly seemed habitable, although she supposed a dwarf might like it. There was the road, if one could call such a steep, narrow, cracked stretch of stone a road; devoid of traffic, it wound its way up from the lower slopes and ran along a cliff before leveling off through the high pass. She didn't see the inn itself at first. There was no building to speak of, no sharp-peaked alpine chalet or thick-walled redoubt; instead, there was a gigantic dragon's head carved into one of the peaks, an angry saurian face with a bony mask and a suggestion of horns curling back into the mountain. The smoke they had seen rose from a pair of cavernous upturned nostrils, the plumes twining together thanks to some twist of the wind. Mercy finally spotted it, carved into the cliff beneath the broad snout: A small door, a few tiny windows, some weathered stone posts for tying horses. As suited a dwarven proprietor, this inn was part of the mountain.

"I have never seen the dragon from this angle," Cynidece said. "It looks even more impressive from above."

"Your dwarf friend carved that?" Nebandalex said.

"No one knows who carved it," the Pelt said. "The fortress existed long before the dwarves occupied it and expanded the tunnels, and they abandoned it hundreds of years before Grunsandrovar arrived and turned it into a way-station. The dragon is not their work. It did give the place its name, though."

Bernard said: "Which is ... ?"

"The Draggin' Inn."

Aldric groaned. Cynidece, evidently pleased by this reaction, laughed. Then, to Mercy, she said: "The dragon-head is our destination, but Goldshine's suggestion about arriving tired and dirty was well-made. If you find us a spot on the road several miles down the slope, we can make sure to get there looking suitably bedraggled."

Still not trusting her voice to make an answer, Mercy allowed the viewport to crash down to the level of the mountain, choosing a location below the level of the inn where the road made a hairpin turn through a boulder-choked defile. She gave the window a quick spin to make sure they weren't going to step through, turn around, and find an astonished-looking mountain troll about to club them with a tree trunk. It looked clear, with nothing but a bit of rubble, frozen mud, spindly leafless bracken, and pockets of crystalline white glimmering from the shadows.

Okay. Now the screen had to change from something they looked at to something they could walk through.

She fell back on her earlier analogizing. Maybe this was a door after all, the kind that opened sideways into a wall. Maybe it had a lock at the bottom and a recessed handle in the middle. She pictured herself releasing the lock, putting her finger into the handle, and sliding it into its pocket until it disappeared. An icy wind began to blow out of the opening, carrying the odor of mud and stone and a few small, hard flakes of dry mountain snow. They skittered across the patio flagstones like harbingers of winter. Aldric and Bertram took a cautious step back, but the others stayed where they were.

"Me first," Cynidece said, heading for the portal. She put first one arm through the opening, then another, and then, with a little laugh, hopped through. On the other side, she turned and looked back at them. "A moment of dizziness, nothing more," she called, her voice oddly attenuated, as if the portal, though without thickness, nonetheless required the sound to travel some great distance in order to reach them.

"Hurry now," Mercy said, wondering if she sounded as strained to the others as she did to herself. "Everyone go, then I'll follow and close it."

"Good luck," Aldric said, as Nebandalex went through and Bernard followed. Not trusting her voice at this point, Mercy turned and gave Aldric a final smile and a wave farewell. She moved forward. A blast of cold air from the other side staggered her as she stepped through. She felt the brief vertigo the Pelt had mentioned, as if her brain thought she was falling; then she stumbled out onto the frozen mountain path, landing on her hands and knees. She rolled over and stood. As she prepared to close the portal, something else came through it, a small grey and white blur; Trouble bounded up onto Bernard's shoulders, snatched the hat off his head, and leapt away again, carrying her prize through the window and back to Aldric's estate. The panel shrank in on itself and vanished, closing off their egress to the lowlands.

After a moment, Cynidece said: "My apologies, Bernard, but the cat has won the day."

FIRST INTERLUDE

HIGH ROAD,
LOW ROAD

Chapter 6

BERNARD LAY DOWN his quarterstaff, stepping on it to keep it from rolling away while he fastened up the double set of loops and buttons that held the front of it shut against the wind. The garment consisted of alternating layers of a wool-like material and linen, with some sort of soft fur on the inside to trap body heat and wick moisture. The hood was lined with the same fur, downy and smooth against his ears and cheeks as he cinched it up. Lobster claw mittens were stuffed into the large pockets. He pulled those on, then picked up his staff; the loops that held it to his back were part of his leather jerkin, which was now covered, so while wearing the coat he had to carry his weapon in the awkward pincer grip of his primitive gloves. He was grateful to Aldric for giving them a place to stay and providing the warm clothing that shielded them from the cold, but couldn't quite ignore an unwonted irritation that the innkeeper's pet creature had ultimately won the Battle of the Hat. It wasn't even really *his* hat, it was Brannoc's, so why should he care about it?

He looked around at the others. Nebandalex was just checking his bow to make sure it was secured to his quiver, no doubt anticipating being assaulted by the wind that howled overhead. Cynidece had vanished already, scouting up the trail ahead, he supposed. Mercy stood off to the side, wiping blood from her nose and chin, leaving a smear on the back of her gloves. They were made of fabric, and, Bernard thought, didn't look as warm as the ones he wore. He moved over to her and said, "Do you want to trade mittens?"

She raised an eyebrow, shook her head, and held up one of her hands, apparently to illustrate how much smaller they were than his.

"Oh. Right. Of course. They wouldn't fit." Then: "Are you ... okay to walk?"

She nodded. Her lips and chin were smeared with blood; it was obvious to Bernard that using the Illata was causing those nosebleeds, and who-knew-what other unseen damage. Now that the Illata had merged with the death-wind it seemed to have an even more nefarious effect, as if Daras-Drûm were still trying to claim the life-force of the one who had imprisoned it. She had to know this already, and wouldn't care to have it pointed out, so he didn't say anything. Perhaps the blood on her face could be offered to Cynidece's dwarven friend as a symptom of altitude sickness, further evidence of their long, arduous journey through the mountains.

"The air is pretty thin up here. When you need to take a break, just say so, okay?"

"I'll be fine," she said in a tight voice. "Let's just go."

Well, he knew she *wouldn't* be fine if she kept pushing herself, and so did she, but he also knew she didn't want him babying her or trying to clean her up or calling attention the fact that she was harming herself with the magic she was using. He would just have to count on her to say when she needed a rest. He went to Nebandalex. "Are you ready?"

The elf raised his hood and tied the straps around his neck. "I am now," he said.

The three of them walked up the narrow pass and around the hairpin, and soon emerged onto an unprotected section of trail. As Bernard had expected, the wind immediately blasted them with staggering force, blowing crossways from a gap in the high peaks to their right. It was even stronger than he'd thought and he wedged his quarterstaff into the ground to catch his balance. Some way in the distance ahead of them, the smear of smoke from their destination spread across the sky, a streak of muddy blackish-brown scraped across the dazzling pale blue of the sky. From here it was much more obviously the output of a fire than it had been when viewed from Mercy's floating window. This must be a welcome sight to the exhausted traveler who had slogged his way up from the plains far below. Grunsandrovar probably charged an extortionate rate for rooms and warmth, and for the first time Bernard wondered what Cynidece was going to offer in exchange for his help. Certainly not money, as she had none of that. Information, then. But about what?

The Pelt stood several yards beyond the end of the defile, seemingly oblivious to the gale, peering up the road. It ran along the top of a steeply-angled ridge, exposed in all directions until it curved to the right and entered the shelter of an overhanging palisade. To either side of the cracked and listing surface, crumbling slopes fell away to the tops of scruffy pines below. He moved up to stand next to her, wondering how she stayed so stable in the shifting, arctic blasts. "This looks familiar, right? This is the road we wanted?"

"Oh, yes. I have been this way many times. Usually it takes much longer to get here from down there."

She kept glancing at the forests below. Bernard said: "Are you looking for something?"

"More than one top-heavy wagon has been overturned by the sudden wind when coming out of the fat man's misery back there. The mountain Pelts like to scavenge along the bottoms of the roadside cliffs, especially after storms or rock slides. They have no reason to be down there now, but I was just having a look."

"Mountain Pelts. Are those friends of yours? Cousins?"

"They know who I am," she said.

That was an interesting and rather tart answer. He looked over his shoulder at the hairpin turns. "Back home, we would blast through those rocks with explosives to straighten out the road."

"*Explosives*," Cynidece said, trying out the word. "Is that some category of magic?"

"You might say that."

"Well, blasting through *these* rocks is likely to result in a collapse. The Fists are old, and crumbly around the edges."

"We have … ah, *magic* … for handling that, too."

"What a wondrous land you must come from," Cynidece said, smirking. "But since we do not have such enchantments available to us, we will refrain from damaging the landscape, and we will stay in the middle of the trail until we get past the ridge."

With the Pelt's advice in mind, they walked single-file, first Cynidece, then Bernard, then Mercy, with Nebandalex bringing up the rear. Bernard found himself continuing to use the quarterstaff as a sort of combination brace and walking stick. Brannoc would never have approved. The shelter of the cliff wall turned out to be farther away than it looked, of course, and the road steeper; the sharp ascent and the thin air had him short of breath before they'd made even half the distance. Mercy had to be about ready to pass out, he thought, but she didn't call for a rest. Maybe she was trying to prove something. As the path began to curve to the right, a gap in two distant, lower mountains came into view, exposing the lowlands of the Slash far below. Although largely hidden by clouds that rolled beneath their current altitude, the green-grey plains were visible here and there, stretching off to the east. He wondered if, on a clear day, one would be able to see all the way back to Aldric's mansion, or even beyond that, to Abacar and the sea. It must be quite a view for those who were inclined to stop and enjoy it.

At last they put the higher slope between themselves and the wind, greatly reducing the buffeting they had been taking. Nebandalex called for a rest at once. Bernard glanced back and saw that he was helping Mercy walk, her arm over his shoulder, his arm around her waist. She was red-faced and breathing hard and Bernard felt a sudden burst of shame that he had not been the one to assist her. He took a step toward them but his help was not required; Nebandalex lowered Mercy to the ground, where she leaned back against the rock wall to catch her breath, then stood over her protectively, as if challenging the wind to try to get at her. Bernard looked a question at the elf, who said: "I asked her, but she would not stop out there in the wind. Too exposed."

"Will she be all right?" Cynidece said. Then, to Mercy: "Would you like me to carry you? Because I can."

"Just need to rest," Mercy said. "Can get moving again … soon. Stupid … low … constitution score."

"Low what?"

"It's a good thing you didn't land us any farther away than you did or you would never make it," Bernard said, not wanting to have to explain what she meant by a constitution score. This earned him a glare, and he realized that she thought he was criticizing her. As he tried to figure out a good way to explain that he hadn't meant to denigrate her portal-opening skills, Cynidece pushed past him, stripped off her gloves, and knelt to examine Mercy. The Pelt pulled down her cheeks to check her eyes, pinched her skin and studied the marks left behind, felt the flesh at her throat. Mercy muttered a weak protest, but didn't offer any resistance.

Looking concerned, Cynidece stood and pulled Bernard aside. "She is showing signs of the mountain sickness."

"She … what? Mountain sickness?"

"Yes. She will not make it to the inn. Not today, certainly not on foot. Nor is it advisable for me to sling her over my shoulder in this condition. She needs to rest and stay warm."

"Rest and … but we can't spend the night here. There's no shelter, it's too cold—"

"Of course, of course. Calm yourself. We are hardly the first to run into this manner of trouble on our way up the mountain. Grunsandrovar keeps a litter for such occasions. You and I will go to the inn and fetch it back here, put her in it, and ferry her to safety." Then, when he didn't reply immediately: "We wanted to make it look as if we had had a hard journey. We have succeeded."

Bernard nodded, then turned to Nebandalex, who crouched beside Mercy. "You heard that, Lex?"

"Yes. I will wait with Mercy for you to return, and keep her as warm as possible."

"Come along, Bernard!" Cynidece called. Fast and silent as a ninja, she was already well ahead of him up the path. "The day is not getting any brighter, nor the air any warmer!"

Leaving the elves behind on the desolate trail, he hurried to catch up with the Pelt.

~~~~

The jagged rock wall of the cliff jabbed into Mercy's back like dull knives; every inhalation of icy air freeze-dried her lungs a little more; the inside of her head felt as if a blender were running at high speed, pureeing her brain. She just wanted to go back to her attic room and crawl under the covers and wait for someone to appear with a bowl of hot soup or a cup of juice. She tried to get up but couldn't; something was holding her down. It took her a moment to realize that this was Nebandalex, restraining her with an arm across her collarbone.

"Do not try to get up again," he said. "You can hardly stand. The last time, you nearly fell off the mountain."

Oh, yes, she remembered that now: She had lurched to her feet and stumbled forward, and Nebandalex had half-tackled her to stop her from going over the edge. She had fallen back and hit the rock pretty hard. Maybe that was why she felt so banged up. She settled back, looked around, realized someone was missing. "Where's Bernard?"

"He and Cynidece went to get help from the inn, remember?" She did, as soon as he said it. "You must rest and wait for them."

She nodded, hugged herself, and tried to remember what she had done to get to this point. Opening the window, moving it around, then the instant transition from the lowland plains to near the summit of the Fists … it had been too much. She had pushed herself too hard. The air was too thin. Maybe if she descended to a lower altitude, she would feel better. She tried to get up again, and again, Nebandalex stopped her. "Insisting on standing is only going to make you feel worse," he said. "Sit. Rest. The others will be here soon."

"Cold," she said.

"Yes, I know." Nebandalex drew her in closer, shielded her from the wind. She leaned into the elf. Even through his coat she picked up some of his body heat, but not enough. Where was her blanket? Oh, right. It was in her room, in the attic, in her house, in another world. The wind just kept knifing across the cliff face from different directions, not letting her forget that her room and her bed and her blankets and anyone who might bring her soup were all far, far away. "This journey was ill-starred," Nebandalex said. "Once we had located the spot, you should have rested another day at Aldric's estate before attempting bringing us to it."

"No time."

"What good is saved time if you kill yourself before you can spend it?"

She grunted and stared out across the sprawling vista of the Fists running off into the distance. Innumerable chimneys of rock with weathered, bulbous tops rose from the slopes near almost every summit, the entire range seemingly ready to punch at the sky. So strange. The hands of buried titans. Was it getting dark already? It was only afternoon, wasn't it? Then she realized the light wasn't fading, she had just started to close her eyes a little. Maybe she was falling asleep. Would sleeping be bad? Nebandalex had told her she should rest. Sleep was rest, wasn't it?

Movement jostled her awake and she realized she was on her back, looking up at a rocky overhang as it scrolled by. She tried to sit up, but couldn't. She seemed to be lashed down to something; even her head was restrained, preventing her from lifting it or turning it to either side, just like in Torgonderrer after the Rittandic—disguised as the elf, Shelliyan, Nebandalex's mate—had abducted her and tied her up. Had it returned and tied her up again? Why not just kill her? Maybe it hoped to pry the secrets of the using the Illata out of her mind, but then, what had it done to Nebandalex? She began to squirm and struggle, trying to free herself, but the restraints were too tight.

"You see? This is why I tell you to use straps!" someone said. "You say no, but now you know I was right!" Low and rumbly, the unfamiliar voice reminded her of the voice of the dwarf who had attended the audience at Korrin's castle. Had the dwarves somehow tracked her to the mountains and captured her? Did they have the Brisindeld? She kept wriggling. Whatever she was tied to shifted a little.

"Mercy. You must be calm." Nebandalex's voice this time. It came from the direction of her feet. "Lay still."

"It's us." Bernard's voice. "We're carrying you to the inn on a stretcher. You're belted in so you don't fall out."

"She is disoriented because of the mountain sickness." A female voice, familiar, but less so than the other two. "It happens up here sometimes. She will recover in a few days, once she rests and gets used to the thin air."

"She will?" Bernard's voice, near her head.

"Yes. Well, or she will die. But we are well below the height where people die." Pause. "Usually."

"Of course she will not die!" That was the new, rumbly voice again, scandalized and booming. "Travelers do not die of mountain sickness while under my care!"

"Of course not," Cynidece said. "No one has more experience treating the effects of altitude than you do, Grunsandrovar."

"No, they do not," Grunsandrovar said, mollified.

So that was Cynidece's friend, the dwarven innkeeper with all the information. It sounded like he was up ahead, leading the way. She finally understood what must be going on: Bernard and Cynidece had returned with the stretcher and the dwarf, and they'd loaded her into it while she was unconscious. She suddenly remembered the Illata. She felt it at her side, tucked away into one of her packs; Nebandalex would have made sure it wasn't visible when the dwarf came around, right? He was smart enough to do that, wasn't he?

She couldn't seem to stay awake to worry about it. She was so very, very tired.

The sky darkened again, and she slept.

~~~~

Mercy opened her eyes. Something smelled delicious.

She lay in a small, dark room—smaller and darker, even, than her attic hideaway back home—on a narrow, lumpy bed, beneath a rough sheet and an even rougher blanket. Her head rested on a pillow that felt like it was full of gravel. She sat up slowly, half-expecting her skull to detach and float away, but it didn't. The air was warm and smoky; a fire burned low in a stove very close to the bed, glowing red through four narrow vertical vents in the iron door. A thin gruel of smoke leaked into the room, but most of it went up through a crooked chimney into the ceiling. If the place had had a fire alarm or carbon monoxide detector, it would probably be chirping its head off.

The bed seemed to be an extension of the stone wall, a ledge left behind when the rock had been chipped away. She turned so that she was sitting on the edge, trying to blink away the graininess in her eyes. Her nose and mouth felt very dry. A stone pitcher full of water sat on a nightstand, within easy reach. She grabbed it, sniffed its contents, and then drained it. The water had a light skin of dust, but tasted wonderful. When she put the pitcher down she noticed that the nightstand was of a piece with the floor; even the stove, she now realized, was part of the rock, except for the grille through which it could be stocked with wood.

She was still thirsty. Mercy picked up the pitcher and stood, stopping just before cracking her head on the very low ceiling. This room obviously wasn't scaled for anyone taller than a dwarf. Stooped like a dowager, she shuffled to the small door, opened it, and stepped out into the much larger room beyond, where she could straighten up. Though much taller and wider than the cell she had left, it was almost as dark, and not nearly as warm. It contained a number of tables, most of which were shoved up against the outside wall, with chairs stacked on top of them and tablecloths wedged like chinking into the gaps. It reminded Mercy of the school cafeteria when the staff was getting out the buffers and the floor wax.

At one of the few tables that hadn't been moved aside, Bernard and Nebandalex sat, eating out of dull stone bowls. Or rather, *not* eating; they had both stopped to stare at her, Bernard with his bowl up near his mouth, tipped as if about to drink from it. Something dripped from its lip to spatter onto the table in front of him.

"Is that dinner?" She followed her nose to the table. "Can I have some? I'm really hungry."

"This is breakfast," Nebandalex said.

"This is the *third* breakfast we've had here," Bernard added, "so of course you're hungry." He put his bowl down and slid it around to an empty space. She sat in front of it, picked it up, and smelled the thick porridge inside. This was not the source of the odor that had penetrated her consciousness as she slept in the small room; apparently something else was cooking. The bowl was heavy, and trembled in her hands. "You might want to start eating slowly, so you don't get—"

"Screw that," she said, taking one huge mouthful, then another. The stuff had the consistency of hot cereal from a packet, flavored with something sweet, like honey. Eyeing Bernard's mug, she said: "Water?"

"Uh-huh." He slid that over to her too.

After she drained the mug, she looked around at what was obviously the dwarf's inn, trying to get a feel for their new surroundings. The room was wide and low, essentially a half-circular slot chiseled right into the mountainside, which would protect it from the storms and cold temperatures outside but deprived it of natural light. Only the front wall had any windows, and they were shuttered against the chill mountain wind, then blocked by the piled tables and chairs. Three thick stone columns had been left standing in a triangular pattern around the room. Each one was inset with a much larger version of the stove that had heated the closet in which she had awakened. Two were lit, the other dark. The back wall was perforated by a couple of openings onto corridors that ran off into black depths, perhaps to storehouses and guest rooms. There were a few other doors like the one she had come through, thick planks bound by black metal, ranging in size from squat and dwarf-sized up to tall and narrow. One door broke the pattern of wooden construction, being made entirely of iron. Maybe that went to the dungeon.

"It's a lot like being in Dolvendelve," Bernard said as she eyed the place. "Took me a while to stop thinking I would get clubbed over the head when I wasn't looking, but Cynidece's dwarf friend seems okay so far."

"Mmm. Where are they? Cynidece and her friend?"

"There." Nebandalex pointed at the iron door. "The kitchen. Apparently she helps him cook when she is here."

"The place is so empty. Does Grunsandrovar stay here by himself the whole winter? I would lose my mind."

"As I understand it, the dwarf is on good terms with some Pelts who live in the mountains nearby, who stop in occasionally regardless of the season," Nebandalex said. "I believe that is how Cynidece originally made his acquaintance."

"She's from around here, then?"

"Well, not originally, but she gets around," Bernard said.

"I'll bet she does," Mercy said, without thinking, earning a reproachful look from Bernard. "Sorry, that just slipped out."

"Considering we wouldn't be here if not for her, I'll expect you to start being nicer to her as of today."

"I know, I know. Sorry. I'm being catty."

"Yes, you are. I mean, if she hadn't led me here to get a stretcher so we could bring you back, you'd be——"

"I *said* I was sorry. So was that like the hospital room I was in?"

"It's Grunandrovar's room, actually Smallest one at the inn, hence the warmest."

"Bernard has spent a great deal of time in there with you," Nebandalex said. "He came out for breakfast shortly before you emerged."

Good old Bernard. "So the iron door goes to the kitchen?"

"Yeah, even though it looks like it goes to a cell block." Bernard eyed it warily. "Maybe it did, once."

"Well," Mercy said, picking up her empty bowl and standing, "I think I'll go meet our replacement Aldric, thank him for his hospitality, thank Cynidece for saving my bacon, and get some more food."

"Wait, I can do it——"

"I'm fine, Bernard. I've been lying down for three days, I need to move around a little." As she tottered off, she heard Bernard trying to explain to Nebandalex what *bacon* was, and why it might need saving.

~~~~

The iron door to the kitchen was every bit as heavy as it looked; Mercy had to brace herself against the wall and push with her legs to haul it open, and when it finally begrudged to move, it screeched its displeasure for all to hear. The room beyond was dim and close, illuminated by firelight emanating from a long, curved hearth—mostly cold at the moment, with only the central fire pit burning beneath a steaming iron pot—on the back wall. Stone countertops with cabinets beneath, all of it carved out of the surrounding rock, lined every foot of wall that wasn't a fireplace or a door. Cynidece stood off to the right, a largish skinned animal in one hand and a sharp knife in the other, with a small pile of bones in front of her. The counter was sized to be comfortably used by a dwarf, and only came up to about Cynidece's calves; she had evidently been deboning the animal in mid-air, which said something frightening about her skill with a blade. At a nearby dry sink, their dwarven host stood, chopping vegetables with a cleaver that might have been stolen from a cartoon butcher. He had skin the color and texture of light sandstone and shaggy hair the dark brown of thick, rich river mud. It ran like fur along the backs of his bare arms to his wrists, interrupted by a number of what appeared to be old burn scars, as if he had caught fire more than once. Both of them stopped what they had been doing to turn and watch the door squeak its way open.

"Why are you exerting yourself like that?" Cynidece said, as Mercy put her back into pushing the door the rest of the way open. "Get one of the men to help you."

"I can ... do ... it." Mercy turned and leaned against the door, panting. It was fighting her, trying to swing shut on its own. She couldn't see any self-closing mechanism but it obviously had one. "Why is ... this ... so hard to open?"

"Is not easy to keep iron hinges greased here!" The dwarf evidently considered booming to be a normal conversational tone. "Dry air, lots of dust, and not much oil."

Mercy certainly couldn't argue with any of those points, although from what Bernard had told her about Dolvendelve, she would've expected a certain level of engineering know-how from Grunsandrovar, such as how to keep doors working smoothly. She braced her feet against the floor, finally in control of the situation, and said: "I wanted to thank both of you. For getting me here and taking care of me."

Cynidece gave her a little nod of acknowledgment; the dwarf said,

"Any friend of the little stone is a friend of mine!"

"Little stone?"

The Pelt chuckled. "He means me," she said, "even though I'm not so little anymore."

"You two go way back, eh?"

The dwarf looked puzzled. "Way back where?"

"Um. Nowhere. It just means you've known each other a long time."

"Oh. Then yes! A long time! Since the little stone was smaller than me!"

Mercy wondered how long that was, exactly. She proffered the empty bowl. "Is there anything in that cauldron besides water?"

"Not yet. We make soup for lunch, but the little stone takes her time cleaning the meat!"

"Soup should only have game in it, not any of the cook's fingers," Cynidece said. To Mercy: "Leave the bowl. We will put a bit more porridge on for you."

"Okay. Thanks." Mercy put it on a nearby counter, which she could reach without giving up her post at the door; Grunsandrovar picked it up and took it over to one of the idle fire pits of the hearth, where he knelt down and set about stacking kindling beneath a small pot that hung from an iron hook. Cynidece went back to deboning the giant squirrel or whatever it was. Mercy watched the activity for a little while, until Cynidece shooed her out, exhorting her to go and sit and rest and catch up with the others and wait for her porridge to be delivered. Finding herself thus dismissed, Mercy stepped back; the eager door happily closed, sequestering the dwarf and Pelt once more.

She spotted a water jug and a few mugs on a wooden stand nearby. She took a cup, filled it, drained it, filled it again, and brought it back to the table where the others sat.

Bernard said: "No porridge?"

"Not yet," she said. "It'll be ready after they're done with their secret meeting."

~~~~

It wasn't long before Grunsandrovar pushed the kitchen door open—even the little bulldozer really had to put his shoulder into the task—and held it so that Cynidece could bring out a tray laden with steaming bowls. Bernard had seen this ritual repeated at every mealtime since they'd arrived, but thinking about Mercy's theory of why the door was so hard to open, it didn't seem as innocently amusing anymore. Surely a *dwarf*, of all people, would be able to keep a door greased and silent if he really wanted to. Mercy had suggested the noise and difficulty involved in opening this one was intentional, as a way to give those in the kitchen time to stop whispering and resume whatever chores they were supposed to be doing. For all he knew, Grunsandrovar could throw a switch somewhere and then the door would open smooth as butter. So if Mercy was right, and the reason for the door's obstinacy was to keep things private, what might they be discussing in there? Had Cynidece told Grunsandrovar about the Illata? What if the innkeeper had some way to get a message to Filothandiar, who wanted the gem back so badly he had tried to burn down the elven forest to get it? They were nowhere near the burrows of Dolvendelve, as far as he knew, but then again these mountains were no doubt riddled with old tunnels, and who was to say the dwarves didn't have some crazy steam-powered underground rapid transit system?

Bernard shook his head. He was being paranoid. Still, it wouldn't hurt to have a look around later, and make sure there weren't any secret ways into the inn by which they might be taken by surprise again, like in Abacar.

Cynidece set the tray down on the table and wriggled herself onto the bench next to Bernard, while the dwarf went back into the kitchen. The door screeched shut behind him. Mercy, half-starved, immediately started eating. Cynidece watched her for a moment, then said: "Grunsandrovar tells me that he had two envoys here several weeks ago. They were on some secret mission from Abacar. One went south toward Dolvendelve, the other went east into the Ravels."

Bernard and Nebandalex had already heard about this, but of course Mercy had been unconscious at the time. "How does he know they were envoys if their mission was a secret?" she asked.

Cynidece raised an eyebrow.

"Okay, never mind," Mercy said. "So, um, yeah. Lord Korrin was looking for help against Banderlund. The dwarves ... well, they didn't react the way he hoped they would." She glanced at the kitchen door. "The reason they stepped up their campaign to get the Illata back was because they thought Banderlund would be invading, and they wanted to shut themselves up under the mountain with the gem. By then they knew Kihantroh had double-crossed them."

"Well, Banderlund *will* be invading, so the dwarves were not wrong about that. According to Grunsandrovar, the 'Lundi are currently engaged in a seagoing blockade of Chasm Bay. The season for seaborne commerce is over, but they intend to make sure it does not start up again in the spring. And to answer your next question, Grunsandrovar knows this because our friend Bernard is not the only Banderlundi wandering around these parts, and is far from the most knowledgeable one."

"Everyone keeps calling me a Banderlundi," Bernard said. "I've never even *been* to Banderlund."

"Mmm. You have missed very little. Cold, rocky, barren, snowbound land, I am told." She looked around. "Rather like this place, in fact."

"So did you tell Grunsandrovar where we're going?"

"In general terms. He would find out anyway, after all, and I had to answer some questions before he would agree to lend me his spyglass."

Mercy looked doubtful. "*In general terms.* I see." Then: "You didn't mention our ... cargo, right?"

Cynidece bent forward and said, in an utterly serious tone, "Oh, yes, of course I did, because I am simply *that* incapable of keeping a secret. No, he knows nothing of what you carry, but I had to tell him *something*. He did not know that Lord Korrin had been murdered nor that the death-wind had nearly escaped nor that Arran Blackhawk is now Lord Arran, so those were valuable pieces of information I could share. I left him with the impression that you lot were dispatched to the Ravels by the remaining Blackhawk to find out what happened to Jordneh, why all of her enchantments collapsed. I adjusted the time frame of these momentous events to make it seem reasonable that we could have traveled here by conventional means." To Mercy: "Your mountain sickness helped to make the story believable, so well-played there." Mercy grunted. "Eventually Grunsandrovar will discover that my tale was not *wholly* accurate, and I will have to account for myself, but that will not occur during *this* visit."

Mercy said: "If Grunsandrovar knows as much as you say he does, he can't possibly believe Blackhawk would send *you* out as an agent of Abacar."

Cynidece laughed. "Not even I would be able to convince him of that! I myself still find it rather difficult to credit. No, I told him that I met you three along the Peltish Way, and offered my services as a guide in exchange for a small payment, and that my *true* intention is to spy on you and discover if you can somehow be of service to the Pettish cause."

"*Is* that your true intention?"

She grinned. "Of course it is. Among other things. Now the

question is, when will Mercy be ready for the next stage of our trip?'"

"Not today," she said. "Tomorrow, I think."

"Don't push it," Bernard said. "You nearly killed yourself getting us here."

"The next jump should be easier. We're going to a lower altitude so I won't have that to deal with a steep climb through thin air after we arrive. And from what I hear we'll be able to see where we're going, so I won't have to play satellite camera, right, Cynidece?"

"I do not know what a *satellite camera* is," the Pelt said after a moment, "but I will say no, because that seems to be the answer you are expecting."

~~~~

By that afternoon, Mercy felt well enough to take Bernard and do a little exploring of the inn and its environs; still concerned about a surprise visit from more dwarves, he wanted to search for secret doors, and she wanted to work out some of the soreness in her muscles and help clear the fog from her brain. Not wanting to spend her energy trying to craft a illumination glamour, Mercy begged a lantern off their host. Grunsandrovar, seemingly amused by the prospect of their spelunking into the depths of his inn, provided one, but made her promise not to set anything on fire. Cynidece, sitting with the dwarf in the common room at the table where they had all breakfasted earlier, watched them debate which tunnel to enter first. She projected the air of a half-bored spectator observing a frivolous polar expedition as it prepared to depart, and finally said: "Those are two ends of a loop. It matters not which you pick, you will still end up back here. Take that one." She pointed to the left.

The matter thus decided, they went through the opening on the left, heading into the mountain. No natural light penetrated to this depth; unlit lanterns hung from regularly-spaced iron hooks in the low ceiling. They threw weird shadows along the walls. The tunnel quickly ramified into a warren of guest rooms and storage areas. Once the maze-like nature of the area became apparent, Mercy shifted into her standard labyrinth-exploration mode, keeping one hand on the surface to her right to ensure they visited every accessible location within the burrow. They entered and exited vacant accommodations, storerooms full of hard bread and dried meat and root vegetables, low arched vaults jammed with redolent kegs of ale and casks of wine, alcoves piled high with well-seasoned wood, and, eventually, a wide dead-end where the tunnel became rough and dark and unfinished before terminating against a wall of black stone flecked with sparkling bits of mineral. An ancient-looking pick was embedded in the rock, as if whoever had originally been chipping away at the stone had left mid-shift and never returned.

Bernard eyed the pick with suspicion, as if it were a lurking monster that might attack them. "What's *this* doing here?"

"It's probably stuck," Mercy said. "That looks like seriously hard rock."

Bernard made a dubious noise, then tried moving the tool in various ways: Up, down, left, right. He pushed it and pulled it and tried to turn it. It didn't budge in any direction. Mercy stood nearby, watching and tapping her foot, and finally said: "Come on, Bernard. Do you really think a secret door would have such an obvious handle?"

He looked at her, his face slightly flushed. "It might."

"Even if it *is* a secret door, what do you think is behind it? Grunsandrovar's treasure vault? A secret communications room where he sends broadcasts to the other dwarves?"

"Maybe."

"Uh-huh, sure. Come on, let's get going."

"In a minute."

Now he was hanging onto the handle, both feet off the floor and braced against the wall, trying to pull it out with leg power. If it popped loose he was likely to fall on his head; if the wall suddenly pivoted, he was likely to go around with it. But neither thing happened. The pick just stayed stuck in the wall like a pick that was stuck in a wall.

At length, Mercy said: "Fun as that looks, I'm tired. Give it up. Let's get back and sit down a while."

"Okay." Bernard returned his feet to the floor and gave the pick one last mighty tug; despite his effort, the putative secret door continued failing to open. Keeping one hand on the wall to her right, Mercy led the way out of the rat's nest of tunnels, eventually returning them to the common room via the other doorway, just as Cynidece had predicted. She and the dwarf still sat at the same table, chatting and drinking what smelled like stale beer. The dwarf was chewing on a gnarled black thing that might have been a root or might have been beef jerky.

"Are you two done exploring?" Cynidece said as they approached.

"Yes. There are a lot of tunnels back there."

"And a lot of storerooms full of stuff," Bernard added.

Cynidece laughed. "What were you expecting? An empty cave? It takes a lot of supplies to get through a winter up here."

Bernard said: "What's the deal with the pick in the wall at the end? Did you leave that there?"

Grunsandrovar snorted. "You go all the way back to *that*? Ha! Many years ago I come along, see opportunity, chase away bears, clean tunnels out, fix them up, turn fort into inn. I find pick then, and I cannot get it out of wall. Pick will still be there long after you and I and the little stone are all dead. It will probably be there until mountain falls down!"

"So there's no secret door back there?"

The dwarf shook his head. "If you can find secret door or get pick out of wall, you are more clever than me and the little stone and all the guests who ever tried to move it!"

This wasn't exactly a denial, which Bernard would realize if he thought about it for more than a second, so Mercy changed the subject. "Where's Nebandalex? In his room?"

"No, he went out hunting." Cynidece sounded like she didn't quite believe it even as she said it.

"Hunting? Ha! What he expects to catch? Anything worth eating is flown away or gone to lower valleys or asleep in a cave for the winter. Why you think storerooms are full of dried meat? Because I *like* eating leather? Bah! But trust elves to waste time, since they have so much of it, eh?" The dwarf gave Mercy a broad grin, fireplug teeth visible between his bushy beard and mustache. "Say, elf, you all live so long, why you make silly houses out of wood and leaves up in trees like bird nests? You should live in caves like dwarves do. Caves last forever!"

She had to smile at the innkeeper's good-natured bluster. "Elves like to be outside. Maybe he just wanted to enjoy the fresh mountain air."

Grunsandrovar blinked in disbelief, then burst out laughing, the sound like rocks being shaken in a metal drum. "Fresh mountain air? What kind of talk is that? Is not fresh, is *frozen*! Give me smoke and fire to warm the heart, not *fresh mountain air* that hurts to breathe!" He looked at Cynidece. "Get the litter ready, little stone. We will soon need to carry another elf back in and revive him!"

Cynidece gave the dwarf a swat on the shoulder, but that just made him laugh even harder.

~~~~

Bernard was still thinking about the pick at the end of the hallway when the front door opened and Nebandalex entered. The elf swept over to the table and sat down, bringing with him a strong odor of wood smoke, as if he had been hanging around too close to a bonfire.

His eyes looked red and irritated. Grunsandrovar would approve. "Ribbit," he said.

"You don't have to say the password every time we see you," Mercy said.

"I thought that was the entire reason it existed, as a code to be given when we are reunited after an absence."

"Well, it is, but——"

"Then I will keep saying it."

"How was the hunting? Why do you smell like smoke?" Bernard said. Then: "Where's your bow?"

"In my room."

"How can you hunt without your bow?"

"I *do* know how to set snares. Why waste an arrow by shooting it at some vanishing rodent so that it breaks on the rock of the mountain?" Nebandalex sent his hand into the table, spreading his fingers on impact, in mimicry of a projectile shattering.

"Okay, so, did you snare anything, then?"

"No. I was not really hunting." Mercy stifled an amused snort. "I have seen nothing furred or feathered in these mountains that I would even consider eating; I just wanted time out from under the weight of all this stone. Are the others in the kitchen?"

"Uh-huh. They're making soup or something. Why, are you hungry?"

"Did you tell Cynidece we would be leaving on the morrow?"

"Um, yes, I said I thought I'd be strong enough to travel soon," Mercy said. "What's with all the questions?"

"I had climbed up to sit on the nose of the dragon sculpture and noticed voices emanating from within, so I decided to explore its interior."

Bernard said, "That thing is hollow? How did you get in?"

"The eye on the left contains a recessed ladder. The inn's fireplaces and ovens vent into the dragon's head and then out the nostrils, which is why I smell like smoke. The space within contains a pile of brushes and scrubbers for cleaning out the chimneys." Back to Mercy: "Inside, I stumbled across a spot where I could hear the others speaking in the kitchen. They were discussing our impending departure."

"Mmm. I see." Mercy gave Bernard a glance. "What were they talking about, exactly?"

"The dwarf wanted to come with us to ensure that his spyglass would not be stolen by Bernard——"

"It's *your* fault everyone thinks I'm a thief," Bernard muttered to Mercy, who shushed him.

"—But Cynidece indicated that she would leave it in some prearranged location. He tried to induce her to tell him why he could not accompany us, but she refused to say. Grunsandrovar was not pleased, but eventually agreed. I am not entirely sure how she persuaded him, as I could not make out all her words. The dwarf's voice carried much better than did hers. She must have promised him something of great value, though. Information, most likely. Evidently the spyglass is an item of considerable rarity and value, and not easily replaced."

"I bet," Mercy said. "Back home you can get them at any department store, but I'm surprised they even exist here."

Bernard shrugged. "The dwarves have artillery and flintlocks and gaslight and elevators. Why not telescopes?"

"They did not use that word, *telescope*," Nebandalex said.

"A telescope is the same thing as a spyglass," Mercy told him. Then, to Bernard: "It can't be easy to get hold of decent window glass here, let alone lenses. It's not like they have optical grinders."

"They wouldn't need those," Bernard said. "Think about it. They have *magic* here. Someone could just, like, *conjure* lenses if they wanted to, right? It's just a matter of knowing what pieces you need and how to put them together. The dwarves are smart enough to figure that out."

"Huh," Mercy said after a moment.

"Sorry to bend the rules of your fantasy land by introducing science," Bernard said.

"The device is of Rittandic provenance, so if this *science* of which you speak exists, it would appear to reside with them, not with the dwarves."

"Well, whoever made it, we'll go to this lookout Cynidece knows about and use the spyglass to pick a target spot close to the Æther, and then she can leave it wherever she wants." She flashed a mischievous grin. "With all of us watching, Bernard won't get the chance to steal it."

"Don't sell a rogue short," Bernard said.

~~~~

Morning. They were supposed to be leaving today, but peering out the front door at the horizontally driven snow, Mercy wasn't sure things were going to proceed according to schedule. She pulled her coat a little tighter and stepped away from the front door. The broad overhang of the draconian snout loomed above her head like a porch roof, providing a little protection from the windblown spindrift. It was already accumulating in dry, sloping heaps against the ruddy stones and the scant, gnarled scrub, lining the delicate, skeletal branches with white. She moved farther out, onto the mountainous track that brought Grunsandrovar his trade. Looking in the direction of Abacar meant putting her face into the wind and being blasted by tiny pellets; she could see them coming at her, a swarm of stinging dots obscuring anything beyond the first few dozen yards. Turning toward the Ravels, icy niblets peppered her neck, and the wind blew her platinum hair out in front of her face like a flag of surrender. She could see a little farther this way, simply because the squall didn't force her to close her eyes, but unless this storm ended or they were going to a spot that was below it, she didn't think they were going to be able to see the Æther, no matter how marvelous Grunsandrovar's telescope was. She lacked the energy for more reconnaissance. What would happen if she just took a chance and opened a portal blindly? Where would they end up?

"What are you doing out there?"

Startled, she glanced at the door. Cynidece leaned against the frame, holding a rather battered-looking metal tube. This, Mercy realized, must be the fabled spyglass. Moving closer to the door, into the lee of a mounded rock that had been carved into the shape of a claw for the dragon, she said: "Checking out the weather. This isn't going to work. Can we expect the snow to—"

"You underestimate the Rittandics," Cynidece said. She proffered the telescope. "Here. Try it."

"Um, okay." Mercy took the device. She had vaguely expected some sort of pirate-movie style spyglass, but this was just an uniform cylinder about as big around as a rolling pin. One end was inset with a smoothly curved glass lens, while the other sported a small protuberance ending in a polished wooden eyecup. Mercy glanced at Cynidece, who nodded. She lifted the tube and put her eye to the cup. It seemed to be designed for a much larger eye than hers, but the edge was rubbery and somehow conformed itself to her face, blocking out external light. She aimed the spyglass toward the west. She couldn't make out anything beyond the drifting sheets of grey. "I just see a lot of snow," she said.

"There is a knob on the side," Cyndice said. "No, the other side. Yes, that one. Turn it slowly."

Mercy did as instructed. The obscuring precipitation faded from view, leaving the distant mountaintops clearly visible. Mercy took the scope away from her eye and looked at it with a vastly increased sense of respect. "Wow," she said. "I bet the astronomers back home would kill to get their hands on something like this."

"I am told the Rittandics use these to look at the stars, or some such silly purpose, and they don't want things like clouds getting in the way." She shrugged. "If these *astronomers* you speak of share that useless interest in the sky then I am sure you are right. The only reason I can think of to look at the stars is for navigating at sea, and I do not sail. Goldshine and I have that much in common."

"What else can it see through? Can it see through rocks?" She turned the knob further; the clouds beyond the mountains fuzzed into obscurity and vanished, then faded back in, followed by the snow.

Cynidece snorted. "*Rocks?* Why would it be able to see through rocks?   The Rittandics do not make their observations from underground."   She held out her hand.   "If you please? Grunsandrovar was quite specific that it must remain in my possession except when in use. He fears Bernard will steal it and perhaps trade it for a new hat."

Mercy gave the telescope to the Pelt, then followed her into the dim warmth of the inn. Grunsandrovar stood near the door to the kitchen, squat and stony and watching the door intently. "Demonstration successful?" the dwarf said.

"Quite," Cynidece said.

"You sure you must go during storm? Paths slippery."

"We will be fine, Grun, really."

"Ha! Of course you will. But if you fall off cliff, try not to take spyglass with you."

"I think we'll just try not to fall off any cliffs," Mercy said.

~~~~

Their final breakfast at The Draggin' Inn wasn't very different from their first one, or at least, the first one that Mercy remembered. She was anxious to get going and paid hardly any attention to the meal or how it had been prepared or how it tasted, and really, as long as it wasn't poisoned or drugged, porridge was porridge.

Once the food had been eaten and the bowls had been cleared, the four travelers gathered just inside the front door, bundled up in their mismatched fur-lined coats. In addition to their original supplies, Cynidece had prevailed upon the dwarf to raid his wintertime cache of hard cheese and dried meat and sturdy bread, so each of them now carried a small snack-bag as if being sent off on a day trip from school.

Mercy only half-listened as Grunsandrovar once again admonished them that if the paths were too treacherous they should turn back, that if they didn't turn back they should be very careful not to cause a rockslide or fall off a precipice, and that if they *did* fall off a precipice they should make sure to hurl the spyglass to safety or he would be very, very disappointed. The Pelt carried it in a protective wooden tube strapped to her back, a setup not unlike Nebandalex's quiver with the arrows taken out; it didn't look like it would be easy to remove, so if they *did* suffer a mishap, Mercy was pretty sure the spyglass was going to be involved no matter how many times Grunsandrovar exhorted them against it.

Impatient and warm, Mercy shifted from one foot to the other and back again. The Illata, wrapped in a rag in a voluminous interior pocket of the coat, shifted with her, concealed beneath the bulky outer garment. She had never suspected that years of smuggling bags of cheap drugstore candy into winter movie matinees would translate to a useful skill. At last, with the final goodbyes out of the way, they exited to face the icy, howling wind. Hoods up, heads down, they trudged west along a slight incline, the lingering warmth of The Draggin' Inn soon erased by the driving squall; the scent of wood smoke faded like a memory of autumn bonfires. After some considerable distance winding through the pass and scrambling around rockfalls, Cynidece guided them onto a narrow trail leading to the southwest that began in the cleft of an arrowhead-shaped boulder. Withered grey brambles scratched at the opening, reminding Mercy of the ravine in Torgonderrer through which Glorian and Meliander had led her to the elven village after rescuing her from those trackless woodlands. As they moved farther from the main road—such as it was—Mercy began to realize why Grunsandrover had been so concerned about their safety, or rather, the safety of his precious telescope. This new trail was much narrower than the one they had left, and soon became a cliffside thread high above a valley whose depths were obscured by mist and precipitation. They stayed close to the rock wall that rose to the left, although Mercy couldn't stop herself from peering over the edge from time to time. There was never anything to see down there, just icy fog and billowing snow and the occasional shadowed hint of trees. Eventually the trail turned a corner and leveled off at a broad shelf of splintered rock and frosted scrub. The mountain interposed itself between them and the wind, providing a small area of relative calm, though powerful cross-gusts continued to buffet them at unpredictable intervals. The trail proceeded up and around the rocky shoulder on its way to wherever it went, but Cynidece took a spur, moving them out toward the edge of the shelf. Mercy could barely see the mountain range dwindling off to the west, and although anything down below remained out of view, she got the general sense that they stood above a vast open area. Somewhere beyond the grey and white lay the grassy lowland where the Rittandics lived; somewhere out there was the castle to which she had been drawn, and to which she now had to return.

At the very edge of the outcropping stood a boulder that resembled a broken tooth. Cynidece, typically unmindful of personal peril, clambered onto it and stood with her feet braced against the crenellated crown of the rock. She removed the telescope from its case and held it up to her eye, sweeping it back and forth, finally stopping with the metal tube aimed off to the far left. The Pelt motioned Mercy forward; she approached warily, the others shuffling along behind, and stopped at the boulder. Cynidece impatiently gestured for her to climb up. Mercy, flummoxed by this request, examined the boulder with no idea how to scale it with her mittens and heavy coat, and not much more idea how to scale it without them. Bernard and Nebandalex ended up giving her a boost while Cynidece reached down to pull her by the wrists, helping her to gain the top. Cynidece kept a steadying arm around her shoulders, which was reassuring; the splintered ridge of stone around the depression stood barely knee-high, tall enough to trip over but nowhere near adequate to stop a tumble down the slope below. It was, at least, less than vertical, and seemed to consist of ancient, snow-covered scree. A tumble down it might be survivable, though it wouldn't be pleasant.

"Look there," Cyndice said, handing Mercy the telescope and gesturing into the fog with her free hand. Mercy aimed the device in the indicated direction, looked through the eyepiece, and adjusted the knob until the obscuring weather faded and their surroundings were revealed. The view was much as she had expected: A series of lower peaks spread out into the distance, followed by foothills, then a broad basin of grey-green grass and occasional clumps of trees. Off to the south, the mountain range terminated as if sliced with a knife; where the peaks ended, one might have expected to spot the blue sparkle of the sea, but instead there was a low, frothy, whitish simmer, as if someone had dumped a vast quantity of dry ice into the ocean and left it to boil forever as a witch's giant cauldron. Mercy swept the telescope back and forth along what she supposed might be considered the coastline of the Æther. Unlike the northern portion of the Ravels, it had a brown, arid character, with little vegetation other than low, gnarled trees and bracken. At this distance it looked like the foggy void was trying to grow a scruffy beard.

Something on the top of a tall, barren hill caught her attention. Wreckage? She stopped, backed up, and dialed it in for a better look. It seemed as if there had once been a small complex there, recently destroyed; the strewn debris and splintered timbers looked fresh, not yet deteriorated by sun and wind. What had it been? An old lighthouse? "There," she said, handing the scope back to Cynidece. "The timbers and stuff. What was that?"

The Pelt put the spyglass to her eye and moved it around a bit. "Perhaps the monitoring post, where the Rittandics keep an eye on the Æther. Or used to, anyway. Grunsandrovar did not mention it had been destroyed, so it must have happened quite recently." She lowered the telescope. "That would be a good place for us to land. A road from there will take us north to Jordneh's castle. Can you open a gateway to that spot?"

"I think so, but I don't want to step out of a window and get smashed by whatever wrecked the place."

"There are no monstrous beasts rampaging through the Ravels stomping on buildings. I suspect your sorcerer friend is responsible."

"Why would it do that?"

Cynidece shrugged. "You tell me."

"Mmm. No idea. Do you think it's still watching the area?"

"No. Nothing comes out of the Æther. There is no reason for it to expect a threat from that direction."

"Um. Well, I guess the plan is the plan. Let's do it."

"All right." Cynidece held out a gloved hand; Mercy handed her the spyglass, which she put back into the case. Then she jumped off the boulder, heedless of the slippery rock, and trudged back toward the cliff face, leaving Mercy alone on the broken tooth of stone with Bernard and Nebandalex peering up at her. She hunkered down, afraid of being blown away, and called: "Hang on! Where are you going? Do you want me to wait for—"

"I am going to put this where Grunsandrovar will know to look for it," the Pelt shouted, neither turning nor breaking stride. "You get started with the hocus-pocus. I will return in time to go through with you."

Mercy watched her go, then looked down at the others. "Well, you heard her. It's time to get started on the hocus-pocus. Help a girl down?" She sat on the crumbled edge of the rock and slid off; Bernard caught one of her arms, Nebandalex the other, and together they lowered her the rest of the way. She settled into the lee of the boulder and pulled off one mitten, then fished the Illata out of the depths of her coat and held it in front of her, savoring its delicious warmth. She closed her eyes and concentrated, remembering the scene she had just viewed through the lens: The hilltop, the surrounding scruffy trees, the smear of debris across the grass, the roil of the Æther beyond. She wanted to deposit them in the center of the ring of bush-like vegetation, near but not, of course, *in* the heap of debris. The portal opened quickly this time. That had been surprisingly easy, almost as if something had guided the creation of the portal to its destination. She opened her eyes and there it was, a tall, slender rectangle just to her right, angled toward the Ravels, through which she could see the hill that was their destination and, beyond that, the Æther, thick as treacle. The others stood nearby gawking at it, as if they hadn't quite believed she would really be able to do it again.

"Well, go on," Mercy said. "I can't keep this thing open forever."

"But … Cynidece isn't …" Bernard shifted his quarterstaff from one hand to the other, glanced uneasily in the direction the Pelt had gone. "We can't just leave you here *alone*."

"Well, one of you go, at least, and check out the other side."

They exchanged a glance. Neither wanted to be the one to leave her; or maybe neither wanted to be the test pilot for the jaunt from the mountains to the far-off edge of the world. Maybe she should just go through it herself. That'd show them. A strange sense of possibility came over her, or of expectation, the sort of unsettled, anticipatory, slightly anxious feeling she got just before they left on a family trip, or near the beginning of summer. She *could* go through it herself. It would carry her to any place she wanted, to any time. It would—

"Mercy," Bernard said.

A warning tone in his voice brought her back from idle thoughts of escape. She realized at once what concerned him: The snow in front of the window had begun to drift toward the opening, moving against the wind, like the dirt and mud in Torgonderrer had done when she'd lost control of the portal she'd used to remove the dwarves from the forest. She looked again at the shimmering portal. Beyond the hill and the scrubby trees of the Ravels, the vapor of the Æther stirred and frothed and swelled like rising dough. She didn't think that was normal. Was it responding to the presence of the gateway?

"Something is wrong," Mercy said.

"What's it doing?"

"It's—" Suddenly Mercy felt the portal shifting and warping like thin metal flexing under pressure. It distended and curved, the bottom part vanishing into the snow and rock of the promontory on which they stood. She had opened the door too soon; she had left it open too long; the Æther wanted to flow through it. "The Æther is … it's doing something to my portal," she said. "Cynidece was wrong. We can't do this. I have to close it."

As if summoned by the sound of her name, Cynidece materialized from the lashing squall, running toward them. "The ledge is coming apart!" she shouted. Mercy heard a cracking *boom* and felt a shudder run through the stone under her feet. The surface tilted and slammed her into the side of the broken boulder as the outcropping splintered into several massive, jagged pieces, each tipping in a different direction. Bernard went one way, Nebandalex another, separated from each other and from Mercy by a series of rapidly widening cracks. They goggled at her, seeming to react in slow motion, as if the Æther had reached through the portal to bend and warp time itself.

Cynidece leaped over a crevice even as it opened under her feet. "Go through, go now, or fall!" she cried as she landed next to Bernard. She grabbed him by the arm and flung him at the window. He twisted into a distorted funhouse mirror shape just before he passed through and vanished. Cynidece lunged for Nebandalex, stretching herself impossibly far, but not far enough. The elf vanished into the mists of the lower valley as the sled-like chunk of rock to which he clung plowed a furrow through the snow and scree. With an animal hiss Cynidece launched herself at Mercy, flying toward the toppling crumb of the mountain where she cowered. An iron grip caught her by the wrist and Cynidece's momentum carried them both through the portsl. She felt like a horrible, wrenching, burning lurch, as if she were a rag being wrung out after an acid bath. Her concentration shattered. She screamed, even while some dim, deep part of her managed to slam the window shut behind them.

A moment later she and Cynidece tumbled to a stop near Bernard's feet, on an arid, sandy hilltop in the quiet of the Ravels.

PART TWO

THE RAVELS

Chapter 7

BERNARD GAVE MERCY a sidelong glance; she stood nearby, leaning against *Cynidece*, of all people, which gave him some idea of just how badly things had gone back there in the mountains. Mercy, battered and snuffling, wiped bloody dust and snow away from her face as Cynidece explained what had happened, what she had seen with those glamour-sensitive eyes of hers. Mercy had lost control of the portal, she said, which had warped into a torus; that was why going through it had felt like being spun on a spindle. She had not been able to save Nebandalex before the misshapen gateway had torn the mountainside to pieces; as the elf was absent, Bernard had figured out that unfortunate fact on his own. When Cynidece ran out of things to say, and Mercy could stand on her own again, Bernard asked a question that he thought had an obvious answer. "So ... We're going back to get him, right?"

Mercy made a choking noise, then said: "I can't. I can't do that again." She sounded stuffy, as if she were fighting a bad cold. "I can't. Not now. Maybe not ever."

"But ..." Bernard trailed off, then slipped off his fur overcoat, shook it out, and slung it over his shoulder, as much to give himself a moment to think as because of the autumn warmth, which felt summer-hot after the alpine frigidity they had left behind. "We can't just *leave* him there." He turned to Cynidece. "You said he was riding on top of a piece of rock. He could still be alive."

"He could be."

"He could be *hurt*."

"Yes, he could be, but the spot where we stood in the mountains is gone. There is nowhere for Mercy to send us back to. She would have to scry a new location, and I doubt she would survive the attempt. With the Æther so close, creating a portal would be dangerous, and leaving it open long enough to find a safe spot to land would be suicidal. We dare not make the attempt."

Bernard rubbed the back of his head, wondering how risky an endeavor had to be for Cynidece to label it *suicidal*.

"I know they seem desolate, but the Fists are not completely uninhabited," the Pelt said, in a softer tone of voice, as if trying to soothe a pet after thoughtlessly scolding it. "Grunsandrovar will be going to collect the spyglass. There are mountain Pelts in the area. Either may find him."

"But nobody is going to be looking for him." To Mercy: "Can't you at least open a window back to where we were, so we can see if he's there?"

"We have to be realistic about——"

"Are you *seriously* going to lecture me about being realistic?"

Mercy shook her head, sending blood flying from her nose, leaving ruddy dots across the amber sand. "Okay. Listen. I know you're upset, but even if I *could* open another window right now without killing myself—which I can't—the Æther ..." She shook herself, as if trying to throw off a lingering chill. "Like Cynidece said, the Æther is too close. I would ... I would lose control again. This time the Æther might just flow right through and into the mountains. I wouldn't be able to stop it. It might rip the whole planet apart."

"Rip the *planet* apart? You can't think ..." He didn't finish; he could tell she did, she really thought it could happen. "But we can't just *leave* him there. He wouldn't do that to us."

"I know." She ran a hand through her hair, which still managed to give off a platinum shine despite being filthy with sand and grit. "But he wouldn't want us killing ourselves trying to get him. He sure wouldn't want us to, you know, destroy the world. It just ... it won't work."

"Okay, what if we look for him after we get away from the Æther? Then it wouldn't——"

Mercy was shaking her head. "The whole reason we landed here was so the interference from the Æther would hide the portal from Kihantroh. If I open one up out there in the plains, it'll be like sending up a flare."

"So we can't rescue him here because we're too *close* to the Æther, and we can't rescue him later because we'll be too *far* from the Æther. Great."

"I'm sorry, Bernard. That's the way it has to be. Nebandalex would accept it."

"He probably would," Bernard said, "but that doesn't mean *I* do."

"Someone lived through this," Cynidece said.

Bernard glanced her way; she had moved off to the side while he and Mercy were talking, and now stood near the line of withered chaparral, bent over something. "What?"

"The destruction of the post. At least one of the monitors survived it. Probably a male. And a female was killed."

The two of them stared at her for a moment; then Mercy said: "And you know this how?"

The Pelt indicated a spot in the scraggly trees. Bernard eyed the location and spotted what looked like a wooden pendant on a leather thong dangling from one of the branches nearby, like a dull Christmas ornament hung on a shabby tree. As he went over to check it out, Mercy said, "Couldn't that have just landed there when the place was destroyed?"

"It could have," Cynidece said. "If it did, someone tampered with it afterwards. But I think it was placed here deliberately."

"How can you tell that from—careful, Bernard! It might be booby-trapped."

Bernard, who had been reaching out to take the pendant off the shrub, stopped and looked back at her. "Booby-trapped how?"

She cocked her head and raised a dirty platinum eyebrow.

"Oh. Right. Magic." He backed off, eyeing the thing warily.

"It is unlikely to be trapped, considering what it is and where we are," Cynidece said, "but still. Use your staff."

That seemed like a good idea. Bernard stepped back and lifted the pendant off the grabby branches with his quarterstaff. It didn't explode. He tilted the staff, but the amulet's strap wouldn't slide along the leather cord wound along its length, so he swung it around and held it out for Cynidece to inspect, as if it were a fish he had taken from a pond and he wasn't sure if it was over the size limit or not. Cynidece, apparently no longer concerned about traps, took it off and examined it. Mercy and Bernard joined her. The strap was made of soft leather dyed blue, while the tag was a flat oval of wood, polished but badly scratched on one side. The other side was inlaid with tiny multicolored beads set in a double helix pattern, originating from two larger stones at the top, with variegated marquetry connecting them. The helix came together in a large, empty socket at the bottom.

"Holy crap," Bernard said. "Mercy, that looks like DNA."

"I know." To Cynidece: "What *is* this thing, exactly?"

"This is an adornment worn by a female Rittandic who is with child. See the empty spot at the bottom? When the child was born, another stone of an appropriate color for its bloodline and gender would be added there to complete it, and the pendant would be saved and given to the child when it became an adult."

"With child? It *is* DNA. How would these Rittandics know about—"

"Not now, Bernard. Cynidece, how does all that add up to someone surviving this—" Mercy gestured at the wreckage all around them. "—and hanging it up on purpose afterwards? It could have gotten into that tree a dozen different ways."

Cynidece turned the tag over in her hand so that the scratched side was showing. "This rune is freshly cut. It says the owner of the necklace died by violence, and …" She hesitated. "No, not *died*. Was lost. Yes, was lost by violence. The Rittandic woman who wore this must have been killed when the station was destroyed, and her mate could not find the body. But he did find the pendant, so he inscribed the rune and hung it up as a memorial."

Mercy looked at the amulet for a long time, then said: "Okay. Then where is he now?"

"Perhaps *you* should be the one to answer that," Cynidece said, handing her the pendant.

~~~~

Mercy eyed the amulet. "Me? Why me?"

"Work a glamour," Cynidece said. "Read its history to find the one who scratched the runes."

"Um. Yeah. My last glamour didn't turn out so well, did it?"

"This will be different. Just a small spell, a peek into the recent past. Can you do that much, without raising the ire of the Æther?"

"I don't know. Maybe." She had done something similar with the arrow back in Abacar, but she couldn't afford to lose control like she had with the gateway. She wasn't sure what would happen if she lost control of an object reading glamour—maybe it would give her all the information about each atom of which the item consisted, and turn her brain to mush—so if she was going to do this, it had to be as narrow and as specific as she could make it. "The stones," she said, letting the amulet sway in her grip. "Who places them, the mother or the father?"

"They both do."

"But you're sure the father scratched the rune?"

"Yes. Reasonably."

"Reasonably. All right." Mercy closed her eyes and asked the pendant to point toward the one who had made the mark on its unembellished side. For a few seconds nothing happened; then the strings that linked the amulet to that individual began to tighten, drawing the pendant in a certain direction. She opened her eyes. The pendant no longer hung straight down. Instead, it pulled forward and to the left, like a pendulum frozen in mid-swing.

It had worked.

She looked a question at the others. "We are in need of allies," Cynidece said; Bernard only shrugged. Noting no objections, Mercy allowed the gentle tug of the pendant to lead her to a break in the scrubby trees, where a path led down the slope toward a dry wash below. The others fell in behind her with reassuring solidarity, but still, she felt Nebandalex's absence. No arrows would be flying over her shoulder at any pop-up threats. He had sat with her on the icy, narrow road through the mountains when she had been too sick to move. He wouldn't have abandoned them if there were any alternative, Bernard wasn't wrong about that; and even though she knew they had no way of getting back to the mountains, she still felt like a heel for leaving him there. Bernard wasn't wrong about that, either.

They soon reached the bottom of the sandy slope. It ended in a dry stream bed; water had once flowed here, though obviously not in the recent past. The pendant pulled her toward a bend in the ravine, where an overhanging bank loomed against the pallid sky and the sandy, pebbled earth lay in shadow. On the end of its tether, the wooden charm stretched toward the undercut, where soil and stones clogged what might have once been an opening. She glanced at the others. "I think he's in there."

Bernard said: "Buried?"

"I guess."

"Alive?"

"I don't know."

Bernard loosed his quarterstaff and poked at the sloping debris. "It's not packed very tight. Can we dig it out?"

"Yes." Cynidece knelt in front of the plug, thrust her hands into the loose soil, and began to excavate, her hands and arms becoming a blur of motion as an astonishing quantity of dirt and rocks flew back over her head. Bernard and Mercy moved to aside to avoid the earthen torrent. The Pelt stretched forward as the hole deepened, until only her legs were visible. Heaps of dislodged soil surrounded her. Finally she backed out of the dark opening she had created, brushed her hands off on her now-filthy mountain coat. Grimy half-moons showed beneath the tips of her fingernails, which weren't split, or even cracked.

"That was …" Mercy trailed off, not sure what it was.

"Impressive," Bernard said.

Cynidece only shrugged, as if burrowing like a giant gopher were no big thing. She moved out of the way. "There is a large open space past the overhang. A storeroom of some kind, I would say. If the one we seek is in there, he is keeping very still."

Mercy got on her hands and knees and peered into the darkness. She could make out the chamber Cynidece had described, extending back under the bank far beyond what water would have carved. She guessed it had been widened and expanded using tools. Barrels, crates, and bags were stacked and piled along the walls. The pendant continued to tug her forward, but if anyone was in here she couldn't see him in the dimness. She thought for a moment, and produced a small, cold spark from her fingers before she had quite realized she planned to do it. The Æther tugged on the light and turned it into a looping flare that she had to extinguish before it ribboned its way through the layers of earth and erupted into the sky like a beacon. Still, the brief illumination lasted long enough to show her a filthy, bedraggled Rittandic lying nearby, half-hidden behind some wooden tuns, apparently unconscious. Now that she knew he was there she could locate him even in the darkness; he was nearly the same temperature as the surrounding material. She had taken him for a lumpy, rolled-up tarpaulin.

Crawling back out of the opening, she turned to the others and said: "He's in there. He's … hibernating, or something."

"Well, let's haul him out and tell him winter is over," Bernard said.

~~~~

Brennendah awoke beneath the open sky.

For a moment he thought he might be dreaming; but he had crafted his enchanted coma specifically to suppress such brain activity, not wanting to be visited by days-long nightmares of being unable to rescue Kaderleh from raging vortices. But why would he dream about an elf, a Pelt, and a human? Why would they be standing in a little line in front of him, looking at him with curiosity and, in the case of the elf and the human, a trace of fear? Then again, how would they have found him, and why would they have troubled themselves to drag him out and wake him up? Perhaps he was dreaming after all.

Brennendah pushed himself to a more upright position and examined his unexpected callers. Why were they dressed like that? What were they doing in the Edgelands? How had they found him? Then he noticed Kaderleh's pendant dangling from the elf's delicate white hand; no, not dangling, *pointing*, pointing at *him*. These intruders had disturbed the meager memorial he had contrived for his murdered wife, they had *taken* her amulet from it and used it to track him to what should have become his grave. A red fog seemed to fill the dry wash, a cloud of anger that obscured what happened over the next few seconds; when the sudden rage faded, Brennendah discovered that he now held Kaderleh's pendant, that the Pelt stood beside him with something sharp at his throat, and that the human was helping the elf stand up from where she lay sprawled in the sandy dirt. Whispering into Brennendah's tympanum, the Pelt said: "I will assume you lashed out because we woke you unexpectedly and you saw the amulet. I do not insult you by threatening your life, which you obviously value not a whit, but if you attack us again I will kill you. Do you understand?"

His anger subsiding as quickly as it had come on, he nodded agreement. The Pelt released him and withdrew a pace, the wicked claw of her fingernail returning to its original humanlike shape and length. Brennendah opened his mouth to say something, but only coughed and hacked, his throat and tongue too dry to form words. A second attempt at speech proved no more successful. The strangers exchanged a glance, and then the human proffered a primitive water bladder. Brennendah had been surrounded by more barrels of water than he could consume in a month, but had not drunk from them because he had not cared to live; had he not put himself into a state of low metabolism he might have been dead of thirst already. Still, if he intended to communicate with these strangers, he needed to soothe his throat. He accepted the skin, and took a few deep draughts. Then, still clutching the pendant in one hand, he looked at the elf and said: "I apologize. I ... overreacted."

"Yeah, okay," the elf said warily. She was nursing a bloody nose, probably caused by the impact of his spell. "What were you doing in there?"

"I buried myself after the storm came from beyond the Æther and destroyed the station and killed ..." He trailed off, started over. "I did not plan to emerge again."

"It seems rather a waste to just give up and dig your own grave," the Pelt said, "especially when you have so much anger banked. You should put it to use instead of burying it."

"Should I?"

"*I* would," she said.

"That, I do not doubt." Brennendah ran his finger over the smooth stones of the pendant, feeling the pattern as the pebbles slid beneath his skin. "Why did you seek me out and wake me, then? To what use would you have me put my *anger?*"

"We would like your help against the one who gave you cause to put a death rune on that birth-pendant," the Pelt said.

This was so unexpected that Brennendah let the amulet fall to the end of its tether and stared at her. "You seek to kill a monster with a slingshot. For that, you do not need the help of a simple observer such as me. You can fail just as easily on your own."

"It's not a monster," the elf said. "It's a Rittandic, just like you. Its name is Kihantroh. We're going to stop it."

"Are you? Did you see the storm? Its speed, its power? You bend your efforts in a hopeless direction. Unless … Is *that* what you would have me do? Write runes for you after you are dead?"

"Consider something, before you answer," the Pelt said. "So far this creature, Kihantroh, has killed Yexandor in Torgonderrer, Lord Korrin in Abacar, and Jordneh here—all the regional leaders except Filothandiar of the dwarves, who never comes out from beneath the mountains, and the Peltish elders, who have no country. This is not random chaos. What—or rather, *whose*—purpose do you suppose their elimination serves?"

"I hardly have enough information to answer that."

"You said the storm came from beyond the Æther. Why would Kihantroh come all the way down here before turning north? Why not strike directly at the castle from Abacar?"

"I do not know," Brennendah said. "Perhaps it was searching for something here."

"Perhaps. Something, or someone. Someone who was lost in the Æther long ago, and who—if she returned—would benefit from the power vacuum that Kihantroh has created."

"Someone?" The Pelt now had Brennendah's full attention. "Untelleh is not to be found simply by *looking* into the mists."

"Ah yes," she said. "Untelleh. Now we are getting somewhere."

~~~~

"Untelleh." Bernard remembered that name. "Cynidece, didn't you say Untelleh used to live down this way?"

"Not just lived, *ruled*. What is now the Æther was once her territory, but she and it were lost centuries ago, so I am surprised that she would immediately occur to our new friend as the person Kihantroh might have been looking for."

The new friend in question said: "You clearly are *not* surprised, given the leading questions you asked." Cynidece grinned and nodded, conceding the point. The alien creature regarded her with huge, unblinking eyes, and finally said: "Let us return to concealment before we discuss this further. I will feel safer out from under the open sky." Without waiting for them to agree or not, he turned and wormed through the tunnel Cynidece had dug into his cave. Bernard looked at the others; Mercy shrugged, got on her hands and knees, and crawled into the opening. Bernard followed, Cynidece behind. It was a quick shimmy into a bunker-like cavern jammed full of supplies: Food, water, hay, building and repair materials, and other things one might need to operate a remote outpost, or to survive an apocalypse.

"I am Brennendah," the Rittandic said, as he settled in among a pile of empty sacks that he had apparently been using as a bed. "My task here is—or rather, *was*—to monitor the Æther. As the Pelt—Cynidece, was it?—told you, this region was once the domain of a sorceress named Untelleh. The Æther did exist in those days, but only as a very small spot, a pool, if you will, of mist and energy. Untelleh studied it, and built her castle around it, and eventually attempted to tap it as a power source. The resulting explosion obliterated her castle and the surrounding countryside, and gave rise the Æther as it now exists."

"*Exactly* as it now exists?"

Brennendah looked at Cynidece. "Are you a barrister? You seem to enjoy asking questions to which you already know the answer."

Cynidece laughed. "I have been called many things, but until now, never *that*."

"Well, you are correct. The Æther was smaller in the immediate aftermath of the catastrophe, and has been gradually expanding ever since. Attempting to understand the nature of that expansion is why we have maintained an installation here. That name you mentioned, *Kihantroh*, is not unknown to me. Kihantroh once monitored the Æther, as I did; I have seen its signature in the writings left by earlier monitors, and have heard it mentioned on occasion in discussions at the castle. When you suggested that it may have been searching for something in the Æther ... There have always been those who theorize that Untelleh is still present within the mists, though no attempt to reach her, or indeed to do any sort of scrying into the void, has ever succeeded. Most who tried to pierce that veil have gone insane, some more spectacularly than others."

"Was Kihantroh one of those?"

"I cannot answer that. Jordneh could." The dark gaze moved among them. "She is dead, you say. You know this? It is a fact?"

"Yes," Mercy said. "I met her ... her spirit, I guess ... in the castle, not long before Kihantroh dispelled it."

"You were in the castle? After the storm? How?" Then: "What are the conditions there?"

"Yes, I was. How I got there is a long story, but the conditions are, um, not good. The village or whatever was around it is completely destroyed, just like your installation here, and as far as I could tell the only thing left alive in the area is Kihantroh."

"You saw no survivors?"

"No, but I couldn't stay long. I grabbed the——"

She broke off. Brennendah watched her expectantly. "You may as well tell him," Cynidece said after a moment.

"Tell me what?"

"Wait, I'll show you." Mercy reached beneath her coat, took out the Illata, and held it up. The reflection of the gem's aura glittered in Brennendah's huge dark eyes, which grew wider still when the stone was revealed. "This is the Illata, or the Brisindeld, depending on your point of view. Lord Korrin had another like it, the Jewel in the Maul. Kihantroh took them both, and used them to make the storm you saw, but I ... Well, Jordneh helped me get this one back. After Kihantroh killed her."

The Rittandic crept forward until he was almost touching the gem, moved his head around it to the left, then to the right, then back to the left, studying it like a jeweler appraising a diamond. Bernard could see Mercy tense up, as if expecting the alien creature to make a grab for it, but then Brennendah withdrew. "The stone gives off an energy not unlike the Æther," he said. "Kihantroh drew on it for power? And you do the same?"

"Yes."

"That is not so different from what Untelleh attempted, is it?"

"Well, so far, I haven't destroyed the world."

"Not very much of it, anyway," Bernard added, earning him a glare from Mercy that told him he was being unhelpful.

"And now you intend to take the gem to the castle and engage Kihantroh in battle?"

"Um, no. I would prefer to sneak the Jewel out without a fight if I can."

"Kihantroh will be watching for this. When I accidentally reached Jordneh's castle with a probe while searching for my wife, it was discovered and there was immediate retaliation." Brennendah indicated the Illata with a tip of his head. "You cannot possibly think to bring *that* anywhere near her walls without being caught."

"I can mask it pretty well. You didn't sense it until I took it out, did you? As long as I leave it in my pack and don't try to draw on it, Kihantroh won't be able to detect it until it's too late. We'll be moving on foot from here. No Illata. No magic."

"No veil?" Bernard said.

"No veil. And if Kihantroh has eyes in the sky, then we'll have to travel by night and stay under cover during the day."

"Which means we will need to know when and where to stop and find cover," Cynidece said, "so we are not caught out in the open when the sun rises. The southern part of the Ravels is not littered with places to hide."

"Right," Mercy said. "So we need a guide. I know you're an expert on everything, Cynidece——" The Pelt snorted in evident amusement. "——but for this, we really need someone who lives around here, who's familiar with the terrain." To Brennendah: *"That's* what we would ask of a simple observer. Get us to the castle without being seen. Be our guide, and help us put an end to this."

"A guide." Brennendah said. He sat quietly for a long while, and finally said: "Very well. I can be a guide. Your friend is right; between here and the castle is largely nothing but empty prairie, but there are places along the way where we might go to ground during daylight. Thickets. Bridges. Washouts and ditches. Ruins and abandoned villages. Moving on foot and only at night, it should take several days to reach the castle, but it can be done." The huge eyes regarded each of them in turn. "And when we get there, what then?"

"We improvise," Mercy said.

~~~~

They departed from the supply cave as dusk transitioned to night, crawling one by one out of the tunnel opening and assembling in the sandy creek bed beyond. They navigate a maze of ravines and wadis and soon reached a hard-packed dirt road that Brennendah said ran north to the castle and south into the Æther, ending in crumbled stone and fog. They went north. Though the night was overcast and dim, everything from the surrounding grasses to clumps of trees and bushes in the middle distance to the far-off mountains remained visible to Mercy's eyes, stark in shades of white and grey and black, like faded pictures from a forgotten newspaper. The land rose ahead of them in low, rolling hills, eventually overtopped by the distant Fists. She wondered if, had she the spyglass, she would be able to peer through it and see the splintered remains of the outcropping from which she had launched them to the Edgelands. Maybe Nebandalex would be standing there waving to her. She doubted it.

They walked for some time through the darkness, pausing now and then so Mercy could rest. No one talked much, as if Kihantroh might have listening posts set up along the way, though Brennendah occasionally made comments about things they passed, telling them that this pile of rubble used to be a a stone shelter built over a well, or that heap of smashed timbers had been an abandoned farmstead. It seemed that when the storm passed through here it had wrought only casual destruction, as a such a storm usually did, rather than the sort of deliberate and thorough scouring visited on the monitoring station and the village outside the castle. Still, Brennendah seemed concerned that some of the places he had thought they could hide were no longer suitable due to the injury they had suffered, and as a pale light began to seep into the horizon, he paused at a small bridge over a narrow stream—made of stone and wood, it did not appear to have been damaged by the wind—and proposed that they spend the day out of sight underneath it.

"Really?" Bernard said. "Under the bridge, like trolls?"

Brennendah said: "Like what?"

"Don't mind him," Mercy said. "This is fine."

The underside of the bridge was cramped and dirty and smelled like mud and fish and seaweed, as if it were a lakeshore where the water level had dropped precipitously and left newly-exposed muck to dry in the sun. There wasn't quite enough bank beneath the span for all four of them to shelter on one side; rather than leave one person alone they divided the group evenly, two on the south side and two on the north. Mercy just sort of assumed that Bernard would pair off with her and failed to invite him to do so, and somehow Cynidece snagged him instead. She was sure it was the Pelt's idea and wondered why Bernard had agreed to the arrangement, but was too exhausted to think much about it right now. Bernard might envy her night vision, but Mercy would have happily traded the ability to see in the dark for a stronger constitution. You would think all the walking and running she'd been doing would have improved her endurance, but no, it seemed she was eternally limited by the scores she had accepted when she'd thought this would be just another game, and had created this version of Ambrosia the Sorceress.

She slept only a little, and not well; unaccustomed to the nocturnal life, she kept waking up with the changing light. Each time, she peered out at a small clump of scrubby, thin-leafed bushes that sprouted not far to the east of where they hid, taking note of the gradual shift in the length and angle of its shadow as the sun tracked across the sky, as if it were the gnomon of a giant sundial. Once, she awakened to Brennendah's soft voice. At first she thought he was talking in his sleep, but when she shifted around to check on him she saw that he had his wife's pendant in his hand and, holding it near to his lips, was addressing it in low, steady tones. Maybe he was singing to it; his words had a certain rhythmic quality, as if following some kind of cadence, although his metallic tone didn't really seem conducive to lyricism. She couldn't understand what he was saying, as if he were speaking in some private, secret language. She turned away and left him to it, realizing that this performance was not meant for an audience.

With the Rittandic's quiet murmur as a sort of lullaby, Mercy finally drifted into a steadier sleep, until she awoke to someone gently shaking her. She sat up and banged her forehead on the underside of the bridge, then lay back down again with closed eyes and a muttered curse. "Sorry," Bernard said. "I was trying not to startle you. I banged my head too when Cynidece woke me up. She thought it was hilarious."

"Of course she did," Mercy said, rubbing her forehead. "Are we leaving?"

"Um. Not just yet. We've all been up for a little while but you seemed really tired and the others said I should let you sleep. We're going to have breakfast now, though, so I thought … Um, I mean, dinner … Well anyway there's food if you want to come and eat."

"Okay, thanks."

Bernard withdrew, giving her room to crawl out from under the bridge. As he helped her to her feet on the grassy slope, Cynidece—who sat at the top of the bank nearby, with Brennendah beside her—said: "I did laugh after he hit his head, but I *tried* to make amends. Bernard forgot that part of the story." Mercy glanced at Cynidece as Bernard turned bright crimson. Neither of them volunteered what form these so-called *amends* might have taken, and she wasn't about to ask.

After eating a meal of hard bread, cheese, dried meat, and some wild root vegetables that Brennendah had gathered, they set off again, trudging up the road into the darkness. Brennendah explained that their next destination, an old grain mill, had long been abandoned and had fallen into ruins; it was his hope that Kihantroh's winds might not have flattened the structure any further. Given what they had seen so far, Mercy wasn't convinced this hope would not turn out to be a vain one. "What are the alternatives if we get there and this mill isn't usable?"

"There is a culvert nearby where the stream that feeds the pond passes under the road. We may find shelter there."

"Great, another night under a bridge," Bernard said. Cynidece chuckled and poked him; Bernard flushed again, and fell silent.

"Why was the mill abandoned?" Mercy asked. "Why doesn't

anyone live around here?"

"These are the northern reaches of what was once Untelleh's territory," Brennendah said. "The region was abandoned after her castle was lost to the Æther. At first, no one was sure when or if the Æther would stop expanding, and it did so erratically. Several of my early predecessors were taken by sudden expansions of the void. In fact it was just such a jump—a relatively small one—that caused me to leave my …" He trailed off, and after a moment said: "Yes. Well. When the Æther finally stabilized and it became apparent that all these lands would *not* be lost immediately, most of those who had dwelt here had established new lives elsewhere and had little reason or desire to return. Dondoleh, who was the witch-queen in the North at the time, encouraged them to stay away, and they did."

"But why?" Bernard said. "People could have come back. Did they think it was cursed or something?"

"Not *cursed* as such, but the evidence was that the Æther could surge across leagues of land in a matter of seconds and so we retreated from it. The northern castle, where we are going, became the heart of the Ravels. Trade routes had changed; nothing could arrive by sea anymore—there *was* no sea, you understand?—so there was no longer any need or, indeed, place for a port city in the South. And even then our numbers were shrinking. No repatriation occurred simply because there was no need." Brennendah lifted his vast dark eyes toward the dark sky overhead. "There are few of our kind left. That Kihantroh should have killed so many more of us … I cannot understand how that could be considered some service rendered unto Untelleh. She would never have countenanced such a thing."

"Why not?" Cynidece asked. "Untelleh is still *far* ahead of Kihantroh when it comes to inflicting death and destruction, is she not?"

"Perhaps. But that was done accidentally, in a misguided effort to benefit her people."

"Was it?" Cynidece said. "So the official histories say, but my experience has been that official accounts are little better than myths and legends that someone has stamped with a seal of authenticity."

Sounding genuinely curious, Brennendah said: "What do *you* think happened, then?"

"I think Untelleh was hoping to use the Æther to boost her own power, the way our friend Mercy uses the Illata," Cynidece said; of course she would know the story and have an opinion on it, walking encyclopedia of intrigue that she was. Mercy was a little bit annoyed about having her name dragged into the theory of conspiracy. "I think she made some small mistake, and the Æther consumed her."

"For what reason would Dondoleh—no friend of Untelleh's, as I am sure you know—lend her authority to a false story?"

"Untelleh's disappearance occurred just before Daras-Drûm first arose and started flowing across the Slash," Cynidece said. "Some suggest that Untelleh tore a hole in the world that allowed Daras-Drûm to slip through. Making her an accidental martyr who was only trying to serve her people is a more palatable tale than making her a power-seeking despot who indirectly caused thousands of additional deaths."

"Some may claim that, just as some claim that elves live forever because they are in league with some dark force," Brennendah said. "Yet Queen Dondoleh expended a great deal of energy to help the people of the Slash contain Daras-Drûm. After that, the neuters began to appear among our children with increasing frequency, a curse on our bloodline that continues to plague us to this day."

"None of that has anything to do with whether or not Untelleh let Daras-Drûm loose on the world in the first place."

After a moment, Brennendah said: "You are correct. It does not. Yet whatever Untelleh did or did not cause to happen, the Rittandics as a whole do not share responsibility for her actions. You, a Pelt, should know that. Do you hold all the men and women of the Slash responsible for abandoning your people in the Downs to be overrun by the death-wind while they retreated across the river?"

"Of course I do," Cynidece said, "and I am always looking for ways to make them pay for it."

~~~~

Shortly before sunrise they reached the tumbledown mill that Brennendah had chosen for their second night's shelter. Made of stone and stout wood, it stood within a long-deserted village. It had endured its abandonment better than the collapsed cottages and outbuildings that surrounded it, most of which had been reduced by time and weather to little more than barrow-like bulges in the tall grass. Brennendah made metallic clucking noises as he looked it over, putting Bernard in mind of a dismayed robot chicken; evidently Kihantroh's winds had smashed the place down further, collapsing the upper floor and pushing the whole second story over into a sideways-sloping heap of rubble, partially filling the weed-infested pond that glimmered beside it. Splintered wooden shafts and gears lay scattered around the wreckage alongside shattered grindstones and massive wheels, as if some giant cat had been batting them around like toys. Still, it looked like there might be places to hide in there, assuming the debris pile was stable enough not to fall on them as they crawled in.

The others moved off to inspect the wreckage for suitability, while Bernard—exempted from this service due to his poor night vision—followed the cascade of debris to the edge of the old pond, choked with bent and broken cattails and reeds. A shape half-submerged in the water appeared to be the remains of the mill's wheel, hurled like a flying disk by the twister that demolished the building. After standing there for a little while, he picked up a nearby piece of rubble and tossed it into the water. It vanished with a satisfying *ploop*, so he picked up another, weighing it in his hand before throwing it. He thought of the way Kihantroh had flung around chunks of broken wood in Yexandor's fallen tree, creating a flurry of dangerous missiles out of anything nearby. Now, it could probably pick up the entire field of debris at once and turn it into a flurry of shrapnel. He really hoped Mercy's scheme for sneaking in and out worked; he really didn't want to find himself on the receiving end of that kind of punishment.

Suddenly a large chunk of masonry flew past his head, raising a huge splash in the middle of the pond. He whirled and found Cynidece standing nearby, grinning; she seemed to have materialized behind him, in that way she had of silently appearing from nowhere. "Did I startle you?" she said. "I apologize. I thought you were undertaking to finish filling the pond with pieces of the mill, and decided to help."

If he *had* been planning to fill the pond, she had leapfrogged his contribution with that enormous piece of wall she'd thrown in. He wondered exactly how strong she might be. "I was just killing time. Are you all finished exploring? What did you find?"

"The mill is suitable. We found a section where a beam fell across the horizontal grinding wheel and created a pocket large enough for all of us to take shelter." She grinned. "It will be close quarters, but that does not bother me if it does not bother you."

He felt himself flush; before he could formulate a proper response Mercy approached, examining the water with a look of grave suspicion on her porcelain features. "What are you looking for?" he asked.

"Giant carnivorous amphibians. What are *you* two doing?"

Bernard and Cynidece exchanged a glance.

"We are testing the pond for monsters by throwing rocks into it and seeing if anything emerges to attack us," Cynidece said. "So far we have been disappointed, but if one comes out, we will be sure to call you over to see it."

"Don't do me any favors," Mercy said.

~~~~

Sunset found Mercy back at the shore of the mill pond. It had been a slightly less uncomfortable day than the one they had spent under the bridge; the ground didn't slope down into water, the sunlight didn't penetrate to keep waking her up, there was no mud or damp, and the main odors were of wood and broken stone. She had felt oddly secure in that dark little pocket, less like she was hiding in an active war zone, and even though they were actually closer the castle now than they had been before, she felt more confident that she could pull this off and take Kihantroh by surprise. If it knew they were coming, it would have struck by now, right?

Gravel clattered behind her as someone approached along the rubble. She didn't think it would be Brennendah coming to see her, and it couldn't be Cynidece, who wouldn't have made any noise. Sure enough, Bernard joined her beside the water, yawning and scratching at his spiky orange hair as if trying to dislodge tenacious unwanted passengers. "You're up earlier than last time. Did you get any sleep?"

"Did *you?*" Cynidece had paired off with him again and she'd heard some odd noises and murmuring from their vicinity.

"Um. I'm not the one who's supposed to be doing sorcerous battle with Kihantroh in a few days, am I?"

"There's not going to be any *sorcerous battling*. I just want to grab the Jewel in the Maul and get out of there."

"I know, but if Kihantroh catches us you still might have to call down some lightning bolts or whatever."

"You call down *one* lightning bolt, and suddenly you're the Goddess of Thunder," Mercy said. "Anyway Brennendah thinks we won't reach the castle in time to sneak inside tonight, so we'll have one more day to rest. I'll get us in tomorrow after dark."

"You will, huh? By yourself? You won't need a rogue to pick locks for you?"

"Well, maybe. But there'll be magical wards too. Taking those apart without Kihantroh noticing will be my job."

"Maybe Cynidece can help. She can see magic. She saw the spell that was holding Daras-Drûm captive in the sea cave."

"You *all* saw that."

"Well yeah. But she saw it better than we did."

"Better how?"

A few seconds of silence told her that Bernard didn't really know the answer to that. "Well I'm just saying, ask her, maybe she can help."

"Noted," Mercy said.

"So, uh, where is Brennendah, anyway?"

"He's over there somewhere, talking to his wife's talisman again."

"Oh, yeah, I think I heard that earlier. Is that what woke you up?"

Actually it was Bernard and Cynidece's canoodling that had awakened her, but she didn't feel like discussing it. "Yeah, sure," Mercy said.

Bernard looked like he was going to say something else, but Brennendah joined them then, emerging from the reeds nearby. "I apologize if I disturbed your rest," he said. "I was just singing Kaderleh the story of our day."

"Not a very interesting story," Cynidece said, suddenly appearing near Bernard. Where had *she* been hiding? "Just a lot of walking in the dark."

"As Kaderleh is dead, and her story is ended, mine is of necessity more substantive than hers. And so I tell her about it."

Cynidece opened her mouth, then closed it again, and actually looked a bit abashed. Mercy was impressed; it was the first time she'd ever seen the voluble Pelt left without a retort.

"Shall we depart?" Brennendah said, tucking the pendant into his grubby tunic. "We have much distance to cover before dawn."

They fell in behind him, Mercy and Bernard in the middle and the vanquished Cynidece bringing up the rear. They trudged through the night across rolling plains of grey-green grass. After some time a light, cold mist began to fall, slicking the road and chilling the air. The mountain coats they'd left behind in Brennendah's supply cave would have been too warm, but Mercy's traveling cloak wasn't quite warm enough. It was easier to dress in layers when you didn't have to haul your clothes along in a pack. She thought of their little boat trip downriver from Torgonderrer to Abacar, floating along the current in that miniature dwarven sailing ship. That had been a much easier journey than this one. She should have used the days spent idly drifting to prepare for what was coming next but, she reminded herself, she'd had no idea what that was going to be. Still, at the time she had been acting as if this whole expedition was a bit of a lark, when she should have realized after that bruising first encounter with Kihantroh in Yexandor's fallen tree that they were up against formidable opposition, that they could fail, they could die. This time, she needed to be prepared, and careful, and not make any more stupid mistakes.

Towards morning, the trail climbed a ridge and the castle came into view. She was startled to see the size of the structure. It loomed silent and dark, totally dominating a pair of plateaus that rose from the center of a broad bowl-shaped valley, surrounded by the wreckage of the village in the broad flatlands. She'd had no idea, standing on the verandah looking out over the destruction, that the building at her back was so extensive. It filled every square inch of the flat hilltops, its two halves connected by a thick crenellated bridge spanning the gap between them. "It's *huge*," she said. "Maybe Untelleh was trying to tap into the Æther for energy because it cost so much to heat the place."

Brennendah, who had been gravely regarding the smashed buildings around the castle, didn't answer at first, and only seemed to hear the question when she repeated it. "Many who lived in the village would have spent their days within the walls going about Jordneh's business," he said. "Its size is not unique; in fact, the histories tell us that Untelleh's stronghold was even more extensive."

"That explains it, then," Cynidece said. "They were competing to see who could have the bigger castle."

"Keeping up with the Joneses isn't easy."

Brennendah gave Bernard a puzzled look. "Who are the Joneses? Some tribe from Banderlund? I have not heard of them."

"Um, no one," Mercy said. "Never mind. So what's the best way to approach from here?"

"The main road enters through the outlet of an ancient lake," Brennendah said, aiming a long finger at a gap in the ridge on which they stood. Mercy could see a road there, passing through what looked to have once been a set of gates, although now they were just rubble. It continued on into the village, becoming a wide central avenue with a central circus, not unlike the broad street that had extended from one side of Abacar to the other. This avenue, though, was choked with the debris of the surrounding structures that Kihantroh had destroyed. "The route we are taking was favored by those on foot or horseback, unaccompanied by cart or wagon. It will take us into the village from the back side, and offers some concealment from the storm-watch towers."

"Is that what those are?" Mercy had noted at least four tall minarets surrounding the castle, and several shorter ones topped with what looked like large belfries.

"Yes. They are used to observe the atmosphere during tornado season, and would be obvious places for Kihantroh to set up glamours to watch for intruders such as ourselves."

"Mmm. Not much reason otherwise they would still be standing."

"Indeed. The destruction is even more complete than I feared." Brennendah's flat tone and alien features concealed whatever emotion the sight of the destroyed village might have evoked, but given his extreme reaction when first presented with his wife's pendant, Mercy had little doubt that it affected him more strongly than she could see. "This valley has been scoured."

"Yeah. I know we were planning to rest for one more night, but where? I don't see anything left standing taller than a footstool."

"Perhaps a storm shelter is intact somewhere," Cynidece said. "You Rittandics have them near most of your buildings, do you not?"

"Yes. If we can locate one that is not full of debris, we could spend the day there unobserved. That is not too much to hope for."

"And maybe we'll even find some survivors?" Bernard said.

"That, I think, is a hope too far," Brennendah said.

Chapter 8

CYNIDECE HAD BEEN right about the storm cellars; once they descended from the ridge and entered the village such shelters became common, ranging from meager bolt-holes beneath flat stones to plank-covered mounds in the earth to half-buried, crypt-like stone cubes with entrances made of iron. Yet without exception, simplest to sturdiest, the shelters had failed. Their doors were torn away or their sides were caved in or their roofs had been peeled away like the top of a sardine tin, and whoever had sought protection inside them had been pulled out and scattered like feathers from a burst pillow. In most cases the shattered cavities had been filled by packed debris blown in from the smashed buildings that surrounded them, as if someone had taken a giant dull knife and smeared the structures across the ground like soft butter over bread.

They finally located a shelter of the buried-cube variety, about the size of a walk-in freezer, that was only partially choked with rubble, leaving enough space for all of them to crawl in and get out of sight. Its door was missing but the opening had been covered by the remains of a roof that had blown onto it and acted as a deflector, preventing it from getting completely filled by debris. After threading through a narrow gap to get into the pocket beyond, they settled in side by side by side like sausages in a flat tin. They passed a long, quiet, uncomfortable day there; no one dared to speak, and they slept fitfully in shifts. When darkness fell on the end of the silent day and they crawled out one by one, Mercy didn't feel much more rested than she had the evening before. She gazed across the demolished village toward the vast unlit castle, wondering if Kihantroh were still within, where it was, what it was doing. Actually there was no question about it. Kihantroh was in there. She could sense the Jewel in the Maul radiating dimly from inside. The sorcerer had never learned how to shield the gem—or perhaps had simply never bothered to try—and if the Jewel was present, so was its owner; she was sure of that.

Mercy yawned and stretched and shook dirt out of her clothes as the others lined up nearby in the wreckage-strewn street, waiting for her cue to move out. When she gave it, Brennendah led them off the main avenue, walking through the debris field out into a meadow, then cutting left toward the portion of the castle that overlooked the eastern side of the village. Even here, away from the buildings, the going was treacherous; scattered wreckage spread by the winds lay half-hidden by the tall, yellowing grass. Bernard soon moved to the front, poking

ahead with his quarterstaff so that no one broke an ankle tripping over
a hunk of chimney. Before long the vegetation gave way to a trampled
earthen path that ran along the bottom of the butte on which the
castle stood. Its weathered sides loomed above them, overhung with
clumps of some grassy plant, long out of flower, deadheads dangling
like grey-green topknots. They turned left and continued along the
path at the bottom of the escarpment, following a downward slope
toward the split between the mesas, finally stopping just short of a
small stream that had once been spanned by a wooden bridge. It had
been smashed into kindling, blocking the current and forming a small
pond. A gated stairway had been chipped into the rock, leading up to
the castle; nearby, an archway in the hillside yawned onto darkness. A
side path had once run alongside the creek, but it was now submerged.
Water had backed up across it and into the opening. Eyeing it, Mercy
said: "I hope that isn't where we need to go."

"No. That is, or rather *was*, a root and cheese cellar. It had a
heavy door, so Kihantroh must have identified it as a possible storm
shelter and destroyed it. We are going up the stairs to the kitchen that
once supplied Jordneh's apartment and the reception hall with meals."

"Okay," Mercy said, although calling them stairs seemed generous;
the steps were so worn they were little better than washboard ridges, a
steep, bumpy ramp climbing the side of the bluff to the base of the
castle. A slice of grey flowerbed sprouted at the top, overhung by the
crenellated battlements of the high outer wall. Looking at the high
wall looming overhead, Mercy imagined that the castle must be a relic
of an earlier, more turbulent time, when there was something out there
in the plains to defend oneself against: Wandering monsters, maybe,
or roving bands of hostile nomads, or even raiders sent north by
Untelleh—though if most Rittandics were like Brennendah she
couldn't really picture them doing anything so uncouth, not to mention
probably suicidal, as assaulting a witch-queen in her castle. Which was
pretty much what they were preparing to do right now, wasn't it?
Belying the place's formidable appearance, the gate didn't appear to be
locked, just latched on the opposite side. How anticlimactic.
"Bernard," she said, "do you think you can open this?"

He came over, examined it, and said: "Sure. Piece of cake. Let
me just—"

"Wait." Brennendah's vast dark eyes regarded the steps. "If
Kihantroh has put wards upon the castle—as we must assume that it
has—then this is where the risk of encountering them becomes great.
We should make sure there is no snare on the gate before meddling

with it."

"Oh. Right." Bernard raised his hands, as if the gate were a superior foe who had asked for his surrender. "Cynidece?"

The Pelt moved up to take his place. She peered intently at the gate, then at the stairs beyond, exercising her claimed ability to be able to detect enchantments just by looking for them; if she really possessed such a talent then this was the time it would come in most handy. Casting a glamour to detect a sophisticated magical trap risked setting it off, while just passively looking at it would, Mercy hoped, leave it quiescent. After a little while, she said: "Do you see anything?"

"No, the gate and stairs seem to be clear, but we should proceed cautiously nevertheless. I will take the lead for now." She glanced at Bernard. "If you would be so kind as to open the gate?"

Bernard stepped back to the front and produced a thin piece of metal—he seemed to have become quite familiar with all the secret pockets and stitched-in tools hidden throughout Brannoc's leathers—which he slid between the bars and used to lift the latch out of the way. Mercy was sure Cynidece could have done it herself, but was glad she'd given Bernard another opportunity to feel useful. The Pelt carefully opened the gate and began picking her way up the steps. Brennendah fell in behind her, then Mercy, then Bernard; they slunk single-file up the weathered stair like truants stealing back into their dormitory just before a bed check. Where were the wards? Where were the traps? This was too easy.

As if Mercy had spoken her doubts aloud, the Pelt, now at the top of the stairs, suddenly held out her arms and said: "Stop."

~~~~

The kitchen Brennendah had mentioned stood slightly apart from the rest of the castle, a small stone box connected to the main structure by a colonnaded walkway ten or fifteen feet long. This was where Cynidece had spotted a trap. Bernard, of course, couldn't see it. He had suggested they bypass the kitchen, slip between the columns, and head directly for the keep, but apparently the tripwire or whatever you called a magical trigger encompassed the entire structure, so that wasn't going to work.

While the others inspected the enchantment, Bernard moved to the back, once again fulfilling the role of hapless human trying to stay out of the way of those better-equipped to deal with the situation. This was a part he knew well how to play. He hung around near the stairway for a while, watching his magically-inclined companions confer and whisper amongst themselves like a little kid listening to the grownups having a party downstairs. Eventually he got bored and crept back to the top of the curving stairway, figuring that since nothing had exploded on the way up, nothing was likely to do so on the way back. He slipped his quarterstaff out of its holster and sat down with the weapon across his knees, waiting for a task to materialize that required him to clobber, climb, or scamper across something. None did. He held the quarterstaff up and sighted along it down the stairs, as if it were a rifle he could use to shoot any imaginary creatures that tried to sneak up on them.

Suddenly he heard a fizzling hiss from behind him, like a damp sparkler trying to ignite on some soggy Independence Day. He jumped and whirled, quarterstaff at the ready, but the sound was already fading; evidently the others had defused the wards surrounding the kitchen, and the noise had merely been its death rattle. He stayed put and waited for a signal to approach, lest he should get shooed away or, worse, break their concentration and cause something to detonate. He watched as Cynidece moved back and forth, eyeing the entire area. Finally she nodded to Mercy. Taking that as the all-clear, Bernard slipped his quarterstaff back into its holster and joined them. "So what was it?" he said. "A bomb? A fireball? Lightning in a box?"

"No, Cynidece thinks it was just like an alarm glamour," Mercy said. "Something to let Kihantroh know visitors were coming."

"Oh, okay." Then: "Wait … Won't Kihantroh notice that you turned it off?"

"I didn't turn it off," Mercy said, sounding rather proud of herself. "I snipped off the ends and looped it back on itself. If I did it right, it'll look like the alarm is still active and nothing is going on."

"And if you didn't do it right?"

"Um. Well in that case Kihantroh would probably be here already."

"Okay. But I heard a noise. That wasn't the alarm going off?"

"Well, yeah, it was, but it was in the section I cut out. So the alarm couldn't get anywhere. Like a phone call that didn't go through."

"Mmm. Neat." It sounded like she knew what she was talking about. "So we can go ahead now?"

"Yep. But we don't need to get into the kitchen, we can just slip through the columns and head straight to the wall. Brennendah says there's a door there that we might need unlocked, so …" She stepped aside and gestured toward the walkway. "After you, Sir Rogue."

As he headed for the columns, Cynidece sidled up next to him and whispered: "What is a *phone call*?"

~~~~

The alarm glamour had completely encircled the kitchen outbuilding and extended along the full length of the colonnades; there was no way would have gotten through without setting it off if Cynidece hadn't detected it. Score one for Bernard's little friend. Now that the alert glamour was harmless, though, squeezing between the posts was easy enough. Mercy felt a little trill of danger as she crossed the detection line, but nothing happened: No horns, no sirens, no, as Bernard kept expecting, lightning bolts or fireballs. The breezeway between the columnar rows was all brick and slate and other nonflammable material, while the doors at either end seemed to be made of slabs of stone bound with iron; obviously it had been built with an eye toward avoiding catastrophic blazes like the one hinted at by the burn marks she had seen in Korrin's castle. The walkway wasn't wide enough for all four of them to line up, so when they went to check the door into the keep, Cynidece and Bernard took the lead, the one to examine the door for additional magical traps and the other to possibly defeat the lock. After Cynidece pronounced it safe, though, it turned out that the only thing required for entry was to press the latch and push. The door swung inward without a sound, letting them through the outer wall and into a small, deserted courtyard. It was dotted with wreckage that Kihantroh's winds had left behind while doing the work of destruction: Smashed furniture carried from who-knew-where, torn pieces of clothing, shredded tapestries, twisted blankets. It looked as if someone's bedroom had exploded. To the left and right, gated openings through interior curtain walls gave views out to other parts of the bailey, while across the open space, a set of stairs ascended to a gap in the looming wall of the keep where a door had once been. It had been blown off and carried away, apparently. Sheets of flagstone had been laid over one side of the steps to form a steep ramp. Mercy remembered Jordneh's wheelchair and wondered if the scattered belongings had been hers.

Now that they were inside, Brennendah took the lead again, guiding them up the uncovered side of the stairway. Cynidece examined the vacancy and pronounced it free of wards, so they passed through, into a severely disarrayed apartment. Nothing inside remained in one piece. Brennendah stopped just past the doorway, eyes wide in the gloom. "This was Jordneh's bedchamber," he said. "I only saw it from her office, there." He pointed a long finger at a narrow portal onto darkness. All that was left of the door was one bent hinge with a bit of wood attached. "We may pass through and enter the castle that way, but as to where your enemy may be found, I cannot say."

Mercy nodded. "That's all right. I can find the Jewel from here." She had deliberately avoided trying to determine its exact location, worried that Kihantroh would sense the attempt, but it was time to let the pull of the stone lead her; otherwise they would be searching this huge complex for weeks.   She moved out; the others followed, including Brennendah. She hadn't been sure the Rittandic would stick with them beyond this point, and was grateful for the assistance. She hoped he didn't end up regretting it.

The office was in a state similar to the apartment, thrashed and demolished, but it also contained a number of scrolls that had been blown into a corner. Funny how fragile scraps of paper survived things that destroyed ostensibly sturdier material. They passed through and entered a corridor scraped clean of adornment, with only a few scraps of fabric or the occasional broken table leg to indicate that rugs or tapestries or furniture had once been there.   Nothing but the faint sounds of their own passage disturbed the sepulchral atmosphere. No torches or candles or braziers remained, nor did any illumination penetrate from the outside.   She reached back and took Bernard's hand to help guide him in the dark; Cynidece already had hold of his other hand, and Brennendah's slender fingers gripped her shoulder, keeping them connected through the inky black.   The Pelt's eyes glittered in Mercy's vision, reflecting light that wasn't there, as she scanned the corridor.   Counting on Cynidece to warn of lurking glamours, Mercy concentrated on finding the Jewel. It eventually drew her to the top of a wide stairway leading downward into some sort of large foyer. A strip along the wall had been converted to a ramp, but most remained uncovered. They descended slowly. Mercy kept one hand on the balustrade.   This would be an excellent place for Kihantroh to strike and send them tumbling to the bottom, but no attack came, and when they reached the end of the stairs they found themselves in a sort of reception area or lobby, with floors and walls of polished marble and blank spaces on the wall from which decorations had been stripped and obliterated. To the right of the landing a set of tall double doors loomed ominous and silent, like the entrance to a museum that had been shut tight to keep the specters of the past penned up within. Each portal was adorned with half of a bas relief depicting raised concentric circles around a central hemisphere. She wondered what the carving was supposed to represent. It reminded her of a solar system, although none of the outer rings including anything that looked like a planet. The convex disc in the center seemed to serve as a handle; dark recessed spaces beneath it looked wide enough to admit slender Rittandic or elven hands, but Bernard's would probably be too big.

The Jewel was nearby, somewhere beyond those doors. They had been left intact, when so many others had been ripped out and smashed, because there was something behind them that Kihantroh valued. "Brennendah, where are we?" Mercy said.

"The outer foyer of Jordneh's audience hall. Her throne is in there."

Of course it was. Where else would Kihantroh sit but in the throne of the ruler it had deposed? Where would it keep the Jewel in the Maul if not in her grand chamber? Certainly it had not wrested its prize out of a subterranean crypt in Abacar just to hide it again.

"Cynidece, do you see anything here that we need to worry about?"

"No," the Pelt said. "There has been nothing since we entered, not even a monitoring glamour. If we are being watched, it is with enchantments I cannot see."

"Something isn't right, Mercy," Bernard said. "This is too easy. We're being played. Kihantroh *wants* us in here."

"Maybe so, but we have to keep going." Motioning for the others to stay back, she approached the enormous doors, only to discover she was too short to reach the hemispherical handles. The outer rings were smooth and solid, with no place to get a grip. Thwarted, she looked back at the others. Brennendah stepped forward, unfolding impossibly long arms from the voluminous sleeves of his robe. Cynidece came along, too, reaching up for the other hemisphere, and although the Pelt stood scarcely taller than Mercy she had no trouble reaching the handle; her arms and legs extended and she became a stretched and gangly thing, as if taking on Brennendah's bone and joint structure within her own body. This was the first time Mercy had actually seen it happen, but she wasn't surprised; she had sort of figured out a while ago that Cynidece could adapt her body, in ways both small and not-so-small, to fit her environment. That was how the Pelt had helped Bernard and Nebandalex escape the sea caves, how she had always kept her footing in the mud, how she easily handled the cold and altitude of Grunsandrovar's inn, how she had excavated Brennendah's hiding place with all the efficiency of a giant gopher. Obviously there must be limits to what she could do, or else she would have grown wings and flown away from the cable in Abacar; but still, she entertained the heretical thought that the next time she was creating a character, if the Peltish species were on offer again, she might just pick that one.

The others were ready to open the doors, only waiting for her to tell them to proceed, or perhaps just to get out of their way. She stepped back, out of the range of swinging doors. Kihantroh was likely to attack them the moment they entered, and she needed to be prepared; she reached into her pouch to pull out the Illata, unwrapped it, held it in her hand. At a nod from her, Brennendah and Cynidece pulled the doors open, legs scissoring as they moved away. The great doors glided a hairsbreadth above the highly-polished floor, with not a whisk of sound between them. The large room beyond was lit with a kaleidoscopic blue-tinged light, the glow of the Jewel in the Maul as it passed through the multicolored translucent gems in the head of the scepter. And yes, there it was, Lord Korrin's ceremonial weapon, near the center of the enormous chamber, set into some sort of stand that held it upright like a tiny beacon. She didn't see Kihantroh, it had to be nearby, perhaps watching from the shadows, waiting for a chance to strike. She had to show it that she was prepared, that she carried the Illata, that she was not helpless before it this time. Mercy took a cautious step forward, then another. She crossed the threshold.

And the Illata was snatched out of her hand, as if it were made of steel and someone had just switched on the most powerful electromagnet in the universe.

Recovering from the shock of losing the Illata, Mercy tried to call it back, but it was already too late and she knew it. The gem was moving too fast, the force that had ensnared it was too strong, and most of all, it *wanted* to go where it was going. She couldn't stop it. It flashed across the room and smashed into the Jewel in the Maul, shattering the metal that held it, scattering the multicolored stones like chips of broken glass. Blinding light flooded the chamber, pallid blue shot with a viridian wrinkle, exploding outward like a bubble before collapsing, gathering itself up again, and finally stabilizing into something cohesive, a luminous globule floating in the center of the wide dark room. Moments later it distended upward, forming a shape like a teardrop; the tip sharpened, spiraled, and erupted in a coherent beam that struck the ceiling and spread across it in a rippling sheet. She heard the barest sound, a faint roar or rumble, heavy rain on a thick, strong roof. Abruptly the apron of light shrank and vanished. No debris fell, but Mercy knew that the light-jet had bored its way through the ceiling and out of the castle. Someone standing outside the walls would probably see a geyser of blue fire scorching the nighttime sky. An odd sort of suction took hold of her then, drawing her toward the column of light. It was only when Bernard grabbed her arm to check her that she realized she had begun to toddle forward like a small child attracted by a shiny, dangerous thing: A knife perched on the edge of a counter, a brightly-burning torch, a colorful wasp.

Not letting go of her, Bernard said: "What just happened?"

"A powerful prepared spell was triggered by our entry," Brennendah said from behind them. "Your adversary was ready for you."

"Okay, yeah, the Illata-stealing thing was a trap. I know. But the light. What is *that* thing?"

A voice from the darkness answered before Brennendah could. "Do you still not understand? It is exactly as it appears to be. It is a lighthouse, a beacon, a marker in the fog. It broadcasts to the Æther with sympathetic harmony, in a language the Æther comprehends, to call Untelleh home!"

That could only be Kihantroh. Mercy looked around. "Where are you? Show yourself!"

"Why?" Kihantroh said. "So that we may do battle? This is hardly a time for fighting. This is a time for celebration! The true and proper Queen of the Ravels returns, and the weeping sore that is the Æther will be closed. The gems you sought to gather for your own aggrandizement will instead return Untelleh and her people to the world, and heal the wound on which the leech-queen Jordneh fattened herself for all these years!"

"Why have you killed so many of your own people if your concern is with *healing?*" Brennendah cried. "Do you think Untelleh would approve? Do you think she will *reward* you for demolishing the village, for murdering the—"

Kihantroh's laugh cut through Brennendah's words. "Of course Untelleh would approve. I acted according to her instructions! Do you think I would have done it otherwise? The way had to be cleared. She told me! The healing could not begin while poison remained in the system, and the poison could not be drawn while the spider's fangs remained embedded."

"This is madness," Brennendah murmured. "It believes Untelleh speaks to it from the Æther, that it can recover her somehow, but that cannot be. She is gone. Nothing returns from the Æther."

"Are you sure? That spell is doing *something* major," Cynidece said. She actually sounded worried, Mercy thought, and if *Cynidece* was worried then the rest of them should probably be downright terrified. "The entire world ripples around it. Can you not feel the—"

The Pelt broke off just as Mercy felt a sudden, wrenching jolt, a shift in the world, as if it had suddenly turned sideways. She staggered into Bernard, and would have fallen if he hadn't already been holding onto her. Whatever had just happened didn't seem to have affected him—he was about as nonmagical as they came—but it had hit Cynidece as hard as Mercy; she was down on her knees, holding her head and keening like a wounded bird. Brennendah bent to help her, but then the world lurched in the opposite direction and Mercy lost sight of him, and of everything else. It felt like she might slide across the room and thud with bone-cracking force into the opposite wall, but she didn't; Bernard held onto her, he didn't move, he was immobile, even as the entire castle was being shaken like a toy in the teeth of a giant dog.

"This must be stopped," Brennendah said. He had somehow gotten Cynidece back on her feet, and was supporting her with a long thin arm around her waist. "Meddling with the Æther—the fool casts a hook into deep water where monsters lurk. What is drawn forth may not be what was sought." The dark eyes turned to Mercy, telling her she had allowed this to happen, and that she had to end it.

Mercy nodded. She reached her mind out to the flaring beacon, trying to find the Illata in the fused, inscrutable, sputtering mass of power from which it blared. The tangle of strings within seemed impenetrable, a ball of steel twine wrapped around a nuclear explosion. She got no distinct reading from either gem, as if the Jewel and the Illata no longer existed separately, as if they had been fused and turned into something else, a radioactive singularity. She moved her probe to the coruscating column itself, only to have it seize her consciousness and sweep it away, up out of the throne room, through the roof, out into the ink black night, carrying her southward across the leagues back toward the Æther, racing toward a dim grey distance where some vast shape rose from the depths, a giant castle built on the skin of an inflating balloon. Was she falling into it, or was it racing up to meet her? Both? Something within was looking at her, it knew she was there, it was *waiting* for her, and—

And she was back in the throne room, on her hands and knees, a sharp pain in her nose and forehead. Bernard knelt beside her, hauling her to her feet, half-dragging, half-carrying her toward those massive double doors that stood just a few yards away, as if safety lay in that direction. "No!" she said.

Bernard didn't look at her. "We are *leaving*."

"No," she said. "We can't! Kihantroh's spell is *working*. It's dragging something out of the Æther. Something huge. An entire *country*."

"You saw that?"

"I saw it," she said.

"If we stay, can you stop it?"

But the light had drawn her in once more, and she couldn't even hear the question, let alone answer it.

~~~~

From the moment Mercy lost the Illata it was obvious to Bernard that they'd been outmaneuvered again; Mercy's scheme to sneak into the castle and steal the Jewel had not only failed, it had failed *spectacularly*. Kihantroh had been waiting for them, it had laid a spell to snatch the gem as soon as it came within range. Now Kihantroh wouldn't even bother coming out of hiding to finish them off. Why should it? It had already won. *Its* plan, unlike theirs, had worked perfectly.

So why were they still hanging around?

Because Mercy, indefatigable adventurer that she was, still thought she could figure out a way to avoid defeat. She just *had* to take her shot at disrupting the sparkling geyser in the middle of the room, and look how well *that* turned out. When he picked her up after she face-planted on the marble floor she seemed lucid for a moment, but then her gaze locked onto the swirling column and she spaced out, maybe remembering whatever she had seen in the Æther. Blood started seeping from her nose again, first a trickle, then a steady flow, the way it did when she was drawing on the Illata to power some spell she couldn't manage on her own. But she wasn't casting anything now, was she? The beacon was doing this to her all by itself, as if it were some kind of vitality tap. They needed to get out of here. He kept an arm around Mercy, glanced at the others, and indicated the exit with a tilt of his head, hoping they would get the idea. The big doors had silently closed behind them while they had been gawking at the spume of light and power, but what had closed could be opened again. He dragged Mercy back that way, turning his back to the massive panels, intending to shove them open with his shoulders.

A shrieked warning split the air, just as Cynidece slammed into him and knocked both him and Mercy sideways. A fresh glare erupted behind them, not the cold pale blue of the gems but a searing red heat. As he sprawled on the floor he half-turned and saw fire blasting out toward them, but something stopped it before it reached them, some force that slammed down like an invisible blast door. The flames roiled white-hot behind it, but no heat or sound reached them. Brennendah crouched nearby, hands outstretched, palms flat, like a mime pretending to be inside a box, and Bernard realized that the Rittandic was responsible for throwing up the unseen wall that protected them from the fiery trap.

The inferno faded from red to orange to yellow, and then it was gone. The protective glamour evaporated. Suddenly the air smelled hot and acrid, like scorched hair and clothes. Brennendah scrabbled on hands and knees across the floor towards Bernard and Mercy, moving like an ungainly spider that had lost a few legs. The Rittandic helped Bernard lift Mercy up and keep her on her feet. He looked around for Cynidece and couldn't find her. A whiff of ozone slid underneath the stench of burnt flesh and skin. He knew what that must mean. The spot where the flames had incinerated Cynidece appeared unmarred, with only a light skein of greyish-black ash to mark where she had stood; the big double doors hung out into the antechamber, smooth and undamaged. He imagined her remains being swept up and tipped into a dustbin as if nothing had happened here, as if it were just the regular sort of dirt and grit that accumulated on a pretty marble floor.

Nearby, the roaring fountain of light continued spewing energy into the sky, and Mercy kept trying to crawl towards it. As he and Brennendah half-dragged and half-carried her away from the thrumming beacon—she didn't make it easy, twisting and squirming, trying to get free, like a moth bent on self-immolation—Bernard could hear Brennendah murmuring, the sound like a tinny radio tuned to a station that specialized in religious chants. What was he doing? Casting spells? Bernard asked, and the Rittandic answered: "I am looking for other wards. It seems the entrance to the throne room was set with a one-way trap that did not manifest until we passed through the first time. Kihantroh wished for us to enter in peace, but did not care for us leave that way."

Of course. Kihantroh wanted them to bring it the Illata, and they had done so. At your service. Can we get you anything else? "So is it safe to go this way now, or is something else waiting to blast us?"

"This trap is spent, but we we must assume others are present throughout the castle, inert until approached from the wrong direction."

"So we can either stay here until Kihantroh decides to kill us, or ..." Bernard trailed off. Something was moving in the foyer out beyond the doorway, a shadow with several other shadows lurking behind it. He reached for his quarterstaff, but stopped as the lead figure moved into the spill of light from the throne room. It had longish hair and pricked ears, and it was holding a bow. Bernard slowly lowered his hand from his weapon. "Nebandalex?"

"Ribbit," the elf said.

Before Bernard could quite process this development, Nebandalex spun to his right and drew, nocked, and loosed an arrow, all in one smooth motion, faster than Bernard's eyes could follow. For a moment he feared the elf had mistaken Brennendah for Kihantroh, but the projectile had been aimed at a far corner of the room; he must have somehow spotted Kihantroh in the distant darkness. A keening cry cut through the dull roar of the beacon; the rippling fountain faltered, but did not stop. Without a word Nebandalex dashed off in the direction his arrow had gone, already pulling another out of his quiver. Bernard shouted a warning about the traps, but the elf didn't come back or slow down or even look in Bernard's direction; the target of his vengeance was too close for that. Bernard couldn't pursue him, not when he was helping hold Mercy up; the last thing he wanted to do was bring her closer to that light. All he could do was watch him go until he lost sight of his friend in the sputtering glare of the fountain. It blinded him to vast portions of the room like a klieg light in the eyes of a suspect under interrogation.

Suddenly the torrent of light flickered and wavered and faded away, plunging the room into darkness. What was going on? Was Kihantroh dead? Had the glamour finished its job, run its course? Things were moving too fast; Bernard couldn't keep up. He turned again, as a much dimmer glow replaced the fountaining glare. Brennendah had created a small illumination at his fingertips, enough to light up their little corner, though it didn't reach into every crevice of the room.

The gems. Even if the beacon was turned off, the gems should still be glowing, right? Why had they gone dark?

Now that the roaring geyser had been extinguished, the figures who had accompanied Nebandalex slipped into the room, one by one. He could see them better now, their rough features, their thick mane-like hair. One of them fell on his hands and knees just inside the entrance, dragged a finger through the swirl of ashes on the floor, held it up to his nose, and then licked the blackened crust. He emitted an animal roar of disappointment or frustration, as if some longed-for reunion had been offered, then snatched away, and it suddenly dawned on Bernard that these must be the mountain Pelts, who liked to investigate landslides in the hope of finding salvage. They had found Nebandalex after all, just as Cynidece had said they might, and apparently had decided to accompany the elf to the lowlands, perhaps in search of Cynidece herself, in which case they had arrived just too late. The screech made him jump and allowed Mercy to wrench herself loose. She stumbled away, heading for the where the stones had been. Bernard started to go after her, but a powerful hand gripped his shoulder and checked him. He glanced back, his gaze passing over thick, hairy fingers with reddish-black dirt deeply ground into the lines of the skin, then along the equally hairy, equally grimy arm to which it was attached, ending at the scowling face of the very large fellow who owned both.

"Let go of me," Bernard said.

The man didn't let go. "Before we dug him out of the landslide, the elf told us he traveled with a Peltish woman." His voice was not quite the guttural rumble of a dwarf, but it was close; it sounded like he'd spent half a lifetime inhaling campfire smoke and the other half shouting at his enemies. "The woman he described was once an agent of ours. She is in arrears to us for information, and not a small amount of treasure. Where is she?"

Of course. Was there anyone in this world who *wasn't* upset with Cynidece about something? "There was a fire trap on the door, and she—"

"The ashes."

"Yes. The ashes."

A grunt. "The elf thought you would come. He thought there would be traps within in the castle. He thought they would be lethal. We did not enter. We waited for you. He thought you would be prudent, but you evaded our watch and blundered in. And now see what you have done."

Well, at least they had escaped *someone's* notice with their sneaking through the village. Before answering, Bernard looked around for Mercy. There she was, still shuffling along toward the dais; Brennendah trailed along behind her, gradually increasing the strength of his light to keep them all in range, evidently having decided he could do so without being struck down by Kihantroh. Much of the throne room was now illuminated, but there was no sign of the sorcerer, or of Nebandalex either. Maybe the elf's arrows had found their mark and Kihantroh was dead, all those it had killed avenged.

Hoping that Brennendah would be able to keep Mercy out of trouble for a little while, he turned back to the waiting Pelt and said: "Sneaking in here wasn't my idea, I promise you that. Nebandalex was right, there were traps. The only reason we made it this far was because of her. Cynidece. She ... died. Saving us. From this last one."

"The woman called herself Cynidece?"

"Yes."

"An alias. That is not a Peltish name."

"Well, it's the only one she gave us."

The man snorted, dismissing Bernard's ignorance of proper Peltish nomenclature. "You say she saved you. You are indebted to her. She was indebted to us. Therefore, *you* are indebted to us."

"What?"

"Information." The Pelt sounded impatient now. "Treasure."

"What makes you think *we* have either?"

"The elf mentioned gems."

Nebandalex sure had gotten chatty with these guys. They must have interrogated him pretty thoroughly. "Um. Right. There *are* gems, but not the kind you would sell. These are—"

"I know what they are, or rather, what they were. You are wrong to think they are not the kind of gems that could be sold. But now their power is used up. Their light has gone out. They are worthless pebbles. Rocks. Trinkets." He finally let go of Bernard's shoulder and turned to look at his followers, who were scraping Cynidece's ashes together, as if they might be able to extract their information and treasure out her cremains if they just assembled a big enough pile. "This journey has been wholly without profit."

"So sorry you came all this way for nothing," Bernard said. He glanced at Mercy, who had by now reached the pedestal, the spigot that had been shooting light into the sky. "I have to go and check on my friend. Are we done here?"

The big Pelt glared at him, but before he said anything, the gems—not pebbles or rocks or trinkets after all—flared back into life, and rendered the question moot.

~~~~

Mercy felt herself severely disconnected from everything that was going on around her, disoriented, her mind somewhere else—still in the Æther, perhaps, down in the foggy depths from which Kihantroh had tried to retrieve the lost castle. She knew, in a vague sort of way, that Nebandalex had shown up, had run off into the darkness, and hadn't come back; she knew that Bernard had been detained by a big, hairy stranger; she knew that Brennendah was following her with a pale light, staying close, though not *too* close, as if he wasn't quite sure what she might do next. But mostly, she knew that the gems had gone dark.

They sat in a shallow bowl atop a low pedestal, dead and drained, imbued with no more power or energy than simple hunks of blue quartz. Kihantroh had used them up in its effort to drag Untelleh back from the Æther. Now they lay on top of the dais Kihantroh had constructed, each in its own socket, the two connected a spidery network of thin, flat gold wire that reminded her of circuitry. The tracery was melted in the middle, the metal scorched and blackened like a blown fuse. The dwarves had powered their entire underground kingdom for years, maybe centuries, with just one gem, until they had lost it to the elves in that cataclysmic meteor strike; yet here Kihantroh had burned two of them out over the course of a few minutes. She could hardly conceive of how much power must have been flowing through those wires. She glanced up at the ceiling, where the beacon had passed through. It remained unmarked, yet there was something *wrong* about it, something off. She fancied she could see the Æther roiling up there, but only when she looked at it sidelong, from the corner of her eye.

She examined the gold lines again, ran her finger along one side of it, where the tracery was intact. Touching the metal made her skin tingle and she withdrew, startled. She paused, squinted, touched it again. Same thing. She hesitated, then reached out and put her finger down on an unblemished portion of the other side.

Energy flooded through her as she reestablished the circuit between the stones. The gems flared to life; the beacon roared back into existence, but it was different this time. Instead of erupting out of the pedestal, it emanated from *her*. All her hair stood on end. Her platinum locks rippled and billowed. If her fingers hadn't been glued to the metal, the energy would have blasted her up into the sky like a rocket, a firework, a shooting star. She felt a pull between the jewels, an attraction drawing them to each other, but the glare of the fountain kept her from seeing what was happening. Then, as suddenly as it had started, it stopped. The light faded. The entire top of the pedestal seemed to have melted into slag. In the center, in a pocket of its own creation, one gem lay, twice as large and four times as bright as the individual stones had been. The Illata and the Jewel in the Maul had fused together. Had she caused that?

She picked up the large gem, and realized only then that a female Rittandic stood on the opposite side of the pedestal, staring at her with huge dark eyes. She wore rich raiments and some sort of diadem on her brow. Long white hair cascaded from beneath her crown, swept back from her forehead, then curled and sculpted into an elaborate braided coif. She looked like a wealthy aristocrat. A high priestess. A princess.

No. She looked like a *queen*.

The newcomer's dark eyes shifted slightly and Mercy knew she was looking at the consolidated gem. A corner of her lipless mouth twitched into the Rittandic equivalent of a smirk. Mercy felt a vertiginous twisting sensation in her gut, almost the same as when the beacon had first begun to flare, except this time it didn't stop; the world tipped and kept tipping, as if the entire castle had been uprooted and pitched onto its side and rolled away, now upside down, now sideways, now upright again. Mercy wasn't standing anymore; she lay sprawled on some hard, unyielding surface, with the strange, immaculate Rittandic looming over her, tall as a sentinel. She had lost her grip on the prize. Now it floated in front of the queen, in the center of a numinous haze, a single large stone that had once been the Illata and the Jewel in the Maul, gently rotating like a small, crystalline, lifeless moon.

"What a *fascinating* gift to welcome me home," Untelleh said.

Chapter 9

WHEN THE BEACON erupted back into life, Bernard lost sight of Mercy in the glare, but it wasn't as if he didn't know where she was. He took off in a flat-out sprint toward the fountain of light, only to be checked by Brennendah, who caught him in a surprisingly strong grip. "No," the Rittandic said. "Too dangerous. You cannot interfere."

"But Mercy is in the middle of that!"

"Yes, she is, and if you interpose yourself in it now ..." Brennendah trailed off as the beacon winked out. It looked like there was only one gem there now, larger and brighter than the two had been; and there was someone new in the throne room, another Rittandic, tall and radiant, standing opposite the dais from Mercy, examining her, or the suddenly-merged gem—or, perhaps, both—with the sort of greedy gleam one might see in the eyes of a child who had wandered into the living room on some summer morning and discovered an unexpected Christmas tree shading a dozen presents, each with her name on the tag.

Whoever this was, Bernard thought, she could not possibly be a friend.

He broke free from Brennendah and ran toward the pedestal, and woke up a moment later crumpled against the wall near the entrance with a throbbing pain in the back of his skull. He blinked a few times, then groaned and pushed himself upright. Where was his quarterstaff? He spotted it nearby, not far from where most of the the the Pelts lay piled up like hairy logs. The big one who had spoken to him wasn't with the others; he lay at the base of a cracked column, his head and back bent at strange angles from each other. Bernard staggered in that direction, noticing that Brennendah was still on his feet off to the left, surrounded by a scrim of dust and debris that seemed to have broken over and around him. He must have thrown up some sort of force field to protect himself. The Rittandic was the source of the light that illuminated the room; the glow he had summoned earlier now hovered several yards above his head, with a greatly increased the candlepower. Beyond him, where Mercy had been, Bernard saw a low, curved rim of rubble, with blast rays extending from it along the floor in every direction. Brennendah must have extended a bit of his protective barrier around Bernard; he couldn't think of any other reason he would still be alive after being so close to such an explosion.

Bernard retrieved his staff, keeping a wary eye on the vast throne room, wondering if Kihantroh was going to suddenly appear and attack. He hoped not. Grunting noises came from the tossed heap of Pelts as some of them began to stir. Their leader still hadn't moved, and Bernard was pretty sure he would never move again, the way he was all smashed up against the column, but at least some of them had survived. Black and grey ash filmed their skin and clothes and everything around them, aerosolized by the shockwave, he supposed; this entire side of the throne room was coated with a thin layer of—

No. He wasn't going to think about that right now.

Quarterstaff retrieved, Bernard limped over to Brennendah. The two of them approached the hemispherical gouge in the floor. It described a nearly perfect circle, aside from the rough edges and slipped rubble one would expect when a crater had been blasted into flagstone. "Did you see her? Was that who I think it was?" Bernard said.

"I can think of no other it would be," the Rittandic said.

"So Kihantroh's spell worked. He brought Untelleh back."

"*Something* brought her back. I am not sure it was entirely Kihantroh's work."

"You mean Mercy finished it."

"Perhaps. Although not intentionally."

"And Untelleh took Mercy and the gems."

"Just one gem now," Brennendah said, "as I recall."

"Okay. Yeah. You're right. One gem" Bernard began a slow walk around the perimeter of the hole. He had no idea what he was looking for. Clues? Brennendah trailed along behind him. At length Bernard said: "We have to rescue her."

"Rescue Mercy?"

"Yes."

"From Untelleh?"

"Yes."

"You considered Kihantroh a dire threat. What sort of enemy do you suppose *Untelleh* will make?"

"I don't care. I'm not going to let her just *show up* and grab Mercy like that and, and, and *keep* her. Look, she only now came back from the Æther, right? Maybe she's not at full strength yet. We're still here after she tried to kill us."

"I do not think this—" Brennendah gestured at the crater. "—was Untelleh trying to kill us. This was incidental. If she had wished us dead, so we would be."

He was right, of course. Untelleh had appeared and vanished with Mercy and the Illata, and the obliteration of a section of the throne room was nothing but a side effect. Such an effortless display of power mere minutes after her resurrection, or whatever you called being reconstituted out of fog and absence, made most of Kihantroh's antics and subterfuges seem like practical jokes; if the witch-queen had wanted them dead, they wouldn't be here discussing whether or not the witch-queen had wanted them dead. "Well, fine. I don't want to make an enemy of Untelleh anyway. She can keep the Illata. I want Mercy back, and then I'm out of here."

"Out of where?"

"This world. This game. I've had enough. I'm done with it."

"Game? You call this a *game*? My queen is dead. My *wife* is dead. My unborn——"

"No … No, look, that's not what I meant. I can't really explain, it's … it's complicated. How we got tricked into coming here. I …" He trailed off as Nebandalex approached, his bow on his back, dragging a ragged bundle——the thin body of a Rittandic——behind him. Bernard stopped and waited for the elf, who circumnavigated the crater to join them near the low ridge of broken stone. He left the corpse nearby, pausing only long enough to pull an arrow out of its shoulder and another out of its chest and return them to his quiver. "Welcome back. I'm glad you're all right. I wanted to open another portal to go and look for you, but the others, they said because the Æther was so close——"

"The risk was too great. I understand," the elf said. "Ribbit."

"What means this word, *ribbit*?" Brennendah asked.

"It's the secret password. Long story. Nebandalex, this is Brennendah. Brennendah, Nebandalex." The elf tipped his head in acknowledgment of the introduction. "Cynidece is dead, and Mercy … You saw what happened to Mercy?"

"Yes. The other Rittandic took her away. Then I woke up out in a hallway, underneath a door, nearby to *that*." He gave the deceased Kihantroh an unfriendly look.

"That other Rittandic was Untelleh. So … We have a new problem to deal with. If you're up for it."

"I am, of course." Then, after a moment: "I am sorry about Cynidece. My *rescuers* were quite eager to see her." Said rescuers had gathered, ululating, around their fallen leader. "It seems our late friend was notorious in many places besides Abacar, though I suppose it matters little enough now."

"I suppose so," Bernard said, watching and listening to the Pelts howl.

"Where do you think Untelleh took Mercy?"

"I don't know. Back to her castle I guess. Mercy said she saw a whole countryside coming out of the Æther. Brennendah, what do you think?"

"If Untelleh's lands have returned from the Æther along with the witch-queen, then I agree. That is the obvious destination." He looked thoughtful. "The storm-watch towers seemed to be intact around the castle. If we ascend one and train its telescope to the south, we may be able to see what Kihantroh has wrought."

"The telescope will let us see all the way to the Æther? In the dark?"

"Of course it will," the Rittandic said. "I know not how it works in *your* world, but here, storms may come by night as well as by day."

~~~~

Brennendah took the lead as they moved slowly through the darkened castle hallways, heading for a side gate that he said would take them to the observation towers. Bernard and Nebandalex followed him, and the Pelts trailed along behind them, two carrying their fallen leader and the other gathering an armload of inflammable material, evidently to be used as the beginnings of a pyre out in the courtyard. It seemed that Pelts wasted no time when it came to the burning of their dead, in which case Bernard supposed that Cynidece had made her exit from the world in precisely the correct way. But, no, Bernard wasn't going to think about Cynidece yet, or about how, if this really had been one of Mercy's computer games, there would have been two inactive slots in the party roster right now: An empty one where Mercy should have been, and an exiled one with Cynidece's name and picture displayed in dull and faded colors, its former occupant never to sally forth again.

They reached the exit without further incident; perhaps when Kihantroh had died, its remaining glamours had evaporated. Once they went out into the bailey, the Pelts split off heading for an open flagstoned space to the left where more potential fuel for the bonfire—smashed wooden furniture, broken timbers, torn wall-hangings—had accumulated, collected by the swirling wind into a dome of rubble and debris. The observation tower stood in the opposite direction, beyond a delta of collapsed masonry where a torn-off roof had taken part of the wall down with it. A black opening in the base of the tower gave access to the interior; like most other entrances in and around the castle, the door had been ripped from its hinges and carried away. They passed unhindered into the tower, which reminded Bernard of a barren lighthouse, containing nothing except a spiral staircase leading up to the platform at the top; the entire structure only existed as a means to support a large telescope high enough in the air to see far across the plains. They took the stairs as rapidly as they could, each limited by his own level of injury and exhaustion; Brennendah and Nebandalex, both long-legged and relatively unharmed, quickly outdistanced Bernard, who arrived at the top sore, out of breath, and last. At the apex of the tower was a circular platform, open on all sides, with a ceiling supported by narrow black bars made of wrought iron. A light wind blew through the space, making a faint whistling sound. At the center of the platform the telescope stood, all gears and tubes and lenses and gleaming blue-grey metal, with an integrated seat where the user could sit and work the controls. The device appeared to be undamaged; Kihantroh had evidently kept the winds from harming it, perhaps expecting it would still be of use to Untelleh after she took over the place.

Bernard joined Nebandalex off to one side as Brennendah prepared the telescope for use. Ensconced in the chair, the Rittandic was carried along with the machine as he spun knobs and turned cranks to orient it towards the south. In the dimness he seemed to have become part of the machine, his cyanotic skin and grey clothes matching the color scheme of the device. Once satisfied with the direction and angle of the spyglass, he folded the handle of the rotational crank down, locking it in place, then took hold of the eyepiece and pulled it toward him, turning a thumbscrew to fix it in a comfortable position. With that secured, he grasped a pair of knurled handles, one in each hand, and dialed them in different directions, nudging the telescope in small increments and bringing his intended target into focus. Bernard found himself unable to do much besides gawk at the unexpected intrusion of science, but Nebandelex said: "You appear to be accustomed to operating this … device."

"I am. We who study the Æther are often drawn from among the weather-watchers." Brennendah finally stopped adjusting controls, and just looked for a moment; then, in the same flat tone he almost always used, he said: "There it is. Untelleh's castle."

"May I?"

The Rittandic looked up at the elf, nodded, and unfolded himself from the chair like a stick-bug giving up its charade; Nebandalex took his place, adjusting the controls the way Brennendah had done, though with considerably less finesse. The knobs and dials were meant for spidery Rittandic digits, and even the elf's relatively delicate fingers seemed clumsy in comparison. When he finally got himself situated, he drew a sharp breath, although he said nothing. "You see?" Brennendah said. "The lands that were lost have been returned; Untelleh's castle once again strides the southern shore."

"Yes," Nebandalex murmured. "It is as if Yexandor had raised drowned Torgon from the Boiling Sea and restored it to leaf and flower."

"Indeed." Then: "Kihantroh must have expected a great reward for its service. Acclaim, riches, a position of power."

"Perhaps." Nebandalex removed his eye from the cup long enough to send a narrow glance Brennendah's way. "But Kihantroh already had power in abundance merely through possession of the gems, and could have used them in myriad other ways to achieve acclaim or riches. Restoring Untelleh was hardly a necessary step along that journey." Then, turning back to the telescope: "I am sure, though, that being struck down by elven arrows and abandoned was hardly the thanks it expected."

"No, I am sure it was not."

"So Mercy is probably down there, then? In the castle?" Nebandalex only grunted; Brennendah apparently considered the question sufficiently obvious as to not require an answer. Bernard waited a while and finally said: "Can I look?"

"Oh, of course. My apologies."

The elf withdrew and Bernard took his place, putting his eye to the lens shade. The rubbery cup, unnecessary in the darkness, warm from its contact with the others, shaped itself to his socket, forming a tight seal. Through it, he could see the landscape of the Ravels illuminated in shades of green and grey, as if viewed through a military night-vision scope. The scene was blurred beyond his ability to make out details; recalling the way Brennendah and Nebandalex had manipulated the knobs, Bernard was able to bring it into focus with only a small amount of fumbling. Soon he was scrolling the circular viewport horizontally and vertically, looking at different parts of the restored terrain to the south. Although the plains had mostly seemed flat when they'd been trudging through them, Jordneh's castle occupied high ground and this tower stood higher still, creating the effect of peering downhill into Untelleh's territory, with few interfering geographical features. The scrubby barrier hills and sandy drumlins where they'd landed after Mercy had opened her portal partially obscured his view of the distant fortress, but he could tell it was massive, just as Brennendah had said it would be. It loomed behind the hillocks like a cresting black wave, an undulating tide of sweeping buttresses and jagged spires, lights glowing from numerous windows, wispy clots of vapor—maybe residue from the Æther, maybe marine fog—clinging here and there like scabs that hadn't fallen off yet.

"It's *huge*," Bernard said. "I've never seen a building so big, not even back home."

"Its size is not its most remarkable feature." Brennendah's metallic voice utterly lacked any trace of soothing reassurance. "Untelleh was known to have mastered the art of instantaneous transportation; it was said that, on a whim, she could change where any door in her castle led. The witch-queen clearly discerned Mercy's affinity for the gems; to keep her secured for study, she may well be shut up in a room that only has an entrance when the Untelleh wishes it to have one."

"So you're saying we could search forever and never find Mercy, because her cell wouldn't even be connected to the rest of the castle."

"Precisely."

Well, that was just great. Mercy's famous maze-traversal technique wouldn't help there at all, would it? Disheartened, Bernard clambered out of the telescope. "I've seen enough," he said. "Let's go." As they descended the spiral stairs back to the grounds, he said: "So what was that you said about Mercy? You think Untelleh wants to study her, to figure out how she used the Illata?"

"Yes, I do. You must understand that it was Untelleh's desire for power—meaning the harnessing of energy—that compelled her to tamper with the Æther, which broke the world and hurled her and her lands into the void. She could have returned chastened and wiser, but judging by what happened here, it seems she did not. The gems radiate a power similar to that of the Æther, and she likely views Mercy as a means to control them."

"Do you think she even realizes she has been gone for centuries?" Nebandalex said. "Does she know it was Kihantroh who brought her back?"

"I do not know what she experienced in the Æther. It could be that, to her, no more time has passed than when one closes one's eyes and unexpectedly falls asleep. Yet immediately upon her return she came to Jordneh's throne room, so she must have felt *something* emanating from here. Kihantroh's beacon had the desired effect; it summoned her across the leagues, if only for a moment."

"I am not sure that was *exactly* the desired effect," Nebandalex said.

"As you say. Yet Kihantroh's intent was to bring her back, and back she has come."

"So she has," Nebandalex said. "I wonder if she is grateful."

Brennendah shrugged his thin shoulders. "She is a witch-queen of the Ravels."

"And witch-queens don't do *grateful*, right?" Bernard sighed. "Okay. Untelleh is back. What's her next move?"

"Who can say?" Brennendah twisted his head around on his skinny neck to look at Bernard. "I imagine that she will seek to consolidate her position in the Ravels before turning her attention to reestablishing contact with the Slash and other lands beyond. She will need to reassert her authority to those who are familiar with Jordneh, and know Untelleh only as a figure from histories and legends."

"Kihantroh already dealt with Jordneh for her," Nebandalex said, "so reasserting her authority should not be difficult."

"True enough. That removes what would likely have been a major impediment, otherwise. Yet she will soon learn that Banderlund is at her door, and that the population of the Ravels is greatly diminished from her time. Despite Kihantroh's work, challenges remain."

"But those Rittandics who returned with her will likely be unaffected by the curse of sterility, as they disappeared before the necromantic war," Nebandalex said. "Perhaps this will turn out to be a blessing for you and your race, eventually."

"Mmm," Brennendah said after a moment. "For my race? Perhaps. Eventually. But for me, and for all those Kihantroh murdered? No. Never."

They exited the tower, and found one of the Pelts there waiting for them. "The pyre burns," he said, looking at Nebandalex. "You will show your respect to the one who brought you safely out of the mountains."

"Of course," Nebandalex said. To Bernard and Brennendah: "Come. We must attend a funeral."

~~~~

While the rest of them had been in the tower, the Pelts had cobbled together their crematory bonfire, piling up all the burnable scraps they could find; from the way the flames were roaring, it was obvious they had a lot of practice building pyres. Had it been daylight, Untelleh could probably have looked southward from a tower window and observed the column of smoke rising into the air. The body of the Peltish leader crackled in the middle of that orange-red inferno. Bernard couldn't see the corpse, but he could smell the acrid stench of his melting flesh mixing with the odors of burning wood and fabric. It made him think of Cynidece, of the enchanted scarlet blaze washing over her, incinerating her in an instant. An odd, sick feeling grew in his stomach. He turned and walked some distance away, off into the darkness, until the sound and smell of sizzling meat became undetectable. He eventually found himself at a well whose wooden cover and winch were missing, no doubt smashed by the winds and, perhaps, appropriated as fuel for the bonfire. He sat down on the ring of stone. The flames were not visible from here, but its glow lit up the night.

Brennendah joined him there presently; it seemed the Rittandic had little desire to stand by to watch and hear and smell a man burn, either. "The Pelts are engaging in a rather unique ritual around the fire," he said.

"Are they? I thought burning was a pretty common thing to do with bodies."

"Burning the dead is not unusual. It is an excellent way to dispose of corpses and prevent contagion. Collecting the ashes afterwards to scatter or bury is also a widespread custom." Brennendah spread his arms wide in bemused puzzlement. "But they are taking turns holding each other over the fire to breathe in the smoke from as near as they can get. They will be lucky to escape with only minor burns."

"Huh," Bernard said. "Maybe they think if they inhale it, they'll inherit some of their leader's strength."

The Rittandic made a noise like a couple of railroad spikes being scraped together; Bernard interpreted it as a snort. "I had surmised it was a sort of contest, to see which of them would dare get closest and stay longest over the fire, but perhaps you are right. It is not the way inheritance works, but I suppose that sort of animistic mysticism is to be expected from wild mountain Pelts."

Bernard decided not to point out that Brennendah—himself a sorcerer of more than middling ability—was a walking advertisement for the fact that in this world *animistic mysticism* was hardly a concept to invite scoffing. He probably shouldn't be surprised that a practitioner of one sort of magic would be parochial about another's. "Are they coming with us, do you think? The Pelts?"

"Coming with us?"

"Yes. South. To Untelleh's castle."

"Oh. Pelts go where they will, as you must have learned by now. I did not ask and they did not say; they were busy coughing."

"Okay. Yeah, I just thought they might want payback for what happened to their leader."

"The Pelts and their ways were never my area of study,"

Brennendah said, "but I doubt they will seek remuneration for their loss from Untelleh."

"Remuneration? That's not what I meant by … Well, never mind. You're right, they'll do whatever they're going to do." He heard a few muted crashes, as if the mounded material had begun to collapse; a burst of sparks rose into the air and faded like feeble fireworks. Soon the firelight began to dim, and not long after, Nebandalex came around the corner, looking subdued and smelling of ignition. "What's going on?" Bernard asked as he approached. "Are the Pelts done inhaling smoke?"

"So it would seem."

"Where are they?"

Nebandalex gave him an odd look. "Gone."

"What, they just left?"

"Yes. These are not creatures of the plains. They came here looking for Cynidece, and with her death and the loss of their leader had no reason to linger. They have already departed for the mountains."

"Can we can catch up with them and convince them to come with us? We could use their help."

"I think you will get no assistance from *these* Pelts. Cynidece chose to involve herself in our affairs for her own reasons, but her purpose is not their purpose is not our purpose, if you take my meaning."

"But——"

"The elf is right," Brennendah said. "Untelleh could dispatch a dozen intruders as easily as she could three or six, and should she deign to release Mercy, it will not be because a few shapeshifters do or do not stand with us. The Pelts were not friendly to begin with. Pursuing them risks a confrontation we do not need."

"Yeah, I guess so," Bernard said. Still, he left the others at the well and went back to the smoke and stink of the bonfire for a quick look. Low though they had become, the flames still reeked of burning flesh; if anything, the stench was even stronger now. Covering his nose and mouth with a leather-clad elbow, he made a circuit of the area surrounding the pyre. The Pelts were, as Nebandalex had indicated, nowhere to be found. If he had really wanted their help, he should have stuck it out and stayed at the fire instead of wandering off, which no doubt had conveyed a dire lack of respect. Brennendah was right; even if he were able to track them, which he wasn't, he could just imagine their dark, unsympathetic, disdainful eyes on him as he asked for their assistance and offered nothing in return.

Retreating once again from the funereal scene, he found Brennendah sitting on the edge of the well staring into the lightening sky and Nebandalex doing some kind of maintenance on his bow, rubbing the string with what looked like a broken candle nub.   As Bernard approached, the elf nocked an arrow and did some test pulls, aiming at nothing in particular; then, noticing him, Nebandalex said: "Did you find any trace of the Pelts?"

"No, they're gone, like you said. I didn't see much point in trying to track them down. What are you doing?"

"Retwisting and waxing the string. My bow has not sung properly since the mountains; I think it found the cold, dry air, and surviving a landslide, to be disagreeable."   The elf looked at the piece of taper. "This is hardly the proper material for doing so, of course, but I found it lying nearby and decided to use it, as I lost most of my own kit in the landslide."

"Sing? Um, okay. I hope it's feeling better now. So it's just the three of us going south, I guess. That's assuming you're coming with us, Brennendah?"   The Rittandic made a noise that sounded like affirmation. "Great. Super. So we'll be more or less going back the way we came, right? If we bring enough food and water to reach Brennendah's old observation post, we can resupply from the cave there before we get to Untelleh's ... whatever that place is.   Her Fortress of Solitude."

Brennendah said: "Solitude? Hardly. All her lands went into the Æther with her, and her retainers, soldiers, farmers, craftspeople, tenants. We must assume that all those who were lost have returned with her from the—"

"It's just an expression where I come from. I didn't mean she was literally alone there."

"That seems an odd expression to describe a stronghold."

"Our friend Bernard often indulges in colloquialisms from his homeland that can be confusing," Nebandalex said as he unstrung his bow and put it away again.   "Mercy as well.   One becomes accustomed to it, and then one ignores it."

"Um.   Yeah.   Anyway, that's the plan, then, such as it is. Southward ho.   Brennendah, this Untelleh character ... I'm not interested in picking another fight we can't win. When we show up at her castle, is she going to cackle and fireball us just for fun like some kind of wicked witch of the Ravels?"

"Untelleh was no more wicked than any other king or queen, I suppose. The histories do not depict her as especially kind, but she has been gone for hundreds of years, and what we know of her has been written and codified by those left behind, who were not necessarily her allies. Who can say what one such as she will or will not do? Not I. You will need a sharper mind than mine to tell you that."

"Well, I just want her to let Mercy go. Do you think she'll do that much, now that she has what she wants?"

"Ah, but does she have what she wants? Remember, Untelleh went into the Æther because she sought to harness the power of a weak spot in the world, and now that she has hold of a source of great energy, she is unlikely to be willing to give it up. She will only release your friend if she is convinced that Mercy has nothing to offer her and poses no threat, or if she believes she stands to gain more by setting her free than by holding her. You will need to be a *very* fine diplomat to convince her of either, I think."

"Right. So what are you saying? That we shouldn't even try?"

"No." Brennendah spread his hands. "All I am saying is that this is a witch-queen who was absorbed into the Æther centuries ago, who should have long since been reduced to atoms; yet she somehow endured, and induced a powerful sorcerer to expend a vast amount of effort and energy to guide her back from the abyss. Untelleh will do what Untelleh will do, and we sad few are quite incapable of compelling her to change course."

"You may be surprised to discover how much a sad few are capable of doing," Nebandalex said.

~~~~

They rested for the night back in the base of the storm-watch tower, and left in the morning after raiding various root cellars and sub-kitchens that Brennendah knew about. The Rittandic was quite familiar with the locations where nonperishable food was stored in the castle; apparently his visits to report on the state of the Æther had also been foraging opportunities, and while the whirlwinds had done a thorough job of trashing and scattering the stock, they gathered enough to supply themselves for the trip back south.

They set out along the main road this time, traveling by day; Bernard saw little point in confining their movements to darkness, as sneaking up on Untelleh seemed an even less viable plan than sneaking up on Kihantroh had been. Without the frequent rest breaks that Mercy's inadequate endurance required—although with a few more than usual for Bernard, who was still feeling a bit banged up—they made better time than on the way up. As they moved through the low, rolling, grassy hills, through patchwork fields largely devoid of trees or settlements, Jordneh's castle remained in sight behind them, looming over the surrounding lowlands; the dwindling column of greasy smoke from the pyre continued to stain the sky with a thinning streak of grey, rising some distance before being scraped into a ribbon by an upper-level wind off the mountains, then swirled into a spiral by a clashing air current from the south. Brennendah pointed that out, noting the opposing winds high above; the vastly expanded Æther had for centuries blocked the flow of air from the sea, and now that it was gone, the natural air flow had been restored. Brennendah seemed to derive some small degree of comfort from that, finding a tiny scrap of good amid all the carnage Kihantroh had wrought, but Bernard was sure the Rittandic would rather preferred having his wife alive to feeling an ocean breeze on his face.

As they walked, Nebandalex told them the story of how he had fallen in with the Pelts who had come to investigate the rockslide and been very surprised to find an elf alive amidst the rubble. It sounded as if that encounter had proceeded much as Cynidece had theorized it might, although as far as he remembered she had never mentioned just how eager the mountain Pelts might be to find her. He wondered what she would have done if she had still been with them when they arrived. Would they have tried to haul her back to the mountains? How would they have tried to collect the information, not to mention the gold, that she apparently owed them? Would she have been able to talk them into joining their little band in exchange for amorphous promises of future rewards, of lands and holdings restored? He wished she were here, ready to offer snarky advice and pull their feet out of the fire when they got in trouble. He was sure she would've had all kinds of information about Untelleh to share, too, just like she did about everything else. But these were all things he would never find out.

The revelation that Kihantroh had been trying to bring the long-departed witch-queen back from the Æther had startled Bernard, and gotten him thinking that maybe, under other circumstances, Mercy and Kihantroh would have teamed up together. If they'd had a chance to actually *talk*, if Kihantroh had been less ruthless and hadn't started right out on the offensive, if Mercy had been less married to her game-inspired belief that every Quest required an Enemy … Well, perhaps things could have turned out differently, but what had happened in Abacar wasn't really their fault; disguised as Rumad Kram, Kihantroh had struck first and struck hard, and after it beat them there it had proceeded to kill hundreds if not thousands of its fellow Rittandics in order to clear the way for Untelleh's return.

Obviously Mercy would never have signed off on that kind of rampage.

And now? Now Untelleh was back, and she had Mercy, and Bernard doubted she would let the rest of them through her castle gate. Why should she? A trio of scruffy vagabonds knocking on her door to beg for a favor? At best, they could expect to be prodded away at spearpoint. At worst ... Well, he didn't know much about Untelleh, but he was aware that aristocrats could be imaginatively cruel when they so chose. He could only hope that despite Brennendah's low opinion of their chances, she would be willing to parley with them once they got there.

The sound of their footsteps changed as they descended into a gully, then trooped across a small wooden arch that carried them over a narrow, lazy stream. Maybe it was the same one that fed that mill pond where they had spent the night before reaching the village around the castle. Bernard paused and went to the edge of the span. The thin chirrups of small frogs—or whatever passed for frogs around here—that hid in the rushes faded as Bernard peered over the side into the dark water. His still-unfamiliar Brannoc face looked back up at him. After a moment, his reflection was joined by Nebandalex's; its mouth moved as the elf said: "Have you been listening to me at all?"

"What? Oh. Um. Sure. Of course I have."

Nebandalex snorted. "I thought those who chose your profession were supposed to be *good* liars."

"Ha, yeah, well, I didn't exactly *choose* my prof ..." Bernard trailed off as the elf pulled back from the edge of the bridge, turning his head toward the south. "What is it?"

"Riders are coming. At least four, I would say."

Bernard couldn't hear anything, but if Nebandalex said there were horses then Bernard believed there were horses. He looked a question at Brennendah. "They could be scouts dispatched by Untelleh," the Rittandic said.

"Scouts?" Members of his almost-chosen class; maybe he would finally get to find out what they did.

"Most likely. Do we stand, or do we hide?"

"Decide quickly," Nebandalex added.

"Okay. Okay." Maybe it was because Mercy had made him a rogue, but Bernard's instincts told him to go to ground. "We hide. Into the weeds. Let's go."

They went, retreating from the bridge, melting into the tall grass and cattails of the marshy area alongside the stream, Brennendah on one side of the road and Bernard and Nebandalex on the other, crouching in a damp, shallow swale that ran alongside the packed hardpan.   Peering at the spot where Brennendah had vanished, Bernard discerned no trace of him; the reedy stalks were themselves a faded grey-green, not unlike the color of the Rittandic's skin and his shabby cloak. The hoofbeats grew very loud, and soon the riders hove into view, riding down into the low valley. Nebandalex had not been far off in his estimate; there were five of them, traveling in a diamond formation. They stopped at the bridge, and after a brief discussion, dismounted. Were they going to search the area? Suddenly afraid of being detected, wondering if they had left behind some trace that the scouts had spotted, Bernard shrank back into the swale. Maybe it was time to sneak away and—

"Stay calm," Nebandalex murmured. "They merely stop to water their animals. They have not seen us. But if you keep moving, they will."

Bernard stopped moving. He watched as three of the Rittandics led their horses down to the black water to drink. The other two knelt on the arch of the small bridge. One of them unfolded a large and rather ragged-looking square of cloth for the other to study. Even from here Bernard could see it was a map of some sort. Unacquainted with the local geography, he couldn't really tell how much it depicted or how old it was, but he figured it must show the Ravels before it became *the Ravels*, back in Untelleh's time, prior to her disastrous experiment and the loss of her castle—which, in an odd twist, probably meant it was more accurate than any recent maps that showed a yawning blank spot where the witch-queen's southern territory had once been.

The three Rittandics brought the horses back to the road, then two of them took the remaining animals down to drink. The map-reader gesticulated to the north with long, spidery fingers. He said something Bernard didn't quite catch, but evidently they were getting ready to move out again; the one who had been carrying the map folded it up into a smallish rectangle, which unfortunately did not fit back into the messenger bag from which it had come. He unfolded the map and then folded it again, properly this time, and tucked it away. By the time that was finished all five horses were back on the road. The travelers vaulted into their saddles and idled at the bridge for a moment, talking amongst themselves. Bernard could make out the metallic buzz of their voices, but not the words. If Cynidece were here, she would doubtless have heard and remembered everything they said, filing it all away for later use, sale, or barter. At last, the riders kicked their steeds back into motion. Hooves clattered and echoed across the bridge and then were gone, thundering off to the north, up the rise and out of the defile to vanish among the innumerable low hills that rolled across this terrain. Bernard waited until Nebandalex gave a slight nod, then the two of them crawled out of the weeds and back onto the road, staying in a low crouch. Brennendah joined them there, the three of them damp and dripping, looking at the dust cloud that moved steadily away from them.

"Brennendah, what do you think?" Bernard said. "Were they Untelleh's?"

"Their garments were of a style I have never seen except in old illustrations, and the map showed southern towns that no longer exist," Brennendah said. "If they did not come from her castle, then they leaped out of an archaic tapestry and onto the road. So, yes, they were Untelleh's."

"Are they looking for us?"

"Doubtful. Why should she concern herself with the progress of our small band? Perhaps she merely sends a few retainers to secure the northern castle. She may be unaware that she has no rival for power at the moment, and in any case she will certainly want to assay the state of the Ravels before taking any action."

"Okay. Well, she's probably sent out more than just them, so we'll need to be careful and avoid getting caught. Maybe get off the road and go cross-country. What do you think?"

"I think your plan was to talk to Untelleh, not to hide from her," Nebandalex said. "We could start by greeting her people, could we not?"

"You're right. We could." Bernard looked off toward Jordneh's castle; at the rate that group was traveling, they would get there very soon. "I just don't know what to say yet."

~~~~

Mercy was back in a tower room, but this one wasn't nearly as sumptuous as Lord Korrin's apartment had been. This one was a prison cell.

The chamber usually lacked a door—except for certain times of day, its walls consisted of nothing but unbroken expanses of stone and mortar—but it did not lack windows, tightly barred and miserly though they were. Peering between the iron bands in a direction she thought was north, Mercy could see rolling green castle lawns stretching out to a distant black wall, and beyond that, fields of planted crops, clusters of small houses, clumps of trees and shrubs, a market square. This was probably what the settlement surrounding Jordneh's castle had looked like before Kihantroh obliterated it. In the opposite direction the black wall was much closer, running along the top of a bluff above a blue-grey sea, below which the surf endlessly hurled itself against a rocky beach. It all looked so normal, so *solid*, that Mercy kept having to remind herself that this castle with its walls so sturdy, and everything in it, all its people, and the hills outside and the trees that grew on them, the village huts, the beach and the ocean and the unseen fish that swam in it: None of that had been here a few days ago. It had all materialized out of the cotton-candy nothingness of the Æther. Although *materialization* wasn't exactly what had happened, was it? Not really. That word implied some sort of agency, as if the thing coming into existence had done the work of appearance through its own devices. No, everything around her had been pulled back into this world, mostly by Kihantroh. But that last small, crucial bit of the reincorporation of Untelleh's realm ... that had been Mercy's doing. She knew that Untelleh realized this, but the witch-queen did not understand it; and that, Mercy had come to understand, was why she was here, in one piece, and mentally intact, more or less.

She did seem to have lost a few hours that had passed after the blast at Jordneh's castle and her awakening here on the floor of her cell. She retained a vague recollection of Untelleh spending that time sifting through her brain, searching for information about how she had reignited the gems to finish the work of restoration that Kihantroh had not quite been able to complete, and what had caused them to fuse together in the process into the single, powerful unit that they had become. In fact, she could still feel Untelleh's presence in her past as an intruding bystander, sort of like looking at a picture and seeing someone in the background who had not been there. The witch-queen had inserted herself into Mercy's memories when she had rifled through her experiences, all the way back to Torgonderrer, when Mercy had first awakened in the forest as Ambrosia. At that point, it seemed, Untelleh had run into a wall she could not break through; fearsome sorceress though she was, she simply could not extend her reach any farther into Mercy's past. Mercy could tell this baffled and enraged her. Untelleh was unaccustomed to obstacles she could not overcome—in the end, even the Æther had been only a temporary impediment—and Mercy had been given to understand that *she*, of all things and creatures, would certainly not become the rare exception to permanently deny Untelleh something she wanted.

From reading her memories, Untelleh now knew that the Illata had drawn Mercy across the leagues from Abacar to the Ravels, allowing her to steal it away from Kihantroh; the witch-queen would certainly brook none of that now that the gem was in *her* possession, and so she had taken steps to prevent it. Mercy was not physically fettered in any way, Untelleh having seen how *that* had turned out when Kihantroh tried it back in the elven forest, but the skin from her hands up past her elbows felt as if it were coated with an invisible layer of thick, gooey grease, impossible to scrape off or remove. Her mouth and throat were similarly clogged, as if she had greedily plunged her arms and face into a giant vat of lard and had never cleaned herself up afterwards. She could breathe, but she could not form a single word or emit any sound more intelligible than a grunt; she could touch and hold physical objects like the bars over the windows, but was unable to cast even the simplest glamour. Even her senses seemed muted. She could see and hear and all that, but she was unable to locate the Illata; its emanations had become invisible and undetectable to her. Untelleh had rendered her as helpless as during her first few hours in Torgonderrer when, confused and amnesiac, she had stumbled through the forest like a small child who had wandered away from the family campsite and couldn't find her way back. At least Untelleh hadn't tried to lobotomize her into compliance, but Mercy was pretty sure that was only because the witch-queen feared that if she misstepped, she would destroy the very ability she sought to study and emulate. And that wouldn't do her any good, would it? No, Mercy was safe from having her brain tampered with further, at least for now.

It wasn't even as if Mercy was deliberately being obstructive; it was just sort of happening. She could remember that other place—home, Earth, the real world, whatever you wanted to call it—without difficulty, and was not making any conscious effort to keep Untelleh from accessing those memories, although Untelleh seemed to think she was. Maybe it was because Untelleh was reading *Ambrosia's* memories, which were not Mercy's, not really; if Ambrosia was only Mercy in the same sense that an avatar in a video game was the player, then some entity within the game might be able to go back and view everything the avatar had done, but that wouldn't tell them anything about the person working the controller other than what sort of decisions they had made and what actions they had taken within the context of the game. Which made one other thing clear: As powerful as Untelleh might be, as desperate as she may have been to escape the Æther by any means available, she was not the one who had brought Mercy and Bernard over to this world. There was some other power involved, one beyond even Untelleh, who had done that.

Somewhere, a wizard still sat hidden and unknown behind his curtain.

~~~~

On the second—or was it the third?—day of her captivity, Mercy noticed that Untelleh's minions were building something out in the yard beyond the walls. It was a strange sort of contraption, all angular crosspieces and pivoting arms and chains running between flywheels, and she had no idea what it was for. She began to get an inkling, though, when they started assembling a cage nearby, a cubical enclosure made of spiky iron bars in preassembled panels that snapped together, sort of like a collapsible dog crate. Once it was complete, spear-wielding guards began to herd prisoners into it. These unfortunates tromped across the grass, blinking and shielding their eyes as if they had spent a good deal of time in a subterranean location and were not used to the bright light of day. The majority were grubby, haunted-looking Rittandics, though she saw a smattering of other races as well: A few humans or Pelts, one or two elves, even a dwarf, she thought, although she only caught the barest glimpse of that short captive among all the taller ones. For the most part, though, the pen was populated with blue-grey skin and white hair and vast dark eyes that regarded the nearby apparatus with the sort of trepidation one might have for a killer robot that, having just been destroyed in an explosion, had begun reconstructing itself before one's eyes. Given the nearby supply of frightened prisoners, this had to be some sort of torture or execution device, Mercy decided; but why would Untelleh come back from the Æther and immediately start building such a thing? Who were those prisoners? Was this a punishment queue picking up from where it had left off before the castle had been lost, or was something else going on?

She heard a whisking sound behind her, and turned around to discover a door materializing kitty-corner to where she stood. It was made of iron-banded wood and painted bright red, and seemed to be being superimposed on the stone blocks that had previously formed an uninterrupted wall in that spot. She heard a key turn in the lock. Such a mundane way to secure a magic door. It swung outward to reveal Untelleh standing there, discreetly flanked by a couple of guards who stayed well back in the shadows. The witch-queen scrutinized Mercy with fathomless eyes dark and shiny as polished, smoky glass. The Heart spun a slow dance around her, never blocking her view or crossing in front of her face; it moved in subtle ways to keep itself in constant close proximity while staying out of her fields of vision and motion. Mercy couldn't help but admire her a little for that casual display of power. Untelleh didn't carry the gem stuffed in a pillowcase or hidden in a sack or wrapped in a towel; she didn't care who knew she had it. Maybe if Mercy had been so bold, things would have worked out differently.

"Walk with me," the witch-queen said, in the same sort of clipped, metallic voice that Mercy had gotten used to hearing from Rittandic mouths. Unable to answer verbally due to the glamour, Mercy moved carefully toward the sorceress, trying not to do anything that might be construed as a threat and get her blasted out of existence or jabbed with a guard's short-handled spear. She stopped immediately in response to a subtle change in Untelleh's expression that told her she had come close enough. Although the fact that the Heart was *right there*, mere yards away, Mercy felt nothing through the layer of enchanted insulating grease Untelleh had slathered on her. The link that hundreds of miles of distance had failed to sever, Untelleh had blocked with ease. Still, it remained apparent that Untelleh could not physically touch the Heart, which maintained a definite buffer space around her as part of its seemingly random orbit. Mercy guessed it would take an incredible amount of force to deflect the spinning crystal toward Untelleh's body, and that it would probably squirt away like a pea squeezed from a pod before the enchantment would allow it to actually make contact with her person.

The witch-queen retreated from the doorway and Mercy followed, emerging into an unfamiliar corridor of sand-colored stone. With Untelleh in the lead and her two retainers nearby, weapons at the ready, they moved quickly along the curving hallway. Untelleh did not speak again. The floating gem stayed in front of her, as if it were a lodestone showing them which way to go. After several short flights of stairs and more twists and turns than Mercy could keep track of, they emerged from the castle and stepped out into the sprawling yard. The apparatus that Mercy had seen from her window stood not far away. It seemed as if they'd had to walk an inordinate distance to get here. From this angle the device looked even more like evil playground equipment than it had from above; Mercy could now identify seats, suspended from chains, on which someone might be placed, but instead of mere flat pieces of wood or metal they were made of barbed black iron and ridged with cruelly jagged teeth which, along with the integrated wrist, leg, and ankle restraints, portended a secure and highly unpleasant sitting experience. A crank and belt assembly, nearly finished, was connected up to the contraption by a series of pulleys. It looked like it would take a couple of operators to run the thing, not including whatever other flunkies would be standing by to add to the misery of the victims by poking them with sharp objects.

"They do not remember the time we all spent in the Æther," Untelleh said, indicating the workers who were busy assembling the device and the fearful prisoners nearby. Her bodyguards were no doubt included in this ignorant grouping as well. "To them, it is as if they passed through a single dreamless night. But *I* remember. They slept; I stayed awake, and spent every fearful moment of those long years struggling to keep my lands and my people and myself from being devoured and dissolved in that realm of mist and nothing. And I saw things. Glimpses. I know what dark wonders lurk out there, beyond the mists." The witch-queen paused, eyeing the progress on her apparatus. Effectively muffled by the glamour that Untelleh had placed on her, Mercy was unable to respond, and after a moment Untelleh continued speaking. "Imagine, if you can, being a solitary conscious entity, trapped for centuries past the veil, alone in the nothing. One could go mad. Perhaps one *must* go mad." She spared a glance for the orbiting gem. "Or perhaps one's mind could ... *fracture* ... into endless pieces. Such a slippery thing, a fractured mind. Like a hundred dozen eels wriggling through the stones of a river bed, searching for the stream where they were born. A few of might find their way back to familiar waters, find someone wading where they do not belong, bite and hold and invite other eels to do the same. Yes?" She looked Mercy up and down, her long, alien face managing to convey a sort of impressed disdain, as if Mercy were a rat that had crawled out of a sink drain and started juggling cherry tomatoes plucked from a colander. "I gather you are an enchantress, of sorts. You comprehend my meaning?"

Mercy guessed that Untelleh was describing, in a roundabout way, how she had managed to ensnare Kihantroh in her scheme to get herself back from the Æther. She made a gesture that she hoped conveyed understanding or, failing that, a death threat.

"Yes, I see that you do. And I have come to realize that you also have some experience with a mind that is broken, or separated, from its true self. Minds are not easily mended, are they? They may be even more difficult to repair than broken bodies. Your remaining friends are on their way here, you know."

That seeming non-sequitur drew a sharp look from Mercy. The others were alive?

"Oh yes," Untelleh said. "They think to skulk beneath my notice, as the fish thinks the river hawk cannot see its ripples in the muddy water. They hope to rescue you from my hospitality. Do you require rescuing, my little treasure?" The dark eyes gleamed. "What shall be done with them when they arrive? Or shall I even *allow* them to arrive? I wonder."

Mercy stared at the witch-queen, mouth agape, wondering what to make of this obvious threat. She could hardly teach the sorceress how to manipulate the gems when she didn't understand herself how she did it. What did Untelleh want from her in exchange for not killing her friends? She made a sound halfway between a squeak and a grunt.

"Walk with me further," Untelleh said. "I would show you something else."

~~~~

Mercy trailed along after Untelleh again, following her out of the warm sunshine and around to the shady side of the castle. The guards did not accompany them this time; evidently wherever they were going now was not a place they were required, or permitted. Eventually they reached a spot where a path turned back toward the vast dark wall, sinking between two grassy berms before vanishing into a squat black opening like the mouth of a barrow. They went between the embankments, passing below the level of the ground. The ambient noise of the stronghold grew muffled as the thick earthen walls rose over their heads. Rust-red iron grillwork, hidden in the overhanging shadows, blocked the entrance. Untelleh waved it open as they approached; the barrier spiraled out of the way like an iris made of spider-legs. Metal clicked and squeaked against metal as the bars closed behind them again, hooks fitting into loops, teeth clicking together, locking them in the dark.

The glow of the Heart lit their way with its ghostly blue-green light. The ceiling was low enough here that Untelleh had to bend over, although Mercy, shorter than the witch-queen, was able to stand up straight. The passage soon narrowed, forcing them both to turn sideways in spots. This catacomb was nothing like the rest of the castle; it seemed older, cruder, and probably predated the structure above. Mercy suspected that, as with many ancient cities and castles back home, the witch-queen had deliberately built atop and subsumed an even more ancient complex. After some considerable time spent ducking and scraping and sidling through cramped passageways, they emerged into a broad, dome-shaped chamber with a roughly circular opening in the ceiling through which nothing could be seen. The floor extended out from the walls for five or six feet, forming a circle around a swirling pool of faintly luminous mist that frothed and writhed like a witch's-brew cauldron. But this was no trick of dry ice, Mercy knew; this was the Æther, or at least a tiny scrap of it. Its emanations, though she could only barely feel them through the smothering glamour that crippled her, were the same as what had permeated the arid region where they had found Brennendah.

"And here you see the reason my stronghold exists in the form and place it does," Untelleh said, indicating the puddle of Æther with a smooth, long-fingered hand. "I discovered this crypt when a tenant farmer, tilling the earth, struck buried stones that turned aside and bent his plow. After learning what secret lay beneath the soil, I raised walls to protect it, and spent decades studying it. And when I thought I knew it well enough to draw upon its power, it swallowed me whole." Untelleh trailed off as she gazed into the softly swirling fog, seemingly lost in thought. Mercy remembered the sensation when Daras-Drûm had surged over her and Bernard, the dreadful isolation of being sealed away from the world, from everything but endless fog and cold, while tiny tendrils sought to burrow into her flesh like rootlets and tear her apart. Was that what it had been like for Untelleh in the Æther? Mercy tried to imagine being trapped for centuries, awake and fighting every second to retain her integrity, to resist dissolution. She would probably have gone insane. She was not at all sure Untelleh hadn't.

The witch-queen shook herself out of whatever memory had taken hold of her and returned her attention to Mercy. "You were touched by the Æther. I can sense it. It clings to you like the memory of a shroud. How is it possible that you escaped, and claimed its power as your own—" Here Untelleh's gaze momentarily shifted to the gem that hovered nearby. "—when you are a sorceress of such low skill? I have searched your past, and I know you have little true ability. Yet a barrier stands in my way when I try to look beyond the elven forest. I would learn whence you came, and how you are able to withstand and manipulate a force that I cannot. If you tell me that, you will spare your friends the suffering that must otherwise await them." Mercy stared at her captor, thinking she had met no one she would trust less with such power than Untelleh; she would rather give the Heart back to Kihantroh than teach the witch-queen how to use it. The Rittandic smirked as if Mercy had said something stupid that she thought was clever. "You will have time enough to consider the matter while your friends make their way here. Fearful of the scouts I sent northward, they have left the road and now travel overland across the plains on their journey to save you. But you need not worry for their safety! I will see that no harm comes to them before they arrive. And once they do, their fate will be left in your fair white hands. I am sure you will decide that I should treat them gently." A long moment passed, during which Mercy, entangled in the glamour, remained unable to respond. Finally Untelleh shivered elaborately. "So cold here, down below, is it not? Let us return to the surface, and enjoy the warmth of this autumn day while it lasts." A bone-thin arm on her shoulder guided Mercy back to the shadowed doorway through which they had entered the domed chamber.

And stepping across the threshold, Mercy stumbled over her bedroll and sprawled, alone, on the floor of her doorless prison cell in the distant tower.

~~~~

Bernard knew they had gotten lucky in the low gulch when the first riders had approached, but the terrain was in general too flat to conceal them consistently, and although the grass was tall enough to tangle up their legs and slow them down it couldn't provide decent cover; travelers on the road, particularly those on horseback, would still be able to spot them easily, and from pretty far away. It wasn't enough for them to be careful. They needed to be invisible. When he raised the possibility of *actual* invisibility, Brennendah seemed rather cool on the idea of keeping a constant veil around them, the way Mercy used to do—evidently it was more of an effort to maintain such a glamour than she had let on—but he said that if they followed the ravine to the east they would eventually enter broken, arid, unsettled terrain, largely devoid of trade routes, through which they could scurry without being seen. And so they spent a few hours trudging along the stream bed, sometimes splashing through the shallow current where the banks were too narrow or too unstable to support them. The Fists grew gradually less distant. The way was generally uphill, though not terribly steep, and after some distance Bernard noticed that the creek had gone dry and become a sandy wash. Not long after that the gully opened up into a sprawling badlands of spiky vegetation and jagged runoff channels that Brennendah said carried alpine meltoff in the springtime. They turned south, walking along shallow, pebble-strewn wadis, winding slot canyons, crumbly alluvial deposits. If he hadn't been traveling with an elf and a blue-grey stick figure, Bernard might have forgotten he was roaming through the landscape of an alien world. The tall, dry grasses that waved grey seed-heads in a steady breeze from the mountains could have been any prairie brush; the small, drab birds that darted throughout it, plucking meals out of the pods, could have been any thrush or sparrow; the unseen creatures and insects that whirred and twittered from the scrubby cover could have been any field mouse or cricket; the occasional unseen raptor that revealed its presence with a keening screech from overhead could have been any familiar hawk or falcon. They made slower progress on these meandering trails, but being well out of the way of any more of Untelleh's patrols seemed a fair exchange to Bernard; he wanted to get to Mercy as quickly as possible, but not as a prize or a prisoner.

The wind shifted as they moved farther south, changing direction and bringing a light but sustained and chilly drizzle in from the sea. According to Brennendah, this sort of autumn shower had once been common at this time of year—not in his lifetime, of course, but it was recorded to have been so in the annals of the distant past, before the Æther's explosive growth—and he took a childlike delight in the mild storm, walking with his arms outstretched as if trying to catch the falling water and store it away for future use. He managed to persuade Nebandalex to do it, too; and soon both of them were spinning around like desert-born toddlers who had never seen any form of precipitation before. Bernard just huddled under his cloak, worried about flash floods that never materialized, and waited for the rain to stop. It didn't. It just kept going, with only occasional breaks, and after a day and a half of it, even Brennendah had grown tired of being cold and wet all the time, and was relieved when the skies cleared towards the middle of the second day. A little precipitation was a welcome novelty, he said, but incessant precipitation was a tedium. Bernard could have told him that.

Soon another novelty replaced the unmourned rain: The sea, which they reached a few hours after the drizzle finally ended. The narrow creek bed they were following had grown steadily deeper, but not any wider, and had accumulated a small amount of current that flowed lazily along its center—runoff from the rain which, though sustained, had never been heavy enough to really saturate the thirsty ground—but Bernard didn't realize they were approaching the coast until they rounded a corner and the small canyon opened up onto a panoramic, miles-wide view of a broad pea-gravel beach. The ocean of greedy, nibbling vapor had been replaced by one of water; grey-blue waves broke and foamed among glistening stones that managed to be both smooth and jagged at the same time. Bluffs rose to a considerable height in both directions, but the weathered gap along which they walked offered a rough scramble down to the sloping, rock-strewn shore. Clumps of prickly-looking pale-green sage dotted the base of the cliffs and grew along the verticals here and there, as if the palisades had done a sloppy job of shaving. Untelleh's stronghold loomed far off to the west, the distant black rampart dominating the top of the seaside bluffs just before the shoreline hooked southward and faded into mist and obscurity. He thought he could make out empty vaulted niches in the seaward-facing side; probably they were for lighting beacons at night, to warn ships away from shoals, but Bernard got the impression they were empty pedestals for carven figures whose occupants had gotten up and gone walkabout. Given what Mercy had told him about the defenders of the Maul in the crypt beneath Lord Korrin's castle, the concept of prowling statuary had a disturbing lack of impossibility. The distant, hulking bulwark made him uncomfortable; grey and washed-out through the miles of thin spray, it bestrode the landscape like the coil of a giant snake, reminding him of the wall around Abacar, as seen from the chasm, where it hugged the edge of the cliff. Bernard found it difficult to imagine that something as plainly massive as that far-off barrier had only days ago emerged from misty nothing. "So that's where we're going, right?" he asked. The question was plainly unnecessary, and no one bothered to answer it.

After ascertaining that no patrols were visible along the shore, they scrambled down from their vantage point, keeping low and moving down the side of the rockfall opposite the keep. Once they reached the bottom Brennendah hurried forwarded and waded into light surf that rose to his knees, scooping up water in his hands and then letting it flow out between his long fingers. Bernard wasn't sure what to make of this behavior, and kept an eye on the Rittandic in case he decided to fill his pockets with stones, swim out past the breakers, and try to drown himself. He seemed only to intend to experience the sea, though. Nebandalex seemed on edge; he stood off to the side nervously nocking and lowering an arrow, all the while scanning up and down the beach, as if expecting a sea monster to heave itself out of the depths and require shooting. Bernard watched the elf for a minute, then turned his attention westward again. "So we'll go along the beach, I guess?"

"It seems the most direct approach."

"There's not much cover down here. They'll see us coming from miles away."

"Of course they will." Brennendah splashed back to join them on the slippery rubble. "Commanding a view of the lowlands is the entire point of building a wall high on the bluffs."

"Can you put a veil on us when we get closer, and hide our footprints?"

"I can cast a concealment glamour, yes, but you must understand that this is not some human king relying on spies and eyes to observe what transpires in his realm. Do not expect to take Untelleh by surprise, no matter how many layers of obscurity you ask me to drape upon us."

Bernard sighed. "I know. I just ... I don't want to get filled full of arrows as soon as we come into range."

"Felling travelers in a hail of arrows before learning who they are and what they want is hardly a usual mode of Rittandic welcome."

"This is hardly a usual Rittandic," Bernard said, "and we're hardly usual travelers."

Chapter 10

IT TOOK MOST of what was left of the day for them to reach the bottom of the bluff where the wall first appeared; following the winding path of the shoreline along its crags and lagoons and miniature harbors increased the distance they had to cover, and in those frequent spots where the beach was buried under rockfalls or simply nonexistent they had to scramble over mounded, shifting debris or wade through deep water. The last few miles, at least, consisted of a straight stretch of smooth, dry, level sand, uncluttered by rubble, unadorned by mounds of sedge; it was so clear and well-groomed, in fact, that Bernard soon realized that it must be maintained by Untelleh's people for the purpose of making it that much more difficult for anyone to approach the stronghold walls unseen. It was definitely time for the veil glamour. Brennendah cast it, explaining that he had been working on it as they had walked, modifying the enchantment so that it smoothed the surface behind them, erasing the signs of their passage with a quiet whisking sound, as if they were dragging one of Aldric's beloved bead curtains along behind them. Bernard had no idea if the glamour would actually fool any observers or detectors, but having it up made him feel a little better, as it always had when Mercy used it.

Ahead of them, the bluff topped by Untelleh's wall grew steadily taller and, it seemed, steeper, as if it saw them coming and was puffing itself up to scare them off. Not wanting to tackle a treacherous climb directly beneath her parapets, Bernard's roguish eyes began searching for a spot where they could get off the beach and back up to higher ground. As they neared the southward turn of the beach, he spotted a narrow, jagged cleft in the bluff, where runoff had exposed layers of shale that formed a rough sort of ladder. The sediment proved crumbly and unstable, and by the time they gained the top all three of them were tired, sweating, and filthy. Here on the plateau, rolling, unmanaged, grassy hills gave way to pastureland in the west and the arid terrain of what had been border of the Æther off to the north. An obvious demarcation existed where the sedge of the seaside cliffs instantly transitioned to a sere landscape of brown scrub and grey earth; Bernard supposed that with the disappearance of the Æther and the restoration of rain from the sea, that desert-like region would bloom again, but for now the ecology remained jarringly different, like new skin next to old where a scab had flaked away. Somewhere in that direction, too, would be the rise on which Brennendah's observation post had stood, now far removed from where the land had once ended: A nondescript hill in a field of other nondescript hills, scrub and sand with no more claim to importance than any other patch of ground. Once special, now ordinary. Perhaps some future explorer would find the ruins and wonder why anyone had bothered to build something in such an unremarkable spot.

They moved off to the west, concealed within Brennendah's veil glamour, towards Untelleh's stronghold and the surrounding cultivated areas. As they circled it to the north, the vast complex of black stone and jumbled towers began to more closely resemble what he had seen through the telescope in the watchtower at Jordneh's castle. A narrow, rocky track skirted the edge of the planted area, splitting into a series of paths that divided it into a grid, with different plants growing in neatly separated rows in each section. A small number of workers, Rittandics clad in shiny hats and silvery outfits that looked like an alien edition of the classic farmer's overalls, prowled the fields inspecting leaves, measuring stalks, and examining produce that was clearly not ripe. The agricultural outlook seemed grim. It was now mid-autumn, Bernard knew, which would put them at or near the end of the growing season for most things; but these plants appeared tender and immature, nowhere near ready to be harvested. He surmised it had been springtime when this region had vanished into the Æther, and now they were back at the wrong time of year, and their crops were going to fail once the weather turned cold. What sort of stockpiles of food did they have? Had they returned from the beyond just to face a famine? Maybe that was why Untelleh was sending riders out across the land; maybe she was looking for supplies to get them through the winter.

They followed a route through the fields that avoided the areas where the Rittandics were working, and eventually reached a major road—the same one they had abandoned in the North, Brennendah said—which sloped down to become a sunken roadway leading to a set of wooden gates in the vast onyx wall. These stood open; through them he could see a rolling, grassy field dotted with small clusters of buildings, and, beyond that, the towering keep and castle complex. That would be where Mercy was being held, of course; you always kept the captive princess in the most impregnable location you could find.

Speaking of impregnable, as they drew closer, Bernard realized that the opening in the wall behind the gates was blocked by a spiderweb of jointed black bars that formed an articulated iron lattice, a geodesic dome flattened into a self-reinforcing panel like some sort of impossible puzzle toy. Bernard had grown accustomed to seeing such archaic barriers to entry as portcullises, gates, and heavy nets, but this was a new sort of thing. Spindly as it looked, he guessed it would prove resistant to battering, and he had no idea how to even begin trying to pick the thing, or even where the lock was, if it had one. Bernard glanced at Brennendah, then at the barrier, then at Brennendah again. The Rittandic shrugged. "I have never seen the like," he said. "It must be some artifact of Untelleh's that fell into disuse with her disappearance."

"Can you open it?"

Brennendah inspected the metalwork, running his long fingers just above the surface but not actually touching it. "It appears to be purely mechanical. I could likely force it to open with a glamour, but that would attract attention."

"We may not have to do that," Nebandalex said, pointing through the gate at a small group of Rittandics who had just come galloping out of the keep. "See? Riders."

It looked like another scouting party. The three of them shrank back into the grassy slope as the clever iron fingers of the barricade twitched, then disengaged and retracted, creaking and clattering with a metallic chatter as they withdrew. The spikes did not completely disappear into the sides or top of the archway, making the door look disconcertingly like a demonic mouth full of needle-sharp black teeth. The riders thundered out of this maw and off up the road; after a few moments the framework sealed itself up again, but not before Bernard and the others scurried through.

They were in.

Now he *really* had to start figuring out what he was going to say to the witch-queen when they knocked on her door.

~~~~

Mercy had spent a good portion of the last few days trying to worry away at the glamour that kept her from speaking or casting spells, to burn it off like grease or grind it off like stone. Unfortunately she had not even come close to succeeding; these bonds had proven much more formidable and resilient than the physical ropes which had restrained her in Torgonderrer, blocking her from getting at any of the strings of the world around her. It was like trying to play the guitar while wearing frozen mittens. So there she remained, helpless and impotent and crashingly bored. Since Untelleh had shown Mercy the puddle of Æther in her basement and then sent her stumbling through a mystical doorway back into her tower prison cell, nothing much had happened; the witch-queen had simply left her there to stew in her own thoughts, doubts, and fears. The only thing that told her she hadn't been completely forgotten was the occasional appearance in one or another wall of a door with a slot-like opening at the bottom, through which flat disk of hard cheese or a trencher of bread smeared with thin gruel would be shoved. She never knew exactly where this portal might appear—once, it had even manifested in the form of a trap door in the ceiling, through which the victuals had simply been dropped, to bounce off into various corners—but she could tell it wasn't random; it never materialized close enough for her to make a grab for the delivery person's arm. She supposed the other necessary items in her cell were being exchanged or emptied in a similar fashion while she was sleeping. With nothing in the room to distract her, with no ability to work glamours, with no jailers to entreat or pester, sleeping became something she did a lot; or at least, it did, until the completion of the evil machine outside brought the hours of unremitting silence to a cacophonous end.

Her room, which until then had been devoid of sounds other than those of her own making, suddenly filled up with the clank and clatter of gears and chains, startling Mercy out of a light doze. After figuring out the noises were coming from outside, she ran to the window to see what was going on, and discovered that they were testing the device, the empty seat sweeping back and forth. What was even worse than the mechanical serenade was the undercurrent of murmuring and gibbering that apparently emanated from the terrified prisoners locked up nearby, watching the instrument of their future torment get put through its warm-up routine like a gymnast getting ready for a round of tumbling. Mercy could almost believe that she would be able to hear the swing set of doom up here, but no way should the voices of the condemned be so loud. Was Untelleh piping all the audio into her cell as some sort of an intimidation tactic? She probably was, the cow. *This is what I will do to your friends when they get here.* Mercy retreated from the window and lay down on her bedroll and covered her ears with her hands, and tried to shut out the pleas and the screaming as the torturers tried out their toy on the prisoners. This went on and on for the rest of the evening and most of the night, finally winding down in the small hours. Then it started up again, exactly the same as before, and continued throughout the day, until finally Mercy went to the window to see how many prisoners were left, how much longer she was going to have to listen to their screams. She discovered that the cell stood empty, the device idle. Evidently Untelleh had captured the sound with a glamour and was playing it back for her on a loop. What a bitch.

Some time later, as the midday sun began to stream through the windows of her prison, the sound ended abruptly just as a new door appeared in the wall opposite where Mercy sad. No bread came through this one; instead, it swung outward to reveal Untelleh standing there, discreetly flanked by a couple of guards. "Good afternoon," she said. "You look rather haggard. I do hope that the tedious business of administering justice did not keep you from your rest?" The witch-queen made a show of looking her up and down. "I see that it did. How sad."

Mercy considered making an obscene gesture, but figured it would be lost on the witch-queen. Nevertheless, Untelleh smirked as if the gesture had been made and appreciated. "I have come to let you know that your friends are here. They loitered indecisive outside my walls until I sent some riders out, that they might have the opportunity to creep inside before the gate closed itself again. Let us go down to meet them, and see what manner of *understanding* we may reach." She stepped back and turned sideways, gesturing Mercy forward; and so Mercy once again followed the witch-queen out of the tower along a different route from before, trudging down spiraling steps that curled counterclockwise around an exposed central shaft. A single misstep could send the unwary walker plunging to the bottom. Mercy wondered what would happen if she tried to push Untelleh over the edge. The guards at her back would certainly spit her on their spears before she could finish making a move against her captor. Maybe she could jump to her own death, sacrifice herself to save Bernard and the others. Would that inspire Untelleh to be merciful? Ha. As if. More likely it would just piss her off.

The witch-queen glanced back at her, and said: "I do hope you are using this time to carefully consider the small favor I asked of you, rather than conjuring futile fantasies of thwarting my will?"

Mercy *really* wanted that woman out of her head.

At the bottom of the stairs, a stone landing and an archway disbursed them into the yard, just like last time. The guards stayed behind when Untelleh guided her out into the shadow of the wall, then extended an arm to stop her. She was gazing off across the expanse of yard, looking toward the distant wall, but Mercy wasn't sure what she was supposed to see besides the small groups of Rittandics moving here and there engaged in what looked like routine inspection and maintenance, though she supposed there was nothing routine about working on a structure that had spent the last half-millennium being chewed over in the Æther like a giant hunk of saltwater taffy.

"You are confused? You wonder where your companions are to be found?" Untelleh said, in the mild fashion of a teacher gently chiding a student who was notorious for overlooking the obvious. "I thought you might be more observant than that. Allow me to show you that which eludes your eyes."

A shimmer flowed across Mercy's vision, shifting her perception of the world from the mundane view to one not unlike what she had seen when she had lowered her consciousness to the level of the strings in Torgonderrer while trying to free herself from the ropes that bound her. This time, though, it was like looking through a lens or a filter that Untelleh had placed in front of her face. She tried to seize on the strings thus revealed, to do something with them, anything, grab them and shake them; but the obscuring glamour rendered her incapable of manipulating them. They slipped away from her clumsy grip, as Untelleh knew they would. She might as well be trying to play the guitar with fake fingers made of rubber bands and sausages.

"You would do well to stop trying to work your skills. You cannot succeed." The witch-queen bent over, leaned in close, and lowered her voice, as if she were a trusted advisor warning Mercy of another trusted advisor's treasonous intent. "You have little time left. Soon your friends will be punished for your willfulness."

What was Untelleh talking about? Where were they? Then the witch-queen pointed with a long finger, slowly moving it, as if tracking the progress of some distant traveler, and Mercy finally spotted the thing that the sorceress wanted her to see: A pocket of blankness moving through the field of reality, a place from which her gaze slid like rain from oiled cloth, over which her mind tried to skip like a flat rock skimming still water. Whatever that mysterious bubble concealed was making its way toward the keep, angling slightly away from them, heading for a wide front gate at a spot where the wall curved outward and around.

Well. She didn't really need to peer into it to know what it contained, did she? She knew who was hiding in there. If only she—

"You would like to see your friends again in the flesh, before they depart from it?" Untelleh said, raising her hands to cast a spell. "I will be happy to grant you this small request."

~~~~

As the three of them neared the front gate, Brennendah suddenly halted and spread his spindly arms out to either side, stopping them all short like a lowered barricade. Before Bernard could ask what was going on, Brennendah's head swiveled nearly all the way around to look back at him and Nebandalex. "We have been detected," he said.

"But the veil—"

"It is being stripped." Even as the he spoke, Bernard could tell the glamour was failing, falling to tatters all around them, a broken shimmer rippling down like drizzle half-seen in refracted light. "Untelleh knows we are here."

"Is she attacking us?"

"Define *attack*," Brennendah said. "The best answer I can give is that we are not dead yet."

Bernard didn't find that very comforting. He backed up into Nebandalex, who backed up into Brennendah, each of them covering a third of a circle around them as the last of the veil faded and left them exposed on Untelleh's front step, unwanted peddlers selling unneeded products. Nebandalex had his bow up and ready to fire, though Bernard hadn't noticed him draw or nock an arrow. He supposed this would be a good time to formulate a new plan, but before he could come up with one, he spotted a large, luminous orb—the gems!—floating some distance away, its cyanotic glow lighting up a shady spot beneath a towering wall. Two figures stood near it; one was tall and reed-thin, the other shorter and fuller; one was a pale grey-blue, the other just pale; one had to be Untelleh, and the other was ...

"It's Mercy," Bernard said.

At his back, Nebandalex said: "What? Where?"

"Over there. I think she's with Untell—" He broke off as Nebandalex elbowed him aside and charged off towards the two figures, loosing an arrow as he ran. It struck an invisible wall just short of Untelleh and was deflected to the side to stick, quivering, in the dirt nearby. The archer was already drawing another one. What the hell did he think he was doing? But then he remembered Jordneh's castle, and how furiously Nebandalex had attacked and pursued Kihantroh; he probably shouldn't be surprised that Kihantroh's boss would receive the same treatment. He glanced over his shoulder at Brennendah, tipped his head at the elf's receding back. "Come on," he told the Rittandic. "Let's go parley." The two of them took off in a sprint after Nebandalex, who continued in a dead run, firing arrow after arrow as he went; Bernard realized he kept aiming at the same spot in the protective barrier, as if he thought that if he hit it often enough one of them might get through. To Bernard's surprise, one finally did; but it stopped just in front of Untelleh's face, as if it had been caught in a net. It fell to the ground at her feet. That was the last projectile in Nebandalex's quiver; Bernard could see he had no arrows left and so, apparently, could Untelleh. He felt a sudden wrenching sensation then, as if one of Mercy's portals had just opened up around them, spun them through like an automatic revolving door, and vanished again. They were suddenly back together, the three travelers, standing amid the snapped and broken arrows that littered the ground in front of the witch-queen.

Mercy opened her mouth, but the only sound that came out was a grunting squeak. Had Untelleh cut out her tongue or something? He didn't get the chance to find out; a small army of Rittandics suddenly swarmed out of a door that just *appeared* in the wall of the keep, surrounding and disarming them before Bernard even thought about reaching for his quarterstaff. Nebandalex's shoulders slumped in defeat as the three of them were forced away from Untelleh and Mercy, toward a large freestanding cage that stood not far off, around the curve of the castle, next to a nasty-looking apparatus that seemed to be a swing set made of iron poles and chains and hooks and blades, a toy built by a demented child to torture his action figures. You wouldn't mistake that thing for a playground amusement, not even in the dead of night. They went past it on their way to the cell. Neither Nebandalex nor Brennendah seemed to have any fight left in reserve. If Cynidece were still here, they wouldn't have been able to contain her; she would have had her claws out, pieces of Rittandic would have gone flying. But she wasn't here, and if she had been Untelleh would have just swatted her down like an annoying fly anyway. Bernard cursed himself for an idiot. He thought he might talk to Untelleh? He thought he might persuade her to let Mercy go? Ha! Brennendah was right all along. Untelleh had never had any reason or motivation to bargain with them for Mercy's release.

But she had every reason to use them as leverage to get Mercy to cooperate.

~~~~

"Well," Untelleh said, "there go your *rescuers*. I hope you did not find their performance overly disappointing."

Mercy, unable to respond or intervene, could only stand and observe as the others were taken away, outnumbered and overwhelmed like sad protesters for an unpopular cause who hadn't been told that their demonstration had been canceled. After a self-indulgent moment of smirking triumph, the witch-queen went back to moving with a purpose; she pivoted and marched back toward the castle, compelling Mercy to follow. They passed through a narrow iron door that conveniently appeared when they needed it in the wall nearby and just as conveniently disappeared after they used it, then strode along a narrow corridor in what seemed to be the opposite direction from the way the others had been taken; but when they turned right and exited through an archway at the end, they emerged onto an elevated pavilion that afforded a full view of the cell and the torture device, as if they were a couple of VIPs who had been given an exclusive perch to watch the day's entertainment. Despite having taken what seemed like a long way round, they actually arrived before the prisoners did. From up there she watched as Bernard, Brennendah, and Nebandalex were prodded along by Untelleh's guards, herded towards the cage below. The show was about to begin. Pass the popcorn, please. But suddenly Bernard tore himself out of the grip of the Rittandics who held him, turning into a blur of flying hands and kicking feet, like a mild-mannered librarian suddenly revealed to be a kung fu master. Maybe in his desperation he had finally tapped into the fighting skills that he hadn't accessed since Brannoc's departure. He somehow managed to get hold of his quarterstaff, wrenching it out of the grip of whichever guard had been carrying it, swinging it wide to clear himself a bit of space. The pikemen regrouped, bringing their spearlike weapons to bear. He was going get himself spitted from half a dozen different directions.

Then Untelleh simply held out her hand, and, abruptly, Bernard's quarterstaff was in her grip.

Deprived of his weapon in mid-swing, Bernard was now overbalanced; he stumbled and fell and was immediately buried in a pile of Rittandic guards. They didn't give him a chance to start fighting again; this time, they picked him up by his arms and his legs and carried his wriggling form toward the cage, where the others were already locked up. The witch-queen paid no attention to any of this, intent as she was on studying her new prize, as if it were a giant stick-insect she had found walking on her bedroom wall. Mercy figured she must be object-reading it, going back through Bernard's history, comparing it to Mercy's, trying to figure out the puzzle of their presence here. Maybe she hoped that Bernard's memories would tell her what Mercy's memories would not, although in this, Mercy thought, she was likely to be disappointed. Untelleh stood there with her eyes closed and the Heart floating around her in its little orbit, her long fingers tapping up and down the leather-wrapped wood like a piper playing a tune. How distracted was she? Mercy experimentally sidled a tiny bit closer; the gem immediately revolved to the far side of Untelleh as if actively avoiding her, which, of course, it was. She stopped moving then, understanding that if she got too near Untelleh would certainly notice and retaliate, and not necessarily against her. She took a half step away from the witch-queen; the stone remained on Untelleh's opposite side, but with a little more range in its drifting. It could move a little more freely while still avoiding Mercy. Then it occurred to her that maybe the Heart wasn't really *avoiding* her as such; maybe it was the obscuring glamour that covered her, which didn't let her speak, which didn't let her touch any strings, that was repelling the gem. But, no, that didn't seem quite right either. The glamour didn't seem to be that active; it didn't radiate. The Heart radiated.

Oh.

Oh, of course.

How could she have been so dense? The *Heart* radiated, and the glamour around her blocked it, and so the Heart pushed itself away from her. An equal and opposite reaction. Could she somehow get the glamour to *absorb* the Heart's energy instead? Mercy glanced at Bernard's quarterstaff. Untelleh was still working on it, holding it horizontally, trying to wring out whatever information could be extracted about its owner. Mercy remembered that he had physically struck the Illata with his weapon at least once. Touching the Illata had changed her, and it had changed Bernard; maybe it had changed the quarterstaff too. She shifted her weight, moved over just a hair, then a hair more, until the near end of the weapon was just in contact with the null field that surrounded her. The other end was close to the Heart, and for the first time in days, Mercy felt something through the weight of the spell that Untelleh had laid on her, a flicker of the Heart's presence, its power. It flowed through the quarterstaff like a dull electric current, conducted along the physical object and across the border of the glamour that surrounded her, like poking an antenna through an insulating barrier in order to get the signal out.

She could use this. Or at least, she could, as long as Untelleh didn't tire of trying to read the quarterstaff, or idly step away, or notice what she was doing and turn off the transmitter. Those were a lot of conditions.

Well, if using the Heart were easy, *everyone* would be doing it, right?

~~~~

Bernard watched through the bars as the sinister device nearby was tested by a small team of Rittandic technicians, or whatever you wanted to call them. It looked like something the dwarves might have invented, if the dwarves had put their engineering skills toward developing new methods of torture. Unlike the dwarven machinery Bernard had encountered, this apparatus was quite noisy, squeaking and rattling as it swung back and forth, the motion engaged by a system of chains and pulleys that caused the blades to oscillate and the manacles to twist and retract in a manner that was sure to be highly unpleasant for whatever unfortunate was forced to sit in it. Getting locked in a drawer by the dwarves like a cadaver in the morgue and being suspended out over the chasm by his wrists in Abacar had been bad, but this ... this looked like it was going to be worse. At least there wouldn't be a death-wind lurking under the sea beneath their feet, waiting for its next meal.

Suddenly he remembered that when the dwarves had rolled him out of that cell to interrogate him, Untelleh had been standing in the shadows behind them, watching, listening. She had been there again when they took him out and brought him to the arena, and later on, when he had met Filothandiar and been sent off on his fool's errand to Yexandor's fallen tree. And, yes, she had been in Abacar, too, hanging from the cable with him and Nebandalex and Cynidece and Poddock. She had escaped with them from Daras-Drûm, she had accompanied them into the mountains, she had stood silently in the shadows at Grunsandrovar's inn, she had walked with them across the plains. In fact, it seemed she had been following him everywhere, from the beginning, but despite her continuous presence everyone always acted as if she weren't even there. Wasn't that strange?

Yes, it *was* strange, because none of it had happened. Untelleh hadn't been present for any of those events, and even though he now remembered that she was, he knew—he *knew*—that he had never seen her until the moment she appeared in Jordneh's castle, blasted a hole in the floor, and made off with Mercy and the gem. Why was he even thinking about all this stuff now? Why was the sad history of their little quest replaying in his mind, featuring the witch-queen as a character who had been retroactively added to the show? He squeezed his eyes shut and shook his head, trying to clear it of the sudden rush of memories, trying to push them out of his head, where they didn't belong. When he opened his eyes again, he found he just happened to be looking through the bars of the cell, straight at the platform where Untelleh stood with his quarterstaff, her body turned towards him, and even though her own eyes were closed he felt bathed in her attention, swimming in it.

So that was it. This was something she was doing somehow; she was projecting at him, making him relive all this stuff, so she could watch and learn from it, and he could do nothing to stop her. She went through his memories backwards and forwards and backwards again, from his caged present to when he had first appeared outside the cliffs of Dolvendelve and the rocks began to fall, but no farther. He knew there was more before that point, memories she hadn't reached, and she knew it too, and he picked up her frustration at her inability to cross that barrier and access the older, longer chain of events that had led him here. She beat against it like a moth trying to get through a window to reach the light behind it. She wanted to know, she *needed* to know, where he came from, where Mercy came from, how they got here, and *she couldn't find out,* and it was driving her crazy. The harder she pushed and failed, the more she became convinced that the information locked away must be vital. She was in his head, filling it with echoes of her agitation. She didn't know that the things she didn't know were dull and useless, that she was wasting her time and attention trying to find out what his life had been before. And not only that: It seemed she couldn't even tell that he was thinking about it *right now.* His real thoughts remained concealed, as if he was a crooked accountant keeping two sets of books, and she was an auditor who knew something was up but couldn't figure out what.

Finally she opened her eyes and met his gaze for a moment; then her glance shifted to Bernard's left and she nodded slightly. The Rittandic guards stepped up to a large black metal disk in the door and did something to it that opened the cell. They dragged Nebandalex out, hauling him toward the dreadful implement, slamming the door behind them. Bernard rogue-ears heard a latch click into place on the exterior of the cube, and his rogue-brain noted that they didn't do anything to secure it: No padlock snapped shut, no key turned, no dial spun. It was just a latch. He took a closer look at the circular plate. Rimmed with saw-edged iron points as big as daggers, it filled the entire center of the door, preventing whatever the opening mechanism was from being accessed from within. And if that surface didn't offer enough discouragement, the interior of the cage itself was inwardly spiked at every intersection of the bars, each a vicious snaggletooth eager for a bite of flesh. If for some reason the ceiling dropped or the walls closed in, the unfortunate occupants would be impaled before they could be crushed.

Under the pretext of staring, terrified, through the bars as they hauled the elf over to the torture device—a pantomime which did not require much in the way of acting chops—Bernard let his leather-clad sleeve run over the jagged edge of the protective door plate. His clothing provided some protection, not much, but perhaps enough. Assuming that he got the opportunity while the guards were distracted, and that he had a limb long enough to reach the latch, he might have a shot at opening the door without getting torn to ribbons; and then he and Brennendah could rescue Nebandalex from the device, and the three of them could liberate Mercy, and the four of them could all scamper off and live peaceful lives as cabbage farmers or something. Maybe they could even have a pony.

Jewel-encrusted, of course.

~~~~

It wasn't easy to ignore the activity around the cage, the plight of her friends, the rattling of chains and gears as they exercised their little machine; it wasn't easy to stand with downcast eyes and an air of defeat, all the while focusing on the Heart and its proximity to the quarterstaff, yet betraying to Untelleh no evidence of her interest; but it had to be done, and Mercy did it, until the witch-queen had finally extracted all the information she could get out of Bernard's weapon. She gave some kind of signal to her flunkies down below, who opened the cage and extracted Nebandalex as their first victim. Untelleh moved a little closer to the front of the platform and cast the quarterstaff aside like a rose from a rejected suitor. The Heart—which, as it often did, was drifting in the vicinity of what would have been Untelleh's right shoulder blade, assuming she had shoulder blades—moved itself out of the way to avoid contact with the discarded item. The end of the leather-wrapped weapon missed it by a few inches.

Mercy's left hand shot out, almost on its own, and caught the other end before it hit the ground.

Now that she had hold of the staff, the flow of current from the Heart's aura into hers increased explosively, becoming a sudden, surging wave. Untelleh's glutinous enchantment actually helped her now, collecting energy like a capacitor or a sail catching the wind. Mercy hadn't expected that. Nor had she expected the energy she had begun accumulating to draw the Heart towards her, but it did, disrupting its usual slow orbit around Untelleh. The witch-queen stiffened, and her head swiveled around to look at Mercy, then at the quarterstaff, then at the Heart. Her dark eyes widened. She took a half step forward before stopping short, unable or unwilling to get closer. She raised her arm and extended a long-fingered hand, then jerked it back as if burned or stung. Mercy felt a sudden resistance, a wrenching sensation in her head; Untelleh was trying to pull the Heart back into her orbit, initiating some kind of mystical tug-of-war. The witch-queen was unquestionably more powerful than Mercy, but Mercy had a head start with the reservoir of power that had accumulated in the folds of the glamour and added its attractive force to her own affinity for the gem. It wasn't a thumb tilting the scale in her favor, it was more like a brick. Mercy saw Untelleh's expression change as the sorceress rapidly assessed the situation and realized that the spell she'd laid on her captive had begun to work against her. Mercy felt the muzzling glamour evaporate and then reconfigure from an insulator into a reflector. The energy that had accumulated erupted in a rush as the capacitor discharged, blasting Mercy backwards across the platform. The blowback traveled into Bernard's quarterstaff, which detonated as if it were an explosive cartoon cigar. The leather wrapping came undone and rocketed away like party streamers, while the core of wood and metal blew apart, sending sizzling fragments zinging every which-way. The Heart itself rocketed into the air in a crazy spin as the recoil knocked it free from anyone's control.

This was her chance. Now. *Now!*

Mercy sent her magical grasp lunging for the Heart, but before she could catch it the accursed glamour fell on her again, as if a truck full of tar and blankets had dumped its load over her head. The opportunity was gone. She had missed it. Mercy pushed herself up to a sitting position, feeling as if the platform bucked and twirled beneath her. Those sensations faded as aftereffects of the blast diminished. Nothing else seemed to be happening. Untelleh wasn't retaliating for her affront, and as her head cleared further, she realized why. The witch-queen hadn't gone after the gem immediately herself; she had first taken a moment to cripple Mercy again, knowing that her link to the gem would prove a formidable obstacle to overcome, and in doing so, she had left her flank exposed, mystically speaking. Untelleh had moved faster than Mercy, but someone else had moved faster than both of them. She followed the witch-queen's gaze to the field below, where Nebandalex had been about to be loaded into the torture device. The elf was gone and Kihantroh stood in his place, wearing his clothes, surrounded by sprawled Rittandics. They had been flattened like trees felled by a pyroclastic wave. The dreadful apparatus lay on its side in a tangle of chains and metal. The Heart slowly spun around

Kihantroh's blue-grey head, reflected in its dark and gleaming eyes, as it silently stared up at Untelleh.

"Kihantroh," the witch-queen said at last, "do you have some grievance you wish to air?"

"I did everything you asked, my queen, and you betrayed me," Kihantroh said.

"Oh, Kihantroh," Untelleh said. "Tell me, is the puppet justified in feeling betrayed when the puppeteer puts away the strings?"

"I am not your puppet."

"Of course you are not. As I said, the strings are put away. Your part in this is over."

"Over? We were going to heal the Æther, you and I! We were going to make the land whole. And instead, you——"

"Such righteous anger! Look around you, Kihantroh. The Æther *is* healed. The land *is* whole. Was this not aught but clouds and mist and nothing only a few days past? Now there is grass and earth and fresh sea air."

"I should hardly be surprised that you still seek to dissemble and misdirect. The wound in the world yet festers. I feel it weeping nearby. If you will not seal it, my queen, then I will!"

"Will you? Do you imagine it to be so simple? Very well, yes, some small portion of the Æther remains, the original well of vapor as it existed before. Yet if you seal the Æther completely, whence will come the threads for us to work our glamours? Hmm? When there is no other thread to be had, you cannot weave a new tapestry without unraveling the old one, at least a little."

Kihantroh's expression narrowed into one of disgust and disappointment. "You would begin the whole thing again. You would make the same error, take the same risk, that caused you and all your lands to——"

Untelleh interrupted with a clipped little laugh. "You are a prophet of such dread portent!" she said. "I have no intention of repeating my earlier misstep. Do you believe I have learned nothing from my … my time away? That gem, and this poor creature beside me, are the keys to safely controlling the Æther."

"The Æther cannot be controlled. It must be closed."

"Is that the sort of martyr you wish to be? You would find no more joy than I to live in the world that you seek to make."

"That is speculation," Kihantroh said. "Where is your proof that it is the Æther that grants the power to work enchantments?"

"Speculation? *Proof?* Feh! You studied the Æther for years. You should know what it is and what it does."

"Yes, I know what it does. It consumes the world."

"But you do not know what it *is*, do you? It is the pivot where realities slide across each other. It is the thin spot where the hatchling pecks to free itself from the shell. And yet you would *heal* it." Untelleh's metallic voice was frosted with ice, like a sword left out in the snow. "Yes, you would *heal* it, and lock all the worlds in place, and forever consign the chick to remain trapped within the egg. You would sacrifice all my magic, and yours, and even what little enchantments this small one can wield——" Here she both indicated and dismissed Mercy with a tilt of her white-maned head. "——So that future generations, who will not even know your name, can live mired in drudgery, but free of the fear of that the Æther may, one day, consume them."

"As it consumed *you*, my queen?"

"As it *tried* to," she said tartly.

"Well then. Let us go to the Æther, and learn what it would consume and what it would reject. Shall we all walk together? You and I and the elf?"

"What a splendid idea," Untelleh said. "Yes, do show us how well you understand the Æther, Kihantroh. Lead us to it. *Educate* us." And, over her shoulder to Mercy, with a smirk on her face: "Come along, my pet. Let us go and watch as Kihantroh mends reality and becomes a legend."

Chapter 11

STUCK IN THE cage, Bernard watched as Mercy grabbed his discarded quarterstaff. He didn't realize she was trying to use it as a crowbar to pry the Heart away from Untelleh until the staff exploded, Mercy went flying, and the Heart rocketed into the air. And while all *that* was going on, Nebandalex suddenly melted and stretched and turned into Kihantroh, scythed down the surrounding guards, and retook possession of the gem. In the space of a second or two, the entire power dynamic had shifted, leaving Bernard agape at his own stupidity. Obviously the Nebandalex who had come back dragging Kihantroh's corpse had not been the Nebandalex who had bounded off into the darkness of the throne room. He had known the password, sure, but wasn't that exactly what Kihantroh had been doing all along, stealing bodies, absorbing their thoughts and memories, using the knowledge gained to infiltrate and play different groups off against each other to achieve its own ends? Kihantroh could have disposed of him and Brennendah any time on their long walk to Untelleh's stronghold, just as it had no doubt disposed of the Pelts back at the castle—it had magicked them into the pyre and buried them in burning timber, Bernard was sure of it—but it had played the part of their friend because they could help it safely reach its goal. Now it didn't need to pretend anymore. It had the Heart, and it was talking about closing up the Æther, and Untelleh was lecturing it on what the Æther really was, leading Bernard to the disturbing realization that the so-called *thin spot in the shell* could be the gap through which he and Mercy had slipped from their world into this one. If Kihantroh closed it, would that leave them trapped here forever? *Now* whose side did they have to be on?

Their grievance unresolved, Kihantroh and Untelleh dragged Mercy off to visit whatever was left of the Æther. Some of the witch-queen's remaining pikemen moved in to gather up the guards Kihantroh had flattened, while others set about righting the torture device. It looked like it would be out of commission for a while. Bernard sidled over to Brennendah, who sat in the trampled grass in the center of the cage, legs bent, head down on his knees, and said: "We're being abandoned." Then, when the Rittandic did not respond: "Can you open the door? It's not locked, I think, just latched."

Brennendah raised his head. "No. The cage is enchanted to suppress the casting of glamours." He turned his eyes in the direction of their departing captor. "Untelleh would never have let Kihantroh out had she known what it was."

"Yeah, well, I guess Kihantroh was better at that impersonation spell than she thought." Bernard ran his fingers along the flat interior of the iron disk; it was almost as tall as he was and twice an arm-length wide, effectively shielding the release mechanism from anyone who didn't have a hook on a pole. "Okay, so, maybe we can open it the regular way while they're all occupied? Except this plate is too big. Your arms are longer than mine, can you reach the latch?"

The Rittandic gave him a look that said he was being dense. "This cell was designed *by* my kind to *hold* my kind. We know how long our arms tend to be."

"Oh. Right. Of course." Bernard stepped back, studying the crosshatched lattice of the bars, the span of the protective plate. Could he work the latch with his feet instead of his hands? He was skinny enough to get his legs most of the way through the openings, but the teeth would make any such attempt difficult and probably quite painful, while the daggers at each joint threatened to pin him like a butterfly. But what other option did they have at this point, besides sitting here and waiting for Kihantroh and Untelleh to sort things out between themselves?

If he wanted to get them out of here, he was going to have to shed some blood.

Backing up to the side of the cage opposite the plate, Bernard took a few steps forward and then leaped, swinging his feet up as if doing a trick jump where he would touch is toes in mid-air. Instead of reaching forward, he reached up. His hands found some holds between the downward-pointing barbs and he swung forward, each of his feet slipping through an oblong opening above the plate. Checking his forward momentum before slamming into the spikes on the front wall, he held himself suspended just above the jagged teeth along the edge of the plate. Well, almost; they weren't all the same size, and he felt a burning pain in several spots along his legs where the sharp metal had sliced through his leather and into his skin. Contorted to avoid further injury on the spikes and teeth, he felt all folded up in strange ways, like a piece of origami or performance art. Three Rittandic guards noticed what he was doing and broke away, hurrying over with their spearlike weapons at the ready. No more time for being careful. He let his knees bend and swung his feet around until he caught the latch between his ankles, then gave his knees a twist and lifted. The latch disengaged. He pushed the door open just far enough so that it wouldn't catch again and held it there for a second as the guards approached, waiting until they raised their spears before yanking his legs back inside——he felt more painful bites as metal teeth sliced bloody furrows along them——and kicking the plate with both feet, as hard as he could. The door swung outward and smashed into the nearest guard, sending him sprawling. Bernard leaped out after it, landing on his left foot while kicking the nearest Rittandic in the face with his right, then somehow continuing his motion into a cartwheel that carried him headlong into the only guard left standing. Before the Rittandic could react, Bernard head-butted him and snatched away his pole-arm. Ignoring the stabbing blade on the end, he wielded it as an impromptu quarterstaff, spinning it around to crack the first guard across the back as he struggled to rise, then smashing the shaft against the side of the third one's head. He spun, barely deflected a blade thrust to the face from the second guard, then ducked and swung his stolen weapon in an arc, sweeping the sentry's feet out from under him and clubbing him hard across the skull before he hit the ground. Finally he flipped the spear horizontal, caught it in both hands, and steadied himself, breathing heavily. Untelleh's three minions lay scattered at his feet. None stirred. He turned to face the larger group over by the apparatus, expecting that they must have noticed the fighting, but they weren't coming this way; instead they were running off toward the front gate. For a second he thought they were fleeing from his mighty prowess, but then he realized they were chasing something, or at least *thought* they were.

"They believe they are pursuing us," Brennendah said from right beside him. "I cast a veil glamour here, and another glamour to misdirect their attention toward fugitives who do not exist." Then: "I have assumed that you and I will *not* be making for that exit."

"No. We won't." Bernard looked at the spear in his hands, then up at the stand, where Brannoc's quarterstaff had been reduced to fragments and a heap of leather ribbon. He almost felt like he should gather up the pieces and bury it or something, but of course that was sentimental nonsense, just like his absurd attachment to Brannoc's hat. Neither belonged to him; neither really mattered to him. There was only one thing in this world that did, and she had just vanished around the castle wall as the prisoner of two powerful sorcerers. Bernard turned and pointed his purloined weapon at the spot where he had last seen her. "We're going that way."

"Of course. And when we catch them?"

"Then we rescue Mercy, and we stop Kihantroh from saving the world," he said.

~ ~ ~ ~

Mercy followed the others away from the platform and across the broad, grassy, park-like lawn. She kept casting glances back at the cage, where Bernard peered through the bars after them, but she couldn't figure out a way to free her friends; the muffling glamour, restored to full strength, prevented her from working any magic on the lock, and if she broke and ran she wouldn't get two paces before Untelleh or Kihantroh stopped her. At least they didn't seem to be in imminent danger of being tortured anymore. Losing the Heart had effectively scuppered that part of Untelleh's plan, at least for now.

Despite the witch-queen's sneering tone, it seemed that Kihantroh really *could* sense the Æther; they were going the same way as when Untelleh had taken Mercy there earlier, around the side of the castle and then toward the sunken walkway that led to the small, strange door at the bottom of the castle. As they approached the grassy berm that rose between them and the path, rather than detour to the end as Untelleh had done, Kihantroh gestured and ripped the earthen bank apart, creating an opening that looked like it might have been carved by a flash flood pushing out from the inside. Grass, roots, and stones spread out in a delta, parting around their feet, leaving a smear of dirt across the once-neat lawn. The witch-queen clapped her hands and said: "You see, Kihantroh, you love the casual exercise of power as much as I do! You will not rob yourself of it by sealing the Æther."

"When we reach the Æther, I *will* close it forever. The only question is which side of it you and the elf will find yourselves on when it closes."

"Mmm. So you claim. But when you stand before the pool of mist, you will change your mind."

"Not all of us are so disappointing and fickle as you."

"I *disappoint* you? Have you forgotten who I am? I was and am the witch-queen of the——"

"You plead royal privilege? Feh. The Tellehi were beings of wonder and innocence, not of self-centered cruelty and malice. Is there nothing of them left in you?"

"The Tellehi you spoke to were but broken aspects of myself. Would you expect one shard of a mirror to reflect an aspect entire? You of all creatures should understand that when a multitude becomes a unit, patterns change. After all, do *you* not contain multitudes?"

"No," Kihantroh said after a moment. "I contain only myself."

Mercy thought she heard a certain brittleness in its voice, something beyond its usual metallic stiffness. Apparently Untelleh did too. "Do you? You contain only yourself?" She sounded amused. "You say *I* am the cruel, self-centered one, but my Tellehi taught you the absorbance glamour, did they not? Oh, yes, they taught you better than I had realized. How many times did you use it?"

"It matters not. Those personas have vanished like stones into a pond."

"A stone cast into a pond leaves a ripple after it is gone."

"Ripples fade."

"Of course they do. But with each stone that sinks, does the water level not rise? How many stones rest on the bottom now? Four? Six? Eight? How many more could be added before the pond overflows its sides?"

"I am more than the lives I took on your behalf."

"Of course you are. And surely nothing seethes below the surface, waiting for a chance heave itself into the——"

"Enough! What I did, I did for you, and now you play the judge? Bah!"

Untelleh fell silent, a trace of a smile playing across her thin lips, and she did not speak again as they followed Kihantroh through the gap in the berm, turned left, and descended into the shadows where the path sank into the earth. At the castle wall, Kihantroh gestured for Untelleh to release the gate. Certainly it had the ability to open the way itself, so Mercy figured this must be some kind of power play, making Untelleh do its bidding. The witch-queen smirked and twirled her finger, causing the spindly iron fingers to disengage and retract. She passed through first, and without a word assumed the lead in the catacombs, guiding them along a tunnel that differed from the one Mercy remembered. The bricks that lined the walls seemed flatter, crumblier, drier; and the way it turned, right then left then right then hair-pinning back on itself, had changed. They never passed through a section where she had to crouch or turn sideways. Mercy thought about the variability of the doors and the passageways each time she had been removed from her tower cell. Evidently Untelleh had reworked the layout of the lower castle, but to what end? Were they going somewhere else? The way was definitely longer than before, and she was starting to think the witch-queen was leading them into a trap, but at last she began to feel the familiar dull emanations through the obscuring glamour; soon they entered the domed chamber that Mercy remembered, with the ring of stone surrounding the round pool of rippling, luminous vapor.

This was definitely the place.

Kihantroh seemed wary, declining to approach the mist when Untelleh did so; it hung back, peering at the vapor with those vast dark eyes. "Why do you hesitate?" Untelleh said. "Here is the Æther, which you demanded to see. Show us how you would repair the world. Seal it."

Kihantroh looked at Untelleh, but said nothing.

"Go ahead. You said you would do so. Oh, but you wished to *learn*, did you not, what it would consume and what it would reject. Perhaps you would like to take its measure first?"

"What order of fool do you take me for, telling me acid is honey and inviting me to dip my finger? You are no better than Jordneh."

"Jordneh!" Untelleh made a metallic retching noise. "Compare me not to that facile parasite! She bled the Æther for years, keeping me from——"

"Keeping you from what? From returning? Yet when I removed her and brought you back, I was rewarded with abandonment, lies, and threats." Kihantroh finally took a small step toward the vaporous pit. "So this is the spot where the world is nearly worn through, as it was before your craft tore it asunder. It seems stable. Quiet."

"It is, and that is why I tell you there is no need to close it completely. It is contained in the well and, harmless. It consumes nothing."

"Yet, as you say, that is precisely what we are here to learn. You claim the mouth consumes nothing, that it has no hunger? Then let us test it."

Suddenly Mercy's feet were yanked out from under her. She found herself being dragged along the floor, then lifted up and carried out over the Æther, where she hung suspended, dangling like a treat held to induce a dog to beg. Fog swirled below her. She could see nothing beneath the surface.

"Let us offer it a morsel and find out," Kihantroh said.

The grip on her ankles was released, and she fell into the mist.

~~~~

Bernard and Brennendah hurried after the others, who had disappeared behind a curve of the castle and were no longer in sight when the two of them rounded the corner, but it was obvious where they had gone: A breach had been opened in an embankment not far away, through which Bernard could see a sunken walkway running perpendicular to the castle. Another earthen wall stood unbroken opposite the gap. Evidently somebody had ripped a hole in the berm and then they had followed the path to the left or the right. Bernard doubted they had gone away from the castle.

They reached the earthworks under the cover of Brennendah's veil, where Bernard motioned for the Rittandic to wait while he peered around to see what was inside. The walkway beyond ran downward to another crazy gate like the one in the outer wall, all clever joints and interlocking hooks and loops, closed up tight as a miser's money clip. It was not guarded. He signaled Brennendah to proceed and they moved cautiously toward the gate. Behind it, a tunnel ran into darkness, illuminated by the barest flicker of blue light. That must be the Heart, he thought, receding into the depths of the castle. It had faded by the time they reached the opening. Bernard had no idea what sort of labyrinth lay beyond the entrance, but maybe they could still find the others in time to intervene in ... well, in whatever was going on. He eyed the complicated barrier, which seemed just as impenetrable as the larger one in the outer wall. Despite its spindly appearance, the way each segment interlocked and braced itself against at least three others made for a very sturdy lattice. The openings, while numerous, were scarcely large to admit a hand, and if it had a lock to pick he couldn't find it. "Can you magic this open?" he said, running his fingers along one of the knobby joints.

"Possibly. It is enchanted, though. It will resist the attempt."

"Is it going to explode and kill us if you try?"

After a moment, Brennendah said: "Probably not."

"Um. Well, okay, good enough. Take a shot. If it doesn't work, or it *does* explode, then I guess this is as far as we go."

"And if we get through, what is your plan?"

"Same as always," Bernard said. "Improvise."

The Rittandic gave a metallic snort, then stepped forward. Bernard moved off to the side as Brennendah closed his eyes and began to move his hands in slight, strange patterns, as if feeling his way through a thicket of hanging vines. Eventually Bernard couldn't stay still anymore and started pacing, but he couldn't go far or he would exit the range of Brennendah's veil. No one was between the embankments and looking their way, but a curious guard could always wander along, wondering what had happened to the witch-queen. So he would take a few steps in one direction, turn, take a few steps in the other direction, and repeat the process. After a little while Brennendah opened his eyes and said: "Please stand still and be patient. You are not an animal in a cage."

"Yes I am. I am *exactly* an animal in a cage. This whole world is a cage."

"The world is not a cage."

"Yes it is. It's just a really big one." Bernard tapped the unyielding iron with the blade of his stolen pole-arm. "We were never supposed to be here, you know. It's like we got caught by a trapper and taken someplace we didn't belong. We're the ... the gorillas performing in the circus."

"I have no idea what a *gorilla* is, or a circus, but I find your behaving like one performing in the other to be distracting. So stop."

"Oh. Right. Sorry." Then: "But what difference does it make? You can't open it. The spell holding it closed is too strong. Am I wrong?"

Brennendah sighed. "You are not wrong. When I release one section, two others reorient to lock it in place again."

"So it's like trying to cut the heads off a hydra."

"I have no idea what a *hydra* is, either."

"Um. It's a monster Mercy told me about once. You cut off one head and two grow back."

"This is a creature she encountered in her travels?"

After a moment, Bernard said: "Uh, yeah, sure. More or less. So you need to unlock all the sections at once, then? Can you do that?"

"No. It is difficult enough breaking open one piece, let alone all of them at the same time. Unless ..." He trailed off and cocked his head to the side, peering intently at the door, or through it, to the space beyond. Bernard started to speak, then checked himself, figuring any suggestions he might babble were unlikely to be useful. Finally Brennendah said, "It does weaken slightly, on occasion."

"It does? Why?"

"I do not know. Perhaps it is something to do with how the castle reconfigures its layout from time to time. If I prepare in advance, and move quickly, I may be able to exploit it."

"Okay. Okay good. Exploit away."

Brennendah didn't answer. His fingers danced through the air as if he were playing an invisible harp. The iron fingers trembled in their lattice, rattling faintly, but did not withdraw. Bernard waited, tensed, ready to move as soon as the way was clear. It took a bit of time, and when it did happen, it was sudden: Hooks disengaged from loops; joints swiveled and pivoted; interlocking barbs pulled free and whisked back from each other. It was not a proper opening of the gate—the gap was barely large enough for a man to slip through—but Bernard didn't wait to see if it was going to retract farther, he just bolted forward, hearing metal groan and creak even as he did. It had already begun to close. He felt a sharp point graze his ankle, a small sting added to his growing inventory of scrapes and gashes. He rolled across the dusty floor and regained his feet, then stood, leaning on his weapon as if it were a walking staff.

Brennendah was looking at him through a spiky network of black iron.

"You're on the wrong side," Bernard said after a moment.

"So I am. But I lack the strength to open it again. It seems you must go on alone."

"Alone? Seriously? I don't have a good track record of getting things done on my own." He turned and peered into the darkness. "I can't even see anything."

"That, at least, I can help you with. Bring your weapon here." Bernard tipped the butt of his stolen spear toward the door, but the Rittandic said: "No, the other end." Bernard turned it around so the point was near the door. Brennendah's thin blue hand snaked through the gate and moved in a little pattern over the blade; beads of blue light flickered along the edge of the metal, eventually joining to limn it with a cold and steady St. Elmo's fire. "Let this light your way."

Bernard extended his arm, pointing the spear down the tunnel away from the light. It seemed to provide about as much illumination as a camp lantern. "Okay, that'll do. Thanks." Then, turning back to his companion: "Wait here for us to come back, okay?"

Brennendah spread his hands wide. "Where else would I go, in this cage we call a world?"

~~~~

Time felt different in the swampy fog of the Æther. Just as the few minutes Mercy had thought she'd spent wandering in the dark space that formed the entrance to Yexandor's fallen-tree home had really been hours in the outside world, the seconds she spent falling through the mists could have been a mere eye-blink to Untelleh and Kihantroh. Or maybe the seconds were days, or years; maybe they were no time at all.

There wasn't anything in here, no surface on which to land, yet something eventually stopped her, as if the accumulated resistance of the vapor had compressed it into a cottony solid that caught and held her weight. Like a caustic bath, once she stopped moving the Æther began to eat away at Untelleh's obscuring glamour. Once that was gone, Mercy felt the full icy, corrosive power of the Æther all around her, reminding her of the sensation when Daras-Drûm had overflowed the walls of Abacar, had poured in and swamped the defenders. She and Bernard had been in the middle of it; with his help, and a boost from the Illata, she had beaten the death-wind back, crushed it down and contained it within the gem. But Bernard wasn't here this time, and neither was the Illata. This time it was just her against the Æther, which was trying to burrow in and split her into pieces, the way tree roots would worm their way into a boulder and reduce it to rubble. But some rock was too hard to break, and could turn a questing root aside, at least for a while.

Remembering what had happened on the platform, when she had accumulated the energy from the Heart in the folds of Untelleh's enchantment, she spread her arms wide, imagining them as sails to catch the wind or fabric to collect dew from thin desert fog. Her hands were spoons, they were paddles, they were collectors suitable for gathering clouds of mist. She swept them in a circular motion, scraping the drifting vapor, bringing it close and packing it into a growing bundle of Æther-stuff as if she were fashioning a star out of cosmic dust. And like a star, when her collection reached a critical mass, it ignited.

She felt it begin to push back against her with the ethereal equivalent of a solar wind, but she kept gathering and packing vapor onto it despite the increasing difficulty of overcoming the outward pressure. It was forcing the surrounding Æther away now; there was less and less within reach to gather, until finally the space around her was clear. She was hoping something more dramatic would happen but it didn't seem like her ball of Æther was quite powerful enough to accomplish anything besides pushing the rest of the Æther away. She couldn't stretch her imaginary arms any farther, and even if she could figure out how to move herself and the sphere to where material was still available, it would just retreat from her. So now what?

Suddenly an idea struck her: She would compress it.

Mercy changed her imaginary sails into an imaginary vise, clamping down from all sides on the sphere of Æther, squeezing it down, smaller and smaller. The glow intensified. Something like the Heart began to form in front of her, a small but potent power source, sealed Æther in a can. If she could master it and use it against Kihantroh and Untelleh, then—

Then it exploded.

Just before the blast, Mercy realized what was happening, that her creation had become unstable. She had packed it wrong, or unevenly, or something. Maybe this was what Untelleh had done all those centuries ago. She brought her arms and legs in, curled herself into a protective ball ahead of the shockwave. It sent her rocketing away in a direction that might have been up, if *up* had any meaning here in the nowhere. She felt a tearing sensation, like passing through a thick membrane, as the force of the explosion caused the Æther to spit her out. She hit something hard and tumbled along a curve, then slammed into a flat, cold surface, where she came to rest, stunned and dizzy.

Mercy opened her eyes.

She was lying at the intersection of the curved dome and the stone ring floor, with the puddle of Æther a few yards from her face. The mist frothed and chopped and glowed with an internal light it hadn't shown before. Untelleh and Kihantroh stood near each other on the opposite side, their faces lit up from below by the luminous vapor, reflected and distorted in their enormous black eyes. Kihantroh's lipless mouth was pressed flat in an expression that may have been shock or dismay; Untelleh's face bore an unmistakable smirk.

"So, Kihantroh, enlighten me," the witch-queen said. "Does this mean that the test failed, or that it succeeded?"

~~~~

All by himself, Bernard scurried along the narrow, dry, brick-lined passageway. Silence lay as thick and undisturbed as the dust on the floor. If the others had come this way, they had left behind no trace of their passage, but there hadn't been another route he could take; this tunnel ran straight back from the gate, no intersections or alternatives. If the corridors of Untelleh's stronghold were on some sort of continuous shuffle, he seemed to have drawn one that had gone unused for quite some time.

He came to a wall with a low archway, sort of like the opening to an oven or an igloo, and had to crouch to slip through it. Beyond was a larger chamber with empty recesses along each wall. It looked like a crypt, but if it was, the bones had been removed; no skulls grinned at him from out of the dark, no skeletal arms dangled over the edges of eternal beds. He passed through several more such rooms in sequence, all of them as empty as the first, before the tunnel closed in again and slanted to the left, trending downward. He began to hear metallic voices and slowed his pace, keeping close to the wall. He was approaching another chamber, he saw, not like the crypts; this was round and domed like a planetarium, except its central pit contained a puddle of viscous fog rather than a star projector. The voices clarified. It sounded like Untelleh and Kihantroh were arguing.

If they were here, then where was Mercy?

He found out soon enough; Kihantroh said something about a test, and then Mercy came sliding in from the side and was carried over the central pool of vapor, where she hung for a moment before falling into the fog and vanishing.   Bernard stared, shocked, at the froth. Kihantroh had just tossed Mercy into the Æther like a piece of trash.

Forgetting about moving silently, Bernard charged down the tunnel. He had no idea what he hoped to accomplish beyond jamming the sharp end of his weapon into the Rittandic's skinny chest. Before he got to the chamber, though, the Æther suddenly lit up from within, as if it contained a bank of floodlights that had just been switched on. He stopped short and flattened himself against the wall again, still concealed by the angle and the shadows, he hoped. He held his breath and started counting the seconds as the dribbled past, not sure how long he should wait, or even what he was waiting for. When he got to three, the center of the Æther bulged upward, then vomited out a mist-shrouded ball. It hit the ceiling and bounced off, landing on the floor not far from the archway where Bernard stood. As the clinging vapor dissipated he realized he was looking at Mercy. The Æther had ejected her. Bernard's grip on his spear tightened as she lay there motionless. Was she dead? No; her fingers twitched and her lashes fluttered. She opened her eyes and moved a little, her head lolling to the side to look at the gurgling fog, which continued to churn like water boiling over a high flame. Something was going on in the Æther, but what?

It seemed the Rittandics didn't know either; Untelleh asked a snark-laden question, to which Kihantroh replied: "Neither. It means we must repeat the test."

No. He couldn't let them throw Mercy into the Æther again.

Bernard took two steps into the archway, and threw his lantern at Kihantroh like the spear it was.

~~~~

Mercy pushed herself up on an elbow, just as a pike flew in out of nowhere and buried itself in Kihantroh's abdomen.

The sorcerer looked down at the protruding, twitching shaft with a shocked expression on its narrow face. It sank to its knees, long blue-grey fingers clutching at the weapon.   Blue-black blood began to radiate from the site, wicking through Nebandalex's ill-fitting shirt. The floating Heart wavered, then thudded to the stones like an anvil. It didn't bounce or roll. But after a moment it began to slide across the rough floor toward the vaporous pool. Mercy felt Untelleh uncoil her power, trying to latch onto the jewel and call it to herself, but it had become unmoored when Kihantroh fell and something else had caught it, something stronger than the witch-queen. The Æther had hold of it now. Untelleh may as well have been a spider trying to catch a runaway horse with a single strand of silk.

Someone took Mercy's elbow. Bernard. He crouched beside her, looking across the Æther at the gem, at Untelleh. The witch-queen's face was scrunched up with the effort of trying to check the Heart. That was probably the only reason she hadn't ground the two of them to paste already. As it approached the edge of the pool, the Heart hesitated, wobbled a bit. Untelleh had managed to gain a bit of purchase on it. Her features quivered into an uncertain rictus of consternation and triumph. If she got the Heart back, it was all over.

Mercy didn't have the strength to wrench the gem away from either Untelleh or the Æther—this was a tug-of-war between two contestants, not between three—but maybe she could lend assistance to one of them. She sent her mind reaching over the Æther, past the gem, beyond Untelleh, taking hold of the spear that had felled Kihantroh. It pulled free of the sorcerer's stomach with a faint sucking sound that Mercy didn't want to think about. She angled it slightly, then shot it backwards. The end of the shaft smacked into the faceted stone like a pool cue.

The Heart tipped forward and sank into the Æther.

Untelleh's expression shifted from tentative victory to horror. Like an angler who had hooked something she couldn't master and didn't have time to cut the line, she, too, vanished into the hungry mist. As the roil intensified, Bernard said: "What did you just do?"

"Eight ball," Mercy said. "Center pocket. Help a girl up, would you?"

He hauled her to her feet, steadied her. She didn't look at him, instead keeping an eye on the Æther, where the previously-random froth and chop seemed to be coalescing into something else, an organized swirl. An eye began to form in the middle. "Is that … Is that the death-wind?" Bernard said, sounding rather concerned about the possibility.

"I, um, I don't know." She hadn't really considered what would happen if the Heart fell into the Æther; she'd just wanted to keep it away from the witch-queen. But what if the nibbling mist took the gem apart and freed the prisoner within? What would Daras-Drûm do if it were unleashed in what Untelleh had called a weak spot between the worlds? All of a sudden, dropping the Heart into the Æther seemed like it might not have been such a good idea.

Now something arose from the center of the whorl: The Heart, resurfacing from the depths, without any clingy witch-queen baggage.

Lights flashed and flickered across the surface and in the depths of the translucent stone, the effect not unlike small, distant lightning strikes. She couldn't sense it anymore. It wasn't hers, it never had been; it wasn't even a heart. Mercy felt as if something within the Æther was looking at her and Bernard and everything else around them. Something was peering through the layers of earth and the massive castle walls at the surrounding countryside, its gaze sweeping across the miles and along the plains and over the mountains, examining the dwarves chipping away at their caverns, the elves at work in and around their village, the citizens of Abacar walking their wide streets, the Banderlundi ships blockading the sea out beyond Chasm Bay. It saw Meliander sitting on a bench outside his fallen tree and staring at the garden of raked stone, it saw Grunsandrovar stoking the fire in his mountaintop inn, it saw Aldric trying on Bernard's stolen hat, it saw Arran Blackhawk standing on the balcony looking at the horizon. She sensed that whatever now occupied the Æther attended to all those things, and innumerable others, and that it was going to unravel every single one of them. It couldn't help itself. That was what it did.

"Mercy?" Bernard's voice seemed to come from very far away, even though he stood right beside her. "What's going on? Is this good?"

"No, it's not," she said.

No it's not it's not it's not.

Her own voice seemed echo out of the Æther, transformed and rendered deep and breathy but given the force of a hurricane. Mercy staggered and tried to steady herself against the wall, only to find that the bricks had gone soft, like warm putty. Some of it came with her hand when, startled, she pulled away; it turned back into stone on her skin, flaked off, fell to the floor like snow, where it once again seemed viscous and unreal. She looked up from the floor, confronted a wall of vapor. She couldn't see anything. Where was Bernard? Where was *everything*? She flailed about and caught onto something solid. She thought it was Bernard's wrist. She clamped on and held tight. A deep rumble rattled her innards. Laughter? Earthquake? But there wasn't any earth here, it had gone away. Mist crawled over her, worrying at her skin, her hair. She felt it prickling over her like tiny hooks, as if it were trying to find something to fasten onto but kept sliding off. Whatever had happened to the Æther, it still couldn't dissolve her. She had fallen into the Æther, or the Æther had fallen into her. She couldn't tell which. Was there even a difference? She supposed not. Something was coming for them, rushing out of the fog, and she didn't think she could stave it off for long, not this time. The only thing to do was escape, but to where?

Mercy turned and ran, blindly, in some random direction, pulling Bernard along behind her, first in a retreat and then in simple panicked headlong flight. Where could she go that this entity, which saw into the world all around them, wouldn't spot them? Where could she hide long enough for her to come up with a plan? She ran, and stumbled, and lost hold of Bernard. She was alone. The walls had disappeared, and the floor, and the ceiling. There was nothing left but fog.

So she was very surprised when she fell flat on her face on a cold stone surface, and even more surprised to discover that the thing she had tripped over was a golden crown.

SECOND INTERLUDE

INSIDE OUT OF YOUR MIND

Chapter 12

MERCY PICKED HERSELF up, and the crown as well, and took a look around. She saw a tray on the ground nearby, round and made of dark, stained wood; scattered about it were strange, bruised, thick-peeled fruits. Nearby lay a toppled cup from which a puddle of dark liquid had splashed across the stone floor. She was standing to the right of and slightly behind a throne. It wasn't a big throne, and it wasn't an ornate throne, but it was definitely more than just an oversized chair. Snoring sounds emanated from it. Confused, she inched forward and peered around the tall back to see who was there. A fat man, hairy, slovenly, but richly dressed, lay sprawled across it, slumped to one side, his mouth hanging open. A king? He looked like someone she should know, but she didn't think she had ever seen him before. She cautiously slipped the crown into the crook of his arm, then retreated a few paces as the man snorted and shifted and began to wake up. Small, piggish eyes opened and, unfocused, darted around in their fleshy home; then he seemed to notice the crown. Taking it in his plump hands, he fumbled it onto his head. With no idea what else to do, Mercy began gathering up the fallen tray and its erstwhile contents, which seemed like a better option than being caught staring at the disheveled potentate.

"Damn Faundren to hell, anyway," the king said, his voice a sleepy growl.

Mercy looked up, startled. Faundren? Had he just said *Faundren*?

"Curse the man. Curse him and flay him and feed him to the hogs. What's that stretch of river to him, anyway? It's mine! Always has been. At least, it would be if old Unglor hadn't lost it two generations ago."

Now Mercy knew why the man in the throne had seemed familiar, even though he was no one she had ever met: Those were words spoken by King Lahr in a story she had written, and had told at Aldric's inn. She looked down at herself. Her elven body, once strange as a new house but eventually comfortable as a home, was gone; in its place was a slim human frame. Her grimy white robes had been replaced by a ratty old tan and brown dress, equally grimy but rather more threadbare, with an uneven hem that ended just below her knees. She shifted her grip on the tray so she could inspect one of her hands. Her knuckles were red nearly to the point of rawness, her nails were short and irregular as if frequently chewed, and her palms displayed a calloused familiarity with broom handles, spit-cranks, or butter churns.

"Cardella!"

The king's roar jolted her from her baffled self-examination. Looking up, she saw him peering at her from around the side of the throne. The crown, small and ridiculous, sat unsteadily atop a mass of greying brown hair tangled into absurd curls, which framed a plump, perspiring, dissolute face. Jowls hung down on either side of his thick red mouth, above which a bulbous nose protruded like a sentinel watching the lips for signs of treason, and which in turn lay under the dominion of a pair of small, dark, watchful eyes. Their focus shifted to the mess on the floor where she had, evidently, dropped her tray. "Clumsy girl. I've a mind to beat you myself or, if you are fortunate, have the guards do it while I offer suggestions. Now fetch me another cup of wine." Then, when she failed to instantly move: "Damn you, girl, go!"

"Um, yes, sire," she said, wondering which exit was the one that led to the wine.

"*Sire?* How many times must I tell you peasants, a *sire* is a horse's father! You may call me *majesty* or *my lord*, but not *sire*. Never *sire!*"

"M-my apologies, majesty," Mercy said, hurrying away from the throne and down the black steps. The audience hall stretched out in front of her, bigger even than Lord Korrin's and boasting row upon row of dark wooden pews for courtiers and sycophants, none occupied; the room was empty except for two bored-looking guards down at the far end, where tall double doors stood closed. She cut right, across the wide area between the foremost bench and the foot of the stairs, heading for the nearest archway, hoping it was the right one.

"Cardella!"

She stopped.

"Fool of a girl! Have you forgotten your way around? Use *that* door!"

Mercy glanced back to see King Lahr pointing at a different dark opening, his face gleefully angry. He was always happiest when shouting at someone. From here she could see his food taster, Toad, lounging on his cushion beside the throne, watching her like a dog mooning after a favorite toy that was out of reach. She sketched a curtsey for the king, or tried to, and pivoted to go the way she had been told.

She felt eyes on her back the entire time, and wondered whose they were.

~~~~

The corridor, not quite as dark as it had appeared from the

audience chamber, was lit at lengthy intervals by torches that guttered and snapped in the incessant, icy draft that stalked the castle halls. She walked slowly, and eventually stopped and leaned her forehead against the cold wall. All right. She had to settle down and think, and try to get control of this situation.

Mercy turned and slid to the floor, hugging her knees to her chest. Her initial disorientation, when she had stood there idiotically inspecting her hands and fingernails, had more or less faded, but understanding eluded her. How had she ended up inside her own story? Where was Bernard? Was he here somewhere, playing the role of some other character? And what was going on with the Æther? Was Daras-Drûm gnawing away at the weak spot between the worlds while she shivered in Caredella's rags here in Humbold's Spire? Where was *here*, anyway, given that Humbold's Spire didn't really exist anywhere outside of her brain? Experimentally, she felt around for strings, but no luck; the borders of this reality seemed smooth and solid, and untroubled by frayed spots she could pick apart and use to knit something new. She remembered what Untelleh had said to Kihantroh, that you couldn't make a new garment without unraveling the old one, and decided the witch-queen had been on to something.

She heard feet padding down the corridor from the direction of the audience hall and hastily stood, not wanting to get caught idling on the floor like a truant. She realized she had forgotten her tray and bent to retrieve it, fumbling in the dimness because she couldn't see it; her excellent night vision had departed along with the rest of her elvish qualities. A hand grabbed her by the posterior and squeezed it appraisingly. Mercy managed to check herself, barely, before whirling and smashing her fondler in the face with the tray. She was only a serving girl here—she was Cardella, King Lahr's illegitimate and unacknowledged daughter—and if she slugged the wrong person, they would throw her out in the snow to freeze, or worse. So instead of breaking the pincher's arm, she simply slapped it away and said: "Don't touch me!"

"Cardella, it's *me*."

From the whining tone she supposed this must be Toad: Nobody important after all. As long as she didn't break his jaw and prevent him from tasting the royal victuals, she doubted anyone would care what she did to him. "So? Why are you here?"

"His Royal Horse's-Father sent me to see why the wine he asked for has been so delayed."

"What? I just left a minute ago."

"Not so. Not so. His Most Broad-Bottomed Highness knows how long it takes to get to the kitchen and back. It may be the *only* part of the operation of this castle that he understands." Then, with a distressed note creeping back into his voice: "Why did you *hit* me? I thought you liked——"

Egad. No. "Whatever you thought, you were wrong. Besides, I didn't hit you. If I had, you would be on the floor." Mercy turned her back on the flustered little man. "And you can tell the king his wine will be along shortly." She continued down the corridor; after a moment she heard Toad's feet slapping on the bare stones as he returned to his cushion beside the throne. She shivered all the way to the kitchen—she hadn't considered the relentless cold when, in her story, she had dressed Cardella in rags—and found to her relief that here, the heat of numerous ovens chased away the winter chill. The place teemed with cooks tending bubbling pots, stoking fires, slicing meat, plucking fowl.

"Well, don't just stand there, girl!" a nearby cook said, startling her. "What does His Most Majestic Sire want now?"

"W-wine," she said. Now that she was someplace warm, she felt a little sluggish, and didn't really want to leave.

"Wuh-wine?" The man cocked his head. "Never heard of it." He called back over his shoulder: "Have we any wuh-wine today?"

A chorus of negative responses and derisive laughter swept the room as the other servants enjoyed the mean little joke, the small humiliation of the king's bastard child. Mercy's mouth tightened. Just as in her story, the rest of the staff disdained Cardella simply for being—and, more than that, for not knowing—who and what she was. Cardella had put up with the condescending behavior of her fellow domestics because she had conceived herself as a kitchen wench with no other options and no horizon.

But this was not a story, and she was not Cardella.

She walked deliberately over to the guffawing cook, who didn't seem to realize she was approaching until she was close enough to touch him. He abruptly stopped laughing and regarded her with wary curiosity, the way someone might look at an unexpectedly bold squirrel. She tipped her tray forward, letting the bruised fruit and empty cup roll off it and against the man's chest, to tumble down to the floor at his feet. The small quantity of liquid that had remained in the goblet left a crimson dribble down his shirt. She nudged the cup toward him with the toe of her slipper. It rolled in a semicircle and bumped up against his foot. Incredulous, the man looked at the fruit and cup on the floor, then at her. Mercy raised an eyebrow: *Are you going to pick that up or not?*

The man reached out with a beefy hand, growling low in his throat. Mercy knocked his paw aside with her free arm, then slammed her tray edge-first into his abdomen. Onion-scented breath came rushing out of him in a great gust as he doubled over. She dropped the tray, grabbed his wrist, spun around, and used his own weight to flip him and send him sprawling across the warm stone floor of the kitchen.

The room fell utterly silent but for the crackling of the flames.

"Well?" she said, kicking the goblet and sending it skittering across the floor towards the gawking staff. "Isn't anybody going to get me something for the king to drink?"

~~~~

Apparently, by pausing in the hallway and then demonstrating her self-defense skills on the obnoxious cook, Mercy had taken quite a bit longer to bring Lahr his wine than Cardella; upon her return, the king's champion, Lortax, was already partway through relaying the tale of Faundren's unstoppable advance up the ravine. "We are slowing him down," the knight said as he kneeled before the throne, "but we are unable to——"

"Stop him!" the king cried.

"He is too strong, sire. His men——each fights like five. And he fights like ten!"

Mercy, carrying a flagon of wine which the suddenly-helpful kitchen staff had procured for her, emerged out of the dark passage from the kitchen, sidled along the wall, and climbed lightly up the steps to the king's platform. Lahr stood near the edge of the dais, and when she passed within reach the king abruptly spun and struck her across the face with the back of his hand. She went stumbling to the side, the clay flagon bursting against the floor and spilling its contents out to wash the stones, the goblet clattering away and bouncing down the stairs. Suddenly the now-silent audience chamber reeked of cheap wine.

"When I say I want wine, I want wine *quickly*," the king said.

"Yes, s——my lord," Mercy said. Lahr was stronger than she had imagined, and much faster. She was going to have to keep that in mind.

"Clean up what you spilled," the monarch said, turning away to resume his conversation with Lortax. Mercy didn't hear the rest of their exchange; she clung to the floor, her face and jaw throbbing, barely able to keep her fury and humiliation in check. She was Ambrosia the Sorceress! How dare he strike her as if she were someone of no consequence? The next time he did that, she would——

Nothing. She would do nothing. She needed to calm down and remember that for the moment, she *was* a slave girl, more or less. Until she found a way out of here, she was Cardella, and Cardella lived and died at the whim of the king. Well, not quite; when Cardella died, it was by her own act, not by the king's. But still. Being driven to jump from the tall tower was not the ending she had in mind for herself.

Lahr had commanded her to clean up what she had spilled, but she had no cloth except the rags she wore and so she used that, dabbing at the spreading wine with the hem of her dress. The material was thirsty, absorbing the liquid and adopting its hue like a white flower taking up colored water. Unfortunately there was too much wine and not enough dress; if she wanted to get it all she would have to roll in it, and that was a humiliation too far. Hoping the mortar between the stones would prove absorbent, she went to work gathering the pieces of the broken flagon, lest Lahr should tread on them and cut his tender feet. As she collected them she placed them on her tray, and by the time she was finished she had a platter full of potsherds. Maybe she could cut Lahr's throat with one of them.

The discussion between the king and his champion meandered to its end as she scrounged the last of the fragments, the tiniest slivers. Lahr commanded Lortax to defend the castle and dismissed him. The big man bowed and scraped his way out of the audience hall. The guards at the double doors opened them to let him out, and closed them behind him.

"Bad news," Toad said.

"Ah, the toad speaks," King Lahr said. "He should beware, for the croaking toad is found and eaten by the hawk."

"Hawks don't eat toads," the food taster mumbled.

"I say they do and that makes it so," Lahr said. Then, turning to Mercy, he said: "So, Cardella, have you made my platform clean?"

"Yes, my lord," Mercy said.

"Have you really?" Lahr walked over, inspected the floor, and then coughed up a tremendous wad of phlegm and spat it at her feet. "I see you have more work to do," he said, turning away to reclaim his seat.

"Up yours, my lord," Mercy muttered.

~~~~

Lahr's lips were shiny with grease; the floor around his throne was littered with bones. In his hands he clutched a brown haunch of meat that glistened in the light of the torches. He worried at it furiously, turning it this way and that, biting off every bit of flesh he could find, as if—despite the fact that he kept shooing Mercy off to the kitchen whenever his stockpile of food got low—he wasn't sure he would ever lay hands on another piece of mutton in his life. When she wasn't being ordered to pick up the bones he had tossed aside or dispatched to retrieve more bones-in-waiting, Mercy couldn't help but stare at the spectacle until, much to her horror, she found herself wondering when *she* might get the chance to have something to eat, and if she could pick a few morsels off the next roast without being caught and struck again; so it came as something of a relief when that evening, as she had known it would, the calling began, and gave everyone something else to think about.

"... *Lahr* ..."

The king paused in his devouring and looked around, eyes narrow and suspicious. He leaned forward—causing his crown to almost slide off his head—and peered sharply at Mercy, who ignored him with studied indifference, holding her platter full of meat, cheese, bread, and wine as if some wizard had frozen her in that position. "Did you hear that?"

"Yes, I did," she said.

"... *Lahr* ..."

The king leaped off his throne and stood in front of it, trembling like a mouse about to bolt. Prince Faundren's voice continued to slide into the castle, a knife between Lahr's fat ribs. He kicked Toad, berating him for a fool, screaming at him to wake up and listen to the ghostly shouts of his enemy; the startled Toad tried to scramble away and sent himself tumbling down the stairs, whining and yelping like a dog. Mercy stared at the high wall, where what she thought was the tall tower could just barely be seen through a frost-shrouded window. The story was moving on to its next stage; she wondered what would happen when they came to the point where Lahr cut off Faundren's head and appointed it his food taster, and Cardella took the opportunity to poison the king, then fled and threw herself from that far-off height. She had no intention of killing Lahr—at least, not until she could find a way to do it that wouldn't be tantamount to suicide—but then what would happen after the victory party? Would everything here stop and cease to exist, or would she remain indefinitely, fated to bring Lahr one turkey leg after another, while her story veered off in unknown directions like a ship on strange currents with no one at the wheel?

No.   That wouldn't happen.   She was no one's kitchen wench.
There had to be some other way out of this.

Suddenly the doors to the audience chamber burst open and
Lortax strode in, ignoring the startled guards, his long hair tousled, his
mustache drooping low. "My lord," he said as he neared the throne,
"Faundren's men are at the gates."

"Well, what are you doing in *here* then? Get out there! Fight them!
Drive them off!'"

"Of course, my lord.   The castle guard is already engaging his
army. Your archers are stationed at the battlements." Lortax paused.
"I thought perhaps my lord King would like to view the battle."

Lahr's skin had taken on a clammy look. "View the battle?"

"From the safety of a tower, of course," the knight added.

"Oh. Oh, yes. Yes, of course." Lahr looked at Mercy. "Bring the
food," he said.

<p align="center">~~~~</p>

Lahr observed the fighting with a large poultry leg clutched in his
hand, but he had ceased raising it to his lips. The meat had to be half-
frozen by now. Mercy stood several feet behind him, but she could still
see down into the bowl-shaped killing ground in front of Humbold's
Spire. It was full of men, Faundren's in blue, Lahr's in green. Swords
clanged against shields; maces thudded into armor; arrows whisked
down to lodge in vulnerable joints; blood both fresh and frozen
gleamed in the snow.

She scanned the field for the legendary Prince Faundren—brave,
noble, mighty Prince Faundren, strong as Lord Korrin, clever as
Brennendah, cunning as Rumad Kram, loyal as Nebandalex, resolute
as Arran Blackhawk, and, no doubt, handsome as a movie star—but
he was not yet to be seen.   He would make his appearance soon
enough, though. The king also seemed impatient for a glimpse of his
great enemy; she occasionally heard him muttering after Faundren's
whereabouts as the battle progressed, as if one of his attendants or
hangers-on might know where the man could be found.

The prince finally arrived after his men had pushed Lahr's forces
nearly back to the castle walls. As the shadows lengthened, a column
of soldiers mounted on large silver lizards scuttled out of the ravine.
At their head was a shining white stallion, the mammal incongruous at
the head of a squadron of reptile-riders.   Faundren sat upon the
warhorse's back. At least, Mercy supposed it must be Faundren; he
wore the black plate mail emblazoned with a rose, but he was much
smaller than she had expected; in fact, it looked as if inside that shell

of mail and metal, he was just a regular person. A glorious mane of amber hair did not flow from beneath his helmet. His armor did not strain with the force of his mighty biceps. He didn't even seem to really want to fight, despite his fearsome reputation. He carried no weapon that she could see, not even a lance. The snow had become a churned mass of slush and blood. Behind him, the ballista emerged from the ravine, mounted on a sled pulled by two massive, blue-furred crocodilians with eyes like crystal ice. Each creature bore two riders, one facing forward holding reins, the other facing backward helping to steer the sleigh.

As Faundren's men cleared a path to the very gates of Humbold's Spire, Lahr rose slowly to his feet; Toad pulled him back down again, whispering something into the king's ear, his thick lips close to the monarch's head as if sharing sweet nothings. Nearing the wall, Faundren reached up and lifted off his helmet. Mercy was surprised he would invite an arrow to the face in such a fashion. She craned her neck and stood on tiptoe, hoping for a better look at the bold and, apparently, foolish Prince. He was scanning the castle as if searching for something. His eyes met hers, passed on, then came back to her and widened. Mercy's eyes did the same.

The mystery of where Bernard was had just been solved.

This was the point in the story where Faundren challenged and personally insulted Lahr, but Bernard, playing the role of the prince, didn't do that; he just stood there, somehow not being hit by anything fired or hurled at him, as if protected by an aura that said he couldn't die just yet, which, she supposed, he was; he had to die later, in the throne room, not here on the battlefield. Finally Lahr stood and flung the chicken leg at the Prince. Unlike every other projectile, that one hit him, but Lahr didn't see it; he had already turned and begun to withdraw, taking his entire retinue, including Mercy, with him. Dismissed along the way, she returned to the servants' quarters behind the kitchen, in a section of the castle that was even more poorly insulated than the rest of the place. The odor of cooking drifted through the chilly halls, but none of the heat. She didn't have her own room, of course; none of the lower-ranking servants did. They slept in nooks that were little more than alcoves with cots and storage lockers, lacking even the amenity of a door for privacy. She picked the first unoccupied niche she found, went in, and threw herself down on the thin, straw-stuffed mattress. She tried to think, to assess the situation, and came up with this: Bernard was Faundren. Crap! *Now* what was she supposed to do?

Mercy got up and started pacing back and forth in the tiny, squalid room—two steps forward, two steps back—listening to the distant clangor of the ballista as it pounded the gates with iron-tipped bolts. She realized that the real question wasn't what they *should* do; it was what they *could* do. Bernard wasn't interested in pursuing this fight with King Lahr, but he was obviously unable to stop it; the siege had its own momentum that carried him along with it. She had tinkered and she had nudged, but so far, she hadn't made any serious attempt to divert the story from the course she had originally plotted for it. That had to change.

It was too late to prevent Bernard from being captured.

She could only hope it wasn't too late to prevent Lahr from cutting off his head.

~~~~

Some time later, Mercy was awakened by a hand shaking her shoulders. Was it time to get up and go to school? She didn't want to. She pulled the thin, rough blanket up over her head and turned away to face the wall, only to have the cover ripped away, allowing raw, cold air to fall on her like the exhalation from a walk-in freezer. She shrieked and curled herself up into a ball, trying to hold onto the bit of warmth that had surrounded her, but it was hopeless; her tiny, temporary pocket of comfort had vanished. Awake now, and remembering where she was and that she had spent half the night pacing and thinking and had still come up empty, she looked to her right. A young page stood there, holding her blanket in his pink hands. "Get up," he said.

"Why should I?" The little punk probably ranked higher on the castle hierarchy than she did, but she was too tired to care.

"His majesty wants you."

"His majesty can just—be patient a moment, and I'll be right there." Apparently satisfied, the page nodded and left. The little bastard took the blanket with him. Mercy sighed, sat up, and rolled off the straw, yelping as her feet landed on the stone floor; it was like standing barefoot on an ice floe. She looked around for her threadbare slippers, which she was sure she had left by the side of the bed, but they weren't there. Seriously? Someone had come in here and made off with her dismal footwear? The indignities never ended. She went to the little trunk at the foot of the bed. This, at least, was bolted to the floor to keep it from walking out of the room, although nothing protected its contents from being rifled, which was her intent. She knelt down, opened the trunk, and rummaged through the sad treasures it contained: A few shift-like dresses that made hers seem the height of formalwear; an even more worn pair of slippers than the ones she had lost; a stale, half-frozen piece of cheese that someone had evidently stolen from the kitchen but had never eaten. The slippers looked like they would fit, so she took them out and put them on. They did almost nothing to protect her feet from the cold, but at least the king wouldn't beat her for disrespecting him by wandering around barefoot. The left one had something inside of it, cold and round like a coin attached to a thong. She took that one off and shook the item out into her hand: A simple wooden pendant on a thin leather strap, smooth and dark and well-worn, featureless on one side, etched with a pattern of concentric circles on the other, like the layers of an onion, with a raised button in the center. It reminded her of the design on the door to Jordneh's throne room. She traced the disk with her finger, feeling like she needed to put the thing on, but who did it belong to? Why had it been tucked into the shabby slippers as if it were some sort of clandestine treasure?

Well, it wasn't as if she had anything to lose, or any powerful enemies to make that she didn't already have. She draped the charm around her neck, slipping the disk inside her dress. It lay cold against her skin like a half-dollar that had been out in the snow for a while. The outline could be seen through her thin clothing; Mercy didn't like that. She glanced out the doorway into the corridor. No one there. She slid her dress up over her head and the cold air rushed at her again, hungry for whatever additional heat it could devour. She threw on two of the shifts from the trunk, then put her dress on again over them. Layers. Maybe they would keep her a little bit warmer. More to the point, they obscured the fact that she was wearing something around her neck. She couldn't say why she wanted to conceal the amulet, exactly, except that it reminded her of the Ravels, and it wasn't something she had written into her story.

Of course, neither was the rock-hard piece of cheese, but something told her the charm was more important.

~~~~

Mercy found Lahr sitting on the throne, waiting for her. He had allowed the tapers scattered about the audience hall to burn down; the only illumination came from the flickering torches that reposed in sconces on the columns. Mood lighting. The double doors were barred now, the guards standing back discreetly. They knew what the king intended. From the shadows of his platform he beckoned to her, his pale fingers wiggling in the darkness like levitating maggots.

"Come here, child," he called.

Ah yes. Yet another fun scene was about to ensue.

Mercy slowly approached the dais. Lahr urged her forward, impatience shining through his ill-fitting mask of false geniality the way a candle illuminated a jack-o-lantern. She climbed the steps, stopped out of reach, and said: "My lord king wished me to attend to him?"

"Yes, child," Lahr said. "Come closer, please."

"How can I serve you?"

"By coming closer," Lahr said.

"Would my lord king like more food? More wine?"

"Cardella—"

"Bread perhaps?"

"Cardella—"

"Perhaps my lord king would like a nice juicy cheeseburger?"

"Enough!" King Lahr roared, slamming his fist on the arm of his throne with such vehemence that his crown slipped off his head, rolled down his belly, and clattered to the floor, then bounced tinnily down the stairs to spin across the flagstones of the audience hall.

"Please permit me to retrieve your diadem for you, my lord." Mercy did so without waiting for Lahr's approval or disapproval. He was standing in front of his throne when she took the stairs a second time, waiting for her at the top step; he snatched the icy golden crown from her hands as soon as she was within reach.

Then he hit her with it.

She saw him draw his arm back, holding the crown with one hand, and she had time to formulate the idea that she should duck, dodge, kick him in the crotch, do something—anything—to defend herself; but the instant that thought came she knew any of those responses could be fatal. Touch the king and be put on the rack; dodge the king and be whipped and beaten; but let the king strike you, and that would be the end of it, probably. So she did. For added effect, she even fell down, rolling with the blow to absorb most of the energy behind it. Still, one of the crown's sharp edges cut her cheek. The metal felt cold, the blood hot, but that was good. Bleeding would help assuage the king's anger.

"I do not know what impish spirit has possessed you lately, Cardella," Lahr said, replacing the crown on his head and smoothing his mussed hair, "but you would be well-advised to act less willful and more aware of your position here. Begone. Clean your face. I will send for you again anon."

"Yes, my lord," Mercy mumbled, keeping her voice as low and as servile as she could stand. She considered pretending to cry, but couldn't bring herself to do it. She crawled backwards down the steps, only standing again at the bottom; then she tottered off toward the corridor, moving with a calculated unsteadiness that she hoped would convey a broken spirit. She felt Lahr's cold gaze on her backside. His lecherous goals had been thwarted this time, but such tactics would likely not work again. She would have to think of something else for next time. Maybe he would wait too long and by then Faundren—Bernard—would be in the castle, giving the king something else to occupy his mind.

Unfortunately Bernard would be in chains, as Lahr's prisoner.

And Lahr would not be feeling merciful.

~~~~

When Mercy entered the kitchen in search of water and a rag, one of the cooks spotted her and brought over a flagon of wine. "Take this to the alchemist," he said, thrusting it into her hands, ignoring or not noticing the blood dripping down her cheek and onto her shoulder, leaving ruddy stains in the dirty cloth.

"The ... the alchemist?"

"Yes, the alchemist." The cook smirked. "You know, the old man. He's probably forgotten he asked for it, but bring it just the same. Go on, girl, get gone!" The cook turned her around and sent her out one of the half-dozen doorways that opened onto the kitchen. This one was low and narrow and slightly crooked, as if whoever cut it had not been quite sober. The hallway beyond was very poorly lit; only a single torch far ahead gave any sense of the direction in which it ran. The walls were close on either side of her, the ceiling just above her head. As she had pictured it, Lahr's mountain stronghold was a maze of tunnels and warrens and dark, narrow, cramped corridors, so this claustrophobic passageway was hardly out of place.

Here was the pivot point of the story. Would Mercy, as Cardella had done in the version she had told at the inn, steal a vial of poison from the alchemist's room and use it to assassinate the king? She could only administer it after Lahr had beheaded the captive Prince Faundren—which was to say, Bernard—and promoted his severed head to the position of food taster; otherwise, she would only be killing the annoying but innocuous Toad, and that wouldn't do anyone any good. She couldn't permit Lahr to kill Bernard, of course, but she still hadn't managed to push events far enough off course to prevent it, and she was running perilously short on time.

The little corridor ended at the glowing light, which hung on the wall next to a door. When she reached it she saw that the xanthic glow came not from a lantern, but from a paste-like mixture contained in a glass bowl that rested in an iron ring at about chest-level. Apparently the alchemist had discovered a way to make chemical illumination. She knocked at the door, waited, got no answer, knocked again, and finally went inside. The mad scientist sat asleep at his table, his head resting on a pile of books amid a collection of phials and ampoules and leather pouches. Mercy examined the stockpile of chemicals. One vial in particular stood out; it was jet-black, with a grinning human skull inlaid in the surface with bone or ivory. Could it be more obvious? She was supposed to pick it up, hide it somewhere on her person, and sneak its contents into Lahr's punchbowl, just like in the story.

Well, she wasn't going to do that. Instead she put the flagon of wine down in a more-or-less empty spot near the old man's chair, then shook him gently. The old man grumbled and kept on sleeping, so she shook him again. It took several more tries before he snorted and his dark eyes opened blearily. He gurgled deep in his chest as if he'd inhaled a gallon of water, sat up, and began to cough. Finally he looked around and fixed his gaze on Mercy. "Oh, hello, Cardella," he said. Then: "You are bleeding. What did Our Royal Doughiness hit you with this time?"

She touched the cut on her cheek. "His crown."

The alchemist sighed and said, "What do you call a fool on a throne, Cardella?"

"What?"

"*Your majesty*. Ah, I see you brought the wine I asked for. Thank you. My throat is always so dry these days." His dark eyes glittered. "Age brings down the best of us, though I'm sure you have no fear of it yet."

"I'm getting older too," Mercy said, relieved that this sage was apparently of the benevolent sort rather than a cranky schemer; in her story, he'd had no dialogue or personality, and she hadn't been sure what to expect from him.

"Pah! If you've seen your eighteenth summer, then I am a snow lizard."

"There aren't any summers in Humbold's Spire."

The alchemist laughed scratchily. "True, my dear, all too true. Here's hoping we won't have to stay in this frigid prison much longer." He picked up the flagon and took a long drink, then offered it to Mercy. She shook her head and asked about the bottles on the table.

"These?" he said. "Reagents, components, chemicals. I've shown them to you before, have I not?" He frowned at the black bottle, picked it up. "But *this* is a dire poison. I should not have left it out." He tucked it out of sight in one of the desk's numerous small drawers.

"So you mix them together?"

"Of course. They would be useless if all they did was sit in their vials." He rummaged in the clutter on his desk, his gnarled hands each selecting a bottle. One was made of green glass, the other of tan clay streaked with blue. "Take these two bottles. If you mixed the contents, you would very quickly get a large and noxious cloud of smoke that would cause all who breathed it to choke and cough. Lortax thought it might make a good battlefield weapon, but the wind blows it away too quickly." He shrugged. "I am trying to make the smoke heavier and stickier, but for now, it just spreads and spreads and spreads." He put the bottles aside. "Other chemicals may explode when mixed, or crystallize, or as you no doubt saw outside the door, produce light. Some merely turn into sludge. Have you intentions of entering the field of alchemy, young lady?"

An idea forming, Mercy eyed the two bottles that made smoke, trying to figure out a way to get her hands on them without getting caught. "Oh, no, I'm sure I couldn't."

"Of course you could. When we return to the regular castle, I can teach you. There I have proper equipment, and more books, and blackboards, and the like." He gave her a critical look. "Despite what you may believe, Cardella, and what others may tell you, your destiny is not fixed. You are not fated to be a serving girl. Do not let whispers and slights limit you. You are clever enough to find your way to better things; you simply must decide what you want to do, and apply your mind to the task." The alchemist sighed and grunted his way to his feet. "And right now, I must apply *my* mind to the task of using the privy. It is not as easy as you may believe." Mercy watched the old man shuffle off toward the other side of the room, where his cot stood against the wall and a partition blocked off the corner where, she supposed, his chamberpot must be. He paused at the divider, gave her a wink and a small wave, and said: "No doubt you must get back to your duties. I am happy that you are taking a bit of new knowledge with you when you go, but please, leave the wine."

As soon as the alchemist disappeared from view, Mercy snatched up the two vials of chemicals that made smoke, slipped them into the front pocket of her shabby dress, and scurried out of the room.

~~~~

Walking back up the long, dark corridor, Mercy could feel the vials bouncing against her waist. She worried that anyone who gave her more than a cursory look would see a suspicious-looking bulge in her pocket, but she had one thing working in her favor: Nobody ever gave Cardella more than a cursory look. Lortax would soon be bringing Bernard-as-Faundren into the castle, and in all the excitement, who would pay any attention to a kitchen rat's pockets? Besides, she was sure it wouldn't be long before someone pressed a tray at her that she could use to hide her illicit cargo. Sure enough, the moment she got within range of the ovens, one of the staff immediately accosted her. "Where have you been?" she demanded, shoving a bowl of fruit into Mercy's hands. "The king has been waiting for this!"

Resisting an urge to make the woman wear the bowl as a hat, Mercy turned and ferried it up the long, dark corridor to the great hall. As usual, Lahr sat alone except for the ever-present Toad snoring on his velvet cushions and the stoic guards standing beside the double doors. She approached the throne platform carefully. Lahr slouched there, looking straight ahead, like a drunken vagabond slumped on a bench staring into some world that no one else could see. As she neared the king his head turned and he glared at her. "Your fruit, sire," she said, not meeting his gaze. Her hand of defiance was played out; now she needed to be patient, and wait for the capture of Bernard-as-Faundred to take the spotlight off of her, at least temporarily.

Lahr reached out and grabbed an apple and examined it as if the secrets of the universe were written on its pimpled skin, too full of anger even to chastise her for the slip of calling him *sire*. That was bad. "I have these imported," he said, apparently addressing the apple, "from the southern march of Bentwood. Faundren has cut us off from there, so when these are gone, there will be no more. It is my prerogative to have fresh fruit from my own orchards in the South, and Faundren is denying me it." He looked up at her with blue eyes that should have been steely, but were simply pale and watery, like melting ice. "It is also my prerogative to have pleasure of anyone I choose. And *you* are denying me *that*."

"My lord, I ..." He glared at her, his eyes hardening, and for a moment her throat went tight and dry, as if she had suffered a sudden attack of strep. Inspired by the thought of being struck down by illness, Mercy continued: "I only seek to protect your august majesty from the sicknesses that plague your ... your *diseased* serving wench."

Lahr's eyebrows shot up, and Toad—who apparently was only

pretending to be asleep—issued an alarmed little grunt. *"Diseased?"* the king said. "What do you mean, diseased?"

"Oh, it's nothing fatal," she said. "Usually. The physician told me so."

"Which physician was——"

"It's sores, you see," she said, lowering her voice to a stage whisper.

Toad gulped loudly and said, in a tremulous voice: "Sores? Where?"

Lahr, looking horrified, dropped the apple as if it were contaminated.

Toad said: "These sores ... are they *painful* in nature?"

"Silence, Toad!" the king roared.

And as if at his command, silence descended, like a thick, heavy blanket thrown over the castle. This, Mercy knew, marked the defeat of the enemy army. Lahr had won the day. He just didn't know it yet.

Maybe she should inform him.

"My lord," Mercy said, punctuating her words with a theatrical little gasp. "The pounding at the gates—it has stopped."

"What?" Lahr stared at her, then jumped to his feet, causing his purple robe to flap and briefly expose plump and quivery legs that ended in small, dainty feet. Standing there, leaning forward, he cupped a hand to his ear and strained to listen. He stayed in that position for an interval during which there should have been at least one report from the ballista; instead there was quiet, as Mercy had known there would be. The king turned to Toad, his face pale and pasty, sweat gleaming from his features, giving him the appearance of uncooked dough smeared with water. "What does this mean?" he said, his voice now as unsteady as his crown. Toad coughed and said nothing. Lahr knotted the fabric of his robe in his hands, twisting it back and forth. Mercy stood where she was, waiting. Lortax would be here any moment. When the pounding started again, it was on the doors of the throne room, and it was delivered not by a ballista but by a fist. "It is Faundren!" Lahr cried. "He has come for me!" The panicked king scrambled off the dais, leaving his crown where it fell, and scampered toward one of the dark doorways, robes flying out behind him like a cape.

"My lord King!"

Lahr froze at the exit; the voice that had just boomed from beyond the huge double doors belonged, of course, to his champion.

"My lord King! Command your guards to unbar the door! I have great news, I bring a great gift!"

Lahr paused, smoothed his robes, and walked back to his platform, then climbed the steps to the top, where he found his crown and put it back on his head. Once settled into the throne, as if he had been sitting there the entire time waiting for the arrival of Faundren and his men so he could spit at them from on high, Lahr waved his hand and called out: "Admit him."

The guards removed the bar from across the double doors and swung them open; Lortax entered, battered and grimy but grinning widely. Blood darkened his mustache. He dragged his prisoner along behind him in fetters and manacles. King Lahr drew a sharp breath, obviously seeing his mortal enemy, the great Prince Faundren, but Mercy saw only Bernard. He clanked and shuffled into the audience hall, wrists and ankles encircled with black bands, the two sets of cuffs connected by links that ran vertically from his hands to his feet. Another length of chain was attached to a ring in the middle of the vertical run; this was what Lortax held as if it were a leash, and his prisoner a dog. So much iron. Did they think Faundren could snap metal simply by flexing his mighty biceps?

Lahr jumped to his feet, elation on his face. "Lortax!" he cried. "You shall be my heir for this! How? How did you perform this feat?"

Lortax said something, and the king responded, but Mercy wasn't listening. She already knew their dialogue. She had written it. Bernard hadn't stopped looking at her since he'd been dragged into the room. His gaze was unsteady, pleading; she wanted to run over and tell him it would be all right, that she had a plan to set them both free, but of course she couldn't approach him. There were archers here now, and more guards, swarming in after Lortax. Cardella might have been invisible, but Faundren wasn't. Everyone was watching. If she made a move toward the supposed Prince, she would be cut down and that would be the end of them both.

"What find you so fascinating in my throne room, oh broken prince, that you cannot look away from it even as your death stands before you?" The king peered around; his gaze swept over and past Mercy, inspecting the back part of the chamber. She was no longer of any interest; she might as well have been a coatrack or a tapestry or a forgotten bone. It never occurred to the king that Prince Faundren would notice a serving girl. Finally Lahr returned his gaze to Bernard. "I see nothing here worthy of your attention. You will look at me."

Bernard, perhaps realizing that focusing on Mercy had been an error, now cast his eyes at the floor.

"I said look at me, not at the ground!" Lahr shouted, waggling a finger at his captive. Then, when Bernard still didn't raise his head: "Who are you who sits before me in chains and ignores my commands? Nothing and no one. You will show me the respect I deserve!"

"That's what I am doing," Bernard said.

"Is it?" Lahr crossed the platform and kicked his food taster, not gently. "Toad, you useless fool! Go and tell the pages, tell the criers—tell them the war is ended. Summon all my subjects, bring them here! We shall have a celebration tonight, and soon we will at last return to the gentle green lands down below." Then, to Bernard: "But you, brave Prince, had best get used to the snow. You will soon be buried in it."

~~~~

Time slid by like sandpaper while Mercy waited for the audience hall to fill up. People arrived in ones and twos and threes at first, but as word spread through the rambling castle the trickle grew into a steady flow of courtiers in their gaudiest dress, craftspeople in the garb of their trades, peasants in home-stitched habiliments, lower-ranking castle staff and functionaries in uniforms appropriate to their tasks and stations. Last to arrive were the basest of the indentured servants in their ragged vestures. To Mercy, who had remained on the platform the entire time, half-hidden behind the throne, the attendees accumulated in layers that were almost sedimentary. Press them together and they would end up like strata in the socio-geological record. She found it difficult to believe that Lahr had hauled this entire vast retinue with him up into the mountains; surely some of them—probably the ones who had, at some point, annoyed the Lahr in some fashion, like by not properly buttering his bread—must be permanent residents of Humbold's Spire, enduring its endless icy chill season after season. She felt sorry for those unfortunates, and didn't want to become one of them.

At length, the crowd reached some critical mass, and Lahr decided it was time for the festivities to begin. He adjusted his crown, then stood. "My people," he said, raising his arms so that the loose sleeves of his purple robes slid down toward his shoulders, "the siege is broken! Here is the one who has kept us all imprisoned here for so long. I give you my captive, your enemy and mine; I give you … Prince Faundren!"

The crowd whooped and hollered; it was like he was introducing some fabled rock star for a final command performance. Bernard scanned the room, his nervous gaze flitting around, never settling in one place. He was smart enough not to stare at her again, but Mercy knew he was waiting for her to do something. It wasn't quite time yet, though; she needed Lahr to have his weapon, so she could take it away from him.

As the approving roar died down, the king signaled to a courtier, who brought over the jewel-encrusted belt and golden scabbard of his royal forefathers. Lahr put it on, fumbling with the buckles and straps as if he were unused to the operation of such things, which, of course, he was. Mercy watched him intently, waiting.

Not yet.

Once Lahr had finally fastened the belt about his considerable girth, Lortax approached, carrying the sword that went in it. The weapon gleamed coldly, sharply, like a piece of moonlight captured and carved into a blade; the belt and scabbard might be purely ceremonial, but the sword had an edge, and it could cut. Oh yes. Mercy adjusted her grip on the bowl, still waiting. With her free hand, she reached into her front pocket to loosen the stopper of one vial, then of the other, getting ready.

Not yet.

Lahr took the weapon by the hilt and nearly dropped it, but managed to catch it without severing a hand or impaling himself through the foot. He lifted the sword up and turned it slowly so the blade caught the torchlight. It glittered as if it were made of ice.

Not yet.

"Behold the sword of my fathers!" he shouted, his voice like a gong in the silent hall. One or two people clapped, realized they were stepping on Lahr's moment, faltered, and stopped. "A sword of bravery! A sword of truth! It once carved a kingdom from the wilderness, and now it will carve the Prince!"

Mercy rolled her eyes, thinking: Please, just *shut up* already.

The king lowered his sword, favored Bernard with a grim leer, and began moving toward him.

Now.

Mercy shifted the bowl to the crook of her arm and half-turned away from the scene, hoping to conceal what she was about to do. She grabbed a container out of her pocket—it was the clay one—and with a twist of her thumb and forefinger fully removed the cork. She tipped the contents of the phial into the bowl; it had a pungent, herbaceous odor, like rosemary mixed with vinegar. She slipped the empty container back into her pocket and took out the glass one. The hall was hushed, everyone waiting, expectant, the only sound the swish of Lahr's robes as he descended.   She glanced at the stairs.   Lahr, moving at a stately swagger, was only halfway down the steps; Lortax stood with his back to her, watching the king.   She could only see Toad's feet as he lounged on his cushion on the other side of the throne.   No one was paying her any mind.   Mercy pushed the crystal stopper off the vial with her thumb, fumbled it, and stared in horror as it fell toward the stone platform.   She moved her feet together and caught the stopper between them just before it shattered on the floor.

She hurriedly dumped the second part of the admixture into the bowl and gave it a little shake to swirl the components together.   For a moment nothing happened and she feared she had taken the wrong bottles, but then thick black smoke erupted from the bowl as if she had ignited an oil well.   That finally drew some notice; a gaudy fop in the front row gasped and pointed, causing others to look her way.   Well, it wasn't as if she'd expected a giant cloud of noxious vapor to go unnoticed; the fact that it *couldn't* was entirely the point of this scheme.

Mercy put the bowl on the floor and kicked it toward Lahr and Lortax.   It wobbled and spun across the stones, spilling some of the contents, leaving a trail of fumaroles in its wake.   She heard Lortax cursing, and someone else cried, "It was the wench!   The wench!" Busted—time to go.   She ducked around the back of Lahr's throne. The smoke stung her eyes and burned her nose.   Heavy footsteps clomped on the flagstones to her right, where she had been standing. She darted left and forward, holding in her coughs.   Quietly, quietly. She had to move like an elf now.

"Find her!" Lahr shouted.   "Find Cardella!"

She reached the top of the stairs.   The bowl was there, overturned; the chemicals had spilled outward in a sheet.   Smoke rose everywhere the liquid flowed, as if the flagstones themselves had caught fire.   She bounded down the steps, no longer bothering with trying to be quiet; the assembled onlookers were coughing and cursing and rushing the exits, the din of their panic drowning out any sound Mercy might make as she pushed on through the smoke, trying to keep to a straight path.   Bernard was up ahead somewhere.   Did she risk calling his name?   If she did, would he even hear her?   Suddenly an apparition appeared out of the smoke, and a hand clamped onto her arm: Lahr, coughing, holding the curving sword one-handed.   He held the blade up over his head, the steel gleaming and unmarked.   He hadn't used it on Bernard yet; he intended to bloody it on her instead.   "Treasonous wench!" he said, raising the weapon yet higher.   "I will have your head for—"

Mercy slammed the palm of her hand into Lahr's fleshy nose, and followed that up with a knee strike to his groin. Blood gushed from the king's nostrils. His grip on her relaxed as his eyes rolled up into his head; he groaned and slumped to the floor. The sword clattered to the flagstones beside him. Mercy picked it up and yelled: "Bernard!"

"Mercy?"

His voice had come from nearby, ahead of her and to the right, she thought. "Keep talking, Bernard!"

"About what?" he said.

"Anything!"

"Okay. Um … I can't think of anything to say."

Good Lord, really? "Just make noise! Sing! Yodel! I don't care!" He didn't answer; he had succumbed to a fit of coughing, which worked just as well as anything else would have. She pressed on through the smoke, taking shallow breaths. Her own chest kept trying to convulse. Somewhere behind her, Lortax was shouting for the king, but Lahr made no response other than a barely-audible groan. She tripped over someone. Bernard. He was down on his hands and knees, coughing like he was about to expel a lung, tears streaming from his eyes. "Hey," she said softly.

He looked up at her. His eyes flicked to the sword, then back to her face. Between coughs, he managed to say: "How did you get hold of *that?*"

"The king dropped it. Hold still." She raised the blade high, then brought it down on the chain between his wrists, letting gravity do most of the work. The steel had a good edge; two more such blows and the brittle chain snapped. She quickly delivered the same treatment to the links between his ankles. The clatter and rush had obscured the sounds, she hoped. The blade was ruined now, dented and bent. She cast it aside as Bernard unwound the other chains that bound him, then gave him a hand up, draping his left arm around her shoulders to help him stay on his feet. She guided him through the smoke toward the corridor to the kitchen. The thunderous racket of the escaping crowd was magnified by the huge open space and reflected by the undraped stone walls, so that the mass of people appeared to be simultaneously rushing toward and away from them. Few if any of Lahr's panicked subjects seemed to be coming toward the kitchen exit, though; going in this direction meant plunging into deeper smoke, which you would only do if you were as desperate as she was. Besides, the aristocrats were up in front; they never used, and had quite possibly never even *noticed*, the small dark opening from which their food and drink materialized, and in the chaos it didn't occur to them to use it now. The servants who might have done so had lined up in back, and were now caught behind a juggernaut of their betters struggling to get out through the double doors in the far end of the chamber.

They reached the wall of the throne room, grey stone smeared with black soot. Mercy put her fingers on the pebbly surface and turned right, following the wall until it fell away beneath her hand. This had to be the kitchen corridor. A cold, weak breeze wafted from the archway, discouraging the smoke from drifting into the hallway. The shoddy construction of the servants' wing was good for something after all. She hauled Bernard into the dim passageway, where the air was cool and impossibly fresh after the choking acrid smoke released by the alchemist's potions. Mercy could smell the aromas of the kitchen—cooking meat and bread, ripening cheese, spilled wine—as well as a scent that belonged to the castle itself, a damp, dusty, stony odor, like mountains after a rainstorm. Beside her Bernard was inhaling deeply, clearing fouled air from his lungs, coughing in short, hiccupy bursts. She gave him a second or two to recover, then said: "Are you ready? Come on." Not waiting for an answer, she dragged him after her as she took off down the corridor. No longer saddled with Ambrosia's feeble endurance, she was the one with stamina now, Bernard the one who struggled and fell behind; he stopped her again after a little distance, leaning against the wall, gasping. Behind them, the tumult of the stampede from the throne room had begun to fade.

"Where are we going?" he asked, after a few moments spent catching his breath.

"The kitchen."

"And *after* we grab a snack?"

She snorted. "You think I planned that far ahead?"

"I wasn't sure you were *planning* at all. I thought you didn't even recognize me."

"Of course I recognized you. I just couldn't give it away or they would've strung me up. You know where we are, don't you?"

"Uh-huh. We're inside your story."

"Yeah," Mercy said. "So how did you like leading an army?"

"Well, I—"

From far behind them, somebody shouted in a booming voice: "The wench has taken Prince Faundren this way!"

"Crap," Mercy said, dragging him onward. "Come on. You can tell me all about it later."

~~~~

In the kitchen, three cooks and various kitchen staff who had remained on duty to supply the king with victuals during his victory celebration stared at them as Mercy dragged Bernard in a hard right turn and darted into the narrow, crooked corridor that led to the alchemist's quarters.   Not long after, she heard an angry, shouted question from the kitchen, which was answered by a babble of voices and, no doubt, accusatory fingers jabbing at the dark archway through which they'd exited.   So much for the solidarity of the working class. Footsteps came pounding down the hallway after them, along with cries for them to stop.   Mercy ignored the orders.   They still had a decent lead when they reached the alchemist's suite. A circle of wood, painted red, hung from a nail in the door. Did that mean there was some kind of dangerous experiment in progress?   Mercy grabbed the handle and pulled, but the door refused to move.

Bernard said: "Mercy, what's——"

"Can you open this? I think it's barred."

"I can't pick a bar from this side. Can't you magic it open?"

"No, there's no magic in this story."

"What? It's *your* story. Just change it."

"I wish I could."   She turned to look back the way they had come. The guards were closing in, dark shapes against the distant kitchen light. She could make out Lortax ahead of the others, just like in her story, except they weren't at the top of the tower and she wasn't going to be jumping off any parapets. She assumed a fighting stance, even though the guards were mailed and would barely feel blows from her bare hands and feet.   As they drew close Bernard snatched the luminous glass globe out of its sconce, spun, and hurled it at Lortax's face.   The fragile bowl of crystal shattered and the luciferous paste inside splattered across the man's face like a puree of crushed glowworm. He pawed at his eyes and staggered backwards, screaming epithets, blocking the other guards for a moment. Bernard stepped in front of Mercy, fists raised, as if he thought he really *was* Prince Faundren and could battle ten men at once. Idiot. He knew she was a better fighter than he was.   And if she only had her magic back, then——

Suddenly she felt a pain at her chest, a burning sensation, like being stuck with a poker fresh from a fire. What now, a heart attack? She pressed her fingers to her thorax and felt the wooden charm beneath the layers of threadbare cloth, warmer than any piece of wood had a right to be. She pulled the pendant out from the front of her shift. The burnished wood was glowing dully, a faint red, like metal cooling after being thrust into a furnace. She thought she saw light flickering along the concentric circles engraved in its surface, tiny foxfire droplets circling the raised bud in the center like planets orbiting a sun. What was it? A diagram? A map? A representation of the solar system? Was one of those planets here? Where *was* here, anyway?

"Mercy," Bernard said. Lortax had cleared the glowing goop from his visage and, snarling, red-eyed, gestured for the other guards to stay back.

There was power in the charm; or not *in* the charm, but *connected* to it. It was a way back, a way out, a way to somewhere else. Bernard had told her to change the story, and she'd told him she couldn't, but maybe she already had.

"Mercy," Bernard said again.

Lortax drew his sword. Bits of glowing paste stuck to his mustache, as if it had attracted fireflies. This was no schoolyard bully, backing down when confronted. This was an angry man-at-arms, and he was going to kill them.

"Mercy! Where's your head? Mercy!"

Her head. Of course. This was all in her head, or rather, *their* heads, hers and Bernard's. She had wanted a place they could hide from the thing that had come out of the Æther, the thing that had been Daras-Drûm, and this was what her desperate mind had conjured up: Not some calm Elysian field, but the icy waste of Humbold's Spire, where she had to once again figure out how to survive. The alchemist had tried to tell her, sort of, but it wasn't until Bernard said it that she finally understood. She had been fighting herself as she tried to alter the flow of events, because, after all, she knew this story, and what she was doing was not the way the story was supposed to go; but on another level she had been helping herself all along.

Yes. That was where the charm had come from. She had left it for herself, a token, a clue. Bernard was right. It was *her* story, and she could change the rules. She had the cheat code for this game. She could enable God mode. Lortax and his men? They were of no more consequence than woven figures on a tapestry. In fact, that was what they were. Her tapestry. She peered past Bernard to where the stitched rendition of the guards snapped and fluttered in the breeze. Bernard looked at her, his eyes wide and, she thought, more than a little bit scared.

"Follow me," she said, pushing the decorative curtain aside.

Behind it was an open window, beyond which lay a realm of drifting, luminous mist.

She took Bernard's hand and led him forward, up and through the window, into light that smelled like dust and sounded like the sea.

PART THREE

THE HEART

Chapter 13

MERCY BLINKED A few times as the light and sound and mist faded. She was standing on a ring of stone; it seemed to be part of the floor of the subterranean pit that had enclosed the well of Æther in Untelleh's castle. In the center, where the Æther had been, a dim sphere luminescence glowed, like the ghostly afterimage left behind from staring at the sun. It looked like the stone ring extended in and downward, forming a cup in the center that contained the glowing remnant. She was like a fly on the rim of a soup bowl. A lid covered it, sort of, another layer of stone, she thought, the inner surface of the domed room, rendered so thin as to be translucent, like a giant soap bubble; beyond was only blackness, empty as deep space. There were no openings to the outside, perhaps because—as with the doors in the rest of Untelleh's castle—those had only existed when Untelleh wanted them to. It was as if they had been shot into orbit in a pod made of rock. This suggested something unpleasant about how long they could expect their life support to last.

"Well, *now* where are we?" Bernard said.

He stood next to her, still holding her hand, of course. He was back in Brannoc's body, all gangly limbs and shocking carrot hair. If he was Brannoc again, then she must be Ambrosia. She inspected her arms, and ran a finger over her pointed ears and down through her platinum hair to confirm it. "I'm not sure," she said. "Nowhere, I guess."

"Nowhere? It can't be nowhere."

"Why not?"

"Because we're here, and if we're here, it has to be somewhere."

"Hmm. I like your confidence, Descartes, but I'm not sure your logic applies in the void."

"The what?"

"The void."

"Um. Yeah. I heard what you said, but not what you meant."

"Oh. So, okay, the Æther was a raw spot where worlds rubbed against each other, right? The void is the space that's left after it's completely worn through."

"What, like a ... like a hole in a pair of jeans?"

"Sure, if that helps."

He looked around unhappily. "So how do we patch the jeans?"

"Good question. The death-wind didn't leave us much to work with, did it?"

"You think this is all empty because we let Daras-Drûm out into the Æther and it … it ate everything?"

"Uh-huh. Maybe." Then: "*Something* did, anyway, and I can't think of any other candidates."

"So that would mean everyone else is …" Bernard trailed off, obviously unwilling to finish the thought.

"Yeah."

"I left Brennendah outside the castle. You're saying he's gone?" She spread her arms but didn't answer, and after a moment he said: "Why are *we* still here, then?"

"I don't know, Bernard. Because we were inside my story?"

"Or because some beasts cannot be destroyed."

"What?"

"Cynidece said that to me once. Why they kept Daras-Drûm penned up instead of killing it. They didn't have a choice, because they couldn't destroy it, so they imprisoned it instead."

"I couldn't destroy it either. I did the best I——"

"No, I'm not talking about the death-wind now. I'm talking about *us*. Maybe it didn't evaporate us just because it *couldn't*." He gestured at the void. "I mean, look around. Were we *really* so well hidden in Humbold's Spire that it couldn't find us?"

Mercy grunted. "You might as well ask, are we *really* so special that we're immune to Daras-Drûm? What makes us any better than what we're standing on?" She stamped her foot on the rim of stone, the tureen that held the last remnant of reality.

Bernard shrugged. "It was touching the Æther. We both touched the Illata. Maybe we're all the same. You and me and the floor."

She stared at him.

"I bet Untelleh was here when she tried to tap the Æther and made it explode," he said, looking into the depression at the center of their refuge. "In this room. I bet being here helped her keep it together all those years."

"She *didn't* keep it together. She was in a million pieces. She told me so herself."

"But she came back. All her stuff came back. If she could do it … why can't we?"

"She had somebody on the outside helping her," Mercy said, even as she started to think that maybe, just maybe, Bernard was on to something. She put her left hand on the inner wall of stone and started walking around the ring, as if she were going to do her maze-traversal technique. That was obviously unnecessary here in this closed circle, this pocket of stone; any labyrinths here were strictly in her head. Bernard watched her, looking slightly concerned, like he thought she might do something reckless. When she was on the side opposite from him she stopped and gave him a closer look. The fuzzy glow in the center of the ring seemed to be acting like a mystical X-Ray device: Instead of Bernard as he was, she saw him as a Bernard-shaped bundle of strings. So many, wound so tightly! How could he even move? He was knit up like the rubber bands inside an old golf ball.

Mercy needed strings in order to work a glamour; well, there they were. But what could she do with them that wouldn't jeopardize Bernard's very existence? Kihantroh had claimed that Jordneh powered her magic by unraveling reality, and Untelleh had all but confirmed it as fact. If she drew on Bernard's strings to try to save the world, might she watch him puff out of existence as she worked? No. Mercy wouldn't risk unraveling Bernard, not even now in the direst of dire straits, not ever. She owed Bernard more than she owed the world.

Besides, there was another source of strings available. Herself.

Mercy closed her eyes and regulated her breathing, trying to put herself into that state she had visited before, when she had burned through her fetters in Torgonderrer; but before she got too deep she became aware of something else making a claim on her attention. Like a flower bending toward sunlight, her focus shifted away from herself and toward a faraway radiation that intruded into the otherwise perfect void that surrounded them. Her mind bloomed and opened as it absorbed the energy that the distant beacon offered. Power crashed into her, over her, through her. She saw it as shapes, interlocking in a matrix of circles and squares and triangles and octagons, forms repeating down to the smallest level, closing all the gaps.

Almost.

Something was missing from the arrangement, some critical piece, leaving a hole through which energy—the energy she was picking up—gushed out like water from a punctured skin. Maybe that was the flaw, the gap, the fissure that Untelleh had created all those centuries ago, that the death-wind had used to slip across to the wrong side of reality and begin chewing it up. That was the way in.

So where was the way out?

Mercy yielded to the flow of energy, letting it whisk her mind away into the void. The current carried her along like a leaf that had fallen into the gutter.   It had to be going somewhere, and it wasn't long before she found out where: It was draining into Daras-Drûm.

The death-wind swirled below her, less like a hurricane now than like a black hole, with a central throat spiraling down into darkness. It ineluctably pulled in and devoured all the energy that crossed its event horizon. She allowed herself to get close to it, probably closer than was safe, because she needed to see and understand what was going on down there. She felt her mind becoming distorted, stretching out like an elastic band. Closer. Time seemed to be slowing down. Closer. Fizzing clouds of energy swirled beneath her. She went with them, spinning around the vortex, hoping the obscuring haze would clear enough for her to finally get a good look. The clouds were made of chewed-up bits of strings, tiny ones, bunched together in loose agglomerations that resembled tufts of cotton or patches of mist. All the colors were there, blended and squashed until they glowed a pale grey-white, the same color as the Æther.

At last she fell below the level of the clouds, swirling downward toward the black center of the death-wind. It yawned beneath her, much larger than when it had slouched across the bay in Abacar, stretching out endlessly in every direction. A mighty current caught and buffeted her; realizing she had come too close, she reversed direction and began trying to fight her way back, to extract herself from the matrix. She failed to make headway. The spiraling thing beneath her had grown vastly more monstrous and powerful than when they had confronted it before. What if she was not as immune to destruction as Bernard had speculated? If she was unable to escape from the vortex, if it pulled her in, what would happen to her? What would happen to Bernard, left behind and stranded? What would happen to *everything*? She had to get away. Out, out, *out*! Energy pummeled her; she fought with all the strength she had left but it wasn't enough. She still moved inexorably closer to the center of the maelstrom. The effort of battling the current was exhausting. She couldn't keep it up. The maw grew and loomed beneath her, a gaping wound. Reality had suffered a fatal gut-shot, and Mercy was about to be bled out through. She struggled against the irresistible force but, like a riptide with a swimmer in its grip, it kept dragging her farther and farther out. It was too strong to fight.

But riptides were *always* too strong to fight. That was why you *didn't* fight them. You went with them. Otherwise they wore you out, and you drowned when you didn't have to.

So she stopped resisting, and turned herself around, and kicked herself straight into the hole in the world.

~~~~

"Mercy?"

No response. She was sitting down, her eyes closed, her breathing regular but very slow. Bernard, having warily circled the ring of stone, knelt beside her, one hand on her shoulder, trying to wake her up.

"Come on, Mercy," he said, giving her a little shake. "Wake up."

Still no response. She seemed to be in a trance. Maybe in a minute she would start channeling some ancient ancestor, wake up and tell him all about her past life as a warrior princess. He sat down next to her and waited for something to happen. Suddenly the pocket flexed and rattled, as if a giant dog had grabbed their sanctuary and given it a bite and a hearty shake. Bernard, startled, braced himself against the floor, which was essentially the same as bracing himself against nothing; he and Mercy both tumbled to one side and piled up against the curved wall of their floating prison. Propping her up against himself, he saw that something was happening to the glow in the center; a swirl of clouds had appeared and began to grow outward into a small, vertical cyclone, complete with an eye in the middle. The Heart materialized there, seeming to spin up out of nothing. It wobbled, steadied, then began to spin slowly, sparking and flickering across its depth. It wasn't really the Heart, he realized, just a three-dimensional image of it, holographically semitransparent. He glanced at Mercy. She was still out, but he had the feeling this was her doing somehow, that her absent mind was off somewhere else, making mischief. It would hardly be the first time that had happened.

The frothy clouds continued to thicken, beginning to form a sphere in the center of the chamber. Through the outer layers Bernard could still make out the ghostly Heart spinning in the center like the rocky core of a gaseous planet. He felt like the coalescing globe was looking at him. A shiver ran through the stone, a shudder and a crack as the accreting vapor gathered density. Little pieces broke off from the inner edge, crumbled and spun off into the fog, spinning away to dust and nothing as they were absorbed. Bernard backed as far away from the interior as he could—which was not nearly far enough—then started edging sideways, dragging Mercy along with him. He didn't know why he was bothering. There wasn't anywhere to go. Through the obscuring clouds, he thought he saw the facets of the Heart slow in their spinning, then stop, then reverse direction to follow him as he moved, as if it were tracking him. It *was* looking at him. He didn't like that, not one bit. He liked it even less when cracks began to spread through the rim along the inside where it edged the cloud. He wished Mercy would wake up. Maybe she could figure out a way to reinforce their little pod, but Bernard didn't know what to do, and couldn't think of any way to reach out and call her back. Maybe he didn't want to. Maybe she was somewhere better than this. She could hardly be somewhere worse, right?

As soon as he thought that, he took her hand and squeezed an apology.

If he had learned anything from this miserable adventure of theirs, it was that there was *always* somewhere worse.

~~~~

Falling through the vortex into the geometric network within was like being shot through a cannon into a room with angled elastic walls; Mercy felt a brief surge of extremely rapid motion, exiting through a narrow one-directional opening, then ricocheting around at lunatic speed from one surface to the next, bouncing and reflecting and bouncing and reflecting. The bits of masticated string that had gotten pulled in with her kept going when they hit a facet of the reaction chamber, but not her; they could pass through, but she was trapped; the walls were porous to energy, but sealed to her. It could bleed out. She was trapped.

The insanity of the motion made it hard to think and impossible to concentrate, so it took Mercy some time, whatever *time* meant here, to realize that she was inside the Heart. The hole in the world led into the very thing that Kihantroh had hoped to use to plug the hole; the glow, the destructive radiation that the Illata and the Jewel in the Maul emitted, the bleeding energy that had powered Mercy's enchantments, that had energized the underground city of the dwarves, that degraded those around it and killed those who touched it: That was the outflow of the matter that both the Æther and Daras-Drûm consumed, digested and channeled and poured back into the world through the crystalline aperture; the wounds in the world looped back around to the gems, converted into something corrosive. No wonder it killed almost everyone who came into contact with it. And then she had dropped Daras-Drûm into the Æther, and the two forces had blended, allowing them to really cut loose and devour *everything*. The Heart couldn't handle that much energy being sucked into it at once. It was approaching meltdown, like some sort of overheated nuclear reactor. It was lousy with frazzled remains of strings that it had drawn in and not been able to shed. They flailed and sputtered like out-of-control fireworks, unrestrained fire hoses, plutonium with the control rods removed, spitting and spraying energy. Nothing could survive in here for long. Mercy felt as if she might splinter into pieces at any moment. Was this what Untelleh had endured and fought against for five centuries? She could hardly imagine. Now she had to be that strong, that determined. She couldn't let the vortex tear her apart. If it did, if she broke down into pieces, then she would bleed out through the walls, too, and she would be nothing.

Remembering what she had done when she'd gathered the energy transmitted by Bernard's quarterstaff and again when Kihantroh had thrown her into the Æther, Mercy stretched out her arms, imagining them as vast winglike things, not for flying but for sweeping up the bits of string that swirled around her. She gathered them up and stopped them from escaping through the walls and vanishing into whatever lay beyond. Soon she had a variegated globe in front of her, molded between her imaginary flippers. She and her ball of string-stuff continued to bounce around the interior of the Heart, moving together, slower than before; the sphere had begun exerting drag on her motion. It was growing on its own now, too, exuding an attractive force that caught the fragments of strings that drifted by, interrupting their journey to oblivion, causing them to slow, quiver, and reverse direction to join the bundle, attaching themselves to its exterior. Mercy soon became entangled in her creation as newly-arriving strings blanketed her arms and legs, sticking her in place. It was as if she'd been glued to a giant ball of yarn and was getting batted around by a lazy cat. It rotated lackadaisically as it traveled between one surface to the next, bounced, and moved on. Mercy began to detect some give in the walls as the sphere collided and ricocheted; the string-globe had become so large that the Heart was having trouble containing it. It hadn't yet hit a wall with Mercy on the striking side and she wondered what would happen when it did. She had no control over the globe anymore, and when she finally felt herself swinging around as it neared one of the facets she couldn't do anything to avoid the impact.

She had worried that it would be like getting caught between a hammer and an anvil, but it was more like riding a cannonball through a pane of sugar glass.

Mercy didn't know if the Heart shattered because the string-ball had gained too much mass and momentum, or because it had pushed her into it with such force that she finally broke through like some piece of debris piercing a screen intended to block it; either way, the barrier buckled and bent behind her back, then breached. The sphere kept going, carrying her with it. Fragments of the Heart spun away, carried on a wave of energy that poured out through the rupture, pushing her along like jetsam in a floodwater tide. The string-ball began to disintegrate beneath her. She couldn't hold it together anymore. With nothing to cling to she found herself flung loose, spinning end over end through the void, wildly tumbling through the slurry of what was left of reality.

Then someone caught her hand and gripped it, and started pulling her down through the storm. Without really realizing what was happening, she felt herself slipping back into her body. She had almost forgotten how well it fit, how comfortable it felt, like old, soft, faded sweats. Sensations crept in. She opened her eyes.

It was Bernard who had caught her. Of course it was. Who else would it be? The two of them sat scrunched up against the wall of the drifting chamber that was the only remaining bit of Untelleh's grand stronghold. In the pit that had held the Æther, something that looked like it a swollen and distorted version of the Heart spun, surrounded by a corona of dying strings that looked like clouds. She could see sparkling little bits of the Heart flying off as it whirled, sparking like tiny shooting stars through the mist. Shards. Fragments. She knew that if she could catch one and look at it under a magnifying glass, it would be a fractal replica of the whole, just like the Illata and the Jewel in the Maul were; but unlike those powerful and coherent crystals, these kept splitting, dividing into tinier and tinier pieces until they vanished below the threshold of her perception, disappearing like a misty summer rain. The Heart was dissolving. What would happen when it was gone?

Then it exploded, and she got to find out.

~~~~

The catastrophic demise of the Heart wasn't a booming, fiery sort death—nothing like a propane tank or a car bomb exploding—but rather a soft, lacerating whisper, sharp and jagged and many-edged, as if just hearing it could cut her to pieces. The remaining crystalline exterior sublimated into sparkling vapor as it burst outward, becoming soft as water, evanescent as fog. It formed a frontal wave that swept out in all directions like a supernova. It passed over and around Mercy and Bernard as they floated in the nothingness. She grabbed his free hand just as it hit, sending them tumbling away together. She held on tightly to him as they flew through the vast, nebulous cloud that the Heart had exhaled as it died, until, finally, they slowed and stopped, halted by the slight drag of the gaseous void-stuff that still surrounded them.

"I don't like this ride," Bernard said. He sounded like he might throw up; his voice was muffled by the pervasive, drifting, nebular cloud that surrounded them, thick and impenetrable. The destruction of the Heart had refilled the void with Æther, but it no longer seemed to be plucking at them or trying to disintegrate them. It had become inert. It refused to encroach, leaving Bernard and her in a sphere of clarity in the middle of a cold eternity of vapor, a couple of tiny refugees from a previous universe adrift in a new one that wanted nothing to do with them.

"Mercy?" Bernard said. "What now?"

What now? Good question. She had been trying to put the Heart back together, not destroy it, but despite—or perhaps because of—her efforts it had exploded, Big Bang-style, taking everything else with it. Yet here they were, her and Bernard, still around. Why could they could touch the Heart and live, while everyone else died? Why had they been able to survive contact with the death-wind? What made them so different? The question had never been answered. She remembered how Yexandor had tried to figure her out by reaching inside her. He hadn't been able to get through her tangle of strings. What had he said about it? Something was blocking him, something that she *was*? That had to be the same blockade that had stopped Untelleh when she'd tried to read back beyond her appearance as Ambrosia. It seemed that nothing in the world of the Slash could get past the barrier that the two of them had gone through to get there. Why? Because they weren't from the Slash. They weren't from the plane that Untelleh had damaged with her attempt to control the Æther. They weren't a part of the reality that Daras-Drûm had fed upon, hadn't been born of the world that the Æther nibbled at like a swarm of immortal mice.

That was what made them different. It was so obvious, she'd completely overlooked it.

"Untelleh told Kihantroh they could do magic because they pulled reality apart a little bit each time, because you can't make a new garment without unraveling the old one," Mercy said. "There's no magic where you and I come from, though. Is that because there weren't enough strings there for magic to work, or because there were too many?"

"What?"

"It's because there were *too many*. Where we're from, the strings are stitched so tight you can't get through the weave. You can't make a new shirt because you can't unravel the old one. I get it now."

Bernard was looking at her, confused, but she was on to something here, she knew it. Those concentric circles that had turned up on the door in Jordneh's castle, on the amulet Mercy had left for herself ... It didn't represent a solar system. It represented a series of realities, one inside another inside another, an onion-ball of worlds where each succeeding layer stretched over and encased all the earlier ones within it. And just in the way the weave of a fabric became more open when you stretched it, the farther from that center world you got, the more space there was between the strings.

"We're from the *middle*," she said. "Do you get it, Bernard?"

"No. What middle?"

"We're from the *middle*." She should have figured this out a long time ago. They were from the middle! They were made of strings that were packed more densely than anywhere else. They may have been drawn through the Æther to reach the Slash, with its magic and its monsters, but they were still from the middle. Probably that was the only reason they could even make the journey. Yes, and she bet it was a one-way trip, that someone from an inner layer could go outward, but not the reverse. That was why the Æther hadn't been able to disintegrate her; that was why Daras-Drûm—and where was *it* from? From out beyond the frontier of the final world, invited in by Untelleh's mistake?—hadn't been able to kill them on contact. They were more real than it was; they were the realest things around. The death-wind could easily snack on the artificial constructs that were Ambrosia and Brannoc, could strip them away like coats of paint, but it couldn't devour the real Mercy and Bernard any more than it could kill them by smashing a mirror that showed their reflection. Maybe, given time, it could have, but with the two of them working together, with the Illata at hand, they had overcome and contained it.

But now, she had really messed things up by breaking the Heart. That was more than smashing a mirror. That was blowing up the planet the mirror was on. But she had touched the Heart before she'd destroyed it, and more to the point, it had touched her. It had left some sort of signature inside her, it had *changed* her, just like it had changed Bernard and everything else that it had touched. She was even more real than she had been before. And she carried a blueprint inside her.

"I'm going back in," she said. "I'm going to reboot the world."

~~~~

Bernard stared at Mercy. "You're going to do *what?*"

"You heard me."

"Okay. By going back in *where*?"

"The Heart."

"But the Heart blew up. There's nowhere to go back to."

"Yeah, it did. But it's not really gone. I've got a copy of it inside me, I think."

"A ... copy?"

"Yes. Like I made a backup." She didn't tell him he probably had one inside him, too; he was freaked out enough as it was.

"So you're going to, what, try to restore it? From the backup?"

"Yeah, you can say that."

"Um. And what's that going to do to you?"

"Er, I don't know. Nothing, I hope. But hang on to me, okay?"

"What else have I got to hang on to?"

She stuck her tongue out at him, then closed her eyes and cut her mind loose from her body again, like when she had sent it into the vortex. What she saw out there was that the Heart was still exploding; even though they couldn't see it anymore, and the main shockwave had long since passed them by, it still pulsed in the Æther, burning with faded power, like a small, dying sun. The last bits of reality swirled in the void, a vast spiral howling with energy at some deep level that couldn't be perceived with ordinary senses. The death-wind had grown and had swallowed the world, and it still screamed for more, an insensible devourer. How stupid she had been, how naive, thinking she had it safely trussed and bound in a glassy prison.

Now that her mind was unmoored from her body, the maelstrom grabbed hold of her and pulled her back into the spiraling dance, sweeping her along with the rest of the flotsam, the stuff of reality boiled down to a broth. She didn't resist the flow this time. The energy came at her and she let it in, let herself unfold as the power surged through her, let it push the envelope of her potential. She was a flower, a tree, growing, blooming; she was a torch, burning, incandescent, and even though she knew that the brighter something glowed the faster it burned out, she didn't try to stop it. This was the way it had to be. She had to use her own essence to stanch the bleeding in the matrix, because there was nothing else left. She would jam it with a mesh of her own reality, of what the Heart had made her. It was too late to *save* the world, but not to late to *become* the world.

She let her strings uncoil, sent them out into the vortex. They remembered the shape of the Heart that she had once carried in her hands. Instead of shredding and vanishing like gossamer in the hurricane, they spread and solidified into unseen anchors, catching and reassembling the broken fragments of other realities as they tumbled by. As the network grew, Mercy felt her consciousness fading; her strings were spreading too far, she was growing too attenuated to sustain the peculiar energy of life and sentience. She was joining with the matrix, insensible, but indispensable; she was becoming an integral part of the process of re-creation, undoing the undoing. She was becoming the Heart herself. The energy of the geometric network would flow along her strings. Reality would be remade in her image, which was to say, in its own image, as it had been when it was imprinted on her, when she had touched the Heart and it had fused its essence with her. It was a rare honor. More than rare. Unique.

A pity that it had to belong to her.

~~~~

Mercy had gone rag-doll limp in Bernard's arms. Her head kept wanting to loll to one side or the other, assuming a rather insouciant position, and he kept nudging it back with his own cheek. He wondered what she was doing, and if he could help her with it. Probably not. If he tried he would just screw something up.

He felt the change in the void before he saw it. His skin grew prickly, as if someone were waving a giant glass rod full of static electricity over his head. The mist began to swirl in new patterns, purposeful whorls and eddies he hadn't seen before. They seemed to be coalescing, but into what, he had no idea. Seconds dragged by, or centuries. Something like thunder boomed in the distance. Energy crackled like lightning. Was the void turning into a thunderstorm? Something tugged on him, pulling him downward. He looked toward his feet and discovered that his legs had stretched out seemingly to infinity, off and gone into a wormhole, a snaky tunnel through the mist. What the hell? How could that happen without his feeling it? As soon as he thought that, pins and needles shot up his legs and throughout his body, painfully intense, jellyfish stings of prickling agony. He held onto Mercy as the wormhole pulled him in, as he had promised he would, bringing her with him, not letting go even as it stretched him out so far his skin separated from his flesh, his flesh separated from his bones, his bones separated from each other. And still he held onto her. Even if he had no fingers or, for that matter, hands, he would pull her all the way to wherever they were going. He would.

He didn't.

One moment she was with him, gripped by nothing except, perhaps, his stubbornness; and then she was gone. She didn't even slip through his grasp. She just wasn't there anymore. It was like trying to hold onto water as it evaporated.

Bernard burst from the far end of the wormhole, overwhelmed by a strange feeling, a sensation of falling and flying at the same time. He was lying on a surface that was firm but not hard. He tried to sit up but couldn't. Something that felt like plastic was fastened over his nose and mouth. Noises. There were noises all around. Flashing lights. People talking.

People?

He was strapped onto something. Was he moving? Yes, the thing he lay on, it seemed to be rolling. He looked around, still woozy, and realized that he was on a stretcher, being transported somewhere. Were they still in the mountains? Had Grunsandrovar and Cynidece come to rescue him in a litter? No: There were people alongside him but it wasn't them. His head fell sideways and someone turned it so he was looking straight up again. The thing on his face was a mask. Air was being forced into his nose and mouth, filling his lungs. The people were still making noises that were starting to sound like words. He heard something about a faulty furnace, something about carbon monoxide. His conveyance rattled and bumped down some steps. The steps belonged to Mercy's front porch. He saw Ribbit, the black cat, watching him with yellow eyes from a nearby railing. Was she going to jump down and steal his hat and carry it away? No, that was another cat, in another world. The cart clattered onto the sidewalk, where emergency vehicles idled, blowing steam into the icy air, as if purposefully creating a screen on which to project their lights. Nearby, in his peripheral vision, he caught a glimpse of another stretcher. They wouldn't let him turn his head, so he rolled his eyes for a better look. Mercy was on the other stretcher. They weren't using a mask on her. Why not? She wasn't moving. Why wasn't she moving? Why was she on a stretcher at all, when she looked so apple-cheeked and healthy?

As he watched, someone pulled the sheet up over her head, and she was gone.

EPILOGUE

APPARENTLY BERNARD HAD been babbling on about elves and dwarves, monsters and magic, when he'd first come out of his hypoxic stupor; it seemed he'd been quite insistent that he had to go back and rescue Mercy from something, despite the fact that Mercy was already downstairs at the hospital lying still and cold and quiet in a drawer. He didn't remember the babbling, but he did remember the eventual visit from the nice doctors who explained that powerful hallucinations were not uncommon with carbon monoxide poisoning and that, whatever he might believe, Mercy's spirit was not trapped somewhere between dimensions waiting to be freed. It sounded pretty crazy hearing it echoed back to him, and he stopped talking about it.

Technicians had examined the furnace and the water heater and the carbon monoxide detectors in Mercy's house, all of which seemed to be working properly; they could not explain why the place had filled up with invisible, odorless, deadly gas or why, when it did, none of the alarms had gone off. No one had an explanation. Settlements were, of course, offered and accepted; most of the money went to Mercy's family, but some of it had come Bernard's way too. It was a hell of a way to pay for college, but it was an even worse way to pay for a wake and a funeral. It seemed like most everyone in the neighborhood and the school had shuffled through Mercy's calling hours and memorial service at one point or another, even Jack and Warren, who kept a prudent distance both from Bernard and from each other, as if Mercy might suddenly return and beat them senseless again if they stepped one inch out of line. He could picture how that might go: One of Mercy's windows would open up and she would storm out, snarking and shooting lightning bolts, sending Jack and Warren scurrying for cover. But of course, that didn't happen. Instead Bernard stood off to the side and watched Mercy's family collect condolences the way Mercy had once collected detention slips, staying until the very end. After they got back he'd excused himself and taken a walk in the woods, still somehow hoping she might appear like a dryad from a hollow tree, carrying a wand and laughing and making the autumn leaves pirouette. But that had been months ago. Winter was well underway now, and as those memories became buried by time the same way those fallen leaves, which never did learn how to dance, became buried beneath an ever-deeper mantle of snow, it grew more and more difficult for him to imagine why such a thing as that had ever seemed within the realm of possibility.

~~~~

The grey sky spat snowflakes the size of rose petals as Bernard trudged through the woods on his way home from another afternoon in detention. He seemed to end up in there rather often now; after having been studious and compliant throughout his entire academic career, at the very end of it he had become inattentive, distracted, disruptive. So said the notes that kept getting sent home, anyway. That was something else the nice doctors had explained: That personality changes could be another side effect of carbon monoxide poisoning, which in his case seemed to have manifested as a decreased ability to cope with stress, frustration, and boredom. For a while the system had cut him quite a bit of slack, letting him skate on the ice laid down by his previous good behavior and the tragic loss of his best friend, but eventually they began bringing punishments to bear. He understood they had to do it; they couldn't allow him to coast indefinitely. Maybe if Mercy were still here then things would have been different, but instead he was alone, out of place, trapped with vivid memories and a missing partner, a sidekick without a superhero.

The wind gusted and whipped the snow into soft, fat bullets, like feathers fired from a gun. Despite the chill and the late hour he paused, as he always did, in the sad little forest between the school and the road, looking at the spot where he and Mercy had stopped to talk about magic the day before the game had arrived in the mail. She had wished for goblins in the earth and dragons in the sky and elves in the forest, and had gotten her wish, sort of; but it hadn't turned out the way she had hoped, had it?

Behind him, a familiar voice said: "Aren't you cold, just standing there?"

Bernard spun. Stopped. Stared.

Mercy stood nearby, giving him that crooked smile of hers. She wore a brown tunic sashed with green; her hair, long and black and lustrous—had she really once complained it was mouse-brown and stringy?—reached to her waist. Loose beige leggings descended to a pair of soft leather boots, while her smoothly-muscled arms were bare from the shoulders to the snakelike gold bracelets around her wrists. She looked like an ancient warrior-priestess or something; not that he had ever met one of those.

He said: "Um. Yes. Aren't *you* cold?"

"I'm not where you are," she said. "I'm on the other side of a window."

"A window?" He squinted at her, then walked in a circle. From the side and the back, she wasn't there. When he got back around to the front, she was smirking at him.

He eyed the supposed window. "But … Where's the thing that looks like a door?"

"It's a window," she said, "shaped exactly like me."

"That's …" He trailed off, not sure what that was. "Tricky."

"*I'm* tricky," she said.

He looked at her for a long time, then said, "The doctors told me what I remembered was a hallucination."

"They would say that. You know how doctors are."

"Maybe *this* is a hallucination, too."

She shrugged. "Maybe."

"You look different."

"I *am* different. When I replaced the Heart with myself, I thought that would be the end of it, but it wasn't. I rebuilt myself."

"Rebuilt yourself." He thought about that. "So you're … back?"

"I'm back. But I'm not who I used to be."

"Who are you, then?"

"I've been watching you for a while," she said, ducking the question. "You don't belong here anymore, Bernard. You know that, don't you?"

After a moment, he shrugged. Then he nodded.

"Yeah. You know it. You belong here, with me."

"Where's *here*?"

"*Here* is *everywhere*." She reached out to him. There was a ripple in midair, as if she were passing her hand through some invisible yet iridescent membrane. He looked at the hand a moment, then at her face. The snow fell down around him, icy on his neck. Fat flakes landed on her arm and melted instantly.

"I might not belong here," Bernard said, "but I don't want to go back to … *that*. All the fighting. Kihantroh. The death-wind. Untelleh. I told Brennendah I was done, and I meant it."

"It won't be like that this time."

"No? Whoever played that trick on us with the game. They're still out there. Right?"

"Well. Yeah, I guess so. Somewhere. But they've been leaving me alone. After all, we did what they wanted. We put the Heart back together." She frowned. "Sort of."

"How do we know that's what they wanted? That stuff written on the game, good gods, bad gods … that was all a lie."

"It was … advertising copy. A hook."

"A *hook*? Like bait? And we were the stupid fish who bit on it."

"We're the stupid fish who saved the multiverse," she said crisply.

"No, *you're* the fish who saved the multiverse. I'm the fish who got picked up by mistake."

"Enough about the fish already. And your being there was *not* a mistake. I couldn't have done it without you, Bernard." Then: "Think about it. Whoever sent the game already knows who you are and where you live, right? If she ever decides to pull you in again, wouldn't you want to have me there with you?"

"Well, yeah. Of course. So why don't you just come home?"

She shook her head. "I can't," she said.

"You can't? Why not?" Bernard heard a distant rumble then, as if a thunderstorm were approaching, thought was hardly likely this time of year. He looked around, then back at Mercy. Her smile had vanished. "What was that? Was that you?"

"Not exactly. But sort of. Listen, Bernard, I ... I have to leave soon. Are you coming with me?"

"What? Why do you have to leave? Why can't you come back?"

"Well, see, it's just ... I can't stay in one place too long anymore. If I do, energy starts to gather. Things ... happen."

"Things?"

"Yeah. Things."

Bernard wondered what sort of *things* she was talking about. Whatever they were, they didn't seem to be good. He said nothing.

"Yeah," she said, filling the silence. "So I, um, I have to move around a lot. But I've got all the worlds to choose from now. *We've* got all the worlds. You and me. If you want them."

"So, what, you want me to leave forever like you did?"

"No, not *forever*. Don't be so dramatic. I can bring you back to visit any time you want. I can bring you back five minutes after we left." Her face darkened a bit, then brightened. "I could visit now and then too, I guess. Short visits. Dinner and a movie. Just not as myself. Since I'm, you know. Dead. And stuff." Then, when he didn't answer: "It happens all the time. Kids grow up, they move away, they see their families once a year at Christmas—"

"This isn't like moving to the next state, Mercy."

"No, it's not. It's better. There's so much stuff to see."

He sighed and shook his head, then raised his gaze to the sky, feeling more than hearing another distant rumble. What might be rolling in behind the clouds? What *things* were going to happen if Mercy stayed?

Finally she said, in a small voice: "Don't leave me alone out here, Bernard. Please?"

He looked at Mercy. Her hand was still extended. He took it in his. Her palm was soft and warm. The window around her expanded, became the sort of door he remembered. She pulled him through. The doorway began to close. Just before it vanished, Bernard's voice came back across: "Wait. The person who sent the game … Why did you say *she*?"

The only answer was the gentle whisk of falling snow as it filled the footprints he had left behind in the empty wood.

ABOUT THE AUTHOR

James V. Viscosi is the author of several horror and fantasy novels. An expatriate New Yorker, he currently resides with his wife and various finned and furry animals in sunny Southern California, where he spends most of his time hiding underneath a very large hat. Visit him online at www.jamesviscosi.com.

www.ingramcontent.com/pod-product-compliance
Lightning Source LLC
Chambersburg PA
CBHW050513110726
47899CB00005B/1444